Angel's Rest

An
Eternity Springs
Novel

EMILY MARCH

BALLANTINE BOOKS • NEW YORK

Angel's Rest is a work of fiction. Names, characters, places, and incidents are the products of the author's imagination or are used fictitiously. Any resemblance to actual events, locales, or persons, living or dead, is entirely coincidental.

A Ballantine Books Mass Market Original

Copyright © 2011 by Geralyn Dawson Williams
Excerpt from *Hummingbird Lake* by Geralyn Dawson Williams copyright © 2011 by Geralyn Dawson Williams

Published in the United States by Ballantine Books, an imprint of The Random House Publishing Group, a division of Random House, Inc., New York.

BALLANTINE and colophon are registered trademarks of Random House, Inc.

This book contains an excerpt from the forthcoming book *Hummingbird Lake* by Geralyn Dawson Williams. This excerpt has been set for this edition only and may not reflect the content of the forthcoming edition

ISBN 978-0-345-51834-7
eBook ISBN 978-0-345-51835-4

Printed in the United States of America

www.ballantinebooks.com

9 8 7 6 5 4

In loving memory of my dad,
John Edward Dawson.
He was the greatest storyteller I've ever known.

Home—
that blessed word, which opens to the human heart
the most perfect glimpse of Heaven, and helps to
carry it thither, as on an angel's wings.

—LYDIA M. CHILD

ONE

Eagle's Way Estate
Outside of Eternity Springs, Colorado

Holding a 9 mm Glock in one hand and a tumbler of single-malt scotch in the other, John Gabriel Callahan stared out the mountain home's wall of windows and knew it was time to take a hike. An hour ago he'd watched a gray cloud bank roll in and swallow the rocky peaks above. The rain had turned to snow twenty minutes later. Now a thin layer of white dusted the branches of the trees that surrounded him in every direction. Evergreens and aspen—yellow, gold, and orange with autumn. It was a breathtaking view. A lonely beauty.

It was perfect place to . . . hike.

He set down his glass without sampling the whiskey, then shifted the automatic from his left hand to his right. He held it balanced on his palm, testing the weight, absorbing its warmth. How long had it been since he'd held a gun? Long enough for it to feel foreign. Not nearly long enough to forget.

Heaven knows he needed to forget.

A bitter smile hovered on his lips. He stuck the Glock into his jeans at the small of his back, and ignoring the jackets hanging on the coat rack, exited the house.

He paused long enough to lock the door behind him

and secure the key in the lock box like a good guest should. Then he paused on the wide wooden deck, surveyed the area, and debated which way to go. Up into the mountains behind him? Along the shallow creek that bisected the high, narrow valley? Across the creek to the tree-covered slopes rising before him? It didn't much matter. Wilderness stretched in every direction. The memories traveled with him everywhere.

He chose to climb the mountain behind him, where the path appeared a little rockier, the forest a bit more dense. The more rigorous the path, the better.

He hiked a long time, his thoughts bouncing between events of his life. His lives. That's how he thought of it. He'd had his life in Texas, then the dark months overseas and his struggle for survival, and finally the new life when he'd started over. The third time, he'd gotten it right. *The third time's the charm.*

Charmed. Magical.

Over.

A bitter wind whipped around him, and he grew as numb on the outside as he'd been on the inside for the better part of a year now. Weariness weighted his legs and his soul.

The snowfall intensified, visibility decreased. As the ground disappeared beneath a blanket of white, he idly wondered if this snow would last until spring. It was early in the season for snow, so he doubted it. Although, at this high altitude, with this low temperature, who knew? Bet it wasn't more than fifteen degrees. A man could freeze to death.

But that way was too easy.

He turned into the wind, and in the echo of wind and memory he thought he heard a sound. Listening hard, he heard it again and his gut clenched. It sounded like . . . laughter. The sweet, familiar notes of laughter. A woman's. A child's. Happy.

Haunted, Gabe closed his eyes and shuddered.

No laughter, just ghosts.

Over. It's over. I'm done. He broke into a jog, chasing the imaginary sound or running from it, he didn't know. It didn't matter. He moved deeper into the forest, uphill and down, paying scant attention to his path until trees gave way to rolling meadow. It was a beautiful, peaceful place.

Their suburban home in Virginia had been a beautiful, peaceful place. A sanctuary.

The imagined echoes of laughter swelled and strengthened into a whirlwind of memory, sweet and pure, and Gabe listened and yearned until the sound transformed and all he heard were screams. He was so very tired of the screams.

In a Rocky Mountain meadow, Gabe Callahan tripped and fell flat on his face. He lay in the biting cold and snow, breathing as if he'd run a marathon, sweat— or maybe tears—running down his face. He wanted to die. Dear God, he wanted to die. Here. Today. Now. Right now.

Today would have been Matthew's sixth birthday.

Enough. He climbed to a kneeling position and reached for the Glock. This time the weapon felt natural in his grip. He flicked off the safety and chambered a round. Shutting his eyes, he took one last deep breath. A sense of peace surrounded him like the snowfall, and he was ready.

The force hit him without warning, a hard body blow to the back that knocked him forward and sent the Glock sailing from his grip. Weight settled atop him. Gabe's thoughts flew like bullets. Not a man. Fur. An animal. Sharp claws dug into his back. Mountain lion? Would fangs sink into his neck?

Instinct kicked in, and in a strange twist of fate, Gabe prepared to fight for his life. He rolled and the animal rolled with him and let out a sound. Gabe froze. This wasn't a mountain cat.

Arf, arf, arf. It pounced again, its forelegs landing on Gabe's chest, and a long wet tongue rolling out to lick his face.

A dog.

Gabe's breath fogged on the air as he let out a heavy sigh, pushed the dog off his chest, and sat up. It was a goofy, too-friendly, starved-to-skin-and-bones boxer with floppy ears and a crooked tail. Gabe turned his head as the tongue came back and bathed his face in slobber once again.

Then, for the first time in months, John Gabriel Callahan smiled.

"You're an angel, Dr. Nic," said the fifth-grader, her arms full of a shaggy-haired, mixed-breed puppy and her eyes swimming with tears. "I love you. I'm so glad you moved home to Eternity Springs. I knew you'd be able to fix Mamey, and that we wouldn't have to put him down like Daddy said."

Nicole Sullivan stood at the doorway of her veterinary clinic and waved at the girl's mother, Lisa Myers, who waited in the ten-year-old sedan on the street, her eight-month-old son strapped into a car seat in the back. "I'm glad I could help, Beth. And I'll enjoy your mom's canned peaches all winter long."

The smile remained on her face until the car drove off and she sighed and murmured, "Too bad I can't pay the electric bill in peaches."

Or baked goods. Or venison. She had managed to barter a case of elderberry wine for a radiator hose replacement on her truck.

"Mom says you have to stop giving away your services," said Lori Reese, Nic's volunteer assistant and seventeen-year-old goddaughter.

"Like your mother doesn't let Marilyn Terrell pay for a portion of her groceries with free video rentals," Nic fired back. "Rentals she seldom uses."

Lori shrugged. "My mom is queen of 'Do as I say, not as I do.' "

"That's true." It was also true that Nic had a severe cash-flow problem. In the five years since her divorce, she'd worked hard to pay down the debt her sleazy, tax-evading ex had dumped in her lap, but she still had a long way to go. Those bills on top of her school loans and a practice whose invoices were paid in foodstuffs as often as currency made meeting monthly expenses a challenge.

"Let's swab the decks around here, Lori, and call it a day," Nic said, checking her watch. "I have an appointment at the bank, and with any luck, I'll be through in time to catch a bite of supper at the Bristlecone Café before it closes." She still had two free specials coming in payment for suturing the cut on Billy Hawkins' chin after his skateboard accident.

As the closest thing this county of 827 permanent residents had to a medical doctor since Doc Ellis died in August, Nic stitched up almost as many two-legged creatures as four-legged ones these days. While she was glad to help with minor injuries, Eternity was desperate for a doctor.

"Mrs. Hawkins is closing for supper?" Lori pursed her lips in surprise as she grabbed the bottle of disinfectant from the supply closet. "Wow. She never does that. I knew this meeting tonight was a big deal, but . . . wow."

"It's an important announcement. Eternity Springs needs a miracle."

Lori wrinkled her nose and squirted lemon-scented spray on the exam table. "I don't think building a prison in town qualifies as a miracle."

"I can't honestly say I'm thrilled at the prospect myself, but it would bring jobs to town and boost our permanent population. The town needs that if we're going to survive."

"Tell me about it." Lori tore a handful of paper towels from a roll and went to work. "Even if they're not going on to college, everyone leaves town after high school graduation because the only work here is summer work. Mom says it wasn't like that when you were my age. I want to go away to college and vet school, but I also want to be able to come back home to live after I graduate. I love Eternity Springs."

"I hear you." Nic had fallen in love with the tiny mountain town when she and her mom moved here to be close to Mom's sister and her husband. Nic's jerk of a father—her mom's married lover—had finally cut all ties with his mistress and their daughter. Nic had been nine years old and devastated, and the place and its people had given her a hug and a home. Years later when her marriage fell apart, she could have gone anywhere to rebuild, but this mountain valley had called to her soul. She'd spent a year at a clinic in Alamosa to reacquaint herself with large-animal veterinary medicine, and then finally she'd come home. She'd renovated her late uncle's dental office into a vet clinic and scraped by.

Nic loved Eternity just as it was, but she recognized that her hometown wouldn't thrive and perhaps not even survive if the local leaders didn't succeed in bringing in some sort of new industry. New jobs meant new residents, which would be good for everyone. A new prison would definitely bring that doctor they needed so desperately to town. If Mayor Hank Townsend relayed a thumbs-up on the prison tonight, she could at least look forward to having that particular burden shifted off her shoulders.

"I don't want to live anywhere else, Lori," she told her

young assistant. "If building a prison in the valley means we get to stay here, then I'll help clear the land for it myself."

Lori sighed dramatically, reminding Nic of the teenager's mother at the same age. Those two were so much alike it was scary.

"You're right. I see that." Lori's expression clouded with worry as she met Nic's gaze. "But I love Eternity Springs as it is. What if we do get the prison and it changes us?"

Nic's stomach gave a little twist at the thought, but experience had taught her how to answer Lori's question. "Change happens whether we like it or not. The trick is to accept it, to make it work for us as best we can. Who knows? Maybe it'll bring that man your mom's been waiting for to town."

Lori rolled her eyes. "Great. I've always wanted a criminal for a stepdad."

"I was thinking more of a tall, dark, and handsome contractor." She waggled her brows and added, "Who wears a tool belt. Sarah has always had a thing for tool belts."

"Dr. Nic, puh-lease! That's my mom you're talking about. Besides, we already have a handful of contractors in town. I can't say I'm impressed."

Nic laughed and carried the trash bag outside, where sometime in the ten minutes since young Beth had left with her Mamey a light snowfall had begun. Years of experience told Nic the flurries wouldn't stick, but this did represent the first snowfall of the season. Winter was bearing down upon Eternity, and Nic recognized the fact with dismay.

Once upon a time, winter had been her favorite season. Cold weather invigorated her. She loved the holidays, winter sports, and cozy nights snuggling in front of a fire with the man she loved. But a series of really

awful winters had all but ruined the season for her. First
she'd found her husband in bed with another woman
two weeks before Christmas. Then a stroke took her
beloved uncle David the following November. The next
winter, the financial fallout from an ugly, prolonged divorce took its toll, and Nic was forced her to sell her
share of her Colorado Springs vet practice. Then, on
New Year's Eve of her first winter back in Eternity
Springs, her mom and her aunt had dropped the bombshell that they'd bought a condo in Florida and moving
day was two weeks away. Now Nic couldn't feel the
sting of a snowflake on her cheek without mourning all
that she'd lost.

And wondering what losses the coming winter would
bring.

Attempting to ward off the melancholy that threatened, she exhaled a cleansing breath and hauled the
trash bag outside to the waste cans, which she then
rolled out to the street for tomorrow morning's pickup.
When she was halfway back to the clinic, an unfamiliar
red Jeep Wrangler skidded to a stop at the curb. Nic's
steps slowed as a bedraggled stranger climbed out of
the vehicle. He was tall, broad, and trim with dark hair
overdue for a cut and a square jaw that needed a shave
even worse. He reached into the backseat to reappear
with an armful of struggling dog—a skinny brindle
boxer whose left hind leg appeared to be bleeding badly.

Nic picked up her step. "Lori? Emergency patient
coming." To the man, she called, "Bring him here."

The stranger followed Nic into the clinic. Lori took
one look and then set about preparing the supply tray
Nic would need. The stranger placed the boxer on the
exam table Nic indicated and held him in place.

"What happened?" she asked.

Concern shadowed his whiskey-brown eyes. "A
damned leghold trap."

"He's your dog?"

He shook his head. "No. He's probably a stray. Our paths crossed a few days ago while I was hiking the backcountry, but he didn't hang around or follow me home. When I was hiking on Murphy Mountain today I heard something howling in pain, so I tracked the sound and found him caught in the trap."

"You poor baby," she murmured to the dog.

"We tussled a bit when I tried to free him. I'm afraid I made his injuries worse."

Nic sedated the suffering animal and made a cursory examination. Lacerations, trauma where he'd chewed himself. Broken teeth. She studied the bone. "Not fractured, believe it or not. Significant muscle damage, but I think we can save the leg."

With that pronouncement, Nic focused on her patient and went to work.

Gabe breathed a little easier when he saw the competent, methodical manner in which the vet acted. Dr. Nicole Sullivan of Eternity Springs Veterinary Clinic— according to the sign beside the door—obviously knew what she was doing. He could leave with a clear conscience.

Instead, Gabe stayed right where he was, watching the woman work.

One minute stretched to five, then to ten. She had good hands—long, narrow fingers that moved with a surety of purpose. Straight white teeth tugged at a full lower lip when she tied off sutures. He judged her to be younger than he was, but not by a lot. Early thirties, he'd guess. She was petite but shapely, fair-skinned with a dusting of freckles across her nose. She wore her blond hair long and pulled back in a ponytail; plain gold studs were in her ears. He saw no rings on her fingers beneath the latex gloves.

She spoke in a quiet, confident voice as she explained her actions to the teenager. A teacher with her apprentice, he thought. She was good at it, too. Gentle and warm, her tone soothing and compassionate. A healer.

Gabe didn't belong here. He should leave.

Only he didn't want to leave.

"So where did you come from, boy?" the vet asked the unconscious dog as she frowned over something on his belly. "He's little more than a puppy. Judging by his body weight and the state of his coat, he's probably been out in the wild for a while."

"Think he could have been abandoned at birth?" the teenager asked. "No collar on him, and I've never seen a boxer his age who still has his tail. This one is crooked, too. If he had an owner, you'd think they'd have docked his tail."

"It's a cute tail," the vet declared. "Gives him character."

Gabe tugged a worn leather dog collar from his back pocket. "Here. I have his collar. It came loose while I was trying to free him from the trap."

He handed the collar to the teenager, who checked its heart-shaped metal tag. "Rabies vaccine is current from a clinic in Oklahoma. Bet he belonged to summer tourists and got lost from his family."

"I don't recall any lost dog notices for a boxer," the vet said. "We'll make some calls. He could have traveled a long way." She glanced up at Gabe. "Where did you find him?"

"Murphy Mountain."

Surprise lit the vet's pretty blue eyes. "That's private property."

"Not private enough, apparently. The owner didn't set that trap."

The teenager's head jerked around. "How do you know? Are you a Davenport?"

"No."

The girl waited expectantly, and when Gabe remained stubbornly silent, she tried again. "If you know the owner didn't set the trap, then you must be a friend of the Davenports. That, or you're just another trespasser."

Gabe gave in. "Jack Davenport is a friend."

The girl's chin came up. "Then would you give him a message for me? Tell him that I'm looking for his cousin, Cameron Murphy."

"Lori," said the vet, a thread of steel beneath the warmth. "Don't."

"But—"

"Lori Elizabeth, no."

A mutinous expression settled on the girl's face, but she went silent. Gabe tried not to be interested in what that bit of drama had been about. Davenport business, obviously. Definitely none of his.

He needed to leave. Should have just dropped off the dog and hightailed it. Why had he hung around, anyway? That wasn't like him.

The *beep beep* of a car horn sounded outside. "There's your ride, Lori," said the vet, lifting a gauze bandage roll from the supply tray. "Tell your mom I'll see her at the school tonight, okay?"

The teenager hesitated and darted a glance at Gabe. "I could stay, Dr. Nic."

"Thanks, sweetie, but you go on. I'm going to wrap this bandage and I'll be done here."

The girl didn't like leaving the vet alone with a stranger, and Gabe couldn't blame her. He should speak up. Say he was leaving, too. Instead, for some inexplicable reason, he kept his lips zipped.

Beep beep. "Oh, all right." The girl tugged off her gloves, then looked him straight in the eyes. "What was your name, mister?"

His lips twitched and he acknowledged her challenge with a nod. "Gabe Callahan."

"I'll tell Mom you won't be long," she said, shifting her gaze to the vet. On her way out the door, she paused and added, "By the way, I think Mom is having supper with Sheriff Turner."

In the wake of the girl's departure, Gabe shoved his hands in his jeans pockets and observed, "That was subtle."

"We watch out for one another around here." She quickly and efficiently wrapped the bandage, released the locks on the table where the dog lay, and rolled it toward a wall lined with crates. When she opened the door to a medium-sized wire box, Gabe stepped forward. "Let me help."

"Thanks."

Careful of the boxer's injured leg, he slipped his hands beneath the dog's torso and shifted him into the crate. When he stepped back, Dr. Nic was frowning at him. "What? Did I do it wrong? Did I hurt him?"

"Before, I was concentrating on the dog. I didn't notice." She gestured toward his chest. "That's your blood, not his."

Gabe glanced down at his shirt. "More his than mine, and my fault for being careless. He got me a time or two before I thought enough to use my shirt to wrap his head while I released him from the trap."

"Why didn't you use your coat?"

"Wasn't mine."

He watched her silently mouth a word that just might have been *idiot*. Gabe almost grinned.

"Scratches or bites?"

"Both."

She sighed heavily. "Go sit on the table and take off your shirt."

"There's no need for that," he said, uneasy over how appealing he found the idea.

"That dog's been running wild. At the very least you need the wounds flushed and examined." She pointed toward the table.

He hesitated, and she scowled at him. "Now."

Gabe gave in to both their desires. He tugged off his shirt and it wasn't until he heard her shocked gasp that he realized just what he'd done. The scars had been a part of him for so long now that he forgot he even had them. He unconsciously straightened, bracing himself against the barrage of questions sure to come. Questions he had no intention of answering. That part of his life was a closed book.

The pretty veterinarian surprised him. But for that one betraying inhalation, her professionalism never slipped. Maybe her gaze was a bit softer, her touch as gentle as the snowfall, but she never once recoiled or eyed him with pity. Gradually Gabe relaxed. For a few stolen moments he allowed himself to pleasure in the sensation of human touch upon his skin.

"I'll quarantine the boxer," she said. "You should drive into Gunnison and see Dr. Hander at the medical clinic. He'll put you on prophylactic antibiotics. When was your last tetanus shot?"

"Last year."

"Good."

Next she ran through a series of basic questions about his medical history, and then asked him to lie on his back. "Your legs will hang off the table, I'm afraid, but this way will keep your pants dry."

His jeans had been wet since he wrestled with the dog, but he kept that detail to himself and studied her through half-closed eyes as she prepared to bathe his wounds with saline. Her beauty was the wholesome, girl-next-door type. He figured the lack of a ring on her finger was due to work-related safety factors rather than marital status. Bet she was married with a couple of kids.

Pain sliced through him as she applied the solution, and Gabe sucked in a breath.

"Sorry," she murmured. "It's important to clean all these scratches."

"Wouldn't want them to scar," he replied, his tone desert dry.

He saw the question in her eyes, and she must have seen the answer in his, because she kept quiet. She moved a step closer and caught a whiff of her scent. Summertime peaches, ripe and juicy. Now there was an incongruous item for a cold autumn day.

Her gentle finger brushed across a hard ridge of scar tissue and she softly said, "More than a hundred and thirty bacterial diseases can be transmitted to humans from a dog's mouth, Mr. Callahan. Dr. Hander will tell you what to watch for, but as long as you take the antibiotics he'll prescribe, I doubt you'll have a problem."

"I'll be fine."

She paused and waited for him to meet her stare. "You're not going to go see Dr. Hander, are you?"

"It's a long drive. Can't you give me antibiotics?"

"I'm a vet."

He held her gaze and said, "Woof woof."

As she rolled her eyes, he pressed, more from curiosity about how she'd react than a desire for drugs. "It's two hours to a hospital from here. I'll bet you have an emergency stash."

"This isn't an emergency."

Her teeth tugged at her lower lip and she looked torn with indecision. His gaze settled on her mouth until Gabe abruptly lost interest in the game. He rolled to a sitting position. "Don't worry, Dr. Sullivan. I'll be just fine. I know. I've had worse."

Her gaze dropped to his chest, and this time he saw a flash of pity she couldn't hide before she finally asked, "What happened to you?"

He pulled on the bloodied, tattered shirt and ignored the question. He needed to get out of here. "What about the dog? Will he be okay?"

She accepted the dodge with a nod. "He'll be uncomfortable for a while, but he should make a full recovery. I'll keep him quarantined in case he has underlying issues we can't immediately identify."

He slipped his wallet from the pocket of his jeans, removed a few bills, and set them on the counter. "Thanks for your help, Dr. Sullivan."

Without another word, he turned and walked back out into the snow.

He had almost reached his jeep when the clinic door banged open and she came running after him. She held cash and a small orange bottle in her hand. "Wait. These were hundreds. That's way too much."

He refused the bills she pushed his way, but took the bottle. "What's this?"

"You told the truth about no allergies, right?" As he nodded, she scowled and added, "Take two a day until they're gone. You didn't get them from me."

Gabe stared down at the pill bottle. She could get in all kinds of trouble for doing what she'd just done. For all she knew, he could be a DEA agent.

It was a basic human act of kindness, and it sliced through the scar tissue surrounding his heart, sparking a flicker of warmth in a place cold for too long. "Thanks, Doc. You're a lifesaver."

T W O

❦

Nic entered the school auditorium through a side door and looked for a place to sit. The place was packed. She'd bet that 90 percent of the residents of Eternity Springs had gathered for tonight's meeting. A fluttering hand on the opposite end of the auditorium caught her attention. Nic waved back to Sarah Reese, whose short cap of dark hair crowned an angular face and whose long, luscious lashes set off Elizabeth Taylor violet eyes that were the envy of every woman in town. Sarah gestured toward the empty seat between her and Eternity's newest permanent resident, Celeste Blessing, who appeared to be having an animated conversation with the man seated to her right, Reverend Hart, the pastor at Community Presbyterian.

"Thanks for saving me a spot," Nic said to Sarah, sinking gratefully into the chair. Her feet were killing her.

"I was hoping you'd show up. I understand you had some excitement at the clinic tonight. Dish, girlfriend."

Nic hesitated. This was more than just a man-with-a-dog story. This was a man-with-a-dog-visiting-the-house-on-Murphy-Mountain story, which made it more than idle gossip to Sarah and involved more scars than those that marred the stranger's chest. "Not much to tell. Guy staying up at Eagle's Way found an injured dog on the mountain."

Sarah studied her manicure and said in a casual tone, "Lori said he knew Jack Davenport and that he looked to be our age."

Nic gave a slow nod. "Maybe a little older. He didn't mention Cam, Sarah."

Her friend momentarily stiffened, then wrinkled her nose and gave her dark hair a toss. "Did I ask?"

"No." But then, she never did. Nic was one of only three other people who knew about Sarah's unfinished business with Cameron Murphy. "Lori said you were having dinner with Zach Turner."

"After this meeting, if nothing comes up," Sarah said. As Nic arched a curious brow, she added, "He's a *friend*, Nicole."

"He could be more if you'd let him."

"We're not like that."

"I don't know why not. He's gorgeous, and he wears his . . . pistol . . . so well."

Up on the stage, the mayor and council members huddled around the sound system while a technician tested the microphone. Nic waited until Celeste Blessing finished visiting with Reverend Hart, then said, "Celeste, I drove down Cottonwood Street today. You did it, didn't you? That new ride in front of Cavanaugh House is yours?"

Blue eyes twinkled as she reached up to adjust the jaunty brim of her white felt hat. "You mean my Honda Gold Wing?"

Sarah leaned forward and gaped at Celeste. "You bought a motorcycle?"

"What can I say? I love to fly."

Sarah groaned, closed her eyes, and banged her forehead against her palm. "My daughter is *so* not allowed to hang out with you anymore."

Celeste laughed softly, and—as always when she heard that particular sound—Nic's tension melted away. The woman had a gift, an air of serenity about her that was contagious. A widowed, retired schoolteacher from South Carolina, Celeste wore her silver-gray hair in a stylish bob, spoke with a delightful, soft southern accent, and demonstrated an old-money class that blended with a youthful sense of fun. Nic adored her. "Have I mentioned how glad I am that you decided to retire in Eternity Springs, Celeste?"

Pleasure warmed the older woman's eyes. "Thank you, dear. You're too kind."

"Nope. Just selfish. Being around you makes me feel good."

A loud squeal blasted through the room. Celeste winced and sighed. "That reminds me of my Fancy-cat when I was slow with breakfast."

Nic gave her new friend's hand a comforting squeeze. Celeste had arrived in town this past spring with a treasure trove of books and a cranky, arthritic Persian cat. When she brought her ailing Fancy to Nic's clinic, the depth of her love for her pet had been obvious, and Nic had hated relaying a terminal diagnosis. Celeste had been working up the nerve to have Fancy put down when the cat died in her sleep just over a month ago. Though the older woman had accepted the loss of her pet with grace, Nic knew she was hurting. "You let me know when the time is right for you, and I'll fix you up with a four-legged somebody needing a home."

She wondered how Celeste felt about boxers.

"You have a good heart, Nicole Sullivan, and I appreciate your sensitivity. I think I'll be ready for another pet sooner rather than later. That big old house is lonely with only my old bones rattling around in it."

"I can imagine."

Upon moving to Eternity, Celeste had purchased the old Cavanaugh estate, the large Victorian mansion built back in the 1880s by one of the owners of the Silver Miracle mine. Cavanaugh House had been a showplace in its time and later additions contributed to its hodge-podge charm. But after tragedy struck the family in the 1970s, the house had sat empty and the years of neglect had taken a toll.

Onstage the huddle broke and the three council members took their seats at a table. Mayor Hank Townsend stepped up to the podium, banged his gavel twice, and declared, "I'm calling this special town hall meeting to order. Thank you all for coming out on such a blustery autumn evening. Looks like winter might arrive early this year. Hope everyone is ready."

From the front row, the owner of Fill-U-Up, Eternity's combination gas station and convenience store, called out, "Quit politicking, Hank, and tell us what the governor's office said!"

The mayor scowled and banged his gavel again for good measure. "You're out of order, Dale Parker."

"Just like the diesel pump at your place," added one of the council members, Larry Wilson, who owned Eternity's building supply store. "I have to go beg fuel for my delivery trucks from the city pumps. When do you intend to get that thing fixed?"

"As soon as I know that my business will survive the winter," Dale fired back. "Just spill the beans, Hank. Are we getting the prison or not?"

The mayor closed his eyes, pinched the bridge of his nose, and visibly braced himself before saying in a flat, defeated tone. "No. No, we're not."

Nic released the breath she unconsciously had been holding as the gathering let out a collective groan. Beside her, Sarah shut her eyes and winced. This was bad news for Eternity. Nic knew it. Yet she couldn't deny that in her heart of hearts, she was glad. No matter how she'd tried to convince herself and others, she never believed that a state prison would be the answer to Eternity's prayers.

"That's it, then," Dale Parker said, his tone morose. "Eternity is done for. Three bad summer seasons in a row and no prison to halt the bleeding. We might as well roll up the sidewalks and hang a Closed sign at the city limits."

A buzz of voices agreed with him. Hank Townsend shook his head. "Hold on now, Dale. Everybody take a deep breath and don't be so negative. Your city council isn't giving up. In fact, we've scheduled a meeting directly following this one to come up with a plan D. Everyone who—"

"That makes me feel better," Dale interrupted. "After all, plans A, B, and C worked out so well."

"Oh, for heaven's sake," muttered Celeste. Sitting catercorner to the gas station owner, she reached out and rapped him on the head with a rolled copy of the weekly town newspaper, the *Eternity Times*. "Let the man speak, Mr. Parker. You might learn something."

Parker frowned over his shoulder. "Beg pardon, Mrs. Blessing, but plan D? It's obvious that we're fighting a losing battle here."

As the audience buzzed mostly with agreement, Hank Townsend shoved his fingers through his hair and grimaced. "All right, all right, all right. I'll admit it. Eternity is looking more like Temporary every day. We have a dwindling population and zero industry. Summer tourism is sick because we're smack dab in the middle of the most isolated county in the lower forty-eight and the price of gasoline skyrockets every summer. Winter tourism is nonexistent. We're too far from the ski resorts, and it's too hard to get here to enjoy what we do have to offer. Once the snows close the mountain passes, we have one way to get in and out of here, and even I don't like facing Sinner's Prayer Pass in wintertime."

"Wussy," called Alton Davis, the liquor store owner,

who supplemented his income by driving a snow plow in winter—over Sinner's Prayer Pass.

"You bet," Hank replied.

A voice from the back of the room called out, "So is your plan D to annihilate the Davenport heirs, Hank? Gonna fix that troublesome will once and for all?"

The mayor froze, blinked, then snorted with amusement. "I have to admit, that idea has some appeal. Sure would solve a lot of problems to be able to cut a road through Waterford Valley and bring Eternity closer to civilization. Unfortunately, murder is illegal."

"Not to mention immoral," added Reverend Hart.

Dale Parker heaved a heavy sigh. "Nice to dream, though. Eternity Springs has been paying for that deal between Daniel Murphy and Lucien Davenport for a century and a quarter. You know darn well that if Murphys still owned the land, they'd have sold access to the mountain and to Waterford Valley at some point in the last century. Instead, ol' Daniel cursed us forever when he sold out to a rich man whose descendants care more about ancient history than they do about progress."

"Oh, please," said Emma Hall, owner, publisher, and sole employee of the *Eternity Times*. "This is a waste of time. The Davenports aren't going to change their position. Even if they did, don't forget who else would have to sign off on any deal involving Murphy Mountain. That would be Cameron Murphy. The same Cam Murphy you all routed out of town when he was little more than a boy. Somehow I doubt he'd be all that anxious to play Eternity's savior."

A drawn-out discussion of Cam Murphy's youthful misadventures followed, during which Sarah steadily slumped in her seat. For about the millionth time, Nic cursed the string of events that had done so much damage to both her childhood friends.

Celeste's keen, blue-eyed gaze shifted between Sarah

and Nic. She pursed her lips and thumped them
thoughtfully with an index finger, then said, "You know,
girls, Eternity Springs doesn't need a savior."

Nic answered with a wry smile. "No. We need a town
psychologist. After all, it doesn't say much about the
collective mental state of Eternity's citizens that we're
clinging so hard to an isolated, financially bankrupt,
long-past-its-prime mountain town."

Celeste harrumphed. "People tend to place entirely
too much importance on so-called prime years. Believe
me, I know."

Sarah elbowed Nic in the side. "I wouldn't argue with
the senior citizen with a new Honda Gold Wing."

Celeste continued. "As for the rest, actually, my dears,
the fact that you do cling to this lovely mountain town
says everything. Eternity Springs might be financially
bankrupt, but its moral coffers are full. The people here
are good folk. After living here six months, I have con-
cluded that this town is worth saving."

"I know it's worth saving," Nic said.

Sarah wearily massaged her brow. "It's a nice thought,
but at this point, I doubt that particular miracle can
happen."

Celeste exasperatedly blew out a puff of air. "This
only proves that you don't have much experience with
miracles. All Eternity Springs needs is an angel."

"That's not news," Sarah said. "I can't tell you how
many corporations, private investors, and venture capi-
talists the mayor and town council members have approached. No one was interested in investing in Eternity
Springs."

"That's why I said you need an angel," Celeste responded as Mayor Townsend pounded his gavel in an
attempt to regain control of the meeting. "Isn't it lucky
you have one?"

With talk of Cam Murphy's misdeeds finally subsiding, Celeste Blessing rose to her feet. "Mayor Townsend? If I might have the floor for moment? I have a plan to share. My own plan A." With a wink toward Nic and Sarah, she added, "*A* for angel, if you will."

"I'm happy to hear what you have to say, Mrs. Blessing." Hank Townsend waved her forward. "You're such a little bitty thing, why don't you join us on the stage so you can speak into the microphone?"

Nic watched in bemusement as Celeste made her way to the podium. The auditorium grew quiet, the air expectant, as the audience focused on the newcomer in their midst. Sarah leaned toward Nic and murmured, "When I grow up, I want to be like Celeste."

"She does have a way about her." Hope flickered to life within Nic as Hank Townsend adjusted the microphone for Celeste. Plan A for angel? Was Celeste Blessing Eternity Springs' angel?

"Think maybe she's more than just a retired schoolteacher?" Sarah asked, her mind obviously taking the same path as Nic's. "Maybe she's an heiress. Or . . . what has she said about her late husband? Could he have been a corporate bigwig?"

"I don't recall her saying much about him. Plus I wouldn't bet against *her* having been a corporate bigwig. Who knows, maybe Celeste landed in Eternity packing a golden parachute."

Onstage, Celeste leaned toward the mike and said, "Thank you, Mayor Townsend, council members, and fellow citizens. I appreciate the opportunity to address you. First, let me publicly thank you all for the very warm welcome you gave me as a newcomer to Eternity. I just knew that a town built along Angel Creek had to be a special place, and you've proved me right. You've been kind and friendly and my move here has been everything I hoped for. I want you all to know that I have faith in this town, faith in the people who live here."

"Hear, hear," called Reverend Hart.

Celeste beamed at him and continued. "Here is the message I want you all to hear. Eternity Springs didn't need the state of Colorado to build a prison here to save the town. Eternity Springs simply needs to free itself from the prison of its past and utilize the gifts a generous and loving God has bestowed upon it. Then, and only then, will this wonderful little town heal and thrive and fulfill the promise of its name.

"Now, we face a long, difficult winter and it won't be easy to overcome our fears, foibles, and failings. Each one of us must reach inside himself and find the will to do what must be done. But know this: spring is within sight. Thank you, and God bless."

Celeste stepped away from the podium and exited stage left.

For a long moment, nobody spoke. Sarah and Nic shared dumbfounded looks. Then the clatter of a metal door opening and swinging shut shook them from their reverie and the audience buzzed. Dale Parker groaned and buried his head in his hands. Mayor Townsend snapped his gaping jaw shut, then turned to his city council members. "That's plan A?"

Parker moaned through his hands. "*A* for angel, she said. Lady is living in la-la land."

"*A* for Alzheimer's, more likely," grumbled a council member.

"That's not funny, Ronnie," Sarah scolded, the remark having touched a sore nerve.

The council member had the grace to look sheepish as the mayor spoke into the mike. "Okay, then. Well. Anyone else want the microphone?" Without allowing a response, he rushed on. "For anyone who's interested, some of us will be congregating at the Pub to further discuss our options. Anyone who wants to put his or her brain to planning . . . uh . . . well, our next move, is welcome to join us. This meeting is adjourned."

He banged his gavel once again and the crowd slowly dispersed. Nic and Sarah both kept their seats, not speaking, but silently communicating in the way that old, dear friends do.

Finally Sarah spoke. "What just happened?"

Nic drummed her fingers against the armrest. "Do you feel it, too?"

"That something significant just took place?"

"And nobody noticed."

"Yeah." Nic drew a deep breath, and then exhaled in a rush. "No. We're just being weird."

"We do that often." Sarah nibbled at her bottom lip.

"True, but not under circumstances like this. Ordinarily when we're being weird, we have the urge to call each other at the same moment or we order the same dress from an online store and wear it to the same event."

"Or remember that time we both got a craving for good Mexican food and drove all the way to Gunnison to get it, and you walked into the restaurant before I'd finished my chips and salsa?"

The memory still nettled, so Nic lifted her chin. "You mean the time I called you to invite you to go with me but you were already on the road . . . without inviting me?"

"Hey, I was supposed to be dieting." Sarah grinned without apology. "But you're right. This was a different kind of weird."

As Nic tried to put her finger on tonight's particular brand of weirdness, a familiar voice called, "Hey, you two."

Nic glanced over her shoulder to see Sage Anderson striding down the auditorium's side aisle, her Gypsy skirt swirling around trim ankles, her long and wavy auburn hair bouncing with her steps. Sage was one of only a handful of permanent, year-round residents to move to Eternity Springs during the past decade. A painter, she thrived on the isolation the little town had to offer, and the work she'd produced of late was quickly making her the darling of the art world.

Sage had her secrets. She rarely talked about her life before the move to Eternity Springs. Sarah thought she was running *from* something. Nic believed she'd run *to* something in the mountains. Whichever way didn't much matter. Sage was their friend. They liked her and respected her privacy, so they kept their curiosity to themselves—even if it was difficult sometimes.

"I didn't see you," Nic said as Sage plopped down in a seat in the front row and twisted around to look at them. "Where were you sitting?"

"I came in late. Stood in the back." Her dangling purple crystal earrings sparkled as her green eyes gleamed. "Am I ever glad I did. 'Eternity Springs simply needs to free itself from the prison of its past and utilize the gifts a generous and loving God has bestowed upon it. Then, and only then, will this wonderful little town heal and thrive and fulfill the promise of its name.' I heard that and . . ." She snapped her fingers. "A visual popped into my brain. I'm gonna head home and get to work, but wanted to say hi to you two first."

"Batten down the hatches," Sarah said. "The creativity wind is upon us. We won't see her again for a week."

Nic nodded. "I'll hang the Do Not Disturb signs around the studio on my way home tonight. I'd rather avoid being called out to treat the wounds of any poor, unsuspecting soul who might hazard a knock upon her door."

"Oh, stop it," Sage said with a laugh. "I'm not that bad. I never draw blood." She beamed at Sarah and Nic, and exhaled a satisfied sigh. "Look, it very rarely happens this way. I am so stoked. Celeste Blessing gave me a gift with that speech of hers. I think she's wonderful. If the mayor and city council and grumpy old men like Dale Parker want to ignore her, then too bad so sad. I think she put the hope back into Eternity Springs tonight, and that's an important start."

Sarah gave Nic a look. "And we thought nobody noticed. Somebody did."

" 'Spring is in sight,' " Nic quoted, giving a rueful smile. "Think we can believe it?"

"I do," Sage declared. "I absolutely do."

"I want to," Sarah offered. "Although believing would be easier if this were February rather than the end of September."

Nic stared absently at the graffiti inked on the seat back in front of her and considered what troubles loomed before her in the coming months. She had taxes due on the house and clinic. The water heater was making funny noises and the furnace had been on borrowed time for three winters now. On a personal front, she faced long winter nights rambling around in a house that should be filled with children and laughter and love, but instead echoed with loneliness and grief over a lost dream.

Was Celeste right? Was spring—the end of her personal winter—finally in sight?

"Plan A for angel," she murmured as, unbidden, the image of a rescued boxer and a haunted-eyed stranger with scars on his chest and wounds on his soul flashed in her mind. *You're a lifesaver.*

"You know what?" Nic said, glancing from one friend to the other. "I believe it. It is weird, but we do weird here in Eternity Springs. I trust in Celeste's insight. I think she gave us all a gift. We just have to be smart enough to recognize it and act on it."

"Works for me," Sarah said.

"Me too," Sage agreed. "That's why I'm headed home to work. See you two . . . well . . . probably in a week or so."

Nic left the school auditorium with a lighter heart and a more positive outlook than she'd had in months. Maybe she was fooling herself. Maybe this was no more than relief over dodging the prison-comes-to-town bullet. Maybe Celeste had some strange hope-creating disease, and by sitting next to her, Nic had caught it.

Whatever it was, she liked the feeling and she refused to second-guess it. Today, for the first time in a very long time, Nicole Sullivan was looking forward to winter.

Gabe held a steaming cup of coffee in his hand as he stepped out onto the deck bathed in morning sunshine and took a moment to appreciate the exquisite view from the northern exposure of Eagle's Way. Above a sea of evergreens, a trio of snowy peaks kissed a robin's-egg sky. Patches of snow clung to the ground in shady spots and decorated the hills like icing. At the base of the mountain, waterfowl floated on the surface of a sapphire lake. The scene was beautiful, peaceful, and serene.

He inhaled a deep breath of crisp, pine-scented air and took stock of his situation.

Today might be a decent day.

Though he took care to keep his emotions locked away, he couldn't deny that something inside him had changed since the day the stray dog knocked his Glock into the snow. He didn't sleep half the day away anymore; he had energy again. For the past week he'd spent much of his time involved in heavy labor.

His breath fogged on the air and he checked the outdoor thermometer. Twenty-two degrees now, but he'd bet that would double by noon. It'd be a beautiful day to sweat.

He'd noted that a section of retaining wall beside the garage needed repair, and once he'd analyzed the situation and double-checked the house plans in Davenport's study, he'd realized that the builder had screwed up. They'd built the retaining wall five feet off the line, and as a result, vehicles entering and exiting the garage had to make a sharp left turn. Judging by the scrapes of paint on the support posts, the error needed to be corrected.

With no more snow in the immediate forecast and plagued by an unusual restless energy, Gabe had called his host and pitched his idea to tear down the wall and rebuild it according to the original design. Davenport had given him the go-ahead without hesitation. Not because he worried about a few paint scrapes, he'd allowed—he himself never messed up that turn, thank you very much—but because he knew from experience that strenuous physical work helped ward off the demons of depression.

Gabe didn't disagree. An hour of hard, physical outdoor labor beat an hour on a shrink's couch any day of the week.

On this particular day, he finished the north stretch of the new wall by late afternoon and decided he'd worked enough for the day. His muscles were sore, his body weary. Best of all, he'd rebuilt mental defenses right along with the retaining wall, and for the past six nights he'd slept nightmare-free. With any luck, tonight would make it seven.

As he tugged off his work gloves, he realized he was hungry. For the first time in longer than he could remember, he craved a real meal. Maybe he'd clean up, go into town, and try out that restaurant Jack had bragged about—the Bristlecone Café. Wouldn't hurt to pick up a few supplies, either.

Twenty minutes later, showered and dressed in clean jeans and a blue flannel shirt, he opened the pantry door to check the cereal supply and heard a scratching sound at the kitchen door. He glanced back over his shoulder and froze. "What the . . . ?"

Having a raccoon show up at the back door wouldn't have surprised him. Or a deer. An elk. A mountain lion. Actually, having a bear come pawing at the door wouldn't have shocked him. But a boxer? *The* boxer?

He wore one of those white plastic cone collars that prevented dogs from chewing at their stitches, and he looked ridiculous. Healthy, but ridiculous. Crooked tail wagging, ears perked, pink tongue extended, panting.

"It's been two weeks," Gabe muttered, thinking aloud. Was that long enough for the dog to be released from quarantine? Maybe. Had the vet brought the dog back to him to keep? Why? He'd told her the dog wasn't his.

Gabe frowned at the dog, then stepped outside, careful to block the boxer from scooting past him until the door was safely shut. "What's the deal, dog? Did you slip your leash and run away?"

He didn't see the vet or anyone else. Ordinarily Eagle's Way's serious security safeguards would prevent drop-in visitors, but for the past eight years Gabe preferred to leave gates and locks open whenever possible, no matter where he was. Memories of the six months he'd spent as a . . . guest . . . in an Eastern European prison were hard to shake, so he initiated Eagle's Way's security system at night but left the place accessible during the day. The vet could have driven right up to the house if she'd wanted, but the drive was empty. She must have parked in the circular drive in front. She'd probably ring the bell any moment now.

Gabe turned to reenter the house. This time the boxer was ready. A brindle blur all but knocked Gabe down as he dashed inside, through the kitchen, and into the hallway, headed for the great room. Gabe muttered a curse and took a quick mental inventory to determine what might be at risk of destruction as he trailed after the dog, wincing at the thought of the crystal collection on the coffee table—exactly at crooked-tail height.

"Hey!" he called as he hurried after the dog. "Stop. Stay. Sit."

He might as well have said "Sing 'The Star-Spangled Banner' " for all the good that did. Luckily, the dog made it across the room without destroying anything, and after a quick sniff he curled up on the rug in front of the fireplace.

"Well, make yourself at home, why don't you?" Gabe muttered as he crossed to the front door. He stared out at the circular drive where he expected to see a car—but didn't. There wasn't a car or truck or any vehicle of any type in sight.

Gabe's frown deepened as he stepped out onto the front porch. No car by the garage, either. "Hello?" he called. "Dr. Sullivan?"

Nothing. Nada. No one.

Reentering the house, he braced his hands on his hips and stared at the boxer. "You did not come all the way up here by yourself."

The dog exhaled a loud, snorty sigh. His tail thumped twice against the rug, and a stray thought sneaked past Gabe's barriers. Matty would have loved him.

Daddy, can I have a dog? Please? Pretty please?

Gabe gave himself a shake, then grimly said, "Well, it doesn't matter how you got up here. You are not staying here."

The tail thumped three times. Otherwise the dog didn't move so much as a whisker. In fact, he looked as if he'd be content to lie by the fire all winter. "Not hardly," Gabe muttered.

Well, he *was* headed to town anyway. A quick stop by the vet's to dump the dog wouldn't be a big deal.

Gabe grabbed his car keys from a nearby table and jangled them. "You want to go for a ride?"

One floppy brown ear perked up inside the silly white cone.

Gabe jangled the keys again. Both ears perked. Gabe tried to recall if he'd seen a dog leash anywhere in Eagle's Way. Maybe in the mud room?

When he returned to the great room with a leash in hand, the boxer leapt to his feet. After fastening the leash to the leather collar and adjusting the white plastic cone, Gabe led him to the garage and helped him climb up into the Jeep. He and the boxer headed into town.

Again.

THREE

Nic gave her reflection in the bathroom mirror one last look and wished she'd splurged on a new shade of lipstick for her date tonight. She'd worn a bronze shade for years. This was a new life. A new man. She should have a new lipstick.

"Too late now," she told her reflection. "He'll be here in ten minutes."

As Nic made her way downstairs, she admitted that referring to Bob Gerard as a "new man" was a stretch, since this was to be their first date and she'd only met Bob four days ago. He was part of the mayor's plan D, a business consultant from Colorado Springs whom Hank Townsend had brought to town to identify any options for saving Eternity Springs they might have overlooked.

Bob had flirted with Nic from the moment they met during a "business leader" luncheon at the Bristlecone. When he called that night to chat, her first instinct had been to brush him off the same way she had every other man since Greg Sullivan broke her heart. Then she'd recalled Celeste's speech at the high school about prisons of the past and she'd taken the leap, dusting off her own rusty flirting skills. Bob didn't seem to mind her awkwardness. When a conversation about hunting led to his admission that he'd never tried game meats, she'd screwed up her courage and invited him to dinner for the specialty of her house—roast venison.

For this casual evening at home, she'd chosen to wear black slacks and an aquamarine V-neck cashmere sweater that Lori and Sarah claimed did wonders for her eyes. Nic just hoped she could get through dinner without spilling anything on it. She'd about ruined the oxford shirt she'd worn while preparing the meal—despite wearing an apron at the time. "I'm not nervous," she said aloud. "I'm not."

When the doorbell rang, she startled. No, not nervous at all.

She put a smile on her face and opened the door, saying, "You're right on time . . . oh. Mr. Callahan."

Gabe Callahan stood on her front porch, the boxer he'd rescued up on Murphy Mountain at his side. "You knew I'd bring him back?"

"No. Not you. I thought you were someone else." She frowned down at the dog and said, "Why is the boxer with you? Is Celeste okay?"

"Who is Celeste?"

Without warning, the dog yanked the leash from Gabe's hand and darted past Nic and into her home just as her telephone started ringing. Flustered, she said, "I'm sorry. Let me get that. Please come in."

Her home was a standard Victorian design with two rooms on either side off a large entry hall with the staircase to the second-floor bedrooms at its center, a narrow kitchen stretching the width of the house at the back. The closest phone sat on a table at the back of the center hall, toward the kitchen. The boxer disappeared into the cozy library, where Nic spent most of her time and where she'd set a small table for two. Her unexpected guest followed the dog.

She grabbed the phone on the fourth ring without bothering to check the caller ID. "Hello?"

"Nic, hi. It's Bob. Look, I'm not going to be able to make it tonight. I'm on my way home now. Had an emergency."

She waited for her stomach to sink in disappointment. To her surprise, all she felt was relief. "I'm sorry to hear that. I hope it's nothing too serious."

"My son had an accident on his four-wheeler. Broke his arm and a leg. My wife is frantic, and frankly, so am I. Do you know how long it's gonna take me to get home? This town of yours is way too isolated."

"Excuse me?" Nic's heart began to pound. "Did you just say 'my wife'?"

"Oh. Well . . ."

Her blood began to boil. "You weren't wearing a wedding ring."

"Yeah. Well . . ."

"You sorry, lowlife jerk. You flirted with me from hello. I can't believe you . . . Listen. You can take your 'consulting' and shove it. We don't want your kind in our town." She started to slam the phone down, froze, and brought it back to her ear. "I hope your son is okay."

After that, she did slam the receiver into its cradle. She stood staring at it, her hands on her hips, breathing hard. Anger coursed through her blood. "What is it with men? Are they totally incapable of faithfulness?"

"Depends. It's a character issue more than a sexual one."

Nic closed her eyes in embarrassment and swallowed a groan. She'd forgotten about her visitor. Lovely. Just lovely.

"I seem to find only the characters without character. Oh well." She shrugged and shook off her discomfort. "Talk to me about the dog."

Gabe glanced at the boxer, who lay curled on a rug in

front of the fireplace. "He came scratching at my door a little while ago, and I'm bringing him back to you."

"He scratched at the door of your Jeep?"

"No. He scratched at the kitchen door at Eagle's Way."

"How did he get up there?"

"I thought you brought him."

"No." Nic shook her head. "I can't keep strays that come to me. It's one of my few hard-and-fast rules, otherwise I'd be overrun with pets. The boxer is on a week-long get-to-know-you visit with Celeste Blessing, who I hope will agree to adopt him. She lives in the big yellow Victorian on the east bank of Angel Creek."

"That's a long way from Murphy Mountain."

She nodded, then tilted her head and studied him, her eyes narrowed with suspicion. "Did he really show up at Eagle's Way?"

One side of Gabe's mouth lifted in a self-mocking smile, and he raised his hands palms out. "Hey, I have no reason to lie. I'm not married, and I'm not trying to date you."

"Ouch," she muttered, embarrassed at the reminder of what he'd overheard. "I need to call and check on Celeste. Would you keep an eye on Tiger for me, please? The way my luck is running, he'll decide to sample the meat I have resting on the kitchen counter."

"Tiger?"

She gestured vaguely toward the dog. "My name for him. It's his brindle coat, the black stripes on brown. Makes me think of tiger stripes."

Nic lifted the phone and dialed Celeste's number, conscious of the quickening in her pulse as she imagined all sorts of disasters that could have happened to her elderly friend. When Celeste said "Hello" following the third ring, Nic exhaled a relieved breath. "Hi, Celeste, it's Nic. I'm calling about the boxer."

"Ah . . . I take it he's found his way home?"

Nic gave Gabe Callahan a sidelong look and responded, "In a manner of speaking. He's here with me now. What happened?"

"Well, we were outside enjoying the sunshine when Archibald walked over, climbed up on my lap, licked my face, then trotted off. He obviously had somewhere to go, so I wasn't worried about him."

"Archibald?" Nic repeated, not certain she and Celeste were on the same wavelength. "We're talking about the boxer, right?"

"Yes, well, he needs a name, and that seemed to fit."

In what universe, Nic couldn't guess. "What time was this?"

"Oh, this morning sometime."

"And you weren't concerned when he didn't come back?"

"No, dear. Archibald is a sweetheart of a dog, but I'm not meant to be his companion. He and I both know that. We had quite a talk about it."

Nic decided then and there that it was time to take Celeste into Gunnison for a thorough medical checkup. She wasn't a dotty-old-dear type at all. Concerned, Nic asked, "Are you feeling all right, Celeste? Any unusual aches or pains?"

"I'm fine, dear. In fact, I'm just about to take a quick spin on my Honda. It's a beautiful evening, and this time of year, each one we have is a heavenly gift. You should make a point of enjoying yourself, too. I recall that this is a difficult day for you."

"Yes, well . . ." Nic glanced toward Gabe and saw that he was perusing the offerings on her bookshelves. The boxer hadn't budged from his position in front of the fire. "Maybe Archibald will help me pass the time. Drive safely, Celeste. I'll talk to you tomorrow."

She ended the call and joined her visitors in the library. Gabe arched a brow her way and repeated, "Archibald? That's worse than Tiger."

"What have you been calling him?"

Gabe glanced down at the dog and shook his head. "I don't name things I don't intend to keep."

She spared him a scolding look before turning her attention to the dog. Since he didn't seem interested in coming to her, she crossed the room and knelt beside him. "All right, Tiger. Let's give you a quick once-over to see how you fared on today's trek. Hmm . . . no new scratches or scrapes that I can tell. And, actually, these stitches can come out. How about it, handsome? You ready to ditch the collar?"

As she unfastened the Elizabethan collar's plastic tabs, she glanced up at Gabe. "I have a yellow canvas bag hanging on a chair in the kitchen. Would you grab it for me, please? It's the room at the far end of the entry hall."

"Sure." When he handed the bag over a few moments later, he said, "I see why you wanted to keep the dog out of the kitchen. Something smells awfully tempting."

"It's my specialty. Pistachio-and-pine-nut-crusted rack of venison with wild mushrooms." As she removed the stitches from the boxer's leg, she said, "Why don't you stay and share my supper, Mr. Callahan? I have plenty, and everything is ready."

He glanced toward the table set for two. "Oh . . . uh . . . thanks, but I don't think so."

"Why not? You have to eat, and it's not like I'm trying to date you, either."

His stare shifted toward the kitchen, and she thought she saw a flash of regret in his eyes before he shook his head. "I thought I'd drop by the Bristlecone Café. I've heard the food is excellent."

"It's wonderful and you definitely need to try it, but it

won't be tonight. It's Tuesday. The Bristlecone is closed on Tuesdays."

"Oh, well . . ."

His obvious reluctance began to annoy her. "Are you a vegetarian? Don't care for game? If that's it, you really should try my venison. I promise you'll change your mind."

"Dr. Sullivan—"

"Nic."

"I'm Gabe. I appreciate the invitation. Your venison sounds and smells delicious, but I'm not much company."

"All right. What's a little more humiliation?" She folded her arms and sighed. "Here's the deal, Gabe. I know I'm being pushy. It's an unfortunate tendency of mine. But the fact is that I really, really don't want to be alone tonight. See, today is . . . was . . . my wedding anniversary. Would have been six years today if the man I married wasn't a lying, cheating snake. Last year on this date I swore I wouldn't spend this year wallowing in another self-indulgent pity party. If you leave me now, I'm liable to do just that. Besides, the way I figure it, you owe me. I saved your life, remember? You said yourself that I was a lifesaver. All I'm asking for in return is for you to sit down and make small talk with me while we share a gourmet meal and a really fine bottle of wine."

Amusement lit his eyes and she could see the subtle lessening of tension in his stance. "Small talk, huh? You don't know how much I hate small talk."

"Deal with it, Callahan. The meat needs to sit another . . ." She checked the mantel clock. "Five minutes. The powder room is beneath the stairs if you want to wash up, and if you'd like a drink before dinner, the piece of furniture against the wall behind you is a bar. I filled the ice bucket earlier, so you're good to go."

In the kitchen, Nic gave her hips a happy little wiggle

as she stirred the sauce. Okay, so this wasn't a date. No doubt about that. Nevertheless, she'd managed to upgrade her dinner companion for tonight in a substantial way, and for that she was grateful. Excited, even. She couldn't have asked for a better distraction on this unhappy anniversary. Gabe Callahan was downright hot. The scruffy, need-a-haircut-and-a-shave look suited him, and a girl could get drunk on those warm whiskey eyes of his.

Distracted by her thoughts and the man in her library, Nic neglected to use her hot pads as she went to pick up her roasting pan. "Yee-ouch!" she cried as the pan clattered back onto the stovetop.

She was shaking her left hand and staring at the venison, grateful she hadn't dropped their dinner on the floor, when Callahan appeared in the doorway to her kitchen. "What's wrong?"

"I'm an idiot. I almost dropped the roast."

"You burned yourself," he surmised as his gaze shifted from her to the pot on the stove. Crossing to the kitchen sink, he twisted the cold water faucet. "C'mere."

When she moved close, he took her arm by the wrist and studied her hand as he guided it beneath the running water. "You grabbed your pan without a pad? You don't strike me as the careless sort."

"I have my moments of ditziness," she replied.

Ditziness fast becoming dizziness. He'd yet to release her hand, so he stood close enough for her to smell the sandalwood fragrance of his soap. It was all she could do not to sway against him.

Nic had always been a sucker for ruggedly handsome men with well-defined abs, but with the wounded-soul thing he had going on . . . whoa. *My oh my, he trips my trigger.*

"It doesn't appear to be too bad a burn," he observed.

You'd be surprised. With a husky note to her voice, she murmured, "It's fine."

Gabe glanced up and caught her staring at the strong line of his jaw. His gaze locked onto hers, and for a long, smoldering moment time hung suspended. Nic thought he might lower his head and kiss her.

Instead he abruptly released her wrist as if it were the hot roasting-pan handle and quickly backed away.

In that moment he reminded her of a cornered animal desperately searching for escape, and the healer in her responded. This man was hurt, damaged in some fundamental way. She saw it not in those scars upon his body but in the haunted expression in his eyes.

She wanted to make him well again. If he had four legs instead of two, she'd know exactly what to do, but humans weren't her specialty, and despite his appeal, she felt out of her league where Gabe Callahan was concerned.

Gruffly he asked, "Can I, um, carry something to the table?"

"Sure. Thank you. The breadbasket is there by the coffee maker. I'll join you in just a few minutes."

He grabbed the basket in full retreat and kept his distance until Nic invited him to pour the wine as she served the meal. Once they were both seated, she attempted to dispel the lingering tension by lifting her glass in a toast. "To scintillating small talk, Mr. Callahan."

After a brief pause, Gabe gave a half smile, touched his glass to hers, and said in a droll tone of voice, "Lovely weather we're having, Dr. Sullivan."

The exchange set the tone for the meal. His interest in her library led to a discussion about reading preferences and she learned they shared an affinity for popular fiction. They both enjoyed thrillers, though he expressed disdain for spy novels and she didn't care for graphic violence. They debated favorite authors for a time, then conversation moved to the meal. He paid flattering homage to her cooking skills, both verbally and by taking second helpings. She considered it a minor victory when he asked her a question that she felt went beyond "small talk."

Nic lifted her wineglass and swirled the ruby liquid as she contemplated her answer. "I chose to return to Eternity Springs because I have a thing for ruby slippers."

He made the Wizard of Oz connection easily. "There's no place like home, Dorothy?"

"Exactly. I can live other places, be happy other places. I certainly would be better off financially if I worked somewhere else. But I don't think I'd thrive anywhere but here. It sounds corny, I know, but I believe that this is where I am meant to be." She sipped her wine and took a risk. "How about you, Gabe Callahan? Where is home for you?"

Slowly, he set down his fork. He lifted his napkin from his lap and wiped his mouth. "The meal was excellent, Nic. I've never tasted venison as delicious as this."

Okay. Great big No Trespassing sign in that window. She considered calling him on it but decided she didn't want to spoil what had ended up being a lovely evening. "Thank you. Would you care for dessert?"

He glanced at the mantel clock and set his napkin on the table. "I should be heading back."

"I have a plate of the Bristlecone Café's famous brownies."

He returned his napkin to his lap. "I guess there's no need to hurry."

Nic grinned as she rose to clear the dinner plates, but the smile died when she glanced out the window and spied an unusual light. "Wait. Look, Gabe. What is that?"

He responded at the moment a bell began to clang. "Fire. I think it's across the creek."

Nic stared, realized what she was looking at, then gasped. "That's Cavanaugh House."

Celeste Blessing's home was on fire.

Gabe started his Jeep and cursed the dog. If not for that dopey, crooked-tailed mange magnet, he'd be holed up on the mountain safely by himself.

He didn't belong down here in the valley having dinner with an attractive woman. He had no business rushing off to the rescue of little old ladies. Interacting with others. Joining in their efforts. He had no business doing any of this. That wasn't why he'd come to Eternity Springs.

It was all that stupid dog's fault.

Yet the moment Nic slipped into the passenger seat beside him, a medical bag in hand, he shifted into gear and headed for the fire.

She tossed a pair of work gloves into his lap. "We're a volunteer fire department here. They'll have some extra gear on the truck, but it never hurts to have your own."

He muttered a few more curses beneath his breath. He had much more experience with firefights than he did with fighting fires.

When they arrived at the scene, it quickly became obvious to Gabe that the first responders knew what they were doing. They worked efficiently and effectively beneath the direction of the man he recognized as the owner of the local lumber yard.

"There's Celeste. Thank God." Nic grabbed her medical bag and hopped out of the Jeep before Gabe switched off the ignition. As she rushed toward the elderly woman seated on the tailgate of a pickup truck, Gabe braced himself, then went to offer his assistance to the lumberyard owner, who was barking orders into a radio. "What can I do to help?"

"You ever done this before?"

"No."

"Then stay back. Help move the hose." He pointed to a man who had the fire hose slung over his shoulder and who moved in coordination with the two men in front at the nozzle. Over the roar and crackle of the fire, the leader shouted, "Cyrus, go spell Frank for a bit. This fella will take your place."

Heat hit Gabe like a body blow as he moved closer to the fire. From the top floor of the grand old mansion, fingers of flame stabbed into the night sky. Gingerbread decorating the eaves flamed, blackened, and disappeared. An attic window popped and men scurried backward as glass rained down onto the yard.

Once the glass settled, firefighters moved forward with their hoses again, water roaring from the nozzles. Gabe hauled and hoisted and hefted. Sweat cascaded down his face and reminded him of a hot Texas summers of his youth. He turned his face away as a cloud of smoke rolled over him and stole his breath. He started to cough, so hard that he bent over double.

It was as he straightened that he recognized the potential for disaster. With the wind blowing the heat and flames away from them, a pair of knuckleheaded boys had kept inching forward, and they now stood too close to the burning house for Gabe's peace of mind. He yelled to catch their attention and tell them to move back, but between his smoke-filled lungs and the chaos of the moment, no one paid him any attention. *Who are the idiots who allow their kids to run loose this way?*

He heaved a grim sigh and set down the hose, indicating his intentions by gesture to the man in front of him. He hurried toward the boys, and he'd just captured the boys' notice when the boom of an explosion ripped through the night. Burning debris launched like missiles into the air above the boys' heads, and Gabe launched himself at the pair.

The boys cried out as they all went down in a heap. Flaming rubble rained down around them. Something hard and hot struck Gabe's back just as a scream alerted him to the fact that one boy's fleece jacket had caught fire. Gabe frantically went to work smothering the flames, and soon other arms reached out to help. As panicked voices rose all around him, he climbed slowly to his feet, breathing heavily.

Someone shuffled the kids off for Nic to check over, but Gabe ignored the instruction that he should do the same. Instead he went back to the fire hose, back to work. The minor burns on his hands didn't rate a break, and he could tell that they were gaining ground on the fire.

All in all, the incident with the boys didn't last a minute. The fire itself hadn't burned for more than twenty. The volunteer fire department had it whipped in half an hour. When the lumberyard owner ordered the hoses shut off, a huge cheer went up from the crowd. Everyone in town must be here.

Gabe stepped away from the fire hose. The townspeople surged forward to inspect damage to a home now lit only by moonlight. Gabe remained stationary, and as a result, he soon stood at the periphery of the crowd. Scraps of conversation drifted over him.

"How did it start?"

"Who was the fella who knocked the boys to safety?"

"She bought the place lock, stock, and barrel. I heard it's still packed full of Cavanaugh stuff. Hope it wasn't all destroyed."

"Well, Celeste can't stay here. Wonder who will take her home?"

"Looks like the damage is confined to the north addition. Lucky break there."

"Who's that man who came with Dr. Nic? I've never seen him before."

"You know, Hank, we dodged a disaster by the skin of our teeth. We have to get the pump truck fixed. Got it running tonight on a lick and a prayer. Hell, the fire could have jumped the creek and burned down the whole damn town!"

Gabe took another step back. Then another. When he saw a trio of matrons eyeing him with questions in their eyes, he pivoted on his heel and headed for the Jeep. Halfway there he stopped abruptly. He'd brought Nic here. He couldn't up and leave without her. His mother—God rest her soul—had branded that into his bones.

Reluctantly he went to find her. A triage of sorts had been set up along the bank of Angel Creek with lanterns and flashlights and car headlights illuminating the space. Nic and a handful of other women were there tending to a variety of minor injuries.

As he approached, an older woman eyed him with interest. "You must be Gabe Callahan," she said. "I'm Celeste Blessing. Nicole tells me that Archibald has decided you are his owner."

Who? Oh. The dog. Oh, no. No. No. No. "I'm just visiting the area, Ms. Blessing. I'm a guest in someone else's home. I can't have a dog."

"Hmm . . ." She offered him a beatific smile before turning to Nic. "Now that things have calmed down a bit, I need to tell you why the accident happened. I'm afraid I knocked over the candle because I was trying to run after the puppy that a fox chased into my root cellar. He was hurt, Nic, and I'm sure he's still down there. We need to go get him."

A pretty brunette about Nic's age shook her head. "You can't go down there tonight."

"It's a puppy," Celeste repeated. "I hope he doesn't die."

The brunette hit her forehead with her palm and groaned. "Now you've done it. Nic won't hesitate to risk life and limb for a puppy."

Celeste added, "They told me the basement wasn't affected by the fire, so the root cellar should be fine, too."

Nic stared toward the house. "I can make a quick—"

"I'll do it," Gabe announced. "Somebody give me a flashlight."

"Thanks, Gabe." She darted a smile. "Two sets of hands are better than one when working with wild animals, and I suspect she saw a coyote rather than a puppy. Let me grab my bag."

He nodded, accepted the offered flashlight, and headed for the root cellar entrance he'd noticed while fighting the fire. She caught up with him halfway to the house. "I'll go in first. If the animal needs sedation, you'll need to stay out of my way."

Gabe respected her professional abilities, but no way he'd let a woman take point position. At the root cellar door he met her gaze and said, "Dr. Sullivan? Sit. Stay."

She narrowed her eyes and said, "Careful, Callahan. I bite."

He switched on the flashlight and stepped down into the inky blackness. The air smelled musty and smoky. He stood still for a moment as he listened for puppy sounds. Nothing.

"Quiet as a tomb," he muttered, playing the light across the floor from left to right. He saw burlap bags and wooden shelves, two wooden barrels, and . . . a caved-in section of a brick wall.

He muttered a curse.

"What is it?" Nic called, descending the stairs. "What's wrong?"

The beam from Gabe's flashlight held steady on the skull revealed by the crumbling brick.

Behind him, Nic gasped. "Gabe? Tell me that's fake. It's a Halloween prop, isn't it?"

Nope. Sure wasn't. "Go back outside, Nicole."

"It was in the wall? Bricked up?" Instead of exiting the root cellar, Nic Sullivan moved forward. "This is so Edgar Allan Poe."

"Careful," Gabe warned as she approached the crumbled wall, pulling a flashlight of her own from her medical bag. She reached out and dragged another row of loose bricks away, then another. Realizing she wasn't about to quit, Gabe stepped up to help her.

They tore the wall halfway to the floor and stepped back. Nic let out a long, shaky sigh. "That's the saddest thing I've ever seen, Gabe."

The skeleton lay stretched out on a wooden table, what appeared to be the tattered remains of a wedding dress draped atop it.

Gabe peered behind the remnants of the wall and added, "Interesting, too. There are stacks of silver bars at her feet."

FOUR

The tantalizing aroma of frying bacon coaxed Nic from her dreams. So unusual was the occurrence that she took a moment to solve the puzzle before bothering to open her eyes. Was she dreaming still? Why would . . . oh. The fire. Celeste. Celeste had come home with her last night. Celeste had cooked her breakfast.

The events of the previous night flooded into her mind. Bob the philandering jerk, dinner with the mystery man of Murphy Mountain, the Cartwright boys' near miss with disaster. Was there a more foolish human on earth than a teenage boy?

And then the disturbing find in the root cellar: a skeleton in a wedding dress and thirty silver bars. Thirty pieces of silver, Sarah had said. Blood money. Nic shivered at the memory even before she threw off the toasty-warm bedclothes and stepped into the chilly morning air.

While she showered and dressed, Nic took a quick mental inventory of the day ahead of her. Today was Wednesday. She had no overnight patients at the clinic, no boarders. Her first appointment wasn't until after lunch. She'd been scheduled to go out to the Double R Ranch this morning, but the foreman called yesterday and moved the visit to next week. She served as backup vet for most of the ranches in the area, and that would continue until Dr. Walsh over in Creede retired in two more years. The Double R was the only ranch around that called her first, but that was because the Double R's owner, Henry Moreland, had had a falling-out with Dr. Walsh.

She probably should check on Dale Parker. The burn he'd sustained on his forearm needed a doctor's attention, and even though he'd promised to make the drive into Gunnison today, she didn't trust him not to weasel out. Other than that, she was free to help Celeste.

Last night Gabe Callahan had quietly relayed news of their root cellar discovery to Sheriff Zach Turner, who had made the decision to wait until daylight to attempt any further investigation. He'd stretched yellow crime-scene tape around the perimeter of the house—cellar included—and used his bullhorn to warn folks to stay away from the damaged building, whose "walls could tumble down at any second." Then Celeste had appropriated the bullhorn, thanked her fellow citizens for their help, and promised invitations to everyone to the party she would throw once repairs to her home had been completed.

Nic donned jeans and a sweatshirt and made her way to the kitchen to find the dirty dishes from the previous night gone and a breakfast of bacon, pancakes, and juice ready and waiting. "Celeste! You shouldn't have cleaned up my mess."

"Why not?" Standing at the stove, Celeste glanced over her shoulder. "You plan to help me with mine, don't you?"

"Yes, but—"

"Excellent. I knew I could count on you. Now, sit down and eat, Nicole, because as soon as we're finished here, we need to drive up to Eagle's Way."

A glass of orange juice halfway to her mouth, Nic froze. "Eagle's Way? Why?"

"I need to discuss my plans for Cavanaugh House

with Gabe, and you need to take Archibald to him. In all the confusion last night, he forgot his dog."

His dog? Nic opened her mouth to protest, but reconsidered and poured syrup onto her pancakes. Celeste had a point. The boxer obviously had chosen Gabe. She'd find it interesting to watch his reaction to the fact. It would tell a lot about the man. "Why would you talk to Gabe Callahan about Cavanaugh House, Celeste?"

"It's part of my Angel Plan. Dear, have you ever wondered what drew you home in the wake of your divorce?"

She gave it a moment's thought. "The people. The place. It's home for me. Eternity Springs . . . soothes me."

"Exactly," Celeste replied with a nod as she filled Nic's sink with water. "Eternity Springs calls to people in pain."

Like Gabe Callahan. It made a weird sort of sense, but . . . "That's a little woo-woo for me, Celeste."

"It's spiritual. You understand. You're a spiritual woman."

"I'm not a New Ager. I'm Methodist."

Squirting green dishwashing soap into the water, the older woman laughed. "Spirituality is part of the fabric of organized religion. Don't let anyone tell you otherwise. Often it's simply not as obvious. The healing energy in this valley is significant, although it's been muted by a sickness of spirit that infected its people long ago. We need to exorcise that sickness and encourage the healing that's available. All will be stronger because of it."

"That's still borderline woo-woo with me," Nic said. Then she addressed another part of Celeste's proposal that piqued her curiosity. "So, what, you want to use Gabe as a test case or something?"

"I want to engage Gabe Callahan's professional services. He is a landscape architect."

"He is? How do you know?"

"I recognized him. Two years ago his firm designed a play area for a children's hospital in South Carolina. I was on the board of directors of another hospital, and we researched his firm while considering a similar project. He's quite well-known in his arena."

A landscape architect. Interesting. But how did an architect get a warrior's scars? "So what do you want him to do at Cavanaugh House?" Then, before Celeste could respond, Nic understood. She'd said healing energy. "The hot springs? You're gonna ask him to design something around the hot springs, aren't you? A resort like they have over in Pagosa Springs?"

"Not exactly. My idea is bigger than that. This won't be a tourist facility for skiers with sore muscles. Cavanaugh House will be the centerpiece of a healing center, Nicole, and I want Gabe Callahan to design the master plan. Yes, I want a spa facility and pools for the hot springs, but I also want a healing garden and hiking trails and terraces of prayer. My vision is to make Eternity Springs the Sedona of Colorado."

Nic set down her fork and sat back in her chair, considering the idea. "The Sedona of Colorado," she mused. She'd visited Sedona, Arizona, one time. It was a lovely place. Not as lovely as Eternity Springs, but then she was prejudiced. The people of Sedona had been friendly. Different, but friendly. Of course, Eternity Springs folks were different, too. Mountain people usually were.

Winter mountain people, especially.

She couldn't be certain that Eternity would be as welcoming to outsiders as Sedona, but a steady supply of tourist dollars would surely smooth the way for that. Celeste's plan would change their town, but after plans

A, B, C, and D most everyone understood that change of some sort was necessary for survival.

A healing center and spa. "It fits with our history. When this area was being settled, people moved to Colorado because of perceived health benefits. The air here was considered good for those with consumption. Even Doc Holliday came here to heal. And of course, the Ute visited our hot springs for a long time before settlers arrived." Her mouth stretched in a smile. "Celeste, I think your idea is inspired."

"I know, dear. Now, finish your breakfast so you can dry these pans I'm about to wash. Then we can share our good news with poor Gabe."

"Poor Gabe?"

"Not literally, of course. The man is quite comfortable financially. I mean poor in spirit. Gabe is a perfect example of someone who needs what Eternity Springs has to offer. Unfortunately, he's too isolated up there, too alone on the mountain. He needs to come to town to work on the project. He needs to be here in Eternity Springs around the people . . ." She paused as Nic rose to let in the boxer, who stood scratching at her kitchen door. "And the pets who will help heal his wounded heart."

She sees his damaged heart, too. Nic slipped Tiger a half slice of bacon. "What do you know about him, Celeste?"

"I know what I see when I look into his eyes. He's haunted, Nicole. You've seen it, too, haven't you?"

She recalled the horrible scars on his back and chest and spoke quietly. "Yes."

"Gabe Callahan's pain makes him uniquely suited for this project. I believe he'll tap into the energy of Eternity Springs and produce a transcendent design. He'll not only change our world, he will change his own."

Hope lifted Nic's heart, but caution kept her grounded. "If you can convince him to give us a chance.

I had to twist his arm to get him to stay for dinner last night."

"Yes, but he did stay, did he not?"

Yes, he had stayed, and she'd enjoyed his company tremendously. Gabe was witty and intelligent and interesting. Heaven knows the man was delicious to look at. He was the first man since her divorce who truly interested her, but Gabe Callahan had issues. That was as clear as the scars on his chest. To consider him a romantic prospect wasn't realistic.

That didn't mean, however, that she couldn't offer him friendship. She suspected that the man seriously needed a friend.

"Your success at arm twisting is why I want you to come with me this morning. I want you to take the lead in this conversation. He said yes to you last night."

"That doesn't mean he'll say yes this time. He's not very approachable, Celeste. His defenses are as high as Murphy Mountain."

"Then you'll have to come up with a way to scale the heights, won't you?"

Before Nic could ask just how she was supposed to manage that particular feat, her front doorbell rang. Celeste said, "You must have an early customer at the clinic."

"No, the clinic bell is a buzzer that sounds in my kitchen. That's the doorbell." Nic walked to the front of the house and identified the figure standing on her front porch: Zach Turner. Opening the door, she said, "Good morning, Zach. Come on in."

"Morning, Nic. Thanks." In her entry hall, he removed his gray felt hat and said, "I need to speak with Celeste."

"She's in the kitchen. Come on back. Can I get you a cup of coffee?"

"Thanks. That would be great."

Celeste offered a sheepish smile to the sheriff as he entered the kitchen. "Oh, dear. Am I in trouble?"

"You gotta be careful with candles, Celeste, but I'll save the lecture for another time. The county coroner is on his way to Eternity to remove the remains, and I have a few questions to clear up before he gets here."

"I'm happy to help any way I can."

Celeste wiped her wet hands on a dish towel and sat at Nic's table. Zach sat across from her and accepted a mug of coffee from Nic with thanks. He removed a small notebook and a pen from his pocket and made notes as he asked her a few general questions about Cavanaugh House and her use of the root cellar. After pausing to sip his coffee, he said, "It's clear that the remains have been entombed in the cellar for a long time, so we're not dealing with a recent crime. The dress is Victorian, complete with a bustle. Also, we found this."

He held up a plastic bag. Inside it lay a silver locket attached to a silver chain. "Look at the engraving," Celeste said. "It reminds me of an angel's wings."

"You're right," Nic said. Then she asked Zach, "Can you tell how she died?"

Zach nodded. "Probably. There appear to be two bullets. What we didn't find was a clue to her identity. I'll probably have better luck speaking to members of the historical society, but I wanted to ask you, Celeste, if you've found anything in the contents of Cavanaugh House that might be of help."

Celeste shook her head. "No, but I haven't begun to go through the contents of the attic or basement. That's a job I intended to tackle over the winter. The place is packed full of interesting boxes and crates, and luckily, the fire didn't reach that part of Cavanaugh House."

"There's certainly no rush. The state lab will work up a forensic report for us, but due to the circumstances, it's certain to be a low priority. I suspect the only way we'll ever be able to put a name to her is to find something in old records."

"What about the silver?" Nic asked.

"My understanding is that you bought the house and all its contents, so the silver is yours. Although before you get too excited, at today's silver prices, that stash isn't worth as much as you might think."

"Yes, I know," Celeste replied. "However, it's reasonable to believe that it's ore from the Silver Miracle mine, so it does have historical value. I'll come up with an appropriate use for it, I suspect."

Zach finished his coffee, and after a few minutes of small talk he took his leave. Nic attempted to take over the pan-washing chore, but Celeste brushed her away as she said, "That young man impresses me. He's rather new to the area, too, isn't he?"

"Yes. He got the job when Sheriff Adkins retired a little over a year ago."

"I don't see him around town very much."

"He's responsible for a pretty large territory. Eternity Springs doesn't give him much business." Nic grabbed a clean dish towel. "Although he has begun spending more time in Eternity the last month or so. I think he's interested in Sarah."

"Oh?"

"Yep. They've had dinner together a handful of times. She refuses to see them as dates, though. She says they're simply casual meals between friends."

"I see." Celeste handed Nic a clean frying pan to dry. "Maybe if she continues to spend time with him, she'll come to recognize what a catch he is."

"She already knows he's a catch, but that doesn't matter. Gabe Callahan isn't the only person toting around baggage in this town. Unfortunately, Sarah has carried hers so long that it's grown to her skin."

As Nic put the frying pan away, Celeste washed the last

dirty dish. After handing it to Nic to dry, she suddenly snapped her damp fingers. "Oh dear. I just remembered that I have an appointment for a perm at ten. I can't go to Eagle's Way this morning. Shall we go this afternoon?"

"I'm sorry, I have clinic appointments this afternoon. I could go Friday morning."

Celeste rinsed her hands beneath running water, gave a thoughtful hum, then said, "You know, I believe that timing and presentation will be crucial in gaining his agreement. He joined in to help last night, and that's an important step for a man in his circumstances. Let's not give him the opportunity to slip back into solitude. Why don't you go on up now? You propose the plan, then I'll follow up and close the deal. We'll give him the proverbial one-two punch."

Nic slowly shook her head. "I'm not sure that's a good idea, Celeste."

Celeste dried her hands, hung up the towel, and said, "Well, I am sure. I want you to take Archibald up the mountain with you and convince Gabe Callahan that he needs to come back down. It's important for all of us. The man needs Eternity Springs, but we need him, too."

Nic considered the idea as she finished drying the dishes and putting them away. "I do think this idea of yours is inspired, and I don't mind going up there and making the pitch on your behalf. It's a great excuse to get a peek at Eagle's Way. The guys who worked on its construction still talk about how elaborate the house is. That said, it's entirely possible that Gabe might not let me in, Celeste. The security around the place is said to be elaborate."

"I'm not worried. If Archibald can get past the gate, I'm sure you can, too."

She had a point. In fact, she had lots of points. This idea of hers was great and it could be huge for Eternity Springs. "All right, then. I'll give it a shot."

"Excellent. Now, I'd best get moving if I'm going to

have time to stop by the house before my hair appointment. I'm almost afraid to go over there for fear that the destruction will be worse than it appeared in the darkness."

"I had an idea about that last night. Although Cavanaugh House is outside the defined historic district, you might qualify for a development grant from the state if—"

"Money isn't an issue," Celeste interrupted, dismissing the subject with a wave of her hand. "Family funds."

Nic wasn't surprised. Despite being neglected for decades, Cavanaugh House had still carried a hefty price tag. "You never speak of your family."

"I had a lovely family, but they're all gone now. I am comfortable financially, so if the subject of fees comes up, tell Gabe I said to name his price. Perhaps that will seal the deal."

Nic recalled the wad of cash he had shoved into her hand the day they met. "Gabe doesn't strike me as being overly motivated by money."

"Then find out what will motivate him and offer him that."

"I barely know the man. How am I supposed to know what motivates him?"

Celeste reached across the table and patted Nic's arm. "Listen to your heart, Nicole. When dealing with Gabe Callahan, you can't go wrong by listening to your heart."

Gabe tugged off his work gloves and surveyed the retaining-wall construction with a practiced eye. "Much better," he muttered. Now Davenport wouldn't have to lie about the scrapes from the turn on the side of his SUV.

He stuck the gloves in the back pocket of his jeans and

shifted his gaze toward the house itself. An unbidden memory invaded his mind. *He was seated at his drawing board in his home office sketching a landscape plan for Eagle's Way when Jennifer breezed into the room, her eyes sparkling, a smile as big as Texas on her face. "Mission accomplished!" she'd exclaimed. "It was a hard-fought battle, but the good guys persevered. Ta-da!"*

She whipped the plastic sack sporting a toy store logo away from a box. "One birthday Xbox for Nathan, coming up."

Gabe shook his head. "Unbelievable. How long did you stand in line?"

"Only five hours. I made the right decision going to the independent rather than the big-box store. Lots less people to compete with."

"You win the Best Aunt of the Year Award with that one, Auntie Jen."

"What can I say? I love my sister's son."

Gabe set down his pencil and studied the box. "You bought games to go with it?"

"Two of them."

"Hmm . . . you know, hon, just to be safe . . . maybe I should hook this up and make sure it works. I'd hate for Nathan to be disappointed if—"

Jennifer tugged the box from his hands, clucking her tongue. "That's pathetic, Uncle Gabe. You have to wait just like all the other boys. Now, get back to your drawing board and design a spectacular pool and spa for Jack Davenport. He's promised me that we can vacation there when construction is done. I've never been to Colorado, and I've always wanted to see the Rockies."

Gabe closed his eyes and swayed as he was buffeted by a wave of grief and regret. Despite Jack's offer, they'd never taken that Colorado trip. By the time Eagle's Way was ready for visitors, Jennifer was pregnant with Matt.

Once he'd been born, they'd decided to wait until he was older to take that particular family vacation.

Until he was older.

His throat tight, his body tense, Gabe sucked in a deep breath of cold mountain air. Memories were dragons and he had not the weapons to battle them. That's why he'd acquiesced to Jack's suggestion that he spend a few weeks at Eagle's Way. Memories didn't haunt every room of this house. Up here in this high valley, even down in town, he could . . . breathe.

Gabe exhaled heavily and turned away from the house. His gaze skimmed across the snow-dusted mountaintops before lifting toward the clear blue sky. Sunshine warmed his face. The tension within him eased. Jack had been right. There was something special about this place. Maybe he'd stay on a little longer.

He'd need another project, though. Something physical. Maybe after lunch he'd give the house a good going over and see if the contractor had made any other mistakes that needed fixing.

He turned to head into the house to make a sandwich, then pulled up short upon seeing the faded blue pickup truck driving the winding road leading to the house. He didn't recognize the truck before sight of it was lost to the cover of the trees. Frowning, he tried to recall if he'd forgotten a scheduled delivery. No, he didn't think so. The housekeepers Jack retained came on Thursdays, so it wasn't them, either.

Gabe kept his gaze focused on the road as he walked toward the drive, and when the truck emerged from the cover of the forest, he was able to make out two figures inside the cab. Looked like a couple of women. And, as the truck drew closer, he saw a third form. A dog.

The dog. Along with Nic Sullivan and a woman he didn't recognize. What brought them to Eagle's Way?

Maybe she was bringing him the jacket he'd left at her house last night.

She waved hello when she saw him, and he returned a nod, then motioned for her to pull around the excavator to park. The moment she opened the driver's-side door, the boxer pushed past her and scrambled out, barking excitedly as he bounded toward Gabe. The mutt looked so goofy with his ears flopping and his crooked tail wagging that Gabe couldn't help laughing—until the dog jumped on him. He pushed him away saying, "Hey, dog. Stop that. Get down."

"Watch out for the mouth," said a pretty redhead whom Gabe didn't know. "He's been drooling on me all the way up from town." She extended her hand adding, "I'm Sage Anderson, Mr. Callahan. Hope you don't mind my tagging along on Nic's errand. I'm a painter, and if you don't mind, I'd like to take pictures of the peaks from this perspective for my work."

"Sure. That's fine." As Sage grabbed a professional-quality camera from the truck cab and headed out across the lawn, he looked at Nic and asked, "What errand?"

"Tiger, get down!" Nic said, ignoring his question to scold the dog. She shook her head and sighed. "He does have more than his share of bad habits. You'll need to give him extra attention for a while in order to break him of them."

Gabe opened his mouth to protest, but she forged ahead. "Wow, just look at this house. I admit I was happy to have the excuse to come up here. I've always wanted to see it. I hope you'll give me the grand tour."

"Whoa. Wait one minute. What do you mean, *I'll* need to give the dog extra attention?"

She smiled sheepishly but didn't respond.

"Explain something to me, Dr. Sullivan. What is it

you don't understand about the sentence 'He is not my dog'?"

"I'm not the person you need to convince," Nic shot back. She gave a significant look toward the boxer, who had plopped down beside Gabe. Actually, plopped down on top of his right foot.

Gabe glared down at the dog. "He's not a person."

"True, but apparently he considers you *his* person."

"That's ridiculous."

"Actually, it's not uncommon at all. I see it all the time in my practice."

"Well, then, he'll just have to reconsider." Watching the boxer, he remembered another pair of big, brown puppy-dog eyes. *Please, Daddy? Please? I'll take care of him. I promise.* Gruffly Gabe declared, "I'm not keeping that dog."

When Nic Sullivan simply stared at him, waiting, he raked his fingers through his hair. "Look, I appreciate what you're trying to do. He's a good dog. Goofy, but I guess that adds to his appeal. I agree with you that he needs a good home, but that home isn't with me. Be reasonable. I'm a guest here. I can't move a dog into Eagle's Way."

"Why not? Does Jack Davenport hate dogs?"

"No. He has dogs of his own. But they are well trained and well behaved, everything this dog is not. Besides, I don't want a dog. Period. Now, can I offer you and your friend something to drink before you head back? The coffee is fresh, or I think there's some packets of instant hot chocolate if you like that stuff."

"Here's your hat, what's your hurry?" Nic responded in a dry tone. "I'd love a cup of coffee if that's an invitation to go inside. I really do want to see Eagle's Way, and I have another reason for coming up here today."

"You brought my jacket back?"

She snapped her fingers. "Well, shoot. I forgot. I noticed it hanging on the coatrack, but I walked right past it."

"So what *does* bring you here?"

She grinned and suggested, "Coffee? And brownies. You didn't have the chance to sample the Bristlecone Café's brownies last night, so I brought them along."

Sighing, he said, "Shall we call your friend?"

"No, she truly did tag along to take pictures, and besides, she has a personal bias against caffeine. She's an artist."

Gabe almost asked what one had to do with the other, but instead he focused on the dog and frowned. "Do you have a leash?"

"Yes."

"Then bring him in. It's not like he hasn't been through the place before." After she grabbed a round dessert tin from her truck and fished a pink-and-purple nylon rope from her pocket and clipped it to the boxer's collar, Gabe turned toward the house and said, "Follow me."

He led her around to the side entrance, and their path took them past the pool area. "Oh, wow," she murmured. "A waterfall into a hot tub? How cool is that? So romantic."

Gabe felt a stirring of professional pride. He'd done a particularly fine job with the landscape design here, and he found Nic's enthusiastic reaction gratifying. It had been a long time since he'd taken any pleasure in his work.

He escorted her inside and gave her the two-bit tour. "I can't believe this is only a vacation house," she said after exiting the media room. "Scuttlebutt in town is that Jack Davenport rarely visits. Only a handful of people have ever met him. If this place were mine, I'd live here permanently. What a waste to have it always sitting empty!"

Gabe knew that in reality, Eagle's Way welcomed visitors quite often, although that wasn't something he could share. "Jack is a busy man."

"Well, I hope whatever he does with his days is worth the sacrifice." She reached down to pet the boxer, then said, "What about your days, Gabe? What brings you to Eagle's Way? Celeste tells me that you are a landscape architect. Are you here working on a new project?"

Avoiding her question, he asked one of his own. "I just met the woman last night. How does she know anything about me?"

Nic explained the older woman's contact with the hospital project he'd done in South Carolina. "A small world," Gabe murmured as he gestured toward the cozy upholstered seating group that offered a spectacular view of snowcapped mountain peaks. "Have a seat, Nic. I'll get our coffee, then you can tell me why you're here."

He took a step toward the kitchen, then paused. "Here. Hand me the leash. The dog probably can use some water."

Gabe detoured to the mud room, where he pulled a dog bowl and a box of treats from a storage closet. He filled the bowl with water and waited for the boxer to slake his thirst. Then he offered up a dog treat while saying, "Don't get ideas. You are leaving when she does."

When he returned to the great room moments later carrying two steaming mugs of coffee, the dog led the way and plopped down at Nic's feet. She accepted her coffee with a smile. "Thanks. Have a brownie."

"Maybe later," he replied, eyeing the tin she'd opened and placed atop a magazine on a nearby table. He leaned his shoulder against the wall of windows and watched her, sipping his coffee, waiting for her to speak, and telling himself he didn't notice the way the sunlight seemed to dance in her hair. When the silence stretched, he finally said, "All right, Dr. Nic. Spill it."

"The coffee?" She was the picture of innocence.

He leveled a chiding look, and she offered up an apologetic shrug. "I'm trying to decide the best way to do this."

Gabe hoped she wasn't working up the nerve to ask him for a date. While he recognized that neither one of them had intended it, the atmosphere surrounding last night's dinner had ended up having too much intimacy for comfort. She was a nice woman, a beautiful woman, but he should have dropped the dog at the door and beat feet last night. "Nic—"

"Gabe," she said at the same time, "I want to ask your advice about an idea Celeste has proposed to help Eternity Springs' economic state."

Oh. No romantic advances. Well, good. Gabe relaxed and reached for a brownie. "My advice? That's easy enough, I guess. I don't know that you should put much stock in it, however."

"I'll keep that in mind. Now, I think it might help if I set the scene a bit, first. Do you know anything about the history of this part of Colorado?"

"A little." Gabe lifted a brownie from the plate. "When I was a boy I was fascinated by the Alfred Packer story."

Nic grimaced at the reference to the only man in American history convicted of cannibalism. "Eew. What is it about boys? My friend Cam Murphy had that same fascination when we were growing up."

Gabe grinned, then tasted the brownie, and forgot all about history. "Wow. Just wow. This is good."

"Sarah Reese bakes the desserts for the Bristlecone Café. Her cheesecakes are even better."

"I have to start eating in town."

Nic sat back against the cushion, a smug smile fluttering on her lips. "That's an excellent idea, but I'm getting ahead of myself. Are you familiar with Eternity's founding fathers or the legend of how the town got its name?"

"I recall that the name was derived from the local hot springs and the area's isolation. Something about it taking an eternity for anyone to get here. I also know that Jack's great-something-grandfather was a miner who discovered the rich vein of silver that provided the base of the family fortune."

"That was Lucien Davenport. He and Daniel Murphy and Harry Cavanaugh opened the Silver Miracle mine."

"So Celeste's place—Cavanaugh House—belonged to Harry? That explains the silver bars we stumbled on last night."

"Money and murder. The sheriff told us that they found bullets with the bones—but that's not why I'm here. Gabe, has Jack Davenport shared details about how his family ended up with Murphy Mountain or the conditions of the family trust?"

"No." Gabe helped himself to a second brownie.

"It's an involved story and I won't go into all of it. If you're curious, you can read the town history that Sarah's father wrote. It's in the Davenport library in town. What's pertinent to my business here today is that Lucien Davenport was an early conservationist. He put the Murphy land in a trust that has prevented road construction or development, which meant that growth occurred in other parts of Colorado. In many ways, Eternity Springs hasn't changed in over a hundred years."

"Colorado's own version of Brigadoon," he interjected. "You do know that Eternity's isolation contributes to its charm."

"Yes, but it's both a blessing and a curse. The town is dying, Gabe. We've been looking for ways to save it, and that's where you come in."

He straightened and moved away from the window. "If you're looking for a conduit to Jack Davenport in order to promote roads to ski resorts, you're wasting your breath."

"No, that's not it at all."

"You want an investor for a brownie business?"

"Actually, that's not a bad idea, but it's not why I'm here. Gabe, Celeste wants to hire you to help design the transformation of the Cavanaugh estate into a healing center."

Gabe opened his mouth to explain that he no longer practiced his profession, but Nic forged ahead. Speaking rapidly and with enthusiasm, she explained the idea. Despite his best intentions, he listened, and for the first time in months his professional interest was engaged.

The plan had merit. With the right marketing and the right facilities, it just might work. Cavanaugh House could be a good foundation for such a facility. From what he'd seen last night, the house had good bones, which for the most part had survived the fire. The surrounding acreage offered plenty of space for what Nic had described. "The hot springs are on site?" he interrupted.

"They sure are. There are natural pools along the creek south of the house. Harry Cavanaugh picked the perfect spot to build because the breeze usually blows the odor from the pools away. The mineral springs stink."

"But people love them."

"True."

He was tempted. He needed something to do. The work on the retaining wall had taught him that. But working again would mean interacting with people. Was he ready for that? He'd managed last night, but everyone's focus had been on the fire. They'd accepted his help, and he'd been spared the questions. He couldn't manage questions.

Nic Sullivan hadn't asked him many personal questions. Yet. He saw them in her eyes, though.

Gabe turned to stare out the window and vaguely noted that the redhead had set up a tripod. Did he want to work again? Was his head in the right place for it? He rubbed the back of his neck. He guessed he was better than he'd been a month ago. He didn't want to die anymore. But he wasn't at all certain that he wanted to live, either. Taking on this project meant interacting, which meant living.

And yet the thought of those springs made his fingers itch to sketch.

He finished his coffee, then set the empty cup atop a coaster on the end table. "If I decide to do this, I would have some conditions."

She brightened, and hope shined in the sky of her eyes. "I can't imagine that being a problem. Celeste has already said you can name your price."

"It's not about money." He folded his arms. "It's about control."

Standing, Nic reached out and touched his arm. "Don't worry. I get creative people. Sage is an artist, a painter, and she—oh!"

He followed the path of her gaze and saw Sage Anderson down on all fours, her head hanging, her body trembling, the tripod and camera knocked to the ground beside her.

In an instant, both Gabe and Nic dashed for the door. She was fast, but his legs were longer and as he pulled away from her, he heard the note of fear in her voice as she called her friend's name.

The woman on the ground shook like a tree in a gale. He saw no blood. No outward sign of trauma. Was she convulsing? "Ms. Anderson?" he called as he neared. He pulled up beside her. Touched her back. "Sage?"

Nic dropped down on her knees. "Sage? Honey, what is it? What's wrong? Where are you hurting?"

"I'm okay," she replied softly. Weakly. "I'm okay."

"No, obviously you're not," Nic snapped. "Gabe, I keep a medical bag in the tool box of my truck. Would you get it for me?"

"No. I'm fine." Sage lifted her head and rolled back on her heels. "Really." Her pained gaze met Nic's, then lifted to Gabe. He sucked in a breath. He recognized that look. It was a unique glaze of horror, agony, and guilt. He'd seen it in his brothers' eyes the night over twenty years ago when they started the fire that almost destroyed a town and did destroy their family. He'd seen it in the eyes of the man who'd confessed the terrible truth about a planned attack on America that ultimately led to Gabe's "death."

For the past nine months, he'd seen it every time he looked in the mirror.

She cleared her throat. "I . . . uh . . . must have been another pesky acid flashback."

"Yeah, right," Nic replied. "This from Eternity Springs' resident health nut. You tell me what happened right now or I'm loading you into the truck and laying rubber to a hospital."

Gabe noted the long-distance lens on the camera as he reached out and took Sage Anderson's hand, helping her to her feet. "You saw something in your viewfinder, didn't you?"

She nodded. Shuddered. "It was . . . nature. A fox brought down a rabbit. I don't know why it hit me that way. I'm sorry. I didn't mean to frighten you."

Nic gave her friend a relieved hug, and while the two women embraced, Sage looked over Nic's shoulder and met Gabe's gaze. Silent understanding passed between them. *Acid flashback, no. Flashback of a real experience triggered by violence, you bet.* "It's survival of the fittest out there," he observed. "Laws of nature are seldom pretty."

"They break your heart."

"That they do, Ms. Anderson. That they do."

Nic released Sage and stepped back, a considering look in her eyes as she studied them both. Nic Sullivan wasn't a fool, and she recognized that something more had happened here. Gabe braced for an intrusive question, but she surprised him. "Guess what, Sage? While you were out here communing with nature, I was busy saving Eternity Springs."

"Oh, yeah? And how did you manage that?"

"I used my charm and my persuasive abilities and my business acumen to convince Mr. Callahan here to design the cornerstone of our revitalization project."

Sage arched a question brow toward Gabe. "Is that true?"

He rubbed the back of his neck and made a show of considering. After a long moment, he shook his head. "No. She's wrong."

He watched Nic's face fall and stilled a grin. His expression serious, he added, "It was the brownies that did it."

FIVE

Over the next few weeks, the riot of fall colors disappeared from the mountains as aspens and cottonwoods dropped their leaves. Winter arrived in Eternity Springs with chilling winds and falling temperatures, but only a dusting of snow. The last seasonal stragglers departed town, and Nic and her fellow year-rounders settled into their winter routines.

Folks tended to congregate at the Mocha Moose, a coffee house and Internet café, and the Red Fox Pub, where they visited with their neighbors and fretted about the scarcity of snowfall in southern Colorado. A slow start to the ski season meant fewer people in the mountains, which meant fewer adventuresome, tired-of-the-lines people wandering into town to spend their precious tourist dollars. Luckily, Celeste Blessing's repair and renovation dollars were taking up the slack. The amount of activity had caused one grateful business owner to wonder if the bars found in her cellar really had been gold bars painted silver as a disguise.

The Cellar Bride and her thirty pieces of silver fired the imaginations of Eternity Springs' citizens. Speculation as to the circumstances that led to the bride's entombment in Cavanaugh House's root cellar was just the sort of mystery people loved to discuss on a cold and otherwise uneventful winter's night.

Once Gabe had agreed to participate in Celeste's healing center plans, he and Celeste had held a series of meetings in Nic's kitchen, where they discussed Celeste's vision of the healing center and hammered out a work agreement that suited them both. Nic believed the final result had to be the strangest contract ever negotiated.

She understood keeping the plan under wraps until his design was complete and the concept ready to present. Asking him to work on-site rather than up at Eagle's Way made sense, too. The more he interacted with townspeople the better he would understand the culture of Eternity Springs. That could have a positive influence on his work—or at least help avoid unforeseen problems.

His demands were more difficult to understand. Gabe Callahan agreed to design the landscape plan as long as he was allowed to lead the work crew doing renovations on the house, too. He wanted physical labor, all the brownies he could eat, and a home other than his own for the boxer. Plus he wanted Sage to create a work of art of her choice for Eagle's Way.

That last request had caused Nic to suffer a brief and shameful bout of jealousy. After all, she'd "not dated" Gabe first. But something had passed between those two up on Murphy Mountain that day. They'd connected in some intangible way, and Nic had felt like a third wheel.

She talked about her reaction with her aunt when she and Nic's mom visited for Thanksgiving. After dinner, while her mom took a nap, Nic and Aunt Janice bundled up and headed outside to walk off their meal. When Janice asked Nic about her love life, Nic spilled the beans about the new man in town.

"At least I had the good sense to keep my reaction—and face it, my attraction to Gabe Callahan—to myself," she said as they walked briskly down Aspen Street headed toward the lake. "I know I'm oversensitive, projecting my own past experience into current events.

Gabe isn't my husband, Sage isn't my business partner, and I'm not going to walk into my own home and discover the two in the midst of betraying me."

"Greg Sullivan better hope he never crosses my path," Aunt Janice declared. "I'll take a tire iron to him."

Nic grinned. That was no idle talk. Aunt Janice would do it.

"It's been four years, and I still have moments where the memories catch me off guard. I guess it's only natural that I'm more wary when it comes to men."

"Between your skunk of a father and snake of a husband, you've had some bad breaks. You need to find a man like your uncle David." Janice smiled wistfully and glanced toward the hill to the north, where her husband rested in Eternity Springs Cemetery.

"Don't I wish," Nic agreed. "Problem is, men like that are hard to find."

"You just have to know where to look." Janice shot her a sidelong look and said, "Your mom can tell you that."

Nic stopped dead in her tracks. "Mom?"

"Yep."

"You're kidding me!"

"Nope. He's a widower she met on our trip to Italy. He lives in Miami and they see each other quite a bit. I think it's serious."

Nic was thrilled for her mom, yet her feelings were hurt. "Why hasn't she told me about him?"

Janice grabbed Nic's hand and squeezed it. "She's afraid. She loved your father deeply whether he deserved it or not."

"Not."

"Trust is a real issue with her as a result. She'll tell you about Alan—that's his name, Alan Parks—when she's more secure in the relationship. I thought it best to give you a heads-up."

Nic understood about trust. It was one of her buga-boos, too—as her reaction to Sage and Gabe's interaction proved. "I'm glad for her, Aunt Janice. Shocked, though. It's been such a long time since Bryce Randall walked out on us. She said she'd never love again, and I believed her. I'm shocked she let this Alan Parks get close."

"He was sneaky about it. I like the man." It had begun to snow, and Janice flipped the hood up on her coat and suggested they turn around. "My blood has gotten thin while living in Florida. So, what about you, honey? Do you see yourself falling in love again? Maybe with this hunky Callahan guy?"

"I admit I thought about it, but I don't think Gabe is the guy. It appears that the walls around his heart are higher and thicker than mine. I do hope I'll fall in love again someday, though. I want to."

Nic tilted her face toward the sky, felt the cold kiss of snowflakes on her cheeks, and smiled. "Bryce P. Randall III and Greg Sullivan played havoc on my past; I don't want to give them the power to ruin my future."

"You go, girl. I'm glad to hear you say that. I've worried about you, you know. When you moved here as a girl, you were like a young Hester Prynne wearing a scarlet *I*-for-illegitimate on your shirt. I don't know that your mother ever realized how deeply affected you were by the fact your mother wasn't married to your father, but David and I saw it."

"We lived in a very conservative town. It was hard."

"I know, dear. And I know that you were hurt by Greg and his wandering penis. I've been afraid you wouldn't stay at the plate and take another pitch."

Nic grinned at the expression her aunt had used, then declared, "I refuse to be a quitter, Aunt Janice."

They reached the corner of Aspen and Seventh and turned toward home. Nic's gaze lifted toward Murphy

Mountain. "That said, I'm afraid that learning to trust a man again will be more difficult than falling in love will be. Trust is a tough one—just look at Mom."

"It'll happen for you." Aunt Janice linked her arm through Nic's. "I believe in that old cliché about time healing all wounds."

Nic nodded and added, "Time, distance, and Eternity Springs."

Ten days later, Nic recalled the conversation as she pulled her truck into the driveway at Cavanaugh House and sat for a moment, looking at the sprawling Victorian. The place looked postcard pretty with snow icing the gables, the mountain behind it, and expanse of yard in the front. "Time, distance, and Eternity Springs," she murmured. That would make a good marketing slogan for Celeste's healing center. She'd have to remember to tell her.

The initial cleanup in the wake of the fire was just about finished. Unfortunate though it had been, the fire had worked magic on the town's off-season economy, providing a windfall to local contractors and the building supply store. The Elkhorn Lodge benefited from visits by various inspectors and historical experts brought in by Gabe, and Sarah said the sales of the cinnamon rolls she baked for the Mocha Moose had tripled in the weeks following the fire.

While the north wing of the house had been a total loss, harm to the rest of the manse was for the most part limited to smoke and cosmetic damage. Celeste had moved home over Thanksgiving weekend. She liked being on-site and in the thick of things, able to interact with the workers as they wired and papered and painted. Because Cavanaugh House's current kitchen facilities—a dorm-size refrigerator, a coffeepot, and a microwave—gave her the perfect excuse to dine out most evenings, she often shared supper with Gabe at the Bristlecone and discussed her ideas for the prayer garden, the hot springs pools, and any other new thoughts that had come to her that day.

Nic exited her truck, then hurried up the walk and onto the Victorian house's sprawling porch. Light from the entry hall fixture shone through the front door's leaded glass. She wiped her boots on the doormat, then stepped inside. The scent of sawdust and popcorn greeted her. As she removed her coat and gloves and hung them on the hall tree, in addition to the banging of hammers from somewhere upstairs, she heard female voices coming from a room down the hall. Sounded like Sarah and Sage were already here.

With her plan moving forward, Celeste had determined that she needed help compiling a formal inventory of the contents of Cavanaugh House, particularly the basement and attic. Nic, Sarah, and Sage had jumped at the opportunity to explore the multitude of boxes, trunks, and chests squirreled away in the nooks and crannies of the Victorian house, and they'd taken to spending a couple of hours each afternoon at the task. The inventory already had unearthed some gems. The vintage clothing had caught Nic's fancy. Sarah swooned over the silver tea service. Once Sage got a look at the art glass they uncovered, she eyed each unopened trunk like a gift box on Christmas morning.

In addition to dozens of pretty things, they had unearthed a mountain of paper. Town records, old newspapers, account books, and diaries offered a potential treasure trove of information. Once they made a master list of everything, they intended to dive into those. They all hoped the written records held the key to the Cellar Bride's identity.

Nic walked into the room to see Sage at the desk in front of the computer and Sarah seated on the sofa, a box of delicate glass Christmas ornaments at her side, a yellow legal pad and digital camera in her lap. "Sorry I'm late," Nic said.

"Lori told us you had to make a run out to the Double R this morning. Is the horse okay?"

"She will be."

"Good." Sage reached into the bag beside her desk, saying, "And, now that we're all here, I want to show you what I found. Wait until you see this."

She held up a small leather-bound book. "Remember that photo album I took home yesterday? This was tucked inside it. It's a diary written by a woman named Elizabeth Blaine."

Sarah carefully set down a hand-blown glass Christmas ornament and looked at Sage with interest. "Elizabeth Blaine married Harry Cavanaugh, one of the founders of Eternity Springs."

"The time period this journal covers is January first to June first, 1892. Elizabeth and Harry are engaged. The wedding is set for August. It's fascinating reading, and I'm only through the first three months."

Sage handed the journal to Nic, who said, "That's after he'd built this house, though. I don't suppose you read anything about the mystery bride?"

"Not yet, but that thought occurred to me, too. Also, it reads as if she kept a journal by habit, so we might find more diaries as we go through all these boxes."

Sarah tucked a short dark curl behind her ear as she said, "Zach Turner told me he heard back from the vintage wedding-gown expert. Judging by the lace on the train and the unique design of the embroidery around the neckline, she dates that gown as late nineteenth century. This is cool!" Her eyes sparkled. "We might solve the mystery before the sheriff's department does. Hmm . . . wonder if I could get Zach to bet me?"

Nic snorted. "Shoot, I'll bet you could get Zach

Turner to do anything your heart desires. I saw his car at your house again last night."

"Why won't you believe that Zach is simply my friend? Nothing romantic going on there. Besides, he didn't come to see me last night. He brought Lori home." Sarah hesitated, then confessed, "She and Andrew had a fight, and he left her without a ride."

Sage folded her arms. "That weasel. I hope she finally dumped him."

"She's okay?" Nic asked as she sank into an overstuffed easy chair.

"Yes. Angry, but okay. She finally came out and admitted what I've suspected for a while now. He's pressuring her for sex."

Nic scowled. "I hope she told him to tie a knot in it. She's been nothing but clear about her views on that subject since she turned fifteen."

"Fourteen. She asked me to buy her the promise ring on my thirtieth birthday. Nothing like being illegitimate to know for a fact you don't want to repeat the mistake."

"Don't talk that way. You've never said that Lori was a mistake!" Nic jabbed a finger at the on button on the laptop she'd left on the chair's ottoman the previous day. "I agree with Sage. I hope Lori broke up with that little slimeball. He knew her stance when he started dating her."

"She's thinking about it." Sarah glanced up at the mantel clock and frowned. "I think she's torn because she's afraid she won't have a date to the Christmas dance and she doesn't want to miss it."

"She should go alone or with a group of girls," Sage suggested. "Girls do that in other parts of the country. They usually have more fun that way because girls actually like to dance."

"I'm afraid Eternity is still behind on that trend," Nic

said as the Westminster chimes of the grandfather clock in the entry hall rang out the hour.

"Enough of reality." Sarah said, standing. She grabbed the TV remote from the mantel and pointed it toward the small flat-screen Celeste had provided for entertainment while they labored. "It's fantasy time. The game is on. Buffs versus OU. College basketball at its finest."

"That's why I smell popcorn." Nic propped her legs on the ottoman, her computer in her lap, and settled in for the show. "Excellent. I'd forgotten we had a game today."

"Not me." Sage tossed her a bag of popcorn, still warm from the microwave. "I came prepared."

As Nic tore open her bag, her gaze focused on the television. Thirty seconds later, the three women sighed as one. "Coach Romano."

"Be still my heart," Sage declared.

Nic clicked her tongue. "Slam-dunk."

"Put me in, Coach," Sarah said. "I'm ready to play."

Standing a muscular six foot five, Coach Anthony Romano had wavy back hair, luscious brown eyes, and a perpetual five o'clock shadow. He was in his second season as assistant coach and recruiting coordinator for CU, and according to his bio on the athletics department website, Coach Romano was a bachelor.

The most devoted sports fan of the three of them, Sarah had been the one to bring the coach to their attention after a three-margarita discussion led to an extended search for the perfect fantasy man. Coach Romano was the only man all three agreed on, and he'd become the focus of their tongue-in-cheek fangirls' club.

It was silly, slightly embarrassing, and fun.

"That's a new suit," Sage observed.

"You're right." Nic took a bite of popcorn. "I don't think I've ever seen him wear blue before."

"He's a god in gray." Sarah clicked her computer mouse and a printer began to hum.

Sage nodded in agreement. "Not many men can pull off the suits-and-sneakers look, but I have to say, it really does it for me."

"It's the artist in you, Sage. You need something with a bit more flair than straight *GQ*." Sarah clucked her tongue. "I wonder how he feels about sperm donation. Don't you think the two of us would make beautiful babies?"

Something in her smile, a wistfulness, signaled to Nic that this wasn't fangirl nonsense for Sarah. "Wait just a minute. Babies? What's that all about? I thought you couldn't wait for your nest to empty. That's all I've heard about since Lori's sixteenth birthday."

"Yeah, well, it was easier to be happy about her leaving home when the date wasn't staring me in the face."

"Sarah, Lori is only a junior. She still has a year and a half of high school."

"Don't you know how fast that year and a half will go? We have to do college visits this spring!"

To Nic's shock and surprise, tears welled in Sarah's violet eyes, then overflowed. Sage and Nic shared a look, and the basketball game was forgotten. Both women crossed to the sofa and took seats beside their friend.

"Honey?" Sage asked. "What's wrong?"

Nic didn't need to ask. She'd known Sarah Reese for most of her life. Despite the struggles she faced as a single mother in the small town, Sarah loved being a mom to Lori. From Girl Scout leader to perennial field trip mom, basketball team mom, and chair of the prom committee, Sarah did it all. Both she and Lori had thrived as a result. "You've had me fooled, Sarah Elizabeth. I really thought you were tired of fund-raisers and sports banquets. I thought you were looking forward to this next stage of your life."

Sarah's lips wobbled. "I lied. I don't want her to be a senior. I don't want her to graduate. I don't want her to go to college. I want her to still be six years old."

"That's a problem," Sage said.

Sarah swiped at the tears with the back of her hand. "It just makes me so angry. I feel old and I'm not even thirty-five yet."

"Close to it," Nic pointed out, trying to distract her.

"Oh, hand me a tissue." When Nic did just that, she continued. "All I've ever wanted to be is a mom. Nothing against you two, but I never needed the validation of having a career outside the home. That was never my thing. Motherhood fulfilled me."

"That's true," Nic agreed. Glancing at Sage, she added, "Her mom always said the women's libbers wasted their burning bras on Sarah."

"I was born to be a homemaker, and I've done a darn good job of it—despite the fact my home was missing a penis," Sarah said.

"The visual on that isn't attractive," Sage observed. "However, you shouldn't be defensive. I think you're lucky that you know what you are supposed to do, what you were born to do. I've spent most of my life trying to figure that out, and I still don't have the answer."

Nic held up a palm. "Okay. Hold on. I'm confused. Sage, you have to be the most self-assured woman I've ever known. I've looked at your work, and I've observed your work method. If you weren't born to be an artist, then I don't know a Holstein from a Hereford. And I'm a vet!"

"It's complicated."

"Excuse me?" Sarah folded her arms. "This is *my* crisis. I would appreciate it if we can keep the focus on me, please?"

Nic sighed. "It's gonna be a long year and a half, isn't it?"

"This is our next-to-last Christmas together!" Sarah said.

"News flash!" Nic waved her hands. "College students come home for Christmas break."

"But it'll be different. I don't want it to be different. I love life the way it is, and it just ticks me off that it has to change. Now, I know that's a bad attitude, but it's my attitude and I own it!"

"Well, that's honest, anyway," Sage said. "Futile, but honest."

"Unlike others among us who pretend they are just fine with being lonely, I choose not to lie to myself."

"Okay, now that's just mean."

"Sorry. Not."

"One good thing about Lori growing up is that with any luck, Sarah will quit talking like a teenager."

"Excuse me?" Sage interrupted. "Can we pause the bickering for more important matters, please? Look. There's a time-out on the court."

Which meant more Coach Romano camera time. The three women focused on the TV.

"OMG," Sarah said, the slang usage obviously for Nic's benefit. On the screen, the man in question had slipped off his jacket and rolled up his sleeves, and he was holding a basketball in a one-handed grip. "Look at the size of those hands."

Sage fanned her face. "Think of what he could do with them."

"At the risk of sounding crude, this is the first time in my life my boobs ever wished they were a basketball," Nic observed.

Out in the hallway, something heavy thumped to the floor. Nic recognized the voice that muttered the epithet that immediately followed. Gabe Callahan.

She glanced in the wall mirror and smoothed her flyaway hair, catching Sarah's knowing smirk as she did so.

She stuck out her tongue at her best friend and sent up a little prayer that his hearing wasn't all that sharp.

"Gabe?" Sarah called out. "Everything all right?"

Footsteps approached and he came into sight, pausing in the doorway. He wore a blue-and-gray plaid flannel shirt tucked into a snug pair of faded Levi's. He had a stained and scruffy pair of lined leather work gloves tucked into a back pocket of his jeans, and his steel-toed boots showed plenty of wear. He might be stopping for dinner at the Bristlecone most nights these days, but he still hadn't managed to find his way to the barbershop. His hair brushed his shoulders now, curling slightly on the ends.

And dang it, her fingers itched to play with those thick silken strands.

Until he turned a wickedly amused gaze her way and dashed her hopes about his hearing. "Sorry about the noise. That piece of lumber slipped right out of my hands. You know . . ." He rubbed the back of his neck. "I have to tell you that, while men are often accused of thinking with body parts other than their brains, this is the first time I've ever heard women admit they have parts that think for themselves, too."

He heard, all right. Nic closed her eyes and flushed with embarrassment. *They not only think for themselves, they blush.*

Sage saved her by laughing. "You like basketball, Gabe?"

"Not the same way you ladies do, apparently."

"We're just having a little fun. Would you care to join us? I promise we'll keep all our leering to ourselves."

"You know, I'd enjoy that, but I'm up to my gym shorts in drywall upstairs."

"I haven't looked beyond this room for a while," Sarah said. "How's the cleanup progressing?"

"Pretty good. We'll finish up restoration this week,

and we should be able to tackle the north wing rebuild right after Christmas."

"That fast?" Sarah asked.

"Celeste was able to articulate what she wanted, and the town delivered the permits all wrapped up with a bow." He focused on Nic as he added, "I was hoping to talk to you, Nic."

Oh?

"You have to do something about that dog."

Oh. "Tiger?"

"What other dog roams this town at will and always manages to get in my way? This must be the last town in America not to have leash laws on the books."

"Actually, I agree with you about that. It's not safe for the animals, and it's something Eternity Springs will need to address once we have more visitors to town. What did he do now?"

"I had a breakfast meeting at the Mocha Moose this morning. He was sitting at the door when I left, and he followed me back here. He's been hanging around all day. You were supposed to find a home for him. That was the deal, was it not?"

"Yes, and I'm still trying." She licked her lips, then offered a smile just shy of sheepish. "Dale Parker has agreed to consider taking him."

Gabe jerked his stare away from her mouth as he asked, "So why is he underfoot every time I turn around?"

"I explained that to you before. He's adopted you."

"He's a dog. It's not his choice!"

"Oh, for crying out loud," Sage said. "Give it up, Callahan. I saw you slip that dog a hunk of your sandwich earlier. Way to chase him away."

Gabe didn't bother defending himself, but watched Nic for a long minute before asking, "And where might I find Dale Parker?"

"He owns the Fill-U-Up."

"That grumpy old son of a gun? No wonder the mutt has taken to hiding out with me. Is he the best you could do?"

She watched it register on his face the moment he realized the mistake. Nic decided to take pity on him, mostly because her embarrassment lingered and she needed distance. "Where's Tiger now?"

"Here, at the foot of the stairs."

"He can stay with us." She lifted her voice and called, "Tiger? Here, boy. C'mere, boy."

Four paws' worth of nails clicked against the wooden floor. The boxer paused in the doorway and rubbed up against Gabe's legs. "Awww," Sage crooned as Sarah said, "He's so cute. Gabe is right. He's too sweet to hang with Dale Parker."

Nic dropped her hand and wiggled her fingers. Reluctantly the boxer approached. "You willing to take him home, Sarah?"

"I can't. Daisy and Duke are all I can handle. You know that." She referred to the three-year-old golden retrievers who refused to leave the puppy stage behind.

Nic scratched the boxer behind the ears and said, "What about you, big guy? Wanna watch the basketball game with us?"

When the boxer climbed up on her knees and licked her face, she smiled and looped a finger through his leather collar. "We've got him. Sorry for the trouble, Callahan."

Gabe nodded, then glanced at the television and fired a parting shot. "You do know that Coach Romano has a twin brother who coaches at Southern Cal, don't you?"

Seated at the lunch counter at the Blue Spruce Sandwich Shop, Gabe sipped his coffee and watched the weather report on the muted television hanging in one corner of the restaurant. "Looks like we might have some weather headed our way," Hank Townsend said as he took the seat beside him. "Finally. Ski resorts need the snow. Other than that storm over Thanksgiving, this has been a scary-dry winter so far."

"Maybe so, but it's worked out for the Cavanaugh House project. We're ahead of schedule."

"You have motivated help. She's paying her contractors top dollar. Folks are anxious to work for Mrs. Blessing."

"That's true." Almost too true, in fact. Most days he had more help than he knew what to do with.

The mayor then asked Gabe's opinion about a proposed park addition at Hummingbird Lake. By the time Hank Townsend's lunch and Gabe's own order of a turkey sandwich and fries arrived, three more business owners had joined them, and he'd somehow ended up seated at the center of a table for eight. He left the sandwich shop forty-five minutes later with one invitation to poker night, one to go ice fishing, three invites to dinner, two to church, and a sexual proposition from a seventy-two-year-old waitress with bold hands and a ready wink.

The temperature hovered in the twenties, and during lunch the snow the mayor had been waiting for had started to fall. Gabe looped the hand-knitted brown muffler Celeste Blessing had given him around the lower half of his face, shoved his hands in his coat pockets, and shivered his way up the street toward Cavanaugh House.

How in the world had a Texas boy ended up living in the tundra?

Gabe didn't let himself think about the days of his youth very often. A couple of times when weakness got the better of him, he had Googled his brothers, but like the ancient mapmakers had written, that way there be dragons. Learning that they'd married and started families hurt more than it helped, and made the lonely hole in his heart grow bigger. John Callahan had "died" a long time ago.

Last winter, after the accident sent Gabe spiraling downward, Jack Davenport had attempted to help him by floating the idea of making contact with the Callahan family. As the CIA superspook responsible for the charade in which John Callahan had died, Davenport had the power to make the resurrection happen. He hadn't gone into much detail other than to say that world players had changed and that it no longer served a useful purpose for John G. Callahan to remain dead. Once, Gabe would have jumped at the chance to reclaim his old life, but times had changed. He had changed. He'd refused his friend's offer.

Gabe didn't want the Callahans in his life. They would love him and expect his love in return. Well, he couldn't do it. He wasn't the same person who had grown up in a little hill-country town in Texas. The six months in an Eastern European prison had damaged him. Losing Jen and Matt had destroyed him.

The familiar cold, dark cloud descended on him, and despite the bitter chill, Gabe's steps slowed. What was he doing down here in town, eating lunch with people who invited him to go fishing? Why was he working again? Sure, he'd decided not to die—for now, anyway—but what about that decision made it okay to start living again?

Stepping carefully around an icy patch on the sidewalk, he scowled. It was one thing to use his professional talents to help Celeste Blessing and Eternity Springs. It was something else to invest himself in the town's recovery, to include himself in its social life. To become part of something again.

The warmth of this town and its citizens threatened to thaw the numbness within him. He could not allow that to happen. That way there be dragons.

Gabe tugged down the muffler and sucked in a deep breath, welcoming the cold sting in his lungs. He ignored the friendly wave from a driver making his way slowly up the block and turned his head away from the laughter of a pair of women struggling to hang Christmas garland around the doorway to their flower shop.

Christmas. He closed his eyes. *Oh, joy.* He might be beyond suicide at the moment, but nothing said he wouldn't welcome a good old fatal heart attack.

In that moment, he found himself bombarded with the Christmas season. Holiday flags on lampposts. Twinkling lights in shop windows. Christmas carols piped through outdoor speakers. Red and green everywhere you turned.

God help me.

He wished he could leave Eternity Springs. Get out of here and go somewhere warm with a beach where dark rum flowed like water. He'd do it in a heartbeat if he hadn't promised to spend Christmas with Jen's sister and her family.

Pam and her husband, Will, had been lifesavers for Gabe during the brutal months of Matty's extended hospitalization following the accident. They'd pitched in every possible way to help, and Gabe owed them. Pam and Jennifer had been closer than most sisters, and as a result, the two families had spent their Christmases together. When Pam called asking him to continue the tradition for at least this first tough holiday, he couldn't refuse her, though no way on earth could he have joined his in-laws at their home. Instead, after an enthusiastic endorsement of the idea by Jack Davenport, he'd invited

Pam and her family to join him at Eagle's Way for Christmas, followed by a few days on the slopes at Crested Butte, going so far—in a moment of strength or weakness or idiocy, he wasn't sure which—as to have the Christmas boxes from his attic at the house in Virginia sent to Colorado. Now, bombarded by red and green and Santa Claus and carols, he feared he'd made a big mistake.

Gabe completed his walk to Cavanaugh House and entered through the construction entrance in the back. Once again the boxer was there to greet him. The two of them had reached a compromise over the past week. Gabe allowed the dog to be underfoot at work, but he made certain he didn't have a stowaway when he headed up Murphy Mountain at the end of the day. Apparently the animal spent his night at Nic's.

This afternoon Gabe had decided to tackle the wallpaper in Celeste's bedroom suite. It was a good time to do it, since she was away for the next three days on what she was calling her undercover trip to Sedona.

He plugged in his iPod earbuds and went to work stripping paper. It was a messy, tedious job, but he was glad to have the distraction. It took him most of the afternoon to remove the old paper and prep the walls, and as he stuffed scraps into big black trash bags, he heard the grandfather clock downstairs chime five o'clock. He eyed the rolls of new wallpaper—a vintage cabbage rose pattern that fit the house but made him wince—and debated whether to knock out a wall or two tonight or wait and do it all tomorrow. Before he could make up his mind, he turned toward the door at the sound of a knock.

Nic stood at the doorway. Forgoing her habitual ponytail, today her golden hair hung loose and flowing. She wore a long-sleeved, V-necked, forest-green sweater dress belted at the waist with a red Christmas-patterned silk sash. The knit fabric clung to her full breasts and hugged her slim hips. The modest hem hit just below her knees and covered the tops of brown leather dress boots that sported three-inch heels.

Gabe swallowed hard and took his earbuds out of his ears.

"Sorry to interrupt," she said, smiling. She wore lipstick, bright red lipstick that matched her sash. "Gabe, when you reach a stopping point, could you lend me a hand? I think I might have located the rest of Elizabeth Blaine's journals in a box in the basement, but I need a piece of furniture moved so I can get to it. Would you help me?"

He cleared his throat. "Uh . . . sure. Let me wash this old paste off my hands. I'll meet you down there in a few."

"Thanks!" She flashed him a smile, her eyes gleaming with pleasure, then spun on those heels and disappeared from view—leaving Gabe standing frozen in place, unaccountably warm, uneasy and . . . *holy crap* . . . turned on.

Guess it wasn't broken after all.

SIX

Nic stubbornly refused to glance at her reflection as she crossed in front of the wall mirror on her way to the staircase leading to the basement. She refused to primp for him. Or flirt with him. He might be the hottest thing in a tool belt this side of the Continental Divide, but too bad, so sad for her. The man made it clear he wasn't interested.

Oh, she'd caught him looking a time or two, but it never went further than that. His wounds seemed to need a medicine she simply didn't have. Better that she keep Coach Romano as the object of her fantasies. It was safer that way. With her heart still tender from its mistreatment by Greg-the-Cheat Sullivan, she couldn't afford any risky behavior.

She glanced down at Tiger, who'd followed her from Celeste's suite, and said, "Maybe if I tell myself that often enough, I'll get around to believing it."

She opened the door to the basement, then, because it tended to flop around, propped it open with an old metal milk can half filled with rocks. At the top of the stairs, she flipped the light switch and made a mental note to ask Gabe about wiring the basement for more light. One bulb in that single socket didn't get the job done, especially with snow and debris covering the basement windows, which was why she'd brought a flashlight with her. Unfortunately, thinking ahead didn't do her much good when Tiger came galloping down the stairs and bumped the back of her legs. Teetering, she grabbed for the handrail to keep from falling and dropped the flashlight in the process. "Tiger!"

At the bottom of the staircase he turned to look back up at her, his crooked tail waving a mile a minute as if to say, *Hurry up, Doc. Let's explore!*

"You are trouble, aren't you?" she said, descending safely to where the dog stood. "Somebody needs to teach you some manners."

She patted his head and scratched him behind the ears. He licked her hand, and she pushed him away when he tried to sniff her crotch. "Stop it, Romeo."

She spied her flashlight and bent over to pick it up. Hearing a boot scrape on the staircase above her, she twisted her head to see Gabe standing motionless at the top of the stairs, watching her intently. Abruptly she snapped up straight. A flush warmed her cheeks, though she lifted her chin and brazened her way through the embarrassment by pretending it didn't exist.

"Hey, Gabe. Thanks so much for helping."

"No problem."

Cavanaugh House's basement was a warren of rooms packed to the ceiling with items that appeared to have no organization whatsoever. Gabe glanced around it and frowned. "Have you gone through all these boxes already?"

"No. We haven't begun to tackle the basement yet. I hit pay dirt in a file upstairs. It's an inventory dated 1936, and it's going to be a great help."

Gabe lifted an old snowshoe from the top of a box. "I'll bet there's a treasure trove of antiques down here."

"That's what makes this inventory job so much fun. It's like Christmas every day."

He set the snowshoe down abruptly. "So where's this box?"

"This way." She talked over her shoulder as she led him toward her target. "The inventory gave the description and location of a box containing the diaries, and when I came down to look for it, I was able to go right to it. I'm really excited, first because I'm hoping the diaries might solve the mystery of the Cellar Bride's identity, and second because Sarah and Sage both had something else to do this afternoon, so I made this find without them. They'll be so annoyed."

"Competitive, are you?"

"Yep. Not as much as Sage, though. She's ridiculous."

Tiger brushed past Nic's legs once again, and as he rooted between a steamer trunk and a stack of hatboxes, she pointed out the chifforobe that blocked access to a plain wooden crate marked *Blaine*. "That's it. I haven't unloaded the chifforobe yet. I didn't expect you to come right down."

"Let's see how heavy it is. Maybe I can shift it out enough for you to slip back in there. You're a little thing. It'll probably be easiest to leave the box where it is and empty it rather than haul out the box."

A little thing? Ordinarily she hated it when people called her that. Coming from Gabe, it sounded flattering.

She didn't think he'd be able to budge the piece of furniture, however. It was solid mahogany, taller than he was, and filled to the brim. She had attempted to give it a push herself before going to him for help, and she'd failed to shift it at all. Positioned behind him, she watched him brace his legs and put a shoulder against the wardrobe. His jeans molded against his rear and the flannel shirt stretched across his broad shoulders as he put weight into the effort and strained. The furniture moved a good six inches. *My oh my. Bet even Coach Romano couldn't do that.*

He braced himself again, pushed, and conquered another six inches. Stepping back, he asked, "How's that? Can you slip back there now?"

"Let me see."

It was a squeeze, but she managed it—snagging her dress in the process. If she'd known she'd be putting her good clothes at risk by scuffing around in the basement, she wouldn't have planned to go straight to tonight's book club Christmas party from here. "I need something to pry open the box."

"Here." He removed a chisel and a hammer from his tool belt. "Hand me the flashlight."

Nic went to work, and in minutes she'd pried the lid off the crate. Gabe aimed the flashlight toward it, and delight washed through Nic as she saw six stacks of leather-bound volumes that probably numbered twelve or fifteen deep. "Jackpot! I'll bet Elizabeth Blaine kept journals for most of her life. Imagine the wealth of information about Eternity Springs in these volumes."

"Do you intend to read all these?"

"Eventually. I've read the one volume we found, and it is fascinating. For now, though, I imagine Sarah, Sage, and I will divvy them up to see what we can find out about the big mystery."

She reached into the box and began handing them to Gabe five or six at a time. He stacked them on the floor between a dress form and a steamer trunk. Tiger padded over to investigate. The dog was sniffing the stacks with interest when above them the lone lightbulb flickered once. Tiger's head jerked up. Gabe glanced toward the socket. "I know there are lightbulbs upstairs, but do we have any down here?"

"Not that I've seen, no. I've intended to talk to the electrician about the light situation down here. We really need more than one light fixture."

"It's on the list." When the light flickered a second

time, Gabe said, "Why don't you hold the stack you have there, Nic, while I run upstairs and grab another—"

She heard a pop and the light went dark. The basement plunged into shadow, and Tiger let out a low-throated growl.

"Bulb," Gabe finished on a sigh. "I'll be right . . . whoa!"

Tiger yelped. Something crashed. Nic couldn't see what happened, but based on the sounds, she made an educated guess. The dog must have tangled himself up with Gabe, one of them knocked over the dress form, and somehow the flashlight went flying. The available light shrank to what filtered through the open door at the top of the basement staircase and the little bit that made its way past the mostly blocked basement windows.

Tiger bumped into something else, and Nic heard the sound of shattering glass. The boxer howled and scrambled up the staircase. "That blasted animal," Gabe muttered, following after him. "If he's not careful, he's going to . . . dammit!"

At the top of the stairs, the milk can teetered and fell. The basement door slammed shut.

Nic squeezed out from behind the wardrobe. It was too dark to see much of anything, but she could hear Gabe's steps climbing the stairs. She waited for the squeak of the basement door. And waited. And waited.

Finally, Gabe said, "Nic? Tell me you have your cell phone on you."

"Um, no. I don't."

"Are your girlfriends coming back tonight?"

Warily, she replied, "No, they're not. Gabe? Are you telling me that we're . . . ?"

"Stuck."

"The door?"

"Won't open. I heard the latch fall. To complicate

matters, the hinges are on the other side, so I can't take it off."

Nic considered the situation. They were alone in the house. No neighbors lived on this side of Angel Creek. It wouldn't do them one bit of good to yell for help. They were on their own. She stared up at one of the basement windows. "How about opening a window?"

"We'd likely have to break the glass. You're little, but it might be a tight squeeze."

My butt would get stuck and I'd smother in the snow. "That's probably not a good idea. Can we break the door down?"

"It's a solid wood door. There's not enough of a landing at the top of the staircase to put much muscle into it. The lack of light doesn't help that prospect, either."

Nic peered around for the flashlight. The stairs squeaked beneath Gabe's feet as he descended them once again. She bumped her shins against the dress form and grumbled beneath her breath as she felt around in the dark so she could lift it out of the way. "This isn't good, is it?"

"It's inconvenient. We won't freeze to death. I doubt we'll be stuck down here until we starve. I don't suppose you had any plans tonight that will cause someone to come looking for you when you don't show up?"

Hope flickered. "I have a book club meeting. This month's selection is my choice, and it's our Christmas party. Everyone will wonder when I don't show up."

"That's good."

"They'll call me."

"What will happen when you don't answer?"

"Well . . ." Nic sighed. "They'll probably think I'm out on an emergency. I don't answer the phone when I'm working."

"Okay, what about tomorrow? Is someone expecting you somewhere?"

"I have clinic hours. I have an eight o'clock appointment to take the stitches out of Steve Cartwright's hand. The idiot boy cut it on a skinning knife. I always leave a note on the door if I'm called out into the field, and Steve's mom knows that. She'll worry when she doesn't find one. Someone will see my truck parked here in the drive, and they'll definitely look for me here." She followed the thought process further and murmured, "Your Jeep is here, too, isn't it?"

"Yeah."

Great. Just great. Nic wanted to bury her head in her hands and groan. The drive was clearly visible from the front windows at the Bristlecone, and Glenda Hawkins was one of the worst gossips in town. She would put two and two together and come up with a romantic assignation.

Gabe must have followed the direction of her thoughts. "That gonna be a problem for you?"

"Maybe the book club might come looking for me. They know I wouldn't miss this month's meeting. I had to fight for this pick."

"What was it?"

"My pick?"

"Yeah."

She hesitated, then named a classic historical romance novel from the 1970s and prepared to defend herself from derision. But once again Gabe Callahan surprised her. With a hint of wistfulness in his voice, he said, "My mom used to devour romance novels. She'd read two or three a week. I remember one weekend when my folks took us to Six Flags and to see a Rangers baseball game. My dad wouldn't go near a roller coaster, but my mom was a roller coaster fiend. She made me and my brothers ride with her. That was cool. What wasn't cool was standing in line with her while she had her head buried in a romance novel. If that wasn't bad enough, she even read at the baseball game."

"I think I'd like your mom," Nic said.

"She died the following year."

"Oh. I'm sorry, Gabe."

"Yeah, well, that was a long time ago." He paused and turned the tables on her. "Tell me about your family. Someone mentioned your uncle was the town dentist?"

She wished the light was better so that she could read his expression. Was this an attempt to steer the conversation away from himself or was he truly interested? She suspected the former.

"Yes," she replied, following his lead. "I was born in Missouri, but my mom and I moved here when I was nine to be close to her sister and her husband."

"What about your dad?"

"I never really had a dad. My biological father was married, but not to my mom. He was part of our lives off and on until I was eight. That's when he traded my mom in on a younger mistress."

"That must have been hard."

"Yeah. When they broke up, she had nothing. No financial support, no emotional support. Nothing. He turned his back on us. I haven't seen him or spoken to him since."

"What a jerk."

"Yep." Her mouth twisted in a wry smile. "Uncle David threatened to go after him with a baseball bat, but Aunt Janice talked him out of it. She was thrilled to have my mom living near her and away from my father. My aunt and uncle were great to me. They didn't have children of their own, and they showered me with love and attention. I had a great life here. It's been a joy to come home again."

"Good for you." Gabe glanced toward the door. "We

probably should look for that flashlight. We may be here awhile."

He was right. Nic could hardly see anything, and it wasn't even full dark outside yet. She dropped down onto her hands and knees and began to feel her way around. "It can't be too far away."

The cold from the basement floor seeped into her bones and caused her to consider how uncomfortable the coming night might be. Cold. Dark. No food.

No bathroom.

Immediately she felt the urge to pee. "This isn't good, Gabe."

A circle of light appeared. He'd found the flashlight. "It's not that bad. We have shelter. We won't freeze to death. I have a nine o'clock appointment here tomorrow morning, so somebody will be around to let us out then at the latest. In the meantime, we might as well see what we can scavenge from these boxes and trunks around us. I'll bet we can find plenty to keep us comfortable enough for one night."

"There's no bathroom down here, Callahan."

"Bet you a hundred bucks there's a chamber pot, though. Let's see what we can find, shall we?"

Over the next twenty minutes, they set up camp in the basement. He brought her a stack of quilts and three bearskins that she stretched out on the floor. He found a candelabrum complete with stubby candles and a case containing three clean, dry matches. He tossed her souvenir pillows from Paris and Rome, and whistled with appreciation when he stumbled across a wine rack. "Excellent. My knife has a corkscrew."

"Lucky us. Don't forget we need a chamber pot."

Two minutes later, he presented her a pot with a flourish.

Nic tucked it away in a corner of the basement. By the

time the grandfather clock upstairs chimed six o'clock, they'd created an amazingly comfortable nest.

He'd switched off the flashlight to save the batteries, and the discovery of a box of unused candles made conserving those unnecessary. With candlelight casting a warm, golden glow that staved off the deepening shadows of night, she produced two stems of crystal, which he filled with Bordeaux, and they each settled down with one of Elizabeth Blaine's journals to pass the time.

The atmosphere was comfortable, the air between them easy, and Nic lost track of time as she sank into the history of Eternity Springs and its citizens.

Elizabeth Blaine had immigrated from Ireland to Chicago in the mid-1880s and taken a position as nanny to a banker's family. When the family moved to Denver with the hope of improving the banker's wife's respiratory ailment, Elizabeth moved with them. She lost her position four years later when the wife died and the banker remarried.

Elizabeth then followed the silver boom to Eternity Springs. She cleaned houses and hotel rooms and . . . Nic pored over the words written on the pages and her heart broke.

"Why the tears?" Gabe asked, jerking her back to the present.

Nic blinked and wiped her eyes, then offered him a tremulous smile. "Okay, I'm an idiot. I can't believe I cried over something that happened more than a hundred years ago."

"Tell me."

"She had a dog. Elizabeth did. His name was King. She brought him with her from Ireland, and he was all she had left of her family. She told a story of how once when the child she cared for was still an infant, his mother had him with her as she worked in her flower garden and a vicious neighborhood dog sneaked up on the baby and the mother didn't notice. King was inside the house and went berserk. He crashed through a window screen to get outside and chased the other dog away. Anyway, she writes in her journal about how King got old and sick and she had to ask a friend to put him down. That's what made me cry."

"You are such a soft touch."

She shrugged and attempted to change the subject. "Any interesting stories in the volume you've been reading? Any clues about the bride or the silver bars?"

"No. Afraid not. This diary covers the months when Elizabeth was falling in love with Harry Cavanaugh."

"Oh yeah?" Nic sat up straight. She shut her diary and set it aside. "Cool! Tell me about it."

He passed her the book saying, "I'll let you read it yourself. Makes me feel like a voyeur to read it."

"Why? Tell me it's not X-rated."

"No. It's . . . mushy."

"Romantic." Nic opened the book and flipped through the pages. One passage caught her eye, and she read it aloud. " 'Harry knocked on my door this afternoon, handed me a bouquet of two dozen roses, and asked me to accompany him on a picnic up at Heartache Falls. He'd engaged the services of a violinist who followed behind our buggy, serenading us with love songs. His manservant prepared our picnic spot prior to our arrival. Fine Irish linens graced a table set for two with fine china. He served us roast duckling and chilled champagne from a silver bucket. My dear Harry quoted poetry to me over our meal, then asked me to dance with him in the meadow. It was the loveliest afternoon of my life.' Ahh . . . ," Nic sighed. "That's so sweet."

"So says the romance novel reader."

"You have something against romance, Callahan?"

"Not at all. I have something against schmaltz."

"Schmaltz! That wasn't schmaltz."

"Darlin', that picnic was the epitome of schmaltz."

"All right then, Casanova. What should Harry have done to romance his lady?"

Gabe stretched his legs out and crossed them at the ankles. He linked his hands behind his head and considered the question. "The bouquet was way overdone. A single rose would be okay, or even better, whatever flower she considered her favorite. Hiring a violinist to ride behind the courting buggy ruined the whole thing."

"Now, why would you say that? It's terribly romantic."

"You like threesomes, do you?"

"What? No!"

Gabe chuckled and continued, "A mountain meadow picnic was good, but a linen-draped table? Fine china? Roast duckling? No. Way too formal. Too stuffy. All you need for a romantic mountain meadow picnic is a quilt to spread on the grass and a picnic basket with finger foods. The champagne was a good idea, but it'd have been better if he'd put it to chill in the creek."

"That's a good idea," Nic agreed. "What about the poetry and the dancing?"

"Depends on the woman, of course. If she's into that, then yeah. Nothing's wrong with poetry or dancing."

"What do you do for music if you've left the violinist back in town?"

"If a guy can carry a tune at all, he can sing softly, or hum. You can dance to birdsong or music in your mind, as far as that goes."

She let that sit a minute, then said, "That's not bad, Callahan. Not bad at all."

He grinned, then reached for the wine and topped off their glasses. She sipped the rich, smooth Bordeaux and studied him. Tonight Gabe seemed approachable, not nearly as uptight as he ordinarily did. Maybe with some judicious questions she could learn a little more about him.

Since the best way to learn information was often to share information, she said, "My ex had a romantic streak in him. At least, that's what I thought at the time. He'd bring me flowers and small gifts out of the blue— just because he was thinking about me, he'd say. Looking back, I suspect that rather than romantic gestures, they were gestures of a guilty conscience."

"You're better off without him."

"Yes, I know that." She blew out a breath, then asked in a bright tone, "What's the most romantic thing you've ever done?"

At first she thought he'd blow her off, the way he'd done all the other times she asked him anything personal. Instead, with a smile playing faintly on his lips, he said, "I took my wife to the mall."

She waited, and when he failed to elaborate, prodded, "C'mon, Callahan. You have to explain that."

"Hey, I would have thought the hot-air balloon ride on the surprise trip to Napa would have ranked number one, but Jen always said that that trip to the mall was the most romantic act ever. See, I hate to shop. And I absolutely despise malls. My wife, on the other hand, loved shopping and enjoyed malls. On that particular occasion, she was three days past her due date with our son, and her doctor told her she could go another week. She was just pitiful. So I offered to take her to the mall. We ate burgers at the food court, browsed the bookstore, bought a couple of baby toys. Then I dragged her into Victoria's Secret and picked out something for her to wear before the baby came and something for afterward."

"Your wife was right. That does top a hot-air balloon ride." When he smiled and remained relaxed, she decided to take the risk. "What happened to her, Gabe?"

A full minute dragged by, then two. He sucked air past his teeth, then exhaled a heavy breath. He closed his eyes and dropped his head back to rest on the steamer trunk behind him. "It was a car accident. She died at the scene. Our son, Matt . . ." He stopped, cleared his throat. "The doctors warned me from the first that he probably wouldn't make it, but he fought hard. So hard."

Reacting instinctively, Nic reached out and clasped his hand, halfway expecting him to jerk away from her touch. Instead he clasped her hand in return. "I lost him last July. He was almost six years old."

"I'm so sorry, Gabe."

Now he did pull away. "I'd rather not talk about it anymore."

"Okay. No problem. I'm through being nosy. I promise. Let me just ask you one more thing." As he shot her a narrow-eyed frown, she said, "If you had the chance to come back as a dog, what breed would you want to be?"

He laughed, just as she'd hoped. Nic sipped her wine and hid her satisfied smile.

Gabe lay in the darkness and recalled another time when he'd attempted to sleep on a cold, hard floor on a bitter winter night. Then he'd had no quilts, no wine, no lovely woman sleeping an arm's length away. It had been another world, another life. Literally.

John G. Callahan had been a State Department associate when he took a bullet on a public street in Sarajevo. Eastern European nutjobs who had a sub-rosa war going on with the CIA and other Western intelligence operations then spirited him away. A palsied doctor removed the bullet in an unhygienic hovel, and then when a ransom demand fell through, his captors sold him off to sadistic Croatian mafiosos who dumped him into an ancient mountain fortress that made the Count of Monte Cristo's Château d'If look like a downtown Marriott.

On a basement floor in Eternity Springs, Colorado, Gabe's lips twisted in a wry grin. That bare, bitter cold made tonight's chill seem like a barefoot walk on a sandy beach in summertime.

What a strange evening this had been. Not only had he thought about his other lives—in Texas with his mom and family, then in Virginia with Jennifer and Matt— he'd talked about them. He'd been able to do it without choking up or breaking down. He rarely said Jen's name. He almost never spoke of Matt. Tonight it had actually felt good to say their names.

What had happened to his lunchtime determination to remain on guard against the appeal of Eternity Springs?

It didn't last past his hard-on. Apparently, having that particular part of his body demonstrate signs of life once again had put the whole notion of facing dragons back on the table.

Not that he was anywhere near ready to actually use the damned thing. Just because he was alive didn't mean he got to live again.

Guilt remained a burden able to drag him down into the black abyss. Grief, on the other hand, didn't weigh him down quite as much as it had just a few weeks ago. It still had the power to strike swiftly and savagely, but those instances occurred less often now and with weaker intensity than in the past. He figured this must be the natural grief-recovery process. Although the superstitious part of him wondered if Eternity Springs and its warmhearted citizens weren't getting to him.

"Brrr," Nic complained, her voice drifting across the darkness. "It's so cold. Do you have a spare bearskin over there?"

An image of naked limbs on a bear skin rug flashed

through his mind. He cleared his throat. "I thought you were asleep."

"I dozed for a bit. My boots were killing me, so I took them off. Now my feet are cold, and that makes me uncomfortable and cranky."

Gabe hesitated a moment before saying, "Well, we can't have cranky. Scoot them over here. I'll rub your feet for you."

"God bless you, Gabe Callahan."

She whipped her legs out from beneath her covers and set them in his lap. She wore thin trouser socks, and when he took her right foot between his hands, he sucked in a breath. "You have ice cubes for feet."

"I told you so."

He tugged off her sock and began rubbing her bare, freezing foot. While he tried to keep his touch clinical and his thoughts impersonal, he couldn't help noticing her foot's slender width, the graceful arch of her instep, the softness of her skin.

It was the most personal touch he'd shared with a woman in months, and damn his soul, he enjoyed it.

While he massaged her right foot, her left foot crept up and rested on his thigh, inches from his torso. Inches from his erection.

He should put her ice cubes right on his crotch, but he settled for the next best thing. He tugged his shirttail from his jeans and yanked her sock off her left foot. "Look, don't take this personally. Consider it payback for doctoring my scratches that day."

He took both her feet and tucked them against his belly, sucking in an audible breath. It truly was like putting ice on his stomach. "Whoa. Have you no circulation in your feet whatsoever?"

"Oh, you feel good, Callahan," she purred. "How can you be so warm? Are you hiding a heater or something?"

A heater? Was that a come-on? Or was she just clue-less? He wished he could see her expression to help him judge. Wryly he replied, "Or something."

Gabe had big hands, and they'd always been strong. They massaged her petite feet with firm, vigorous mo-tions while keeping them nestled against his skin. "You should be wearing heavier socks."

"You're right. I dressed for book club rather than the weather. Sheriff Turner's sister is visiting from Boston for Christmas, and she's going to be there. Last time we met I'd just helped a horse give birth and I was a mess. Vanity is my downfall tonight."

Gabe smoothed his thumbs along her instep and tried to recall if vanity was considered one of the seven deadly sins or not. He knew that lust was.

"I want you to know that I'm usually better prepared than this," Nic continued. "Shoot, I carry chemical hand warmers in my purse this time of year."

"Too bad you didn't bring your purse with you to the basement."

"Tell me about it. I also have an emergency candy bar tucked inside." She let out a sigh, then added, "I'd let you have the whole thing. I'm starting to feel my toes again."

Conversation lagged following that exchange, and eventually Gabe decided she'd dropped off to sleep. He relaxed, dropping his guard. His hands continued their ministrations, never straying beyond her ankles, but his thoughts began to wander.

What if this were summertime instead of the middle of winter? Would she wear sandals on these feet? Would she wear shorts? Form-fitting tanks? Or maybe a short, flirty sundress? He loved sundresses on beautiful women.

Just when his touch shifted from therapeutic to inti-mate, he couldn't say. He explored her. He learned that her ankles were slim, her toes long and slender. He discovered she was ticklish on her instep. He deduced she wore polish on her toenails, and he contemplated what color. Fire engine red, he'd bet. Like her lipstick.

Time ticked by. Her feet warmed beneath his touch. A gradual awareness that her muscles had grown taut distracted him from his musings.

Nic Sullivan wasn't asleep. She was awake and aware and . . . tense.

Gabe's hands froze. He held his breath. He sensed rather than saw her come up on her elbows.

Her voice held a husky note as it emerged from the darkness. "Gabe?"

He hesitated a long moment, aware that he stood at the edge of a dangerous precipice. Yearning tempted him, pulled him forward. It had been so long. The warm human touch felt so good. It would be so easy. And yet . . .

He spoke past a lump in his throat. "I miss my wife."

The moment passed as she exhaled a shaky breath. "It's hard to be alone."

Then Nic sat all the way up and tugged her feet away from him. He felt the loss of contact keenly. As she pulled on her socks, Gabe dropped his head back, shut his eyes, and gritted his teeth.

A good five minutes passed before she spoke again, her voice soft and gentle and warm with compassion. "Thanks for taking care of me, Gabe."

Thankful for the shadows that hid the single tear trailing down his cheek, he replied, "My pleasure."

The book club saved the day.

Nic realized help had arrived when she heard the boxer's excited *arf arf* on the other side of the basement door. She quickly rose and ran up the stairs in her stocking feet. Pounding on the door, she called, "Hello? Hello? Is someone out there?"

A minute later, light spilled into the dark basement as the door swung open. "Here she is!" Sarah called out. To Nic she said, "I knew you wouldn't miss the chance to talk about Ruark Beauchamp. He has to be the hottest man ever— Oh. Hi, Gabe."

"You are a welcome sight, Sarah," he said as he started up the staircase.

Nic stepped into the entry hallway, explaining how they'd ended up stuck in the basement as Sage joined them.

"When you didn't show up, Glenda Hawkins said she'd noticed your truck was still here when she locked up the Bristlecone," Sage said. "I thought you'd forgotten the meeting."

"I knew better," Sarah said. "Although we almost didn't come look for you."

Nic frowned and started to ask why not, but Sarah's significant glance toward Gabe answered the question. Undoubtedly Glenda had mentioned seeing his Jeep, too.

Gabe slipped past the women, saying, "I appreciate the rescue. It was cold down there. I'm going to head out. G'night." He looked at Nic but didn't quite meet her eyes. "You'd better get something on your feet before you're walking on ice cubes again."

"I will." She smiled, but he didn't see it since he was already heading for the front door. When it shut behind him, Nic said, "Well, that was awkward."

"A locked-in-the-basement-together story," Sarah said, her eyes gleaming. "Spill the details. Was it romantic? Did he tuck you against him and keep you warm? Or maybe . . . did you play Shanna and Ruark in the prison? You can be witchy like Shanna, Nic. I think

Gabe has what it takes to be Ruark, but I really need to see him without his shirt first."

"Oh, stop it." Nic wanted to leave right then, but she had to return to the basement first. "My boots are downstairs. You stay here so I don't end up trapped again."

Gabe had smothered the candles, but he'd left the flashlight shining. Nic hurried down the stairs, grabbed her boots, then turned around—and ran into Sarah. "Of course you followed me."

"Bearskins? Wine? Candlelight? Nicole Sullivan! Tell me this was as fun as it looks."

Nic pulled on her boots. "You want the truth or fantasy?"

"Hmm . . ." Sarah tapped a finger against her lips as she followed Nic upstairs. "I have fantasy waiting at book group in the guise of Ruark Beauchamp, so I guess I want the truth."

Stepping out into the hallway, Nic looked at both her friends and sighed. "The truth is that the man is still in love with his dead wife."

"That's so sad," Sage said, handing Nic her coat.

"Well, shoot," Sarah added. "In that case, there's only one thing left to do. Let's go to book group and drink rum punch."

"Rum punch?" Nic asked.

"Hey, it might be the middle of winter here, but that novel you picked took me to a lush Caribbean paradise. With a shirtless stud. What else would we drink?"

Nic laughed and followed her friends out into the cold winter night. Later that night she went to sleep and dreamed about Caribbean beaches.

And a shirtless hero with scars on his skin . . . and on his soul.

SEVEN

❦

Demon dreams woke Gabe a week before Christmas and sent him down into town even earlier than his norm. He almost took the day off completely to spend it skiing or hiking or chopping wood—anything physically demanding that would purge the ghosts from his mind. But since today's chore was hauling rocks, which would both serve his physical needs and create something worthwhile in the process, work held more appeal than sports.

The morning dawned in a palette of pinks and purples above evergreen mountains dusted with snow. The air was cold, the wind quiet. It was a place of beauty and peace, and Gabe sensed the tension within himself easing as he approached Eternity Springs.

For no real reason, he decided to take the loop around the lake on the way to Cavanaugh House.

Formed hundreds of years ago by an earth slide that dammed Angel Creek, Hummingbird Lake was one of the most picturesque places Gabe had ever seen. A little less than a mile around, the lake had been sapphire blue and surrounded by the golds and oranges and greens of autumn when Gabe arrived in town. Today it was an expanse of white ringed with Christmas trees and brought to life by a slight figure dressed in red and black.

Gabe watched the skater fly across the ice. He needed to try that. He'd been on ice skates only twice in his life—both times as boy when his folks took the family to the indoor ice rink in downtown Fort Worth. Competent Rollerbladers, the Texan Callahan boys had all taken to the ice like Minnesotans. Surely he could pick it up again without too much effort.

The skater straightened out of a tucked position, and in that moment he knew it was her. Knew he should stay away.

Drawn by forces he had no will to resist, he turned in to the park on the west side of the lake. He pulled up beside her truck, grabbed his cup of coffee, and stepped out into the cold. Leaning against the front of his jeep, he watched Nicole Sullivan skate toward him.

"Good morning," she called, smiling brightly, her breath creating clouds of vapor on the air.

"Hi."

It was just about the only word he could manage. The woman wore leggings and a sweater that clung to her ample, tantalizing curves. She was breathing heavily.

"Did you come to skate?" she asked, tugging off red-and-black earmuffs.

He shook his head, took a sip of coffee, then asked, "Should you be out here by yourself? Isn't that dangerous?"

"I'm not alone," she replied, pointing toward the shoreline across the lake and waving. Two figures waved back. "Sarah and her daughter, Lori, are with me."

"Oh. I didn't see them." He'd had eyes for only Nic. It was the first time he'd seen her since being trapped in the basement four days ago.

She skated to the edge of the lake, then stepped onto land, walking as naturally in skates as she did in high heels. "They challenged me to a race, but then gave up when I took a substantial lead." The grin she flashed was saucy and warmed him as surely as the coffee. "I am good, Callahan."

"I don't doubt that one bit."

She walked to a nearby bench piled high with shoes and outerwear, sat down, and unlaced her skates. Gabe's gaze focused on her foot, and for a moment he was back in the basement with his hands on her leg.

"So what brings you to Hummingbird this early in the day?" she asked.

Distracted, he said, "Hmm?"

"If you didn't come to skate, are you here to go ice fishing?"

"Oh." He shook his head. "No. I was just taking the long way to work. It's a pretty morning. Beautiful."

Beautiful. She was beautiful, with her cheeks rosy, her blue eyes sparkling, and her blond ponytail sliding like silk over her shoulders. Her petite but lush curves were on glorious display in the tight-fitting clothes. His fingers itched to reach out and touch.

His own body had gone hard as a rock, and he knew he needed to leave. Right now.

"It is gorgeous today. When Sarah called and said she'd decided to let Lori cut class this morning so they could go skating and they wanted me to tag along, I couldn't say no. I haven't enjoyed winter very much lately, and I'm determined to change that this year.

"If the hot springs weren't overrun with contractors building your park, I'd insist we hit the pools next. A long, hot soak sounds heavenly right now." She extended her leg and wiggled her toes. "My feet are freezing again."

Gabe took a step back, both mentally and physically. "I would think you'd learn to keep your shoes on."

"Good point, Callahan." She shoved her feet into sheepskin-lined boots, then stood and pulled on a coat, which allowed Gabe to breathe easier. "We're heading over to the Mocha Moose for breakfast. Would you like to join us?"

He glanced out at the lake and spied Sarah and her daughter skating toward them. They were laughing and holding hands. Gabe realized he wanted to say yes. He wanted to say yes so badly that there was really only one response he could give. "No, thanks. I'd better get to work."

He retreated to his Jeep, gave a wave, and said, "Enjoy your day."

He accidentally spun the tires as he left the park's parking lot. As he drove toward the heart of town, he had to consciously loosen his viselike grip on the steering wheel. "What's the matter with you?" he muttered aloud.

Oh, he knew what the matter was with him. After almost a year of absence, his libido had awakened. Fierce. Ferocious. Hungry.

He filled his lungs with air, then exhaled in a rush. His body wanted sex. Sweaty, physical, down-and-dirty sex.

His mind wanted sweaty, physical, down-and-dirty sex with Jen.

That he couldn't have. Never again. Jen, his beloved Jen, was gone.

So what are you going to do about it, Callahan? the devil on his shoulder asked.

The still-grieving husband answered aloud. "This morning I intend to move a ton of rock." After a glance at the dashboard thermometer, he added, "In twelve-degree weather."

On the afternoon of December 23, Celeste Blessing invited the entire town of Eternity Springs to a Christmas open house, to share company and good cheer and to see the progress of the renovations. Evergreen garlands and wreaths sporting big red bows welcomed visitors as they arrived. Rumor had it that she'd imported the life-sized crèche erected on the front lawn from Italy.

Inside Cavanaugh House, the aroma of hot ginger-bread perfumed the air and holiday decorations abounded. Most were true Victorian antiques unearthed from the boxes and crates now cleared from the downstairs rooms. Celeste had added her own touches, however, and as a result, angels in one form or another could be found in every room.

With kitchen renovations completed and with Sarah's and Lori's help, Celeste had baked for days in preparation for the party. Tables all but groaned beneath the weight of cookies and cakes, fudge and candy. Throughout the afternoon, Nic hovered near the sugar cookies on the entry hall table, not because of a sweet tooth attack but out of a desire to keep a close eye on arrivals. The person she waited for never arrived. When she heard the grandfather clock strike five, she finally admitted to herself that Gabe wasn't coming.

He'd pulled away from both her and Eternity Springs in recent days. Now he habitually wrapped up his work day at Cavanaugh House prior to Nic's afternoon arrival. He left more of the renovation work to hired help and stopped eating his meals in town. Guides saw him snowmobiling in the back country a couple of times, and Dale Parker swore that the crazy ice climber spotted near Sinner's Prayer Pass during the snowstorm last week had been none other than Gabe Callahan.

Since their meeting at Hummingbird Lake, Nic had seen him only once, at the town meeting on the twentieth when Celeste publicly announced plans for her healing center and Gabe showed up at the older woman's request. He'd brought preliminary sketches of his hot springs park and had gone out of his way to avoid Nic.

As Nic eyed a plate of chocolate fudge a few feet away, Celeste approached carrying two crystal punch cups filled with eggnog. Handing one to her, she said, "I had so hoped Gabe would join us today. He should hear the compliments everyone is paying his design now that they've had the opportunity to look over his plans. Your idea to create the display in the music room was inspired."

"If I'd known he'd be AWOL, I'd have reconsidered. People are excited, but now they have even more questions. I expected Gabe to be here to answer them." Then, because his absence made her sad and this was supposed to be a party, she deliberately turned her back to the door and changed the subject. "Tell me about your angel collection, Celeste. You must have hundreds of them. How long have you been collecting them?"

"Heavens, I don't know. Decades, certainly. I never made a conscious decision to create a collection. Actually, the vast majority of my angels have been gifts from friends and acquaintances. It seems that people simply like to give me angels."

Nic smiled wryly and sipped her eggnog. The gift she'd placed under Celeste's tree was an angel she'd picked up at an arts-and-crafts fair over in Durango.

"Now, back to Gabe," Celeste said. "Nic, that poor man shouldn't be alone on Christmas. I've invited him to join our services tomorrow night, but since he has skipped the open house, I don't hold out much hope."

She touched Nic's arm, and a solemn look replaced the usual twinkle in her light blue eyes. "Nicole, I think you should go up to Eagle's Way tomorrow and personally invite Gabe to join us. Bring him down from the mountain to church tomorrow night, dear. He shouldn't be alone."

He shouldn't be alone.

The statement played through Nic's mind the rest of the night and was the first thing she thought of when she awoke Christmas Eve. She didn't know what to do. While she hated the thought of his being by himself on this first Christmas without his family, she also respected the man's right to privacy. If he wanted to hole up in his mountain retreat and grit through this holiday, who was she to suggest otherwise?

She understood that feeling. Hadn't she been the same way that first Christmas after her divorce? She'd wanted to spend the day in bed with the covers pulled over her head, and she'd almost done just that. Except she'd had a friend who wouldn't allow it. Sarah Reese had poked her and prodded her and all but dragged her by her hair to Christmas Eve dinner with her family, followed by midnight services at St. Stephen's.

It had been there, in a tiny old candlelit church on a snowy Christmas Eve, with the fragrance of incense drifting on the air and the dulcet strains of "Silent Night" rising toward the rafters, that she first experienced not just a lessening of pain but the healing peace she'd come to associate with Eternity Springs.

Gabe Callahan needed that healing peace more than anyone she'd ever known.

He'd lost his wife, his little boy. Maybe Celeste was right. Maybe she should be a friend to him the way Sarah had been to her.

Nic considered it throughout her morning as she made appetizers to take to Sage's open house that evening, while she wrapped the last of the gifts she intended to deliver after lunch, and while she tended to a sick dog at the clinic. When her mom called to wish her a merry Christmas from aboard ship on the Caribbean cruise she'd taken with her sister and friends, Nic poured the whole story out to her and asked her advice.

"Honey." Mom clicked her tongue. "It's Christmas in Eternity Springs. That's like magic for the soul. Go get him, sugarplum. This is your chance to change his life."

Twenty minutes later, with a Santa hat on her head

and a prayer on her lips, Nic Sullivan headed up to Eagle's Way.

When Gabe woke up and realized it was Christmas Eve, he considered heading out into the forest to find a bear's den where he could huddle up and hibernate for the next week or so. Unfortunately, he had company coming, so he couldn't do that. But as he threw off the covers he admitted to himself that this plan of Pam's had merit, and a slight sense of anticipation ran along his nerves. As much as he dreaded this Christmas holiday, he would be glad to see Pam and Will and their son, Nathan.

The idea of facing Christmas alone made him cringe. While his head was in a much better place now than it had been back in September, that deep, dark pit was always out there waiting for him.

His visitors' flight was due to arrive in Crested Butte at two o'clock this afternoon. Gabe planned to leave here by eleven, giving himself plenty of time to get there before the plane landed.

He rolled out of bed, then stopped short and sighed. The dog lay curled up in front of the floor vent, as close to the heat as possible. "Why won't you stay where you're put?"

The boxer perked up his ears and thumped his crooked tail but didn't lift his head from the floor.

Gabe shook his head and headed for the shower. The dog had managed to hitch a ride with him following the town meeting the other night, and he hadn't noticed until he'd parked the Jeep in the garage at Eagle's Way. "That's what happens when you let yourself get distracted by a woman," he muttered as he gave the hot water spigot a twist.

And yet, as he showered and shaved and dressed in jeans and a sweatshirt, he couldn't find it in himself to care that the dog persisted in pestering him. Not today. Truth be told, he'd be glad to have the company when he tackled the task that awaited him downstairs.

Yesterday he'd hiked up the hill behind the house, cut down a ten-foot fir tree, dragged it downhill and inside, and set it up in the great room. He hadn't had the guts to approach the boxes he'd had sent from Virginia. They sat on the floor like booby traps waiting to explode.

Gabe fortified himself with two cups of coffee and a bowl of oatmeal before making his way to the great room. His gaze took in the tree, then settled on the boxes. He could wait until the others got here to do this, but there was no sense putting them through the pain. Besides, this felt like something he should do himself.

"Ah, Jen," he murmured. "This is so hard."

Bracing himself, he opened his pocketknife and slit the sealing tape on one of the boxes, then pulled back the flaps. The red cardboard box lay nestled among white Styrofoam packing worms. Gabe exhaled a heavy sigh and lifted it free. A familiar hand had written the words *Ornaments, stockings, tablecloth* in permanent marker across the box. He removed the red box and set it aside. He'd take on the other box first.

The second box was green and contained lights for the tree. *You can do this.* His throat tight, Gabe started with the multicolored C-4 bulbs, then proceeded to the twinkle lights and finally the bubble lights. Memories tested his mental defenses, but he battled them back, knowing the danger of starting down that road. *That way there be dragons.*

With the last string of bubble lights fixed to the tree, he stepped back and observed his work. Despite his best efforts, a tiny voice ghosted, *Daddy, Daddy, look! They're starting to bubble! Bubble bubble bubble bubble.*

He had to turn away.

He wandered to the window, shoved his hands in his back pockets, rocked on his heels, and stared blindly out at the brilliant white peaks as memories bombarded him. Jen had loved Christmas. Shoot, she'd been a bigger kid about the holiday than Matt. Every year she'd helped Gabe hang the outdoor lights the weekend after Thanksgiving. Every year they decorated the tree on December first. Every year they lit candles on an Advent wreath and followed a seasonal prayer guide at the beginning of their evening meal.

And Matty . . . oh, dear Lord, Matty. His joy during the Christmas season knew no bounds. He scrambled out of bed every morning and opened the appropriate door on the Advent calendar even before he dashed to the toilet to pee. He walked around the house yelling "Ho, ho, ho, Merry Christmas" for weeks, and he could quote an amazing amount of dialogue from the Rudolph the Red-Nosed Reindeer movie. For as long as he lived, Gabe would never forget his son on his last Christmas morning. Dressed in the goofy Santa's elf pajamas—complete with a pointy hat—that his mother had bought him, Matt had stood before the Christmas tree totally silent. He visibly shook with excitement.

Tears stung Gabe's eyes. He closed them and rested his forehead against the cold windowpane, wondering if he could talk his in-laws into skipping Christmas, just pretend it wasn't happening. They could all hit the slopes tomorrow and wear themselves out. Avoid the holiday altogether.

The idea held an undeniable appeal.

He glanced back over his shoulder toward the Christmas tree and wished for the millionth time that God would turn the clock back, let him have that moment over again when he'd reacted just a tragic moment too slow.

He felt a nudge against his legs, and Gabe smiled

down sadly at the goofy-looking boxer dog. The dog licked his hand, then Gabe scratched him behind the ears and sighed. "Might as well get this over with, hadn't we, dog?"

Gabe heaved a heavy sigh, braced himself, and returned to work. Lifting the cover off a box, he absorbed the impact of the contents. Reverently he lifted from the box the tablecloth they'd signed with their names, date, and a message or drawing with paint pens every Christmas Eve. He swallowed hard when he uncovered the three stockings Jen had made from red and green felt. His lips twisted with a crooked smile as he brushed his thumb over the tiny charcoal grill she'd made for his stocking.

Next he tackled the box of ornaments and reached for a crystal heart engraved with the words "Our First Christmas Together" with a trembling hand.

He got it on the tree. He managed the Baby's First Christmas ornament and a dozen other memory-laden decorations. Just when he thought he might actually make it through the task, he found Matt's Rudolf. Made from a white paper plate colored with brown crayon, it had a red felt circle for a nose, plastic glue-on eyes, and antlers formed by the outline of a kindergartner's hands. Of Matt's hands.

"Dear Lord." Gabe's knees gave out. He sank to the floor, breathing as if he'd run a marathon. He wanted to curl up in a fetal position and whimper.

Instead, when the dog approached him and attempted to lick his face, Gabe wrapped his arms around the boxer's neck and held on, hugging him tight. He allowed the memories to come.

How long he sat there, lost in the past, he didn't know. It must have been awhile. At some point, though, he heard his cell phone ringing. He was tempted to ignore it, but with his family traveling, he didn't dare. He fished the phone from his pocket, checked the display. Sure enough, it was Pam.

He tensed and dragged his hand along his jaw. "Hello?"

"Hi, Gabe."

"Hey, Pam. Are you calling from the airport?"

"I wish." She hesitated just long enough that his heart sank. "I have crummy news. Nathan broke his leg. We're not going to make it to Colorado for Christmas."

"Ah, Pam. That poor kid. What happened?"

"He wasn't paying attention and slipped on the ice. He'll be okay, but he's really uncomfortable and traveling is out of the question. I'm so sorry, Gabe. We really wanted to be with you today and tomorrow. I needed to be with you."

Gabe braced himself and asked, "Do you want me to come there?"

"No, we'll be okay. I'm worried about you, though."

His gaze drifted toward the half-decorated tree. "I'll be okay, too," he told her, knowing he lied. "You just take good care of Nate. Tell him I said he's supposed to break his leg when he's on the slopes, not before he gets there."

They spoke a few more minutes, then ended the call. Gabe gave in to the craving and poured himself a stiff drink.

It wasn't until he'd finished his first and started on the second that he sank onto the sofa in the great room, torturing himself with more memories sparked by decorations on the tree. He was sipping a third drink when he spied his laptop sitting on Jack Davenport's desk. His gaze locked on the computer, never straying as he finished his scotch.

Then, motivated by a self-destructive need he didn't understand but could no longer fight, he poured a fourth drink and connected the computer to Davenport's home theater system.

It was 12:43 P.M. when Gabe clicked on My Videos.

Nic stared at the gate that barred access to Murphy Mountain and Eagle's Way. The other time she'd traveled this road, the gate had stood open. Today it was locked up tight.

Good thing she'd come prepared. Before leaving home, she'd phoned Alton Davis, the snowplow driver Jack Davenport contracted with to clear the private roads on Murphy Mountain, for the current gate code.

Nic rolled down her window, punched the numbers into the keypad, and waited for the gate to swing open. She drove over the bridge spanning the creek and headed along the road toward the sprawling log house.

The afternoon was cold and gray with the promise of snow at any moment. Eagle's Way was bright with light, and smoke curled from one of four chimneys rising above the green metal rooftop. As she parked her truck in the circular front drive and opened the door, she heard the faint sound of Christmas carols drifting on the air. That surprised her. The first Christmas after her marriage broke up, she did everything she could to avoid the sounds of the season.

Maybe Gabe wasn't as upset as she and Celeste had expected.

Nic retrieved the wrapped gift she'd brought him—one of Sarah's Black Forest cakes—and made her way up the front steps. She rang the doorbell and waited.

The door swung open. A handful of seconds dragged by like hours as Gabe stood watching her and not speaking. He looked . . . disturbed. Finally he took a step back, gestured for her to enter, then shut the door behind her, all without saying a word.

Nic gazed around the great room, and her hackles

went up. A hidden stereo played instrumental carols. Lights blinked and bubbled on a ten-foot-tall spruce standing before the wall of windows. Flames danced and logs crackled in the huge stone hearth on the back wall of the great room, and from its mantel hung a pair of stockings. Nic read the names. Mom. Matt.

Something hard and brittle glittered in Gabe Callahan's eyes. He had a drink in his hand and danger oozed from his pores.

Suddenly Nic felt more like Red Riding Hood than one of Santa's elves. She licked her dry lips, then held out the package. "Merry Christmas."

When he didn't move to take the gift, she set it down on the table beside the door and waited.

A muscle jerked at his temple. Finally, just when she thought he'd never speak, he asked, "Why are you here?"

She smelled the alcohol on his breath. She opened her mouth intending to invite him to Christmas Eve services, but as their gazes caught and held, different words emerged. "I didn't want you to be alone," she told him. "*I* don't want to be alone. It's Christmas."

"Christmas," he repeated after a long moment, the word sounding like a curse on his lips. His gaze never left hers as he tossed back the rest of his drink, then set the empty glass on top of the package she'd brought. "What Christmas is, woman, is hell."

He moved toward her and she instinctively backed away until the door was at her back. His voice sounded low and gruff and a little slurred as he added, "And I'm feeling like the damned devil himself."

Then he kissed her.

His mouth was hot and savage, and Nic's senses reeled. Part of her was frightened. He was bigger than her, stronger than her. They were alone, miles away from anyone, and Gabe Callahan could do whatever he wanted with her. She was totally at his mercy.

Except she wasn't afraid. She was . . . excited.

This was the man who'd rescued a wounded dog from a bear trap. The man who'd put himself at risk to save two boys from a fire. The man who had warmed her feet against his bare stomach.

He would not hurt her. He was missing his family and he needed a human connection. He needed her.

So Nic kissed him back. Her hands moved to his shoulders, and she met his thrusting tongue with her own. He tasted of whiskey and loneliness, of anguish and despair. He was another wounded animal, and in this moment, if only for a moment, she had the power to soothe his pain.

His hands gripped her waist, and he lifted her off the floor and back against the door, pressing his body against hers and holding her aloft.

His kiss was carnal and hungry, and when he finally released her mouth, it was to feast at her neck. She felt the scrape of his teeth against her skin, and skitters of pleasure assaulted her. Nic arched her neck, gasped for breath, closed her eyes, and gave herself up to the magic he made.

She needed this, too. She needed to be needed. Greg's betrayal had damaged her, and she wanted to feel wanted again.

Gabe's hand cupped her breast, kneading and squeezing, almost too hard, but not quite.

She slipped a little and he yanked her back up, pressing his hips hard against her. His erection felt like steel. His fingers curled around the placket of her oxford shirt and he yanked, sending buttons flying. He ripped her bra, exposing her breast. He lifted it, took her into his mouth, and sucked her hard.

She shuddered. She wrapped her legs around him,

wrapped her arms around him, and held on for dear life. Nic moaned, long and low in her throat. He answered with a growl.

At some point they slid to the floor and lay atop the braided rug that decorated the entry. At some point he stripped them both naked. Cold rose from the floor beneath her. Heat radiated from the man rising above her. When he plunged into her, Nic was on fire.

He took her fast and hard and rough, his hips pumping, his breathing harsh. Tension built within her as she watched him, wild, angry animal that he was. Eyes closed, he threw back his head, cords of muscle in his neck, shoulders, and arms standing out in hard relief as he drove himself into her, again and again and again.

Her own passion swelled and answered his thrusts. The delicious tension stretched. Grew taut. *Almost. Almost. It's been so long.*

But even as she hung there at the very edge, he plunged one final time and cried out through gritted teeth. Cried out in pain and found release within her.

Heart pounding and aching for completion, Nic held her breath and watched him. The moment felt dangerous somehow. She didn't dare to move. On the stereo, Frank Sinatra sang "O Holy Night."

Slowly Gabe lowered his head. He opened his eyes and looked at her, dazed, as if he didn't know who she was or where they were. Then, slowly, he focused. The dry, empty pools of brown filled first with pain, then with horror, and finally with tears.

Gabe Callahan wrenched himself out of her, away from her, rolling over onto his back. He flung his forearm over his eyes, breathing hard as if he'd run ten miles. His shoulders shook.

His whole body shuddered. The sound that escaped his lips was the most raw, mournful noise she'd ever heard.

It shook her from her stupor. She sat up. She touched him. Scooted beside him. She gathered his head and shoulders to her breast, rocking softly, saying softly, "It's okay, Gabe. It's okay."

He shuddered silently.

She stroked his back and murmured soothingly, repeating over and over again, "It's okay."

He turned and wrapped his arms around her, buried his head against her, and cried harsh sobs that tore from his heart and ripped from his soul. Hot, bitter tears flowed from him like poison. Nic cradled him against her, rocking him, cooing soothing sounds, stroking his head and his shoulders. Her own eyes filled and overflowed.

How long they cried together, she would never know. Two minutes? Ten? Two hours? It was a moment out of time. The most intimate moment she had ever experienced. It was the saddest moment she'd ever known.

Until the afternoon got even sadder, when Gabe finally quieted, when he rolled away from her, turned away, and said in a quiet, raspy voice, "Please leave. I'm sorry. But please. Just leave."

It hurt, but Nic understood his need to be alone. She wiped off her tears, gathered her clothes, and slipped quietly out into the cold.

EIGHT

The first time Gabe had met Jack Davenport was when he'd sauntered up to his isolated prison cell, announced that he was a colleague of Gabe's brother Matthew at the CIA, and asked if he was really worth the $3 million ransom Jack had just paid his captors. When Gabe responded that he might not be, but the prisoner in the next cell who wanted to renounce his terrorist ways and reveal some particularly valuable secrets most certainly was, Jack did some quick thinking, scheming, and executing—in both a literal and figurative sense.

By "killing" both John G. Callahan and the recalcitrant terrorist and silencing some of their captors with bullets and others with cash, they had managed to protect the information in such a way that enabled the eventual apprehension of four sleeper cells on American soil and the disruption of terror plots that would have cost thousands of American lives.

Jack Davenport was a true unsung American hero. He was also Gabe Callahan's best friend. Pam knew that, too, so he wasn't too terribly surprised to hear the *whoop whoop* of helicopter blades on Christmas Day or to see Davenport land the bird on the helipad next to Eagle's Way.

Just because he wasn't surprised that his friend had come, however, didn't mean he was happy to see him.

Gabe was in a full-fledged funk, and it had nothing to do with the fact that today was Christmas Day. Gabe hadn't managed to get past the events of Christmas Eve.

A whole soup of emotions flavored his mood. Embarrassment. Anger. Guilt. Shame. Mortification. Guilt. Humiliation. Guilt. Guilt, and more guilt.

He couldn't believe how he'd acted. He'd all but attacked Nic, ripping her clothes right off her body. He recalled the shock in her eyes. Her tears.

He was a sorry son of a bitch. What he'd done to her was unforgivable. It went against everything he believed, and the only saving grace was that she had responded enthusiastically.

He'd picked up the phone half a dozen times to call her and apologize. He'd picked up his car keys more times than that, thinking to do it in person. Each time he'd chickened out.

What could he say to excuse himself? He'd taken her like an animal, then told her to leave. He simply couldn't find the words to express his sorrow and his shame.

Which meant he could add coward on top of the other charges stacked against him.

As he watched Davenport power down the bird, he tried to banish all thought of Nicole Sullivan from his mind. The last thing he needed was to spill those particular beans to Jack.

Knowing his friend, he went into the kitchen and put a pot of coffee on to brew. Jack strolled inside a few moments later, and as a way of saying hello, asked, "What do you have to eat in this shack?"

"How about a Denver omelet? Appropriate, wouldn't you say?" Gabe was finally hungry himself.

"Excellent choice. I'll chop peppers. You do the onions."

As Gabe handed over bell peppers from the fridge, he

decided that Jack Davenport must have been born giving orders. A tall man with movie-star looks—Jen used to say that he had no choice but to become a spy because he looked so much like a young Sean Connery—Jack was the definition of a leader of men. Brilliant, decisive, cold-blooded when the situation required, and loyal to a fault, Jack earned the respect of everyone who knew him. Gabe would gladly follow him into any battle.

After breakfast, he followed him into the great room, where Jack sat in an overstuffed easy chair, kicked off his shoes, and crossed his feet at the ankles atop an ottoman. He eyed the boxer, who hadn't bothered to lift his head off the dog bed Gabe had added to the room's decor. "Looks like I need to charge you a pet deposit. What's his name? Lazy?"

"He's a stray who won't stay away. Not my place to name him."

Davenport snorted, then sipped his coffee and sighed with satisfaction. "Eagle's Way is one of my favorite houses. I should spend more time here."

"How many houses do you have?"

"Four, domestically. If you count internationally, that brings it up to six."

"That's obscene."

"Hey, you don't have room to talk. You're no pauper."

"I don't have six houses."

Jack shrugged. "What can I say? It's the life of an international playboy."

Now it was Gabe's turn to snort. Jack Davenport was the most dedicated, hardworking American patriot Gabe had ever known.

He wondered when Jack would get around to telling him why he'd come to Colorado on Christmas Day. He had no intention of asking. Experience had taught him that Jack Davenport did things at his own pace, and that the fastest way to get the information he wanted was to keep his mouth shut.

"What can you tell me about Celeste Blessing?" Jack asked.

Okay, he'd surprised Gabe with that. "What do you want to know?"

"I read the local rag. I know about the spa venture and that she talked you into some design work. What sort of person is she? Is she a player?"

Gabe considered the question. "She's unique," he finally replied. "I like her a lot. I've never seen her be anything but kind. I wouldn't call her a player, but I do think there is more to her than meets the eye. She claims to be a retired schoolteacher, but she apparently has serious cash. There's no denying that she's been a force for good in this town."

"Interesting." Jack took another sip of his coffee, then his mouth twisted with a rueful grin. "I can definitely tell you there is more to her than meets the eye. I don't know whom she knows, but she managed to track me down."

"You're kidding." Gabe was shocked. Jack fiercely protected his privacy. "I didn't tell her anything."

Jack waved that away. "Never thought you did."

"What did she want?"

"She asked if my family had any journals, diaries, or other written documents that might contain clues about the town's big mystery."

"The Cellar Bride?" Gabe pursed his lips and nodded. "Smart thinking. Did you have anything?"

"Possibly. I found a stack of letters from Daniel Murphy to my great-great-grandfather. One of them told of a runaway bride. I didn't look into it any further. My plate is plenty full from dealing with contemporary murders—I don't have time to concern myself with historical ones. We've had a really sticky situation going on of late with some of your old friends in the Balkans."

"We should have killed more of those dirtbags when we had the chance."

"I completely agree. Anyway, I brought the letters with me. Figured the local historical society had more use for them than I do."

Jack drained his coffee cup, then set it aside. Gabe sensed the change in subject even before his friend said, "Pam called me."

"I figured as much when you showed up here out of the blue. Don't you have something better to do on Christmas than babysit an old friend?"

"Actually, I do." Jack shifted his stare away from the sad excuse of a Christmas tree and met Gabe's gaze. "I'm headed to one of those other homes I mentioned for a week or so of R, R, and R."

"Rest, relaxation, and . . . ?"

"Rum. It's my place in the Caribbean. I just stopped by here to see if you wanted to tag along."

Gabe rose to his feet. "When do we leave?"

"As soon as you can throw your swimsuit, flip-flops, and a toothbrush in a bag. Although"—Jack gestured toward the tree—"it's probably best to go ahead and take that down before we go. Fire hazard, you know."

Emotional hazard, he meant, and he was right. No sense running away from Christmas just to find it waiting for him when he got back. Half an hour later, all sign of the holiday had been returned to boxes and stored out of sight. "What about the dog?" Jack asked. "If he was smaller, we could take him with us, but he won't ride easily in the bird."

Gabe looked at the boxer, who responded with a lazy thump of his tail against floor. The obvious person to call for help here would be Nic, but he'd rather eat glass than make that call here in front of Jack. "I'll text some-body in town to come get him. The letters, too."

"Excellent. Then let's roll. I want to watch the sunset from my beach cabana with an umbrella drink in my hand."

As they left the house, Gabe turned to his friend. "Jack . . . I . . . thanks."

"Merry Christmas, Gabe," Jack Davenport said with a grin. "You can call me Santa."

The mouthwatering aroma of roasting turkey wafted through Sarah's house early in the afternoon on Christ-mas Day as Nic heard her cell sound the arrival of a text message. She flipped open her phone, checked the mes-sage, and her chin dropped. "A text? He sends me a text?"

Sarah looked over her shoulder. "Who sent you a text?"

"That jerk!"

"Your ex?"

Apparently. If she even could be considered an ex. After all, it hadn't even been a one-night stand. She hadn't even had a night. "Gabe Callahan."

"You're calling Gabe a jerk? Why?"

"Look."

Nic shoved her phone at Sarah who read aloud. " 'Leaving town. Dog @ EW. Code 195847362. Pls get him & letters for C.' I guess EW means Eagle's Way, and I guess C is for Celeste? What letters?"

"I don't know. I don't care. He's got a lot of nerve. This is Christmas! He shouldn't expect me to drop what I'm doing and run up to his precious estate."

Sarah handed back Nic's phone. "Maybe it's a trick. Maybe he's trying to lure you up to his lair. I think he has a thing for you. He looks. I've caught him watching you."

Nic stared at the screen on her cell. She hadn't told the

girls about the Christmas Eve event. What had happened at Eagle's Way was personal and private and . . . devastating. For that short time, she'd become a part of Gabe's pain, and it had destroyed her.

It wasn't the sex that had left her quaking like a stand of aspens on a breezy day while she drove back to town yesterday. To be honest, sex with Gabe Callahan had been the most thrilling—if not satisfying—of her life. But afterward, to see him lose it, to watch him break down and mourn from the depths of his soul, had literally changed something inside her. Yesterday, through his grief, Gabe had shown her love with a capital *L*. Love like she'd never experienced.

If it hurt him that much to lose it, think of how wonderful it must have been to live it. How different from her own marriage it must have been.

She'd mourned her marriage and the dreams it had represented when it ended. She had loved Greg, or at least she'd loved the man she'd believed him to be. But even at the very worst of it, she'd never felt even a tenth of the emotion that Gabe had demonstrated yesterday. It had taken her years to recover, to get to the point where she could be ready to try again. If she'd needed years, Gabe Callahan would need decades. Chances were he'd never be ready to love again.

She wasn't willing to play those odds. How could she compete with a dead woman? She couldn't, so she wasn't going to try. She'd played second fiddle enough in her life already. She refused to do it again.

"He might look, Sarah. He might even be willing to taste. But I want more than that. I deserve more than that. I won't risk my heart for anything less."

Sarah's eyes widened and she drew back. "Whoa there, girlfriend. I wasn't suggesting you fall in love with the man. I was thinking more along the lines of a kiss beneath the mistletoe."

"Yeah, well, mistletoe can kill you."

Sarah tilted her head and studied Nic for a long minute. "All right. What am I missing here? What aren't you telling me?"

Nic debated how to respond. She and Sarah had a long history of sharing the highs and lows of their love lives. Ordinarily she would at least admit that something had happened, even if she didn't provide details. This time was different. She didn't have the words to explain what had happened yesterday even if she'd wanted to do so. Instead, she dodged the question by saying, "Believe me when I say that Gabe Callahan is unavailable. I didn't realize just how unavailable until lately. I don't think that sending me this text was his ham-handed way to ask me for a date. I think it's just what he said. Gabe Callahan has left the building . . . and he's neglected to take along his dog."

The skeptical look in her best friend's eyes told Nic that Sarah wasn't buying her claim. "I'll let it go for now. It is Christmas, after all. That said, I'm no dummy. I know there is more to the story of this text message than what you are telling me. Don't think that we won't revisit the subject."

"I wouldn't dream of it. Now, in the meantime, speaking of mistletoe . . ." She nodded toward Sarah's entry hall, where one of the more interesting residents of the county, the mountain man known by only one name—Bear—crooked his finger in an attempt to lure his woman beneath the mistletoe. Patricia Robertson, who prior to joining Bear in his yurt northeast of town had worked for NASA as an honest-to-God rocket scientist, giggled like a schoolgirl as she allowed her lover to bend her over backward in a thorough kiss.

"Isn't love amazing? You know what Patricia told me this morning when I asked how she could stand living on the mountain in winter with only a wood stove for heat? She said all she needed was a rug, a blanket, and a Bear to keep her warm."

"Ahhh . . ."

When the kiss broke up and Bear set Patricia back on her feet, they saw Sarah and Nic watching. Bear winked, and Patricia said, "Missed your chance, girls. He's mine."

Nic thought about that moment an hour later as she drove toward Murphy Mountain. How powerful the force must be to have compelled Patricia to abandon her career to live in the back of nowhere with a man who considered indoor plumbing a luxury. She envied those lucky enough to find it. She wondered if they realized just how blessed they were.

She wondered if Gabe considered himself blessed or cursed.

In the big scheme of things, which was worse? To have that sort of love for a short time and lose it, or never to have known that depth of love at all? Obviously the answer would be different for different people, but since Nic believed that life should be lived to the fullest, she'd rather have a great love and lose it than never experience it. Of course, what she wanted most of all was a grand love that lasted the rest of her life.

"Hey, it could happen," she murmured aloud as she stopped at Eagle's Way's gate and rolled down her window to input the security code. "Just not with the likes of Gabe Callahan."

And yet, as she continued up the drive toward the house, a subtle tension stirred within her. Could Sarah have been right? Would he be waiting for her, an apology at the ready? If so, how should she respond? What should she say? What did she *want* to say to him?

Except for telling him what she'd thought of his text message, Nic drew a blank. She'd have to see what he said first and go from there.

As it turned out, she need not have concerned herself with the question. Unlike yesterday, the house was dark. No smoke rose from the chimney. No Christmas carols floated on the air.

Taped to the front door, she found a folded note with her name written across the front. She yanked it off the door, opened it, and read: *He's in the mud room. Same security code as the gate. Sack of letters on the workbench. G.*

"I was right the first time. He is a jerk."

For the next week, Nic quietly fumed and tried her best to put Gabe Callahan, jerk, out of her mind. She told herself that she refused to let him ruin her holidays, so on New Year's Eve, when she would have preferred crawling into bed early with a good book, she packed an overnight bag and joined her friends at Cavanaugh House for a previously planned event.

As she donned the Christmas gift Sage had given her in the bedroom Celeste had assigned to her, Nic glanced in the mirror and finally shook off her blue mood. Okay, maybe Sage's idea wasn't so stupid after all. Feeling delightfully silly, Nic headed downstairs. At the second-floor landing, she paused and eyed the banister. Dressed like this, she was tempted to slide her way to the ground floor.

"I know what you're thinking," Sarah said from the ground floor below. "I wanted to do it, too."

Nic looked at her friend and laughed. "Oh my gosh, Sarah. You look ten years old."

Like Nic, she wore fleece footed pajamas, green frogs against a pink background print. "I think I look darling."

"You do look darling. We both look darling."

"That yellow looks good on you. I love the puppies."

"Thank you." Then, indulging in her inner child, she

balanced her butt on the banister and slid her way to the floor. She and Sarah both were laughing when they entered Celeste's drawing room to find Sage and Celeste already waiting for them. Noting the prints on their pajamas—butterflies for Sage and angels for Celeste—Nic shook her head and asked, "How perfect. Where did you find these, Sage?"

"A little store in New England. The owner bought one of my butterfly paintings, and she sent me my pair with a note saying that my work inspired her."

"Well, I love my pair," Celeste said, holding out a foot and wriggling it. "They're so soft and warm and perfect for a slumber party. Now, y'all take a look at the sideboard and tell me if I've forgotten anything."

Nic spied chocolate chip cookies, chocolate cake, pimento cheese sandwiches, popcorn, peanuts, chips, crackers, and party mix. "I get a stomachache just looking at all that food."

"Not me," Sarah said, filling a plate with fats and calories. "I'm starving. I was running late leaving Gunnison, and I didn't stop for dinner."

Celeste offered her a kindly smile. "I'll bet your mother loved her room. Meadows Place is a wonderful facility."

Earlier today, Sarah had taken her mother to a memory-care assisted-living facility for a week of respite care—Sarah's Christmas gift from Celeste. Sarah had been reluctant to keep the reservation until Nic and Sage lobbied long enough to convince her that Ellen Reese would enjoy the activities the five-star facility had to offer. "It's a great place, Celeste, and a too-generous gift."

"Nonsense. Every woman deserves a week of pampering now and then."

"Here, here," Sage said, snagging a cookie off Sarah's plate. "Now, what's this big surprise you promised us,

Celeste? The one that's supposed to make us forget we are sitting in footie pajamas drinking hot cider with nary a man in sight on New Year's Eve?"

Nic tossed a piece of popcorn at her. "Hey, correct me if I'm wrong, but wasn't this sleepover your idea? Didn't you buy these PJs specifically for tonight?"

"Yes. You're right. My bad. It's because of the date from hell last New Year's Eve."

Sarah spoke to Celeste. "If we stay up late and get silly, ask her to do her imitation of Gareth Hollingsworth the Third."

"No." Now Sage threw popcorn back at Sarah. "I promised I wouldn't make fun of him anymore. It wasn't kind."

"He's a man. You don't have to be kind." Nic dropped down into her favorite chair in the room, the wooden rocker that felt like it had been made for her butt. "Except when it comes to Colt Rafferty. I love this chair. The man is an artist with wood."

Sage wrinkled her nose, her usual reaction to the mention of Colt Rafferty. The woman had a competitive streak a mile long when it came to her art. Nic found it amusing to watch.

"The surprise, Celeste?" Sage repeated before Nic could think of a good way to tease her further about Colt.

Celeste nodded and lifted an envelope from the mantel. "As you may know, a few weeks ago I contacted Jack Davenport in search of any information he might have regarding our Cellar Bride. As a result of that query, he provided me letters written by Daniel Murphy to Jack's great-great-grandfather, Lucien Davenport. One of them proved quite illuminating."

"Awesome," Sarah said.

Celeste continued, "Nic, would you read it aloud for me?"

Nic wiped her fingers on a paper napkin, then accepted the envelope from Celeste. Paper crinkled as she carefully removed a folded sheet of paper and opened it. She read aloud:

> *Dear Lucien,*
>
> *I hope this missive finds you and your family well. For my part, I have some hard news to share.*
>
> *Previously, I mentioned I had met the love of my life, a bonny lass by the name of Miss Winifred Smith, whom I came to call Angel after hearing the sweet, celestial sound of her voice as she lifted her voice to the Lord in church. On the day we were to wed, my angel disappeared. She is lost, Lucien. My angel is lost.*
>
> *I am lost.*
>
> *My world is ended and Eternity Springs has assigned the blame to me. They believe she forsook my love for another, and in a jealous fit I pushed her off the falls above town. They name me a murderer. It is a lie, Lucien. A brazen lie. I loved her more than life itself.*
>
> *I am heartbroken. I am lost. As lost as my lost angel. Please pray for me.*
>
> > *Your friend,*
> > *Daniel*

"Wow," Sage said.

Nic blew out a breath. "There's a photograph in the envelope. Look."

Nic held up a sepia-toned photo of a lovely young woman. Around her neck she wore a silver locket engraved with the silhouette of an angel's wings. Sarah said, "That's the locket Zach found with the remains. It's her. The Cellar Bride was Winifred Smith."

"Daniel Murphy's lost angel," Sage spoke in a soft tone.

As Nic stared at the photo, sadness filled her heart. "She's been here all along. At Cavanaugh House."

"Not Cavanaugh House," Celeste said. "Not any longer. I've been searching for the perfect name for our healing center and spa, and now I have found it. My dear friends, though our winter is far from over, spring waits on the horizon. Old wrongs will be righted and healing will come to Eternity Springs. The first step has been taken here, at Angel's Rest."

"Angel's Rest," Sage repeated. "I like it."

Sarah pursed her lips in thought, then nodded. "It's a great name. It's a perfect fit."

Nic met Celeste's gaze. "We need to tell Zach. We need to bring her back and give her a proper burial."

"We will." Celeste's smile warmed the room. "In good time. As soon as Eternity's long winter is over."

For a long moment, the room remained silent but for the hissing and crackling of the fire. Then Celeste, being Celeste, shifted from wise woman to girlfriend and said, "Now, how about we pop in the DVD? I have a hankering to see the new year in with Bond, James Bond. Sarah? Pass me the cookies, would you, please?"

NINE

February

Nic gave the pastry bag in her hand another twist to move the pink icing toward the tip and asked herself one more time why she'd volunteered to help Sarah bake cookies for the Father-Daughter Valentine's Day dance. Ordinarily she enjoyed the event, held annually at Eternity Springs Community School. She adored seeing the little girls all dressed up and standing on top of their daddies' shoes as they danced around the gymnasium. It brought back good memories of Uncle David and the way he'd stepped up to the plate, insisting she attend the dance with him her first year in Eternity Springs despite the fact she'd considered herself too old for such nonsense.

Secretly she'd been delighted. Her father certainly never would have participated in such an event. Even before Bryce P. Randall III turned his back on Nic's mother, he'd had little to do with his accidental offspring.

In contrast, Uncle David treated her like a princess. His princess. That first year he had bought her a wrist corsage for the Father-Daughter Valentine's Day dance, led her out onto the dance floor, and taught her the basic steps of a waltz. She'd fallen head over heels in love with both her uncle and the annual event that night.

This year was different. This year the very concept of Valentine's Day left her feeling a little sick. Mostly, though, she was angry. Fiercely, hotly, savagely, insanely, every-appropriate-adverb-she-could-think-of angry.

She needed a good, complicated animal case at the clinic to distract her. Instead, all she had on her books were shots for a cat and boarding for two dogs. It was difficult to make a living as a vet this time of year in Eternity Springs.

As she traced pink icing around the edge of a cookie, her telephone rang. She set down the pastry bag, sucked a smear of sweetness off her finger, and rose to answer it. She didn't bother to check caller ID before lifting the receiver and saying, "Hello?"

"Nic. Hi. This is Gabe Callahan."

Gabe. Her fist tightened around the receiver as she calmly said, "Hello."

"I, uh, returned to Colorado last night. I left in a hurry and forgot my phone. Thanks for picking up the dog, by the way. My trip came up out of the blue. I hope you've been able to find a home for him since I've been gone. Anyway, now that I've recharged my cell, I see that you called?"

Only two dozen times. At least. Nic's gaze fastened on the water bowl on her floor as she asked, "Can we talk? In person?"

Again, another pause. "Okay."

"I'm making cookies for an event at the high school the day after tomorrow, so I'm tied to my kitchen for a while. Can you come by here?"

"Sure. When?"

"As soon as possible."

After a moment's pause he said, "I'm in town. I'll be there in a few minutes."

Nic closed her eyes. Okay. All right. She was ready. No, she needed more time.

You don't need more time. You've been trying to reach him for the past two weeks. "Good. I'll see you then."

She thumbed the disconnect button, then stood for a moment, staring at the phone. "Heaven help me."

Like a prisoner approaching the gallows, she climbed the stairs to her bedroom. There she made a quick swipe through her hair with a brush and added a little blush to her uncommonly pale cheeks. She glanced down at her shirt, frowned at the icing smudges, then moved to her closet and perused her choices. She picked black. It suited her mood.

When the doorbell rang, she straightened her spine, squared her shoulders, and lifted her chin. *You can do this. You know what you want, know what you need. You can do this.*

He wore faded jeans and a blue chambray shirt. He'd had a haircut since Christmas and he looked tanned and rested. Rested! He was rested, and she hadn't slept for weeks.

"Hello, Nic."

"Gabe. Come on in." As he stepped inside, Nic was tempted to slam the door behind him. He paused in the entry hall, and while his expression remained impassive, she recognized his discomfort at being here. It was obvious. He looked anywhere but at her.

Tiger came galloping down the stairs from his favorite afternoon lying-in-the-sunshine-spot in front of the window in her bedroom. He jumped excitedly around Gabe, who looked happy for the distraction of the dog.

"Hey there, boy," he said, scratching the boxer behind the ears. "How you doing? Have you been behaving while I was gone?"

It was the most attention she'd seen Gabe pay the dog since the first day she'd met him. The boxer's tail wagged so fast it stirred up a breeze.

As Nic waited for the lovefest to end, the timer buzzed

on her oven, so she turned and headed for the kitchen. The pale yellow tile and muted green cabinets dated to the fifties, and while not the epitome of fashion, the room served as the very heart of her home. Here she was comforted. From here she drew strength. Strength she knew she'd need in the moments to come.

Gabe trailed after her and stood poised in the doorway as she set a hot tray of cookies on a rack to cool. He folded his arms and leaned against the doorjamb. "Cookies smell good."

If that was a hint, she was ignoring it. He could just starve.

He tried again. "I heard that y'all solved the big mystery and identified the Cellar Bride. Good work."

Nic wasn't in the mood for small talk. "Where have you been?"

"The Caribbean, then South America. I tagged along with Jack Davenport on his work trip. It took longer than we expected." He took a deep breath, then added, "Nicole, about what happened Christmas Eve—"

"Don't." She cut him off. "Please, just let me say this. I've been trying to reach you the past couple of weeks. I didn't know how to find you. I began to think this would be a rerun of Sarah's situation. I need to tell you . . ." She closed her eyes, exhaled a heavy breath. *Say it. Now. Just say it.* Nic squared her shoulders, stared him straight in the eyes, and announced, "I'm pregnant."

Gabe closed his eyes. The unacknowledged dread that had swirled in his gut since he'd turned on his phone to see he'd missed a number of calls from Nic swamped him. *No. Please, no.*

Maybe he'd heard her wrong. Hadn't he heard her wrong? Or could it be a joke? A really bad joke?

He looked at her. She didn't look like she was joking. She looked upset. Annoyed. A little scared.

Whoa.

"Did you hear me?"

He didn't respond. He couldn't have forced words out of his mouth right then if his life had depended on it. He blinked hard. His heart pounded. Blood roared in his ears.

She's pregnant? He closed his eyes and dragged a hand over his face. *No. Dear Lord, no.* Let him be asleep. Let this be a dream so that it wasn't a nightmare. She couldn't be pregnant. This wasn't happening. *I can't do this again.*

Daddy, look! They're starting to bubble! Bubble bubble bubble bubble.

He filled his lungs with cookie-scented air. He'd gone cold and clammy inside, but his mouth was desert dry. This had to be a joke. It *had* to be! With effort, he croaked out a reply. "You're kidding, right?"

She folded her arms. "No, I assure you, I'm not kidding. We had sex. We didn't use anything. I'm pregnant."

Gabe raked his fingers through his hair, locking his fingers atop his head as scenes from Christmas Eve flashed through his mind. He'd been drunk but not that drunk, cold and dark and desperate. She'd been blond and beautiful, light and bright and oh so hot. "Okay . . . yeah . . . we were careless. But I did think about it afterward. You're on the pill."

"What?" Shock registered on her face. "Why in heaven's name would you think that?"

"I saw them. The blister pack. In your purse."

"And what were you doing in my purse?"

He took another deep breath and blew it out hard, clearing the fog from his head. Panic rushed into the void as his thoughts spun back to early December. Restlessly he paced the small kitchen. "Remember that day at Cavanaugh House when the dog got mud all over you and you wanted to go home to change? You asked me to bring you your keys out of your backpack. I saw the package. Not in your purse, but in your backpack."

"I don't know what you're talking about." Baffled, she shook her head. "I didn't have . . . oh."

"You remember?"

"That wasn't birth control. That was Celeste's blood pressure medicine. I'd picked up her refill when I was in Gunnison."

"Oh."

"So that's why you didn't bother with a condom? You thought I was on the pill?"

He hesitated, then confessed, "Honestly, on Christmas Eve . . . I didn't think at all, Nic."

She closed her eyes and sounded defeated when she said, "Yeah. Me either."

Gabe began to pace the small kitchen. "I'm sorry I didn't call. Afterward. I tried to make myself call you Christmas Day, but I hadn't quite worked up the nerve by the time Jack arrived. We left shortly thereafter."

He'd been running away. Away from Christmas. Away from the anniversary of the accident. Away from his own behavior with Nic. He'd spent two weeks on a Caribbean beach, then when Jack got called to assist in a hostage rescue operation in Bolivia, he'd gone along to help. "I was ashamed, Nic. I pretty much attacked you."

Nic shrugged.

"I wasn't fighting you off. It wasn't a fine moment for either of us."

Gabe linked his fingers behind his neck and stared down at the floor. "I swear, I don't believe this. Jennifer and I tried to get pregnant for a year and a half before it finally worked. I can't believe that only one time . . ."

"You are not questioning your paternity of this child, are you?" she asked, a cautionary note in her tone.

He waved his hand. "No. No. Not at all. I just can't believe the bad luck that—"

"Whoa." Her chin came up and challenge lit her eyes. "Stop right there. Let's get something straight right from the beginning here. You will not refer to this child as bad luck or a mistake or any other negative term. My own father did that, and it's an ugly thing."

"You're right. Sorry. I wasn't thinking. I just . . . my wife had so much trouble getting pregnant. Are you absolutely sure about this? Maybe stress has delayed your period. Maybe—"

"I took four pregnancy tests," she interrupted. "Then I saw my ob-gyn in Gunnison. You gave me a gift Christmas Eve, Santa Claus, and just in case you're wondering, I'm not giving it back. I'm having this child."

She was having this child. His child. A baby. Another baby. It was a done deal. Cells dividing and multiplying. Way too late to go back and grab a rubber. He pulled the chair out from the table and sank into the seat. He didn't want this. Absolutely, positively didn't want another child. He couldn't bear to love another child.

Couldn't bear to lose another child.

Then you should have kept your dick in your pants. In a low, disgusted voice, he murmured, "I've done some stupid, irresponsible things in my life, but this one takes the cake."

Nic sighed and took the seat across from him. "Look, you and I both know that you weren't in your right mind that night. The fact is, I wasn't, either. I could have said no. I should have said no. But I was lonely and sad and it was Christmas. The situation got out of hand. We got out of hand. We're both responsible. We were both wrong."

She folded her hands atop the table and leaned forward, her tone earnest, as she continued, "But, Gabe, this child isn't wrong. This child can *never* be considered wrong. I can't emphasize this enough. I know what that's like, and I *will not* have it for my baby."

They sat in silence then for a long moment. Gabe tried to think the situation through, but he was having trouble thinking at all. A baby. She was having a baby! Finally, he asked, "What do you want from me, Nicole?"

"Only what you're willing to give. Freely and without rancor. It's important to me. I was illegitimate, and my father didn't want me and he made sure I knew it. I won't expose my child to similar hurt."

"Wait a minute," he protested, annoyed at the implication. "I would never be cruel to a kid."

"I'm not saying you would be. It's just, well, children are easily disappointed. Their hearts are fragile and easy to break."

She sucked in a deep breath, then exhaled in a rush. "Look, Gabe, I'd like you to be part of this baby's life, but if you choose otherwise, that's okay. I don't need you. But I do need you to make a choice and stick to it. I know from my own experience and watching Sarah raise her daughter that it's better for the child if no ambiguity exists. Unless you can commit to being a real father to our baby, she's better off without you. We'll get by just fine. I don't want you to feel trapped."

Our baby. He rubbed the back of his neck and grimaced. "I don't know what I feel, to be honest." *Other than scared.* "One thing I can tell you now, though, is that you need not worry about money. I'll take care of you in that respect."

She nodded. "Thank you. I admit that eases my mind. I was a little worried about how we'd make it financially when you disappeared on me. I figured that if I had the chance to tell you about the baby, you'd come through in that respect. I always knew you were a good guy, Callahan."

"I'm an idiot. I got drunk, had unprotected sex, and got caught."

"Gee, thanks."

Again he winced. "Hey, that's not a dig at you. You got caught, too."

"True. I don't even have alcohol for an excuse. I let emotions carry me away. You'd think a woman my age would know better."

"It was Christmas Eve. It's an emotional time for everyone. I was mourning my family. You walked in and . . ." He shrugged.

After that, neither of them spoke. The moment drew out.

Eventually she picked up a knife and resumed decorating her cookies. Though outwardly calm, telltale little signs betrayed her emotional turmoil—the slight tremble of her fingers as she moved cooled cookies ready for decorating onto wax paper, a deepening of the little worry line between her brows, the nervous tap of her foot.

Gabe watched Nic and thought of Jennifer, mourned Jennifer. The night she'd announced her pregnancy, he'd been over the moon. They'd both been thrilled. They'd celebrated with sparkling water and chocolate ice cream, then they'd gone to bed and made love. That's the way it was supposed to be. Not like this.

He swallowed a lump the size of a baseball in his throat and watched Nic spread white icing across the surface of cooled, heart-shaped cookies with hands that trembled. Unexpectedly, a little wave of compassion lapped at his heart. This was her first pregnancy. Her first baby. She must have had some tense weeks. What had she thought when she realized she'd conceived and the father didn't answer his phone?

His gaze settled on her stomach. A baby. Their baby. *His* baby.

No. Matt is my baby. Sweet little Matt, who loved to growl like Cookie Monster.

The memory hit like a sucker punch to his gut. He had to get out of here. Had to get away. Grief forced out his deepest feelings in words just above a whisper. "No. I can't, Nic. I'm sorry, but I can't be part of this baby's life. You deserve better and so does this child, but I can't do it. Not again. I buried a child. I can't do this again. I won't do this again. I don't want another child."

With that, there was nothing more to say. He rose and fled like the low-down, yellow-bellied coward that he was.

TEN

Two days later, on the evening of February 14, light reflected off a seventies-era mirror ball hung from a rafter on thirty-pound-test fishing line in the center of Eternity Springs Community School gym. Crepe-paper streamers swagged the bleachers, and pink and white helium-filled balloons rose from the backs of folding chairs set at round tables covered with white cloths. Candles floating in clear glass bowls served as centerpieces. Music selected by the disc jockey, Reverend Hart, ran the gamut from Sinatra tunes to country and western to hip-hop and the bunny hop.

Nic stood behind the refreshment table dipping pink punch into paper cups. She poured herself a cup of punch and tossed it back as if it were whiskey. She *so* didn't want to be here.

Sarah sidled up beside Nic and said, "Am I glad you made cookies for us, Nic. The cakes are almost gone."

"If you weren't a master at baking, your treats would last longer."

"Thank goodness we have yours, then. They'll last."

"Bite me."

Sarah laughed and gazed around the gym, her violet eyes gleaming with satisfaction. "Doesn't everything look pretty tonight? The mirror ball is inspired. The kids love it."

"Where did it come from?"

"Bear brought it by."

"Bear?" Nic shook her head. "You're kidding. Where did Bear get a mirror ball?"

"I don't know. Even more curious is where he keeps it. He lives in a yurt."

Nic pictured a year-round universal recreation tent with its circular wooden platform, lattice framework, and conical roof covered with heavy wind- and water-proof canvas. "If his yurt has a mirror ball, I want to see it."

As Nic and Sarah shared a grin, Reverend Hart introduced Maurice Chevalier singing "Thank Heaven for Little Girls" and the dance floor swelled with daddies and daughters. Nic watched Alton Davis lift his five-year-old into his arms and twirl her around, and from out of nowhere, emotion hit her like a truck. She closed her eyes and fought back tears.

"Nic?" Sarah touched her arm, concern clouding her eyes. "What is it? Are you okay?"

"Sure. I'm fine." She tried to smile, but her lips began to tremble and she finally gave up. A tear spilled from her eyes and trailed down her cheek. She grabbed a napkin off the refreshment table, wiped it away, and began to babble the disjointed thoughts that spun through her mind. "You've done such a great job. I can do it, too. I love my mom. Truly, I do. I just never wanted to be like her. At least I won't have to worry about the cost of braces."

Sarah frowned. "I saw you drinking punch. Someone must have slipped past you and spiked it. You're talking nonsense."

"I'm not drinking spiked punch," she replied, a hint of hysteria in her voice. "I can't. I'm pregnant."

As her friend's jaw dropped in shock, Nic fled, pushing past Sarah and heading for the gymnasium doors. Out in the hallway, she spied a group of people congregated in front of the building's exit, so she turned in the other direction and walked toward the classrooms.

Eternity Springs Community School served grades K–12 and currently had a student body of 102. The building was new, less than five years old, with three separate wings that housed younger grades, middle grades, and high school, each wing connected to the gymnasium. Nic had fled into the high school wing.

She turned a corner so that she wasn't visible from the gym doors, stopped, and put her back against the wall. She closed her eyes and clenched her teeth, trying to find her composure and will away the tears. She'd held it together after Gabe left and all day yesterday, but now it appeared that her composure had evaporated. She hung on the brink of a full-fledged meltdown.

"Here she is, Sarah," she heard Sage say.

Of course they'd followed her. Sarah, Sage, and Celeste rounded the corner, looking worried. Well, good. Maybe they could talk her down off this ledge. "Approach at your own risk," she warned them. "I'm borderline crazy at the moment."

Celeste said, "In that case, I suggest we find a more private place to talk. Sarah? You know the school, do you not? Where can we go?"

"Right here." Sarah nodded at the nearest door as she dug in her pocket and pulled out a large ring full of keys. She searched their labels, saying, "It's the chem lab."

"Why do you have keys to the chemistry lab?" Sage asked as Sarah fitted a key into the lock.

"I'm here so much doing such a variety of volunteer work that the principal figured it was more efficient just to give me a set of keys." She opened the door and flipped the light switch.

Sage took hold of Nic's arm and pulled her into the classroom, then froze. "Oh, my. This is frightening."

Celeste clicked her tongue. "I'm glad I didn't wander into this room alone."

The note of alarm in her friends' voices distracted Nic and made her smile. "This is part of the local wildlife collection Bear donated to the school. He's a taxidermist."

Celeste made a slow visual survey of the room. "Why do they keep the animals in the chemistry lab? Why not the biology lab?"

"They do keep them there," Sarah explained. "This is the overflow."

"Bear is one interesting man," Sage observed, approaching the stuffed bear standing on its haunches.

"Yes," Sarah agreed. "But I'm more interested in a polecat. Nic? You ready to talk?"

"Yes. No." She grimaced. "I think I need to sit down."

"Of course, dear." Celeste took Nic's arm and guided her over to a table with four chairs. "Can I get you some water?"

"No, thank you."

Sage took the chair next to Nic, saying, "I'm gonna sit here where I can keep an eye on that bear."

Nic recognized Sage's comment as an attempt to lighten the mood and she appreciated the effort. Celeste sat catercorner to Nic, and Sarah took the opposite seat. She reached out, took Nic's hand, and said, "Talk to us."

"I'm gonna have a baby."

"Gabe's?" When Nic nodded, Sarah gave her hand a squeeze. "I didn't know you were seeing him."

"I wouldn't call it 'seeing.' It was a onetime thing."

As Sarah and Sage shared a look, the story poured out. Her friends, being her friends, punctuated the tale with comments throughout.

"I could tell he had his eyes on you."

"You liked him from the first."

"Christmas is tough under normal circumstances."

"In the foyer!"

"I'll bet you were worried, not knowing how to reach him after he left."

"Dodging your calls? What a jerk!"

"My blood pressure pills? Oh, dear."

Then, finally, all three of her friends spoke at once. "He said no?"

"That's right. He doesn't want to be part of my baby's life."

Sarah's eyes flashed. "That sorry skunk. I thought better of him than that."

Nic tugged a tissue from the box Celeste offered to her and dabbed at an escaped tear. "It'll be okay. We will be okay." After a moment's hesitation, she asked, "Won't we?"

"Absolutely," Sarah declared. "And I ought to know because I speak from experience. I won't lie and say it's not a struggle being a single parent, but you're a strong woman, Nicole Sullivan. You'll do just fine."

"If that's how it shakes out," Sage said. She drummed her fingers against the table. "I think he'll come around."

"He said—"

"I don't care what he said." Celeste gave the surface of the lab table a little slap. "The news was undoubtedly a shock to him. I agree with Sage. Don't give up on him yet."

"I don't know. He seemed pretty certain."

Celeste dismissed her argument with a wave. "You caught him off guard. Be fair to the man. I am certain he simply needed a little time to process the information. Gabe is a good man. Once he's had time to think it through, he will do the right thing."

Turning to Sarah and Sage, she continued, "Now, that

puts us under the gun if we are going to make Nic's wedding the thing of her dreams. Nic, you attend St. Stephen's, don't you? Such a lovely old church. I can see the altar decked out with wedding flowers now."

"Whoa. Stop." Nic shook her head. "Wait just one minute. No one said anything about a wedding."

"Do you want your child to be illegitimate?"

"No, but it won't be the end of the world. This isn't the 1950s, you know."

"Or Regency England," Sarah added. "He's not going to lose out on a title or a fortune."

Sage sighed heavily. "Reading those historical romances again, aren't you, Sarah?"

Nic rubbed her eyes. "Mostly I don't want my baby to be hurt. If Gabe can't be in our lives all the way, then we're better off if he's not in them at all. Rejection by one's father is a cruel burden to bear. I won't have this child feel unwanted and unloved."

"I understand your caution," Celeste said, reaching out and patting Nic's hand. "I just think you're a bit premature. Gabe Callahan is not your father. He has a good and loving heart, but it's been damaged. It's still healing. And you know what the best medicine for a wounded heart is, don't you?"

When Nic didn't respond, Sage answered, "Love."

Celeste nodded. "Allow yourself to love him, Nicole. That's one of the greatest gifts a mother can give to her child, you know. To love her child's father. I firmly believe that once Gabe's heart heals, he'll discover that you and your child already have a place there."

"I think Celeste is right," Sage agreed. "Give him time, Nic. He'll come around."

"It's a big risk for her," Sarah cautioned.

"But the potential reward is great," Sage returned.

Nic sighed heavily. "Look, there's no sense straining

my brain about it. The man said no and walked out. He wasn't wishy-washy about it one little bit."

"Nevertheless, what's the harm in being prepared?" Celeste asked.

"I appreciate the thought, but again, this isn't the 1950s. Pregnancies don't necessarily equal weddings anymore. It's the day of the baby mama, not the wife."

"Not in Eternity Springs," Sarah said. "Not for you."

"Not for Gabe Callahan, either, I suspect," Sage added.

Nic sighed. "Even if Gabe and I were to decide to marry, we wouldn't have a wedding. We'd get married at the courthouse."

"Why?" Sage asked.

"Because I won't marry in a religious ceremony unless love and commitment are involved."

"Oh, Nic." Celeste clicked her tongue. "God's blessing upon a marriage is never inappropriate."

"Maybe so, but I'd feel like a hypocrite."

Sarah met Celeste's and Sage's gazes. "I've known her since she was nine years old. No sense arguing with her about this one."

"That's right." Nic smiled around at her group of friends. "Thank you all for helping me through my meltdown. I'm calmer now. I can think more clearly. You are dear, dear friends and I am so glad you're in my life. Now we should probably get back to the dance. The cookie plate is liable to be empty by now."

"Wait," Celeste said, holding up her hand. "There is one important thing we neglected to say."

She took Nic's hands in hers, gave them a squeeze, and said, "Congratulations, Nicole. I wish you great joy with your little one. Children are a blessing from God."

"She's right," Sarah agreed. "Congrats, girlfriend." She gave Nic a hug, then moved aside so Sage could do the same.

"Be happy, Nic," Sage said. "I can't wait to see the baby you and Gabe produce. He's bound to be gorgeous. Having the two of you as parents, he's hit the genetics jackpot."

With the mood lightened, the women headed for the door. Sage paused beside the elk placed in a corner at the back of the room and observed, "I couldn't concentrate to learn anything with all these glass eyes staring at me."

"You should check out Linda Horten's fourth-grade class," Sarah told her. "She has dozens of the smaller animals around her room—five times the number of eyes."

Sage shuddered and linked her arm with Celeste's as they entered the hallway. "Maybe it's my city-girl upbringing rearing its head, but personally, I'd rather learn animals from pictures in a book."

Celeste laughed. "As a newcomer to Colorado, I'd prefer learning what a black bear looks like this way as opposed to the way I was educated. I'll never forget opening my front door last fall to put a letter in the mailbox and finding a bear on my porch."

"What did you do?" Sarah asked.

"I explained to him that I'd forgotten my return address label and I darted back inside."

The picture coaxed a laugh from Nic and was the reason why she had a smile on her face when she reentered the gymnasium.

Her smile died when she spied the man leaning against the wall of folded-up bleachers on the east side of the gym.

Gabe.

ELEVEN

Gabe wore a gray suit, white shirt, and red tie. Seeing her, he straightened away from the wall. He looked somber and serious, and her stomach sank.

"Whoa," Sage murmured behind Nic. "Be still my heart. He's even sexier than Coach Romano."

"Mm-hmm," Sarah hummed. "He is a handsome polecat. I'll give him that."

"I'll bet you the keys to my Honda Gold Wing that he's here to propose," Celeste declared. "You'll excuse me if I say I told you so."

Nic's stomach took a nervous roll. "Don't be silly. He's probably bringing me contact information before he leaves town for good."

"He's carrying a rose," Sage said. "I don't think a man brings a woman a red rose to kiss her off."

Sarah shook her head. "The roses are a freshman class fund-raiser. They probably tackled him coming inside. Still, he could have tossed it."

Nic stood frozen in place, only marginally aware that her friends dropped back as Gabe approached. He carried a long-stemmed red rose tied with a red satin ribbon in his right hand, and when he stopped in front of her, he held it out to her. "Hi."

"Hi." She accepted the flower. "Thanks."

When silence descended awkwardly between them, she twirled the rose between her fingers and thought,

School gym. Red rose with a tacky ribbon. Awkward conversation while my best-friends-forever are watching. Junior high déjà vu. "I . . . um . . . didn't expect to see you here tonight, Gabe."

"Well, yeah." He shoved his hands in his pockets. "Can we talk? I want to—"

He broke off abruptly and scowled at something behind Nic. She glanced over her shoulder and saw that said best friends had moved within listening distance. Celeste smiled, her eyes twinkling. Sage gave a little finger wave. Sarah winked at Nic, then shot Gabe her best dirty look.

Nic tried to shoo them away by making a sweeping motion with the back of her hand, but of course they didn't budge.

Gabe sighed and asked, "Why don't you give me a tour of the school?"

"Okay." After requesting the key ring from Sarah, she led him toward the door she'd entered moments ago. He walked at her side, his hands in his pockets, a troubled expression on his face. Nic twirled the rose stem nervously with her fingers. "This is the high school wing."

"Okay." He didn't bother glancing around.

In the dim light of the hallway outside of the biology lab, shadows accentuated the hard angles of his face. He had a fallen-angel look about him, and his declaration on Christmas Eve flitted through her mind. *I'm feeling like the damned devil himself.*

Nic drew in a lungful of formaldehyde-scented air and felt a little nauseated, so she continued to lead him up the hall and into another wing of the school until he paused in front of a bulletin board decorated with colored chalk drawings of Hummingbird Lake. He studied the students' drawings for a few moments before saying, "I took a snowmobile out yesterday. Went up into the back country and eventually ended up at a spot that overlooked Eternity Springs."

He fell silent then, and after a long moment, Nic felt compelled to speak just to fill the void. "You had perfect weather. Bet it was gorgeous."

He nodded. "Six months ago I wouldn't have seen it. Shoot, six months ago I might have juked the gas and driven the snowmobile right off the edge of the cliff. Yesterday it was different. I was different. I could see the beauty in the blue sky and the sunshine and the pristine snow. Eternity Springs looked like one of those Victorian villages that department stores sell at Christmastime."

He turned his head and his solemn, brown-eyed gaze held hers. "This town has been good for me."

She wanted to ask, *Even considering the consequences?* Instead, she kept it neutral by saying, "I think Celeste is on to something about the healing energy in our valley."

Gabe shook his head. "See, that's the thing. Being better and being healed are two different animals. That's basically where I'm at."

He stuck his hands in his pockets and resumed walking. "For you to understand my position, I'm going to have to talk about myself. I really hate to do that."

"I noticed," she commented dryly.

His mouth quirked. "I have told you a little. You do know I have baggage. What you don't know is that it's enough to fill a container ship."

Nic had to bite her tongue to keep from telling him to just get over it. A whole cruise ship full of baggage didn't change the fact that they were having a child together. Their child's needs had to come first—baggage be hanged.

Choosing her words judiciously, she replied, "Everyone has baggage. Personally, I have a matched set. With pink pompoms tied around the handles."

They reached the end of the high school wing, and she turned toward the small lounge area in front of the cafeteria and school offices. Nerves were making her knees a bit shaky; she might need to sit down.

He paused in front of another bulletin board, this one decorated with third-graders' Valentine-themed artwork. "The cold air cleared my senses, and I was able to think clearly. I was able to figure out what I can offer you, Nic. And what I can't. You'll have to decide if it's enough for you. Is there somewhere we could sit down?"

Just say it already, she wanted to scream. The tension was driving her nuts.

When his gaze focused on her hands and his mouth twisted, she glanced down to see that she'd mangled the flower. Lovely. "Follow me."

She led them to the lounge, where she took a seat in an armchair. She watched him pace the lounge and waited for him to speak. It seemed to take forever, but he finally took a seat in the chair opposite her and said, "So here's the deal. I think we should get married."

Nic narrowed her eyes. "Have you been talking with Celeste?"

"Um, no," he warily replied. "Not since you dropped your bombshell. Why?"

"It doesn't matter. Never mind." Now Nic was the one who stood up and paced.

"Explain something to me. If you're not willing to be a father, what good does it do for you to become a husband?"

"Because it's the right thing to do. I'm the baby's father whether or not I ever become his daddy. I have a responsibility to him. He's an innocent in all of this—the only innocent, really. We have some time, Nic. Seven and a half months of pregnancy, then another chunk of months before I could cause him any real damage by bowing out."

But what about me? she wanted to ask. Big girls had tender hearts, too.

"Look, I'm a bad bet," he continued. "Don't have any doubt about it. My head is pretty messed up. However, it's not nearly as messed up as it was when I came to Colorado. Right now the idea of a baby makes me break out in a cold sweat, but maybe it won't always be that way. I'd like time to try to figure that out."

"We don't have to be married for that. If you're worried about my reputation, well, don't. We're not going to fool anyone. Eternity Springs' residents might not be the most sophisticated people around, but they do know how to count to nine."

Gabe leaned forward and rested his elbows on his knees. "I've done a lot of lousy things in my life, but I've always taken responsibility for my actions. Marrying is the right thing to do, the responsible thing to do."

Responsibility. Great. He made marriage sound as pleasurable as a toothache.

Doubt assailed her. Marrying him could be a huge mistake, not because of the baby—he had a point about having time—but because she was susceptible to him. She could love this man. Shoot, she was halfway in love with him already.

Celeste's words echoed through her mind. *He has a good and loving heart, but it's been damaged. It's still healing. And you know what the best medicine for a wounded heart is, don't you?*

Love.

Nic returned to her chair and sank into the seat. "If we did this, what sort of arrangement are you proposing with this proposal?"

"What do you mean?"

"Would this be a marriage in name only or the real deal? Would we live together? Share our meals?" She paused, licked her lips, then added, "Share a bed?"

He went very still for a moment, then shook his head. "I won't use you, Nic. I did that at Christmas and it was wrong. Honestly, my head is kinda screwed up where sex is concerned. I was a faithful husband and . . . well, I guess you could say I haven't adjusted to my change in circumstance. If you have a spare bedroom, that would probably be best. At least for now."

Nic shut her eyes. How humiliating was this? He wouldn't be her husband. He'd be her roommate. *If I wanted a roommate, I'd have taken out an ad.*

"If I were to agree to this," she said slowly, "there is something I refuse to compromise on. If you decide you're, um, adjusted again, don't let me walk in on you and another woman. Like they say, been there, done that. Totally no fun."

"Hey." He put a finger beneath her chin and tilted her face up, then stared deeply into her eyes. "That's one promise I *can* make you, Nic. I will not be unfaithful. Put that worry out of your mind. You have my word."

She believed him. After all, he was still struggling over faithfulness to his first wife a year after her death.

"Say yes, Nicole," he urged. "Let me do this much for you, for the baby. Let me give him, give both of you, my name."

"Why do you care, Gabe? I don't understand."

"I'm not sure I understand either, to be honest. What I do know is that as I stood on that mountaintop yesterday, I understood that this is the way it's supposed to be. Maybe it's because it's the way I was raised. Maybe it's because this is one thing I know I can do for this baby. If, in the end, I have to walk away, at least he'll know I respected his life and his mother enough to do this."

Nic thought about it for a long time. If she agreed to

marry him, she would be taking an awful risk. What if she fell all the way in love with him and he never healed enough to love her back? Or, even worse, his heart healed and he decided he wanted someone else?

But, like Sage said, the potential reward was great. They could have a happy marriage. Her baby could have both her parents.

Gabe Callahan could fall in love with them.

"If I were to agree to this," she slowly repeated, "I'd want a kill switch."

"Excuse me?"

"We can't have an open-ended agreement. That doesn't work for me. I need to know that if you can't commit to us by the time the baby is, say, six months old, you'll leave. That you'll go away and stay away so that I . . . we . . . can get on with our lives."

He considered it, then nodded. "Okay. We can do that. I don't have a problem with that."

Nic looked at Gabe for a long minute. He really was a good man. Troubled. Damaged beyond repair, perhaps. But when he loved, he loved with a capital *L*. He could be her brass ring, but marrying him would require a leap of faith on her part. Could she do it? Dare she do it?

Again, Celeste's voice echoed through her thoughts. *Allow yourself to love him, Nicole. That's one of the greatest gifts a mother can give to her child, you know. To love her child's father. I firmly believe that once Gabe's heart heals, he'll discover that you and your child already have a place there.*

"Okay," she said, expelling a heavy breath. "I'll do it. For the baby's sake, I'll marry you."

"Good. I'm glad." He wiped his palms on his pants legs, then stood.

If he tries to shake my hand, I'll kick him.

He took her hand, but didn't shake it. Instead, he

tugged her to her feet, leaned down, and placed a chaste kiss on her lips. "Thanks, Nic. I'm honored."

He's honored, and I'm a goner.

"So, how do you want to do this?" he continued. "You go to St. Stephen's, don't you?"

"No. Not at the church. Let's just go to the court-house. In Gunnison. I don't want to do this in Eternity Springs."

He shrugged. "That's your call."

She considered her appointment schedule for the com-ing week and frowned. "This week is bad for me. How about next week? Maybe Wednesday?"

"Sure. That's fine. Whatever you want." He gestured toward the hallway. "Ready to go back to the dance?"

"Guess I'd better. I'm supposed to be guarding the punch bowl."

They didn't speak as they returned to the gym. Sage was standing at the refreshment table, and when Nic gestured that she would take her friend's place, Sage shook her head and waved her away. That left Nic standing awkwardly with Gabe. She expected him to say good night and escape, but instead he surprised her—shocked her—by asking, "Would you like to dance?"

She smiled at him. "Look at the gym floor, Gabe. This is a father-daughter dance."

"Yeah. Well, so what? Consider this my first dance with my daughter."

At that, Nic went all gooey and some of her lingering doubts eased. Gabe Callahan *was* a good man. She tilted her head at him and asked, "What if she's a he?"

"Well, I grew up going to dance halls in Texas, and believe me, it's never too early for a guy to learn to two-step."

Gabe was up on the ladder cutting in paint in a guest room at Angel's Rest the next morning when his cell phone rang. His sister-in-law was returning his call. He set down the paintbrush, blew out a breath, then answered the phone.

The connection was lousy and he could barely hear Pam's voice. "Let me call you back from a landline," he told her. "Give me ten minutes."

He descended the ladder and tended to his painting supplies, then exited the bedroom. He'd use the phone in the hallway. Celeste had left half an hour ago to get her hair done. He'd have privacy for another half hour at least. He didn't expect the call to take nearly that long.

He'd be surprised if Pam didn't hang up on him within two minutes.

Jen's sister would see this as a betrayal. She might well cut off all contact with him. He could very well lose the only family he had left.

Except you'll be gaining a new family, won't you?

"Maybe yes, but maybe no," he muttered.

Gabe wiped his hands on the rag hanging from his pocket. This phone call would be the most difficult one he'd ever made. At some point during his mostly sleepless night he'd tried to write dialogue for this conversation. It hadn't gotten much beyond, *I'm an idiot.* He couldn't believe he'd been so careless as to put himself into this spot. Pam would rightly give him hell—if she didn't hang up on him upon hearing that Gabe "had to get married."

Marriage. He swallowed hard.

He believed he and Nic were doing the right thing. Despite trends in America, illegitimacy could still be a confidence killer for a small-town kid who lived in a fly-over state. Gabe had grown up in a small town, a small town even more conservative than Eternity Springs. There had been a couple of kids of divorced parents who'd gone to school with him. He couldn't think of any whose parents had never married.

He did recall his mother's reaction when the older sister of one of his friends turned up pregnant in high school and a wedding wasn't immediately in the offing. A good Catholic girl, his mom had been scandalized. He'd never forget her comment at the dinner table one night when the topic came up for discussion. She'd sniffed with disdain, then said, "First babies can come anytime. The rest of them take nine months."

That one had him confused for days before one of his brothers explained it to him.

That memory of his mother had helped him make up his mind about what to do. He'd gotten a girl pregnant, so he needed to marry her. Like it or not, he was a responsible party here, and he didn't shirk his responsibilities. His mom would rise from her grave and pull his ears off his head if he tried. She'd be right to do so.

Downstairs, Gabe eyed the phone on the table as if it were a snake. He absolutely, positively did not want to make this call.

Nevertheless, it had to be done. He had to tell his sister-in-law that he'd slept with someone other than Jennifer. That he'd made a baby with someone other than Jennifer.

That he was marrying someone who wasn't Jennifer.

Gabe was tempted to lean over and beat his head against the banister. A baby. Against his will, Gabe remembered holding Jennifer's back as the labor nurse ordered, *Push, Jenny, push*. Bringing Matt home, setting him in the nursery's bay window to let the sunshine do its magic on his jaundice. Jen in the rocking chair, a madonna with a babe at her breast.

He had a mental flash of Nic's bare breasts, then he closed his eyes and groaned. He needed a shrink. Of course, he was out of luck in that regard here in Eternity

Springs. Closest thing they had to a psychologist was a vet. The same vet who'd created his need for a doctor in the first place.

Gabe picked up the phone, dialed the number, then stretched the long phone cord to take a seat on the stairs four steps from the bottom. Pam answered on the third ring. They spoke about Nathan and the rehab on his leg for a few moments, then, when Gabe was trying to find the words to get started, Pam said, "Okay, Callahan. You obviously have something on your mind. What is it? Spill."

Holding the phone to his left ear, his elbows propped on his knees, Gabe held his head with his right hand and closed his eyes. He should have snagged a water bottle before making this call. His mouth was as dry as the West Texas desert.

"Gabe?"

"Okay. Yeah. Well, here's the deal. Don't hang up on me, Pam. Okay? Promise me you'll hear me out?"

"You're scaring me, Callahan."

"Sorry. It's just that this is hard. See, I'm ashamed." *Shame doesn't even cover it.*

"Is it another wreck? Did you hurt somebody else?"

He winced, taking it as a barb despite knowing she didn't mean it the way it sounded. *Yeah, I hurt someone else, but not in the way you think.*

"No, no wreck. Listen, Pam, I'm not going to try to excuse what I did, but I do want to explain it. It happened Christmas Eve. I wasn't thinking straight." He told her about trimming the tree and the effects of seeing all the family decorations. "After you called to tell me you guys weren't coming to Colorado, I went a little crazy. I started drinking. You know what it was like, how hard it was."

Warily his sister-in-law said, "Yes."

"I did something I should not have done, and now I have to face the consequences."

After a beat, Pam asked, "Are you going to jail, Gabe?"

"Jail?" Gabe repeated, barking out an unamused laugh. "Not exactly, but then, there are all sorts of prisons, aren't there?" He blew out a breath and ripped off the bandage. "I got a woman here in Eternity Springs pregnant on Christmas Eve. I'm getting married, Pam."

Nic carried two lightweight but bulky shopping bags in her hands as she approached the back porch of Angel's Rest, where Sarah and Sage waited for her the morning after the dance. She waved and saw both women do a double take. When she drew close, Sarah said, "Nicole, my friend, green is not your color. Not for your complexion, anyway. Are you okay?"

"I'm an idiot. I felt really good this morning and I decided to walk over. Remind me to tell Gabe and Celeste they need to consider building a footbridge for expectant mothers that crosses Angel Creek a little farther down from the hot springs."

"Smell got to you?" Sage asked.

"Something got to me. I ordinarily have morning sickness in the afternoon, but I got one whiff of sulfur and my stomach started spinning like Bear's mirror ball in the gym last night."

Sarah shook her head. "I remember morning sickness. It's too bad God didn't give it to us as a precursor to sex instead of the result of it. There would be a lot fewer unplanned pregnancies that way."

Sage and Sarah shared a look, then Sage asked, "So, are you ready to talk about it this morning?"

"Being nauseated?"

"Wedding plans."

"Not really. No." Gabe had taken his leave after their

dance last night, and the moment he left the gym her friends had swooped down like hawks on a field mouse for details. Pleading exhaustion, Nic had shared only the fact that they had agreed to marry. "We're here to decorate Celeste's office for her birthday, and besides, I have no wedding plans to discuss."

"You are no fun, Nic Sullivan," Sarah groused.

"Deal with it. Now, we'd best get to work if we're going to have everything ready before Celeste comes home from the beauty shop." She opened the door, stepped into the kitchen, and set her bags down on the kitchen table. "I have streamers and balloons, fishing line, and some other sundry stuff. Could have done better if Celeste hadn't been so stingy with information."

Last night Celeste had mentioned in passing to Sage that today was her birthday, though she neglected to reveal just which birthday it was. Once Sarah learned the news, she'd decided the time had arrived to welcome Celeste into a tradition she and Nic had shared for years, one they'd introduced Sage to after she'd moved to Eternity Springs.

"I brought the bananas," Sarah said.

"I have markers and paints—and a list of things I want to write. We don't have time to be, uh, as creative as we were for your birthday, Sarah."

"Besides, I can't drink alcohol," Nic added.

Sarah smirked. "I knew my bananagram had been done in an alcohol daze. Some of those messages were X-rated."

The silly yet enjoyable tradition between the adult girlfriends had grown out of slumber-party activity for Lori and her friends when they were seven years old. "Bananagrams" back then were messages like "Happy Birthday" or "Congratulations" written in black marker on whole bananas. The bananas were then hung from trees in the honoree's yard with fishing line—usually in the middle of the night.

In the past ten years, Nic and Sarah had added their own special touch to the tradition. When Sage moved to town, she'd been happy to join in the festivities.

"I'm going to write something about her motorcycle," Nic said. "Break out the pens, Sage." To Sarah, she added, "Did you bring any rotten fruit?"

"Absolutely. What's a bananagram without at least one 'It's rotten to be so old' message?"

"Celeste is gonna love this." Nic met her friends' gazes and added, "It's just what I needed. Thank you."

They spread their supplies on the table and went to work. They had a lot to do. Not knowing Celeste's age, Sarah had decided on an even hundred for their banana-gram. They'd be hard pressed to have everything ready by the time Celeste returned home.

So intent was Nic on the task at hand that it wasn't until she heard a man—Gabe—spit out a particularly foul curse that she realized they were no longer alone. He was in the hallway beyond the kitchen. Talking to someone, probably on the hall phone. Noting the worry in Sage's and Sarah's expressions, Nic set a banana marked with "Happy B'day Motorcycle Mama" aside and tuned into what Gabe was saying.

"No, I don't *want* to marry her. A baby is certainly the last thing I wanted."

Nic sucked in an audible breath.

"You matter to me, Pam. You and Will and Nathan. You made in-law jokes a joke. You became not just Jen's sister but my sister, too."

Sister. He was talking to his sister-in-law. Telling her about the wedding. The baby. She rose to her feet, then closed her eyes and an emptiness yawned inside her.

"Yeah, well, you're right. I was stupid. I wasn't think-ing. It was sex. Just sex."

Nic's nausea came roaring back. Sarah put her hand on Nic's shoulder.

"I know, dammit. I know! I was an idiot, all right? But what other choice do I have now? I made my bed and now I have to lie in it. I have to marry her. It's the responsible thing to do."

Nic felt the color drain from her face. She was beginning to hate the word *responsible*.

She moved to the doorway, where she could see him. Gabe sat on the stairs, his shoulders slumped, his expression stark. Anguish and anger vibrated in his voice as he stared down at the wedding ring he still wore on his left hand. "No, Pam, of course not. I don't love her. I love your sister. I'll always love your sister. She was my soul mate. Nicole and I . . . we just . . . we had sex and now we have to deal with the consequences."

A little mewl of pain escaped Nic's throat as he added, "Oh, Pam. Don't say that. Not after all we've been through. Please, I can't lose you. I'll have nothing. Let me—"

He let the receiver fall away from his ear and she could hear the dial tone. He muttered a vicious curse and banged his fist against the wall.

Nausea churned, threatened to erupt. She clapped a hand over her mouth and he looked up. Their gazes met and he repeated the curse. She dashed for the powder room beneath the stairs and lost her breakfast.

By the time she emerged, he was gone.

Nic insisted they complete their birthday surprise for Celeste. Wonderful friends that they were, Sage and Sarah added a few succinct bananagram messages for Gabe, which they left with his painting supplies upstairs.

Nine days later at the courthouse in Gunnison, with Sage Anderson, Sarah Reese, and Celeste Blessing in attendance, John Gabriel Callahan married Dr. Nicole

Sullivan. He dressed in a suit. She wore jeans and a baggy brown sweater and accepted the rings he offered with a silent nod.

She hadn't brought a wedding band for him. Nor had she appeared to notice that he'd finally removed Jennifer's ring from his left hand. It had taken him half a bottle of scotch to work up the nerve to do so, and now he felt naked without it.

Until the moment Nic said "I do," he'd expected her to call it off. She'd thrown up on the way into the building. He'd stumbled over her name when introducing her to the judge. Following lunch at the women's favorite Mexican restaurant, where Sarah continued to give him the evil eye and privately threatened to take a rusty knife to his nuts if he didn't treat his new wife right, Nic had hugged her friends and thanked them for coming as they climbed into Sage's car and waved good-bye. He'd pretended not to see the tear that slipped from her eye to trail down her face as she joined Gabe for the two-hour drive home.

Gabe swallowed a sigh, then glanced at Nic. "If you need to stop, just let me know."

"I'll be fine."

Whoa, three whole words. Almost a record.

After she'd overheard his phone call to Pam, all sense of ease between them had disappeared. Their relationship headed downhill. On skis. On lightning-fast skis on fresh powder. Now she avoided him, seldom met his gaze, and spoke to him primarily in monosyllables. Her smiles never reached her eyes. It made him feel like a heel.

He'd attempted to talk to her, to explain about his relationship with Pam and her family, but that had been a big fat fail. Really, what could he say? What excuses could he give? She'd heard what she'd heard—and it had been the truth.

Frustration nipped at him. And it wasn't as if he hadn't warned her. He'd been totally straight with her. Now he was the villain her girlfriends wanted to castrate, and he felt like he'd kicked a puppy.

The woman had lost her spirit, and he knew it was his fault. She wasn't the same Nic who had stood up to him in her kitchen or danced with him at the school gym. He'd bet that if he listened hard enough, he could hear her heart breaking.

He stole a glance at his new wife and noted her stoic expression. His hand tightened on the steering wheel. He'd given her a set of wedding rings at the courthouse earlier. He'd spent a pretty penny on the stones. She'd accepted the rings with a tepid smile, thanked him politely, but never looked at them once he'd slipped them onto her finger. Nic was suffering some real buyer's remorse about this marriage while he enjoyed one more round of guilt. Guilt over Jen and Matt and the accident. Guilt about causing his sister-in-law additional pain. Now guilt over Nic and the baby she carried. He was never free of it. He was a guiltaholic. *Wonder if there's a twelve-step treatment program for this. If so, sign me up for the meetings.*

He was tired of this. Bone weary of feeling guilty every second of every day.

He glanced at the odometer. Two-thirds of the way there. Should be just enough time for him to clue her in on the arrangements he'd made. He lifted his water bottle from the cup holder, took a long swig, then said, "Open the glove box, Nic. Take the envelope and put it in a safe place. I've executed a new will, added you and the child as beneficiaries. Same thing with my insurance policies—the information is in there. So is my attorney's name. I opened a bank account in your name and there's a couple of credit cards."

Her mouth formed a silent O. "Credit cards? Gabe, I

admit my finances have been tight, but I don't need all that."

"Look, it's no big deal to me. My profession pays well, and one of my technology investments paid off big-time last summer. Money is not a concern of mine."

She removed the papers from the glove compartment, looked at the numbers on the bank statement, and her eyes went wide and round. They rode another five minutes in silence before she said, "Thank you, Gabe. I appreciate your making changes to your will and insurance in order to protect our baby's financial future."

For crying out loud, she sounded like a commercial. It annoyed him. The whole day annoyed him. He didn't want to live like this.

Gabe waited until he'd negotiated Sinner's Prayer Pass to say, "You need to give me a clue here, Nic. Please tell me what I can do to make this right. Look, I know the phone call hurt you and—"

"I don't want to talk about it."

"Let me say this," he snapped. "You've dodged talking about this with me for more than a week. It's surprised me, Nic. I didn't take you for a coward."

Her jaw went tight and she stared straight ahead, but she remained silent, so he pressed on. "I'm sorry you overheard my conversation with Jennifer's sister. I'm sorry I embarrassed you in front of your friends. But this is no way to start a marriage. Where do we go from here, Nicole? I need a little help here. I don't know what you want."

She was quiet for a long time before she replied. "That's part of the problem. I'm not sure what I want. I'll be honest with you, Gabe. I feel like my world has been turned upside down and I don't know which way is up. Sarah says it's hormones, but that seems like an excuse. I'm . . . sad. I think I need a little time to adjust to everything."

He spied a herd of bighorn sheep in the road ahead, braked, and honked his horn. He didn't know what to say to her. "Nic, I'll say it again. I'm sorry."

"No. Don't." She shook her head. "I understand, Gabe. Truly, I do. And I'm the one who is sorry. I know I'm being a pain. You're not responsible for my feelings or emotions or neurosis. I think I simply need a little time to . . . well . . . let go of my dreams."

Great. Guilt, guilt, and more guilt.

He negotiated the curve of a switchback, and then the rooftops of Eternity Springs came into view. Time to fish or cut bait. "Okay, then. That brings us back to the original question. Where do we go from here? Friends? Awkward acquaintances like we've been this past week? Do you want me to leave town and you'll call me when the baby is born?"

"No," she said softly. "I don't want you to leave town. We need to be friends. That's what is best for the baby."

"Then this tension between us needs to end. That can't be good for the baby, either."

Tears flooded her eyes yet again. "I'm not trying to be awkward and tense. I am trying not to cry. I want to cry all the time, and it's making me crazy. It's not like me. I've never been a needy, clingy, whiny female, but that's what I'm becoming. I can't stand it. I can't help it. I don't know how to fix it."

Gabe did. He set his mouth in a grim line and considered the situation. What they needed to do was spend time together among other people, but away from the prying eyes of Eternity Springs. They needed to do what all brides and grooms do—to a point. They should go on a honeymoon.

A honeymoon without sex. *Oh, joy.*

He shied from the thought but knew it was a good

idea. Where would he take her? Somewhere fun but not romantic. It couldn't be isolated. They needed to be around people. Somewhere warm. He could use a shot of sunshine about now, and he bet she could, too.

He could think of only one place that would fit the bill. As they approached her house, he asked, "What is your schedule like the rest of the week?"

"Light. Why?"

"Any animals in your clinic that need special care?"

"Not special care. Lori is a great vet tech, and she handles most everything. Why?"

"I want you to clear your calendar. We're going to deal with this, put the awkwardness to bed once and for all."

Her eyes rounded with wariness and surprise, then she whipped her head around to frown at him.

"The awkwardness," he explained. "Not you and me. We'll have separate rooms."

"Separate rooms? What are you talking about?"

He drummed his fingers on the steering wheel. "Listen, Nic. For better or for worse, we got married today. We're husband and wife, and now we need to find our way back to being friends. Do you agree with that assessment?"

She pursed her lips and thought a moment. "Yes."

"Then let's make an effort to do just that, and let's do it away from everyday pressure and prying eyes."

"How? We live in Eternity Springs. It's the definition of prying eyes."

"Then we get away from Eternity Springs. Look, Nic, just because we're not having sex doesn't mean we can't have a honeymoon, does it?"

"A honeymoon?" she repeated, her eyes round with shock and maybe a glimmer—just a tiny little spark—of anticipation.

He stopped the car in her driveway and pulled out his phone. "Go pack a bag, Nic. I'll stay here and make the arrangements. We'll leave from Eagle's Way."

"Leave for where?"

"Pack your sneakers, Nic. We're going to Disney World."

TWELVE

§

Nic blinked. "Disney World? You want to go to Disney World? On a honeymoon?"

"Yeah. It'll be great." He gave her an encouraging smile. "Warm weather, plenty to do. It'll be fun."

Nic opened her mouth, then shut it. Opened it again, then shut it again. Disney World.

"I'll book us into one of the hotels on the resort property. Do you have a favorite?"

"Actually, no," she said, her tone wry. "I don't have a favorite Disney hotel. Or park. Or movie. Or character. Or song."

"Oh," he said, darting her a look. "You're not a Disney fan?"

"I was an undergraduate double major in college. Biomedical science and business. I did an internship at Disney one summer. For two interminable weeks, I worked the It's a Small World ride. A guy I worked with told me he'd been assigned to that ride for three years straight. Can you imagine listening to that music all day, every day? I'm telling you, it's places like that where serial killers are made. Someday we're going to read about that guy burying people under his house."

Gabe's lips twitched. "Let me guess. You'd rather not go to Disney World on our honeymoon."

"Give the guy a set of mouse ears."

"Okay, then, you pick a place."

Against her will, traditional honeymoon destinations spun through her mind: Mexico, the Caribbean, Paris, London, Rome. She gave her head a shake. "Gabe, I appreciate the thought, but we don't need to go on a wedding trip." Then, deciding the moment needed honesty, she added, "It would be awkward."

"Beginning this marriage beneath the watchful eyes of Eternity Springs is what would be awkward. The more I think about it, the more I believe this is the right thing to do. C'mon, Nicole. Let's pick a place neither one of us has ever visited. We'll be tourists together."

He was trying, trying hard, and Nic appreciated the effort. She decided she should do the same. Besides, the thought of discovering a new place along with Gabe had a definite appeal, as did the idea of a break from winter weather. Unfortunately, finding such a place new to them both proved harder than she'd expected. "This isn't going to work," she said after naming a dozen possibilities. "You've been everywhere."

"Not everywhere. Let's do this differently. What activities do we both like? Scuba?"

She shook her head.

He scowled. "Sailing?"

She thought of the delicate state of her stomach and knew she didn't want to spend hours on a boat. "Sightseeing."

"Sightseeing works. What else?"

Another *s*-word came to mind, but she knew better than to mention sex. She changed letters. "Tennis."

He shrugged. "Tennis is fine, too. Golf?"

She wrinkled her nose. "I've played a few rounds, not often enough to be any good. My ex was a scratch golfer, but he didn't play with me. We'd go to golf resorts and I'd do the spa while he golfed. I love pampering as much as the next woman, but . . . wait." An idea occurred and she rolled it around in her head for a moment before voicing it. Would this be something she truly wanted to do? Thinking about it did give her a devilish bit of pleasure. "Do you play golf, Gabe?"

"I'm not a scratch player and I haven't picked up a club in over a year, but I don't embarrass myself."

"Have you ever played Pebble Beach?"

"No. Have you?"

"Nope." She gave her first spontaneous smile in days. "But playing it was Greg's number one golf goal. The Monterey peninsula is supposed to be gorgeous. There's the aquarium, Carmel . . . the weather might not be as warm as Florida, but it won't be twelve degrees." Glancing at the dashboard thermometer, she corrected, "Ten degrees."

Gabe gave her a sidelong look. "I don't believe I've ever seen that particular wicked glint of delight in your eyes before, Mrs. Callahan."

"I admit I wouldn't mind exorcising an old ghost."

His mouth twisted, and she wished she'd chosen a different metaphor, but then he nodded once, forced a smile, and said, "Go pack your bag, Nic. California, here we come."

They arrived in Monterey shortly before sunset. He'd booked them into an ocean-view suite at one of the famous Pebble Beach properties. She'd tried to act cool during the obsequious welcome by the staff upon their arrival, but she'd abandoned all pretense of sophistication when she walked into the spectacular sitting room. The furnishings, fabrics, and finishes were like nothing she'd ever seen.

At Gabe's instruction, the bellman placed her bags in the bedroom, where a king-size bed was dressed in sumptuous linens. Gabe carried his own bag into an adjoining room. Nic stifled the urge to go bounce on the mattress. Next she peeked into the adjoining bathroom and spied a huge whirlpool tub. This place was a palace. For the first time she didn't look forward to her "wedding night" with dread.

Actually, she was almost tired enough to start it right now.

Gabe came to stand in her doorway and must have read her mind—or the exhaustion on her face—because he said, "It's been a long day. How about we order room service rather than try the restaurant tonight? We can watch the sunset from the balcony and turn in."

"That sounds perfect." She beamed a grateful smile his way.

He smiled softly in return. "I'll call room service. How about we meet on the balcony in twenty?"

"It's a date," she replied, then immediately wanted to bite her tongue. They'd been easier together the last few hours. With all the fun stuff taking place, she hadn't dwelled on the bad stuff. She didn't want this slip of the tongue to ruin that. "I didn't mean . . . it's just an expression. I say it all the time to Sarah and . . . well . . ."

"Nicole, I get it. See you in twenty." He reached to shut the door to her bedroom, then stuck his head back in and added, "No need to parse your words around me. It's a date."

She relaxed. Good—she was tired of living in a minefield. She emptied her suitcase and cosmetics bag, then gave in to the urge to test the mattress. She stacked the pillows against the headboard, then kicked off her shoes and curled up atop the coverlet. The pillow case smelled of lavender and sunshine, she thought. It was pure heaven.

Heaven brought to her by her very own angel, Gabriel.

She snickered at her own nonsense and closed her eyes. Except for being exhausted, she felt better than she had in weeks. Her problems were far from solved. Yet she no longer wanted to either cry or commit murder every time she looked at Gabe—a huge improvement.

She'd had a long talk with herself during the flight to California and she'd made some decisions. She was determined to forgive and forget all the past hurts, both real and imagined. She was prepared to do her part to see that this trip accomplished its purpose, and they could return to Eternity Springs having established a comfortable, compatible relationship going forward. As long as she kept her emotions and expectations under control, they should be able to make this work.

Nic stretched like a cat, then snuggled back into her pillows. She awoke ten hours later to find the down comforter spread over her, a plate of cookies, and a small carton of milk chilling in an ice bucket beside the bed.

"Well, shoot," she grumbled. She'd missed both the sunset and the bath she'd craved. But on the positive side, she hadn't spent a single second sulking over the circumstances of her wedding night. All in all, she'd come out ahead.

For the next five days, they played. The weather cooperated, giving them blue skies, sunshine, and unseasonably warm temperatures. He rented a Ferrari and they drove Highway 1 along the Big Sur coast. They played golf, making sure to have their picture taken together at the famous eighteenth hole at Pebble Beach, then she made an e-postcard with the photo and sent it to old friends in Colorado Springs by way of a wedding announcement. She felt a shameful bit of glee in knowing the news would get back to Greg. They toured the famous aquarium in Monterey and wandered through the quaint shops in Carmel. Gabe played more golf while she indulged in some serious pampering at the spa.

It was a lovely trip, and Nic told herself to be happy. She was a guest in a gorgeous hotel in a part of the country whose beauty rivaled the Colorado Rockies. She'd been pampered and spoiled, her every whim indulged.

Well, not every whim. He'd said no sex, so of course all she thought about was sex.

It was hard not to think about it. She was on her honeymoon, after all, and her husband was drop-dead gorgeous. But he'd gone out of his way to avoid any hint of romance on the trip: no candlelit dinners, no dancing cheek to cheek to soft music, no moonlight walks on the beach. Nevertheless, she couldn't seem to look at him without imagining him naked.

Her hormones were obviously running amok.

When he downshifted the Ferrari and shot her a grin, or sank a six-foot putt and gave her a cocky wink, or threw a stick for a sandy dog on the beach and laughed, Gabe Callahan exuded sex appeal. She found herself wanting to touch him, to sink her fingers into his hair. To fit her mouth to his, her body against his heat.

Gabe, on the other hand, showed no sign of suffering a similar desire. He was casual with her, relaxed. Friendly. She told herself to be happy for it, to be glad that the awkwardness and tension between them lessened every day. She warned herself not to expect too much too soon. The goal had been for them to return to Colorado at ease with each other and their situation, and in that respect the honeymoon had been a success.

She just wished he didn't turn her on with a glance.

Pesky hormones.

Gabe needed to run. Or swim. Or run and swim. And lift weights. And do sit-ups. Or take a cold shower. Or jump in the very cold ocean. Or do all of the above.

Something, anything to distract him.

Well, except for the obvious anything.

This honeymoon had been a disaster. Oh, he and Nic got along better. Their conversation never got much beyond small talk, but the awkward moments weren't happening as often. Over the past few days they'd learned to get along more like friends than like enemies. She didn't seem as angry at him, didn't appear to be so sad. Their time together this week had made Gabe feel better, too. His heart was lighter, his outlook more positive.

But he had to quit noticing her jiggle and swish. The object of this trip was to create friendship, not destroy it again. Bringing sex into the situation now would do just that.

Now being the operative word.

Someday, he knew, he'd be ready to resume that part of human existence. The day would come when having sex wouldn't make him wallow in guilt, but that day wasn't here yet. He had already damaged Nic because of it. He couldn't, he *wouldn't* hurt her again that way.

He couldn't give her his heart, but he could give her his respect. He wouldn't take her to a bed where another woman's ghost still lingered.

Nevertheless, as he waited for her to join him on the balcony of their suite so they could watch the sun set on this, the final night of their trip, he was acutely aware of the nearness of a bed. Actually, of two beds.

It would be so easy to fall into a physical relationship with her. However, he'd promised her he wouldn't use her, and having sex tonight would be nothing more than that. Unless he could give her more, he couldn't take more from her.

When she stepped out onto the balcony, however, he took one look at her and smothered a groan. She wore the filmy, flirty strapless sundress she'd purchased this morning at a shop in Carmel. It complemented her curves, showed off her legs, and made him want to grind his teeth in sexual frustration.

This was going to be a very, very long night.

"You look like you're feeling better," he said, referring to that afternoon's bout of nausea.

"It's amazing what a bath in a whirlpool tub will do for a girl."

Oh, great. Just great. That's exactly the picture I didn't need in my mind. He attempted to counter it by saying, "I'm glad you made it to the bathroom before tossing your Cobb salad."

She grinned. "The stomach-settling smoothie you ordered for me from room service almost made it worth losing my lunch. I don't know what they put in it, but I swear I licked the glass clean."

He almost leaned over and banged his head on the balcony at the visual image of that.

She stood at the balcony railing and stared out at the ocean. "Mother Nature is glorious. So much beauty in the world. So many different kinds, too. Here and at home it slaps you in the face."

"Yeah," he murmured, not taking his eyes off her.

As she glanced back at him, her hair spilled like a waterfall of gold over shoulders tanned by five days in the sun. "You've been a lot of places. What's the prettiest ugly place you've ever been?"

So glad was he of the distraction that he spoke without filtering his words. "Far west Texas in July. You have to look for the beauty, but it's there. The land is as flat as a pancake and dry. Brown. In July, all the vegetation is brown. Heat rises from the ground in visible waves. But the sky is so big. The sunset we're watching is spectacular, true, but it doesn't have anything on the desert plain of far west Texas. Because it has the sunrise, too. As pretty a sunrise as I've ever seen."

"Is that where your home was?"

"No." His lips twisted in a wistful smile. "Our home was at the northern edge of the Texas hill country. It was pretty. In its own way, just as pretty as here or even Eternity Springs."

"Because it's home?" Nic asked, displaying an insight that caused him to think.

He shrugged. He'd lived dozens of places since leaving Brazos Bend, Texas. He'd made a life for himself in a few of them. Was Brazos Bend still home after all these years?

While he considered that question, Nic said, "You seldom talk about your family, Gabe. How many brothers do you have?"

After a moment's pause, he answered, "Three."

"Are you a close family?"

"Not anymore." He studied her over his coffee cup and realized that by asking about his family, she'd helped him step back from the edge of doing something stupid. "I need to tell you about my family, but it's not a subject for today."

Then, prodded to flee thoughts of the Callahans, he said, "Want to walk down to the beach?"

Her smile was as pretty as the western sky. "Sure."

As they walked through the hotel lobby to reach the beach-access boardwalk, Gabe watched three different men give Nic the once-over. Whether it was the clichéd pregnancy glow or the easing of her fears of the future or simply the effect of a good vacation, his new wife glowed. She was as relaxed and carefree as he had ever seen her—beautiful, vivacious, and sparkling.

He could just imagine how she'd look after an orgasm.

Gabe grimaced and stepped gratefully out into the fading light of day. The sooner it got dark, the better.

A boardwalk led across the delicate grassy dunes to the beach where a gentle surf lapped against the sand. Gabe took Nic's hand for balance as she stepped down from the boardwalk and then paused to remove her sandals, and he didn't let it go.

They walked without speaking, hand in hand, the haunting notes of a bagpipe drifting on a salt-scented breeze as the inn's piper saluted the end of day. As the golden sphere of the sun dipped into the sapphire ocean, Nic halted and faced the sea, where streaks of mauve and purple and pink painted the sky. Gabe watched his new wife's face as she smiled with gentle delight. Softly she said, "Thank you, Gabe. This trip has been lovely."

"Lovely," he repeated as something new flickered to life in his heart. Guided by instinct and a freeing sense that this much, at least, was right and good, he tugged her into his arms and kissed her.

A real kiss. Not a chaste peck or a friendship kiss or an alcohol-blurred assault. It was their first real kiss— a second-date sort of kiss. A kiss with no ghosts between them.

This was Nic. She tasted both sweet and sultry, and Gabe allowed himself to become lost in the sensual pleasure of the moment. He explored her mouth with his tongue, nipped her lips with his teeth, and encouraged her response with a low-throated groan. He held her tight, wishing to pull her even closer. He stroked his hand down the curve of her waist and across her hip, resisting the more intimate embrace his instincts urged.

He drew back, ending the kiss, and held her for a long moment as he soaked in the sensation of having a woman in his arms. It felt so good. Nic felt so good. He had been alone for so long.

As the shadows deepened around them, time hung suspended. She waited for him to speak. He waited, wanting her, wondering just how far to take this. Was this the right time?

But even as the question formed, he heard the whisper of ghosts on the soft ocean breeze and knew he couldn't do it. He leaned forward, rested his forehead against hers, and spoke from his heart. "I'm sorry, Nic. I wish . . . I just . . . I'm sorry."

"Me, too, Callahan," she said with a sigh. "Me, too."

Nic awoke the next morning to a gray sky and a blue mood. The evening had ended abruptly last night. Right after the kiss on the beach, right after she'd realized that she'd fallen in love with Gabe Callahan, he'd gone into full retreat.

True, she'd been cold in her sundress after the sun went down, but she knew that Gabe's insistence they return to their suite had more to do with his comfort than with hers. Claiming tiredness, he'd turned in early, but she'd heard him leave his room an hour later and watched him return to the beach for a solitary walk.

She'd gone to bed alone and lonely once again, grateful that at least she had her pride to keep her warm. Thank goodness she hadn't confessed what she'd realized was in her heart.

As she packed to return to the real world and Eternity Springs, Nic admitted that as much as she'd loved the trip, she was ready to go home. She missed her work, fretted about how Tiger was doing at Sarah's with her goldens, Daisy and Duke. He'd been with Nic since Christmas, and she'd given up finding a permanent home for him with someone else in town, at least until the seasonal residents began arriving in May. Technically, he was still on the adoption list, but since he slept in her living room every night, everyone considered him hers.

She believed he still considered himself to be Gabe's pet. She wondered where he would end up once Gabe returned to Eagle's Way.

That's where her husband intended to live upon their return to Colorado. They'd talked about their living arrangements over breakfast this morning. That is, he'd talked and she'd listened. Apparently the separate-bedrooms arrangement was off. Now he wanted separate houses. He'd offered up a list of reasons why they'd both be better off living apart, but Nic saw past them to the heart of the matter. Gabe was pulling back. He had spent this time in California working on their friendship, not their marriage. Sharing a home in Eternity Springs, even if they didn't share a bed, would take it too close to a real marriage for his comfort.

She was adding the last of her clothes to her suitcase when he rapped on her door. "Nic?"

"Come in." She took one look at him and saw his worry and concern. "What's wrong?"

"Jack called. My—um, Jen's husband is in the hospital. Heart attack." He ran his hands through his hair and frowned. "I have to go . . . Pam has been through way too much. She was there for me, especially with Matty. I'm sorry, Nic. I'm gonna have to send you back to Eternity Springs by yourself. I'll catch a flight to D.C. I hope you understand. They're my family."

And I'm not. "Of course I understand," she replied, ignoring the pang of hurt. Now was the time to be his friend. "Don't think twice about it."

"Thanks. We can catch the shuttle from here to San Jose. It leaves in twenty minutes. If we hurry, we should be able to make it."

"Give me five minutes and I'll meet you at the door."

"Thanks, Nic. You're the best."

His words rang in her ears as she gathered up the rest of her belongings. *"You're the best."* Yeah, right. She wondered if the day would ever come when the man didn't make her feel like second best.

At the Mocha Moose coffeehouse and Internet café in Eternity Springs, Sage Anderson responded to an email from a gallery in Savannah, then sent off an e-card birthday greeting to an old friend from college. Finished with email, she checked the ESPN site for updates on March Madness standings, then sighed to see that the number twelve seed had whipped the number five seed and busted her East Region bracket. "Shoot, Sarah is going to kick my butt again this year," she muttered.

Rising from her corner table, she wandered toward the bakery case, where a selection of cookies tempted her. The shop's owner, Wendy Davis, was the only woman in town who could hold her own against Sarah when it came to baked goods. Her raspberry jam pinwheel cookies were as much works of art as Sage's watercolors.

"Change your mind?" Wendy asked. "I have a batch of pinwheels hot from the oven."

"You are a wicked woman."

Sage took the warm cookie and her second cup of herbal tea back to the table and the computer. She clicked away from ESPN, and then her fingers settled on the keyboard as, from out of nowhere, the urge struck her to check up on the organization that had once meant so much to her. She even went so far as to type "www.doc" before good sense prevailed and she jerked her hands away from the keyboard as if they'd been burned.

What was that all about? Rattled, she brought her hands up to her face and massaged her temples. She could almost hear the monkeys chatter right now.

The lack of sleep must be getting to her. Nightmares woke her often, and in the small hours of the night she would try to exorcise the demons by painting, in the grip of a dark creative energy.

The work she produced those nights differed substantially from the bright, fanciful paintings that were attracting attention in the art world. That the midnight paintings frightened her was no great shock, since the scenes came right out of her nightmares. That she never wished them to see the light of day held no surprise, either, due to the personal nature of the subjects. Almost always, she painted over the images in daylight.

She had kept a couple whose images were impressionistic rather than detailed. Those she kept facing the wall and covered with a tarp. She knew they were the best work she'd ever done, but they were, and would remain, her dirty little secret.

Bells rattled as the café's door opened, distracting her from her dark thoughts. Sage looked up to see Celeste arrive for their strategy session regarding Eternity Springs' local arts and crafts show, held each June in Davenport Park. As part of her Angel Plan, Celeste wanted to elevate the status of the event by holding a juried show of Colorado artists in conjunction with it. The idea was meeting some resistence from a few locals who preferred the flea market crowd to gallery patrons, so Celeste had appealed to Sage to help win them over.

"Hello, hello," Celeste said, tugging off her gloves and earmuffs. After placing her order with Wendy, she joined Sage at the table and set a large shopping bag on the floor. "I am so glad you suggested meeting here. I needed to stop by and place a cookie order for next week. I'm having a special visitor."

"Oh? An old friend?"

"No, I've only spoken to her on the phone, but she seems like a lovely person. Her name is Alison Timberlake." Celeste paused, preened, then announced, "Alison *Cavanaugh* Timberlake."

"Of the Eternity Springs Cavanaughs?"

"If one goes back far enough, yes. Her branch of the family was a distant cousin to the Eternity Springs Cavanaughs. Our library has tremendous historical archives of the area, and our librarian, Margaret Rhodes, knows them forward and backward. Once I discovered that Cavanaughs settled in Denver, it was easy to track down Mrs. Timberlake. She lives there, is married to an attorney, and they have three children. I have a few ideas I'd like to discuss with her regarding family heirlooms. She jumped at the chance to come for a visit."

Sage tucked an errant strand of hair behind her ear and frowned at Celeste. "You are still trying to solve the Lost Angel murder, aren't you?"

"Not really, no. I admit that I have an interest in seeing that historical records reflect the truth, but in this instance I'm more concerned about the proper dispersal of Cavanaugh family treasures."

"Hmm," Sage said, her tone noncommittal. Their inventory of the contents of the old Victorian mansion had turned up a number of valuable items, and the fact that this Mrs. Timberlake's husband was associated with the legal profession sent up a red flag, or twelve. She'd hate to see anyone take advantage of Celeste or draw her into a lawsuit. Concerned, she asked, "Your sales contract for the house was specific in regard to the contents of the house, right? You do own them."

"I do. Nevertheless, some things should remain in the family, and after speaking with Alison, I think she would welcome the opportunity to reconnect with her roots. Her visit ties into one of the reasons I've asked to meet with you today. Sage, I'd like to commission the design of a piece of jewelry."

She sat back in her chair, surprised. "That's flattering, but I'm not a jewelry designer, Celeste. I wouldn't know where to start."

"Just hear me out. I want a symbol that represents the healing energy of Eternity Springs. I'd like it to be adaptable for use as a small item of jewelry for both men and women—a charm or cuff link or pendant. These items will be made from the silver found in my cellar, and I will give them as gifts when time and circumstances are appropriate."

"You mean the thirty pieces of silver?" Sage said, her brow furrowing. "That's . . . symbolic."

"I think so."

Sage's creative mind engaged. Treachery and betrayal transformed. *Hmm*. Okay, so maybe she did know where to start. A variation of the angel's wings on Winifred Smith's locket formed an image in her mind, and her fingers itched for a pencil and sketch pad.

"Please say you'll do it, Sage. You must do it. You are meant to do it. I know this at the bottom of my heart."

In that moment, Sage knew it, too. "All right. On one condition, though. No commission. This will be my personal contribution to the effort."

"Excellent." Celeste sat back in her chair, her weathered face wearing a satisfied smile. "Mark my words, dear. I have a feeling this particular work will effect a wondrous change in your life."

Before Sage could pursue that curious statement, Wendy Davis approached the table carrying Celeste's coffee and two huge soft ginger cookies. "I hear work is progressing well at Angel's Rest," she said.

"We are ahead of schedule, believe it or not."

"The contractors who come in here say they've never seen anything like it. They've not had a single weather delay."

Celeste smiled beatifically. "The weather has been a gift from God. We have an excellent shot at holding our grand opening by the Fourth of July."

"You're kidding." Sage gaped at her friend. "That fast? I don't believe it. No building project gets done that fast in this part of the world."

"My contractors are motivated. Gabe helped me build premiums into the contracts for speed of completion, and so far my plan A is working out splendidly."

The mention of Gabe Callahan tugged Sage's thoughts in another direction. "Speaking of Gabe, do you know if Nic has heard from him or not? Any idea when he's coming home?"

"I don't know about Nic, but I heard from him yesterday. He called to update me on the building plan for the springs. He told me he'll be returning later today."

"Finally!"

Celeste nibbled at a cookie. "He said his brother-in-law is doing better, thank the Lord. I guess it was touch and go for a time."

"I've felt bad for Nic," Sage said after glancing over her shoulder to make sure they weren't being overheard. "She's put forth a brave face, but I know the gossip has been brutal. First the hasty wedding and then coming home alone from her honeymoon. I hope Gabe sets the record straight about why he's been away."

"Nic isn't much for gossip, is she? Especially in regard to anything dealing with Gabe. It's an admirable trait."

"A frustrating trait," Sage responded with a grin. "Now, since I'm not opposed to gossip, what's up with the summer theater? I heard the Historical Society is pitching a fit after the theater group decided to produce *The Lost Angel Murder*."

"As well they should." Celeste sipped her coffee, then said, "The script is pure conjecture. Margaret and I have pored over every book, journal, and letter in the library. We've found nothing to support the charge that Daniel Murphy murdered that poor woman. He went to his grave declaring his innocence, and I think it's wrong for the theater group to take creative license in a way that disparages a man's reputation. I have to say, Sage, that in my experience with creative personalities, you are the exception to the rule. The scriptwriter is—oh, look. There's Nic coming out of the library across the street."

"She looks happy," Sage observed. "Considering that Gabe is coming home, that's a good sign, don't you think? I sure wish she'd been more forthcoming about the honeymoon. I worry that—oh, no!"

Sage surged to her feet, watching in horror as out on the sidewalk, Nic slipped on a patch of ice. She slid into a bench, then tumbled over it and the bicycle chained to it. She fell, the bike coming down on top of her.

Her head hit the cement curb, and she lay still.

THIRTEEN

Sage grabbed her coat and rushed for the door, shoving her arms into the sleeves even as she sent up a prayer. When she was halfway across the street she saw blood staining the snow, and instantly she froze. In that instant, she was back in stifling heat on a dusty dirt road.

Bullets whizzed past her head. Clouds of flies buzzed around her. Slick, sticky blood coated her hands, her arms, even her face where the spray had splashed it.

The gun swung in her direction.

"Nic? Nicole?" The sound of Celeste's voice jerked her back to reality. "Dear Lord, we need a doctor. Sage, help!"

Sage shuddered. Her knees felt like butter. She had the weight of Murphy Mountain on her chest. *Nic is your friend. You have to help.*

She forced herself forward as Celeste pulled the bike off Nic, then knelt in the snow beside her. "Nic? Nicole?" The older woman placed a hand at Nic's neck. "She has a pulse, thank God. Nic? Nicole?"

Seconds ticked by. Another minute. *Too long.*

As Sage drew near, Nic's eyes fluttered and she moaned.

Bob Carson rushed from the bank, a first-aid kit in hand. LaNelle Harrison flew out of the quilt shop, asking, "Is she all right?"

Celeste repeated, "Nic?"

Sage stood just beyond the circle, her hands clasped in a white-knuckled grip. She willed herself to go forward, but her feet remained cemented in place even when Nic's pain-glazed eyes opened and she rolled onto her side and threw up.

Celeste asked, "Where do you hurt, honey?"

"Ohhh," she moaned. She rolled back onto her back and closed her eyes.

"Nic? Nic!"

She isn't tracking.

"Where is the blood coming from?" the banker asked, setting the first-aid kit on the ground.

"Looks like she has a gash on her leg."

Bob Carson said, "Let's get her inside and we can tend to her out of the cold."

"I don't know," LaNelle responded. "Maybe we shouldn't move her."

Nic's eyes fluttered open again and she struggled to sit up, grimacing in pain. "Oh, that hurts."

"What hurts, dear?" Celeste asked.

"My whole leg."

"We need to get her to a hospital. Can someone call Alton Davis to drive the ambulance?"

That finally propelled Sage out of her stupor. "No!"

She strode the last few steps forward and all but pushed the banker out of the way, then knelt beside Nic. "Call for CareFlight."

Celeste met her gaze with a wide-eyed look. "The baby?"

"I'm not as worried about the baby as I am about Nic. She was out for a couple of minutes. Nauseated. We need to make sure she doesn't have a blunt force trauma injury, and time is of the essence." Glancing up at Celeste, she said, "Will you make the call?"

"Absolutely."

"I'll do it," Bob Carson offered. "I have the number posted in my office."

While Bob hurried off, Sage first checked Nic's head for a lump and was glad to find a large goose egg. Better that it swelled outwardly rather than inwardly. She studied her friend's eyes and was gratified to see the pupils react to light. Next, with methodical, practiced motions, she went to work on the bloody injury on Nic's left leg. Using the scissors from the first-aid kit, she sliced open the bloody pant leg, revealing a deep gash and a swollen knee and ankle. Sage winced. The cut would need stitches.

Nic groaned, then a moment later, exclaimed in a panicked tone. "The baby!"

She's thinking again. That's good. "Any cramping?"

Nic moved a hand to cover her stomach. "No."

"I saw you fall, honey. Watched you hit. The baby should be fine. How's your head? Pain? Throbbing?"

"Yeah." She lifted a fearful but clear gaze toward Sage. "You really think the baby's okay?"

"I do." With practiced movements, Sage cleaned the cut. "This needs stitches, Nic."

Nic's voice emerged thready and weak. "Great. Get LaNelle to do it. Her stitches are prettier than mine."

"I think it can wait until you reach Gunnison." Sage wrapped gauze around her friend's leg and covered it with a pressure bandage.

"You're very good at that, Sage," Celeste observed. "Maybe you can fill in for Nic at the clinic."

Not hardly. "No way. My Girl Scout nursing badge only takes me so far. Besides, I heard about that wounded ram Nic treated yesterday. She's crazy."

"I'm freezing." Nic shuddered, and her teeth began to chatter. "My pants are soaked through. Can you help me stand up?"

LaNelle asked, "I could bring my car around, get her

out of the cold. We need to transport her to the helipad, anyway."

"Thanks, LaNelle," Sage said, tugging off her own coat and wrapping it around her friend. "That'd be great."

When it was just the two of them, Sage asked, "Still no cramps, honey?"

"No." Nic's teeth tugged at her lower lip. "She's okay, don't you think? She has to be okay."

"She's small yet. You didn't hit your tummy. I don't think you need to worry. Besides, any child of yours is bound to be strong."

"That's a nice thing for you to say." Nic tried to smile, but it appeared more like a grimace. "I don't feel good."

"Your head? Are you nauseated?"

"My leg."

It wasn't the leg that worried her. With that thought in mind, she reached for Nic's purse. "You still carry a pen and notepad in here?"

"Yeah."

"I'm going to write a note for the ER doctor. I want to make sure he takes good care of you. Do you want us to let Gabe know what happened?"

"Yes. Thanks, Sage. You're a good friend."

No. Actually, she wasn't. A good friend wouldn't have stood back and left her bleeding in the street, untreated.

Not when once upon a time, said friend had been a surgeon.

Gabe Callahan hated hospitals. He hated the smell of them, the sounds in them, the physical and emotional pain that filled them from wall to wall, floor to ceiling. As he parked his car and rushed inside the medical facility in Gunnison, he said a silent prayer that this particular hospital visit would be as short as Sage had promised it would be when he arrived at Eagle's Way and found her sitting on the front porch, a tote bag at her side.

From there, it had been a mad dash on the twisting, turning mountain road. Two hours in which to worry, remember, and brood.

"Nicole Sullivan?" he asked the middle-aged woman wearing a volunteer badge seated at the front desk.

She frowned. "I'm sorry. We don't have a patient named Sullivan."

"What? You . . . oh . . ." He silently cursed his stupidity. "Callahan. Nic Callahan. She arrived on CareFlight from Eternity Springs."

"Ah." She pointed down the hallway to the right. "She's in room twelve."

Gabe nodded his thanks, then strode down the hall toward Nic's room. The door was partially open. He peeked inside and saw her reclining in bed, wearing a hospital gown and flipping through a magazine. He rapped on the door with his knuckles. "Hey there, pretty lady. Hear you had a hard landing."

"Gabe!" Nic's expression brightened, then she offered him a rueful grin. "I get this month's clumsy award."

He strode into the room and gave her a thorough once over. He could tell by her eyes that she was tired and in pain, and he hurt for her. Taking a seat in the chair beside the bed, he took her hand in his. His tone serious now, he asked, "How are you, Nic?"

She thumbed the control on her bed and raised herself to a seated position. "I'm okay. Nothing is broken. Knee and ankle are both sprained, ankle worse than the knee. I didn't jar my tummy."

"Sage said you had a concussion."

"Yeah. I got a lecture in the ER about the danger of neglecting blows to the head, but everything checked out okay. They want to keep me for another hour for observation, but then I can go home. Can I hitch a ride with you?"

"Absolutely." He gave her hand a squeeze, then released it and sat back. "Sage described what happened. You're lucky you weren't hurt worse."

"I know. I was scared about the pregnancy there for a while. Believe me, I'm going to be much more careful from now on. Especially since I'm going to be on crutches for a few weeks." She closed the magazine she'd been reading, and set it on the bed tray. "Now, tell me what's up with you. How is Will?"

Gabe drew a deep breath, then exhaled in a rush. He'd been so consumed with worry that it took him a moment to adjust to the change of subject. "First, are you telling me everything? Is there anything we need to be concerned about?"

He tensed when she hesitated before saying, "You know about all my injuries. I promise. I'll be just fine in a few weeks. Now, tell me about your brother-in-law."

Hmm. Why did he think she wasn't telling him everything? Unwilling to press the point right now, he responded to her request. "Better. Much better. This has been a wake-up call for him. He's always been a workaholic, but this scared him enough to make some lifestyle changes."

A rap on the door caused them both to look up. A woman wearing a lab coat entered the room saying, "Nic, I have those photos you requested."

Gabe didn't miss the nervous glance Nic shot him before saying, "Thanks, Liz. Gabe, this is my obstetrician, Dr. Elizabeth Marshall. Liz, my husband, Gabe Callahan."

"Nice to meet you," the doctor said, shaking his hand. Handing Nic the photos, she added, "I know this was a scare for you today, but your wife and babies are doing just fine."

From the corner of his eye, Gabe saw Nic grimace. Why would she . . . His heart began to pound and his eyes flew open wide. "Excuse me? Did you just say . . . ?"

The doctor pursed her lips in dismay. Looking at Nic, she asked, "Did I speak out of turn?"

"He just got here a few minutes ago."

Gabe cleared his throat. "Nic?"

She tried to smile, but it was a sickly effort at best. "I had a sonogram today." She held up the pictures. "Gabe, we're having twins."

He exhaled as if she'd punched him in the gut and closed his eyes. Twins. He dropped his chin to his chest. Twins. He leaned over, propped his elbows on his knees, and cradled his head in his hands. Twins.

His stomach rolled and his skin grew clammy. Without saying a word to the women, he rose and walked into the room's bathroom, where he turned on the cold water, leaned over, and splashed his face for a full minute. Then he shut off the water, gave his head a shake, and looked up, staring at his reflection in the mirror. He was as white as the snow atop Sinner's Prayer Pass. "Twins," he murmured.

"You're not going to faint, are you, Mr. Callahan?" Dr. Marshall asked from the doorway. "We don't want you to bang your head today, too."

"I'm fine," he lied, grabbing a white hand towel off a towel bar and wiping his face. He replaced the towel, took a bracing breath, and exited the bathroom.

Nic watched him with an anxious expression, her hands clasped and resting protectively over her stomach. Was she worried he'd be upset? Angry? Maybe he would get angry later—at fate, not at Nic—but right now he was too numb for that.

Twins. Double the risk. Double the responsibility. Double the potential loss.

Great. Just great.

He addressed the obstetrician. "Do you have any special instructions for Nic I should know about? Any limits to her activities?"

"Only those dictated by common sense. She's now classified by my office as a high-risk pregnancy, but don't let that worry you. It's the norm for all my moms carrying multiples, and it means we'll follow her a little more closely, see her more often, do a few more tests. You can probably plan that she'll deliver early."

"Here at this hospital? Does she need to be at a neonatal center?"

"Not unless problems develop later on. I've given Nic a packet of literature to take home. It'll answer most of your questions, and of course you're always welcome at her prenatal appointments."

A pager's beep sounded from the doctor's lab coat pocket. She checked the message, then said, "I've got to go. Nic, I'll see you in two weeks. You be careful on those crutches, you hear?"

"I will, Liz. Thanks."

Silence descended on the hospital room in the doctor's wake. Nic plucked at a loose thread on the blanket on the bed while Gabe stuck his hands in his pockets, rocked on his heels, and tried to come up with something to say.

Finally Nic blew out a heavy breath and said, "This is awkward, isn't it? Gabe, I'm not going to say I'm sorry, because that would be like wishing away the existence of one of my children. I will say I'm sorry you learned about it this way. I seem to have fallen into a habit of shocking you."

"Life around you is certainly not boring."

"That probably won't change anytime soon." She stared down at the sonogram images that her doctor had given her. "Twins. I'm having a hard time wrapping my mind around it."

He could definitely relate to that. He looked away from both her and the photos and cleared his throat. "The good thing is we have some time to get used to it."

Which meant he didn't have to think about it anymore right now. He really, really didn't want to think about it anymore right now.

"So there's probably paperwork that needs to be signed so you can get sprung." He escaped toward the door, saying, "Let me see if I can do anything to speed it up."

An hour later, they were on the road headed for Eternity Springs. Like the last time they'd made the drive from Gunnison, the mood between them was tense rather than relaxed, their conversation stilted rather than easy—absolutely not what Gabe had hoped for in the aftermath of their trip to California. When Nic fell asleep twenty minutes into the ride, Gabe breathed a little easier. Unfortunately, he also started thinking.

Today's events had definitely changed his plans.

He had returned to Eternity Springs with a strategy in mind for managing this marriage. He'd decided to remain at Eagle's Way until he found a place closer to town to buy. He figured he'd ask Nic out to dinner, spend time with her at town events, take things slow.

Gabe had done a lot of soul-searching during his weeks away from Nic. Intellectually, he understood that he wasn't cheating on Jennifer by having sex with another woman. Emotionally, he wasn't there yet.

The accident had complicated the mourning process; sex and guilt were interwoven in his brain. It was life and death and responsibility for death, for Jen's death. How could he enjoy sex—one of life's best gifts—when his wife lay in her grave and he was the one who'd put her there?

He'd thought about Nic and the marriage a lot while he'd been gone. The trip to California had been an eye-opener for him. His wife was smart, definitely sexy, and fun to be with. He admired her loyalty, her enthusiasm, and her determination. In another time, another life, he could have fallen for her.

That, in a nutshell, was the problem. While he could envision a time when the physiology of basic human drives might overcome his reluctance to engage in sex, he was dead solid certain he'd never again open his heart to love.

And Nic deserved to be loved.

He glanced over at her. Even in sleep, the strains of the day showed on her face. She probably still had a headache, and he knew her leg was hurting. She'd refused to take any more than the mildest of painkillers and even then had to be reassured multiple times that they posed no threat to the babies.

Babies. Jesus.

Now he had three people whose lives he could screw up.

He couldn't love Nic. He couldn't love those babies. He thought Nic's issues with her own father skewed her thinking about what was best for the children she carried. She'd have been better off showing him the door and finding a guy who could give her the love she deserved, who would love her little ones like his own. Nic would have been better off looking elsewhere for a dad for her children, a husband with whom to create a family. Nevertheless, she hadn't, and it was a waste of time to look backward now.

Looking backward was a bad idea all around. That's why he resisted Pam's suggestion that he see a shrink. He had no desire to lie on a doctor's couch and babble about the losses in his past. He had no desire to tear down the walls that he'd spent a lifetime constructing. Been there, done that, and look where it had gotten him—on his knees in the snow on a mountain a twitch away from eating his gun. He'd let Jennifer breach the walls around his heart. He couldn't, wouldn't go there again with Nic.

I'll do my best, Nic. It won't be good enough, but it'll be the best I can do. For you and for the baby. Babies.

He shuddered. Twins.

I'll be there to help. I'll be there to support you. I'll be your friend. Then, if the right guy comes along someday, a man who can love you like you deserve, I'll shake his hand and step aside.

Maybe in doing so, he could redeem himself at least a little.

Nic let out a little sleepy sniffle and shifted in her seat. Her foot kicked her purse and some of its contents spilled out onto the floorboard. Gabe locked his gaze on the road before him as his sense of self-preservation demanded he ignore the sonogram photograph lying right there in plain sight.

Nic didn't stir until he slowed to pull into her driveway, and when she opened her eyes and started to move, a groan escaped her lips. "Ow." She grimaced. "I forgot."

"You're due some aspirin."

"Acetaminophen," she corrected. "I'll take a couple as soon as I get inside."

As Gabe exited the car, Sarah Reese opened the door to Nic's house and the boxer streaked outside. He barked twice in welcome, ran three tight circles around Gabe's legs, his crooked tail wagging like a sorcerer's wand, then bounded over to the passenger-side door, ready to pounce on Nic. Gabe called out to Sarah, "You want to grab his collar? The last thing we need is another fall."

As Sarah hurried forward to corral the dog, Nic swung her car door open, then visibly braced herself to swing her knees around. Gabe said, "Hold what you have, Nicole. Let me help."

"My crutches . . ."

"How about I carry you into the house? Then you can tackle the crutches."

"My hero," she said past gritted teeth as he slipped one arm around her waist, the other beneath her thighs, and lifted her up into his arms.

Sarah held the dog and fretted aloud. "Thank God you are okay. Oh, Nic, I feel like this is my fault. If I hadn't forgotten I said I'd meet you at the library, you wouldn't have gone looking for me."

"Don't be silly, Sarah." Nic smiled wanly at her friend. "I have no one but myself to blame for my clumsiness."

"I feel terrible. Lori does, too, because the reason I forgot about the library is because she and I were arguing. We made you a cake."

"Butter pecan?"

"Yes."

"In that case, it was your fault, but being the wonderful friend that I am, I forgive you. Can I have a piece of cake now?"

Sarah scratched the boxer behind the ears. "Not until after your supper."

"You are such a mom."

"Yeah, well, you are too, aren't you? That's why you can't have cake before supper. Nutrition, nutrition, nutrition."

With the women's lighthearted bickering ringing in his ears, Gabe carried his wife into the house, where the aroma of chili spices teased his nostrils and reminded him that he hadn't eaten since breakfast. He settled Nic into the overstuffed chair in the parlor that he'd figured out was her favorite, then returned to the car for her crutches . . . and his suitcase.

When he carried them inside, Nic's smile of thanks faded upon spying the case. Her brow furrowed with confusion. "Gabe?"

He set the crutches beside her and the suitcase at the foot of the stairs. Looking at Sarah, he said, "Do I smell that supper you mentioned?"

"Chili. Cornbread is in the oven. Should be ready in twenty minutes."

"Excellent. That should give me just enough time to grab a shower and stow my things."

"Gabe?" Nic repeated. "Are you staying here tonight?"

He shoved his hands in his pockets. "You can't manage by yourself. Not while you're on crutches. I'll stay as long as you need help."

A flurry of emotions flashed across Nic's face, and Gabe feared he read them too easily. Relief was okay. Gratitude wasn't a problem. It was the hope that sent unease crawling up his spine.

"Thanks, Gabe," Nic said softly.

He searched for words to warn her against making too much of this, but came up empty, so he simply nodded, then headed for the stairs. When he reached the second-floor landing, he heard Nic say, "Guess what, Sarah? We're having twins."

Gabe's stomach took a roll. *Wonder if morning sickness is contagious.*

FOURTEEN
❦

By suppertime the following day, Nic was ready to declare the honeymoon officially over. Her husband was a tyrant.

First he demanded she hang a Closed sign on the clinic door and refer her patients to the vet hospital in Creede. No amount of calm, collected insistence that she could still perform her job while on crutches moved him. Next he refused to leave the bathroom while she hung her head over the toilet for her daily dose of morning sickness. Even if she did appreciate his steadying hands at her waist and his help keeping her hair out of the way, that didn't mean she shouldn't have control over who accompanied her to the bathroom under what circumstances. Finally, when she mentioned her intention to go to Cavanaugh House after supper for a meeting Celeste had requested, he took it upon himself to arrange for the meeting to be moved to Nic's house without even asking her if she cared.

"Of all the nerve," she grumbled as she sat in the overstuffed chair in her living room, her injured leg propped on an ottoman, flipping through the mail he'd brought in from the mailbox moments before.

The worst part of it was that she knew he was right about just about everything. She'd awakened stiff and sore this morning and hadn't wanted to move, much less work. He'd filled the bathtub with warm water for her, and when she'd gone shy about getting naked in front of him, he'd shown amazing sensitivity and promised to keep his eyes closed while helping her in and out of the tub. She hadn't caught him peeking, either.

She told herself she was glad about that.

She also told herself she shouldn't be so grumpy, that she should be grateful to him for his help, and that it wasn't his fault that it was snowing again and she was sick to death of winter. If she was honest with herself, she'd have to admit that the only reason she felt so put out was because she had planned a different beginning for their marriage when Gabe returned to Eternity Springs.

She'd spent a lot of time thinking about their situation while he was in Virginia. He'd called often, keeping her apprised of his schedule, sharing bits and pieces of his days, and nurturing the friendship growing between them. She'd enjoyed the phone calls. Each one left her feeling hopeful about the future and cautiously optimistic that her marriage just might take.

Aware that he was as skittish as a wounded fox, she'd known she would need to proceed slowly and carefully. She'd planned a strategy intended to nurture their relationship that included inviting Gabe over for dinner, spending time with him at town meetings and events, and, when the time was right, inviting him into her bed.

Her plan hadn't included her being black-and-blue with bruises the first time he saw her naked.

Nic sighed heavily, set the electric bill and a postcard from her vacationing mother and aunt aside, then threw the junk mail in the trash just as her doorbell rang. Gabe stood up from the drawing board he'd set up in her library and answered the door, the boxer at his side. "Hello, Celeste."

"Hello, dear." Celeste went up on her tiptoes and gave Gabe a kiss on his cheek. "Welcome home."

His expression registered surprise, and he smiled crookedly before saying, "Thanks."

Next Celeste patted Tiger's head and cooed, "Hello, puppy dog. Look at that tail wag. I bet you're happy your daddy is home, aren't you?"

Gabe rolled his eyes but refrained from the usual he's-not-my-dog protest when a second woman Nic didn't know followed Celeste into the house. She and Celeste both carried bulging tote bags.

"Gabe and Nic Callahan, I'd like to introduce you to Alison Timberlake. Alison *Cavanaugh* Timberlake. Ali is my first guest at Angel's Rest. She's coming to reconnect with her family roots."

As Gabe said hello and shook the newcomer's hand, Nic waved a hello to the attractive, classy-looking blonde wearing black slacks and a carnation-pink sweater set. "Welcome to our home and to Eternity Springs, Ms. Timberlake."

"I'm Ali."

"Ali, then. I'm Nic, and I'd get up, but my dictatorial husband has threatened me with torture if I rise from my chair in the next hour."

Alison grinned and repeated, "Torture?"

Gabe nodded. "We had a discussion about bad disco music this morning. I promised to sing 'Dancing Queen' if she doesn't behave."

"I rest my case," Nic said.

"As long as you rest your ankle and my back, that's all I care about," he fired back before offering to take the visitors' coats.

Celeste laughed. "Ah, acting like old married folk already, I see."

"Nothing old about it," Gabe drawled. "Since she's been acting like a five-year-old, it's more realistic to say she's my child bride."

Nic decided to ignore that and changed the subject by

asking Ali Timberlake, "Has Celeste told you about the journals we found that were written by Elizabeth Blaine Cavanaugh, who would be your great-great-grand-mother?"

"Yes, she did." Ali slipped leather gloves into the pocket of her cashmere coat and handed it to Gabe. "I've glanced through a few of them, and I'm anxious to read them. From what I understand, my branch of the Cavanaugh family descends from Elizabeth's younger son, Lawrence, who married and left Eternity Springs. Her older son, Harry junior, remained in Eternity Springs."

"The journals make fascinating reading. You'll enjoy them." Nic wondered if Celeste had mentioned Angel and the silver bars to the newcomer yet, and if Ali had any new information to offer about the mystery of Angel's death. Knowing Celeste would share any news at an appropriate time, she addressed another curiosity. "What's in the bags?"

"Supplies." The older woman tugged off emerald-green knit gloves and a matching brimmed stocking cap, then allowed Gabe to help her out of her ski jacket. "LaNelle loaded me up. I hope we have enough for everyone, but tonight's meeting is more organizational than anything. I don't expect we'll get down to work until next time."

"What are we organizing?"

"A quilting bee. I've brought rotary cutters, cutting mats, cutting rulers, needles and threads, thimbles, scissors—lots of fun stuff."

"Quilting?" Nic smirked with doubt. "I can't even sew a hem."

"No, you simply sew stitches in animals who are hurting," Gabe pointed out.

Celeste crossed the room to Nic, placed a hand on her cheek, and looked deeply into her eyes. "How are you feeling, dear?"

"I'm fine." At the older woman's chastising look, she conceded, "I still have a bit of a headache. I'm achy and sore."

"And grumpy," Gabe called from the hallway, where he was hanging up coats.

Celeste clucked her tongue, then took a seat on the sofa and patted the cushion beside her for Ali to join her. "I hear that you received joyous news yesterday, Nic. You're a mother to twins. How exciting. God's blessings are indeed bountiful."

Nic's hand drifted to her stomach as her gaze cut toward Gabe. They hadn't discussed the babies since leaving the hospital. He was doing a masterly job of avoiding the subject, and Nic saw no reason to force a discussion. After all, no immediate decisions regarding the babies needed to be made. He had months to grow accustomed to the fact that he'd soon be the father to two instead of one. "The news was certainly a surprise, but I think I'm up for the challenge."

Ali Timberlake spoke up. "Two of my children are only eleven months apart in age. I often wished they'd been born twins. They were just far enough apart to always be on different schedules when they were little guys."

"How many children do you have?" Nic asked.

"Three. Two boys and a girl." Ali's smile grew wistful. "My youngest, my girl, will be a senior in high school this fall, so the emptying of my nest is looming. I miss my babies. Enjoy your time with yours, Nic. It goes so fast. Too fast."

Ali's comments surprised Nic. She had guessed Ali to be no more than a year or two older than herself. Either the newcomer was quite a bit older than she looked or she'd started her family at a young age. "My friend Sarah's only child is the same age as your daughter. She's starting to go a little crazy thinking about Lori going off to college."

The doorbell rang, and Gabe tended to the new arrivals. Sage plunked a hip on the arm of Nic's chair and asked a few quiet questions about the babies and her pregnancy. Before long, eight women and Tiger were crowded into the living room. Gabe picked up the tray of sweets Sarah had brought and took them to the kitchen, then retreated to the library and his drawing board. After a few minutes for people to say hello and be introduced to Ali Timberlake, who bonded almost immediately with Sarah, Nic said, "Okay, Celeste, the floor is yours."

"Thank you, Nic." Celeste smiled around the room and continued, "Thank you all for coming tonight. I know you're all curious why I called you all together, and I apologize for being cryptic with my invitation, but I wanted to present this idea face-to-face. You see, I'd like to invite you all to join me in establishing a quilting bee."

"A quilting bee?" Sarah repeated. "Celeste, I swore off needles when I tried to make Lori a poodle skirt for the fifth-grade sock hop."

"Just hear me out, Sarah. This idea is part of my vision for our healing center. I want to have a special quilt for each room, and I'd like them to be made from the fabrics of our lives in Eternity Springs. Fabrics like these."

She reached into one of the totes and removed a stack of fabrics, which she spread out on the floor. Satins, silks, and laces, all in shades of white.

"Those look like pieces of wedding gowns," Sarah said.

"Give the girl a bouquet." Celeste pointed toward an off-white satin train. "That's from Marlene Hart's gown. The silk is Lisa Cartwright's. The bodice with all the embellishments is Margaret Stewart's."

Nic said, "Each of those ladies has celebrated at least her silver anniversary. Margaret and Jess Stewart had an awesome golden anniversary party last year."

"So you think it would be, what, a magic marriage quilt?" Emma Hall asked.

"No. The snow-white satin is Monica Brown's. I understand that her marriage lasted less than a year."

"Okay, then, I'm confused," Sarah said.

Sage knelt on the floor and began examining the fabric. "I think I get it. A quilt made of wedding gowns would be symbolic of hope and happiness—that dream that every bride has on her wedding day."

Not every bride, Nic thought, stealing a look at her husband and discovering that he was stealing one back at her, too. She quickly turned her attention back to Sage.

"That's right," Celeste agreed. "I do see the quilts as a symbol of Eternity Springs and the positive energies of its people. Take this wedding gown quilt, for example. Think of all that will go into it. Not just the love and hopes and dreams represented by these lovely fabrics, but the friendship, companionship, laughter, and love we will share as we work to create our quilts. It's the compassion we feel for those who will come to our healing place with troubled souls and wounded spirits. Imagine being in a painful emotional place and snuggling up in a beautiful representation of the special life force that this town, this valley, has to offer."

"Okay, I'm sold," Emma Hall said. She glanced at LaNelle Harrison. "I trust you are going to teach us what to do and how to do it?"

"Of course. I have ulterior motives, you know. I figure I'll get you all hooked on quilting and it will triple my business."

"I want to play, too," Sarah said. "However, I need to know what sort of time commitment we're looking at. I'm stretched pretty thin already."

Celeste nodded. "I'd like us to meet once a week, but don't let that stop you from joining. I think we should be flexible. Our group should be something that's fun, not a burden. If you know of anyone else you'd like to have join us, please feel free to invite them. We'll have plenty of projects to work on."

Sarah glanced at Nic and asked, "Do you think we could talk Lori into joining? I think it would be nice for us to participate in an activity as equals, not as mother and daughter."

"That's a great idea," Nic replied. "I think she'd love to be part of this group."

"Will all the quilts be wedding gown quilts?" Wendy Davis asked. "I'll be happy to contribute mine to the cause. It's just hanging in my closet gathering dust."

"We can certainly make more than one wedding gown quilt, but I'd also like to make quilts from other fabrics of Eternity Springs. I'd like to see quilt tops made from kitchen curtains and children's clothes. Happy things. Happy themes."

"I love it." Sage looked up from the length of lace she'd been studying. "How do we start?"

Celeste smiled at LaNelle. "That's your cue, my friend."

"We start by making some decisions. We must decide on our project's size and pattern. I've brought pattern books for us to peruse." LaNelle reached into the tote bag she'd brought along and passed around books and magazines. "Since we are making quilts for a healing center, I've marked patterns I think are appropriate for our theme. However, if everyone wants to do something different, that's fine, too."

The women pored over the pattern books, picked favorites, and discussed possibilities, then chose the Star of Hope pattern as the most appropriate design for their first bridal gown quilt. They settled on Tuesday night for their meetings and accepted Nic's offer to meet at her home until she was back on her feet. After that, they'd move their meetings to Angel's Rest and the room Celeste indicated would be dedicated to their effort.

As Sarah took a bite of one of Wendy Davis' pinwheel cookies, she asked, "Shouldn't we have a name for our group? Is this a guild or a bee?"

"A bee. A guild is a group of bees," LaNelle said. "I do think we should choose a name. Any suggestions?"

Conversation lagged as they considered the question. "We could be the Eternity Quilters," Sarah suggested.

Nic wrinkled her nose. "That's boring."

"Then you suggest something."

With the disco song Gabe had teased her with earlier still playing through her mind, Nic came up with, "Okay, how about the Quilting Queens of Eternity Springs?"

Sarah gave an exaggerated roll of her eyes. "That's stupid."

Leaning against a cabinet and sipping a glass of water, Sage surveyed the room. Her gaze lingered on Celeste a moment, then she smiled. "I have it. I think we should call ourselves the Patchwork Angels."

Celeste gasped and clapped her hands, her sky-blue eyes gleaming with delight. The name was adopted by acclamation and the Patchwork Angels Quilting Bee got down to work.

As spring finally arrived in the Rockies, ice cracked and creeks began to flow. Cottonwoods and aspen budded and bloomed, and the world turned green once more. Patches of snow would remain into May and sometimes even till June, but in Eternity Springs, citizens declared the official arrival of spring when Zach Turner posted signs forbidding skating on Hummingbird Lake.

Gabe and Nic had settled into a routine of sorts. In the mornings, he awoke ahead of her and showered and dressed first, then knocked on her bedroom door on his way downstairs to make coffee. Once Nic had washed and dressed, he carried her downstairs. Two weeks after the accident, Nic resumed clinic hours on a part-time basis. Gabe grew increasingly busy at Angel's Rest as the healing center took shape.

In addition to refurbishing the main house, Celeste's plans called for the construction of three slightly smaller Victorian-style structures to provide rooms for up to thirty guests on the property, along with a separate dining facility. By the first week of May, those buildings, including the spa facility that was part of Gabe's design for the hot springs pools, were ready for finish work inside. Outdoors, landscape construction proceeded at such a pace that Gabe came home marveling about the progress almost every day. He'd never had a job go as smoothly as this. Of course, he'd never seen working conditions quite like this before, either.

To say that the citizens of Eternity Springs were grateful for the activity was an understatement of epic proportions. Local enterprises reported that business had more than doubled in March and April over the previous year. Townspeople were happy, and they showed their gratitude to laborers by being friendly and welcoming and by offering treats like cookie breaks in the afternoon and complimentary rounds of Miracle Mead microbrew at the Red Fox Pub. As a result, happy laborers worked harder and the project took shape ahead of schedule. Mayor Townsend's favorite saying of late was that this was shaping up to be the greenest spring the town had ever seen. Crusty old Dale Parker even went so far as to rename the Fill-U-Up, calling it Eternity's Angel Gas and Grocery Emporium in Celeste's honor.

On an afternoon in early May, while finishing up a phone call with the chemist who had done the water testing for the center, Gabe glanced out the library window at Angel's Rest and saw Nic sitting in the front porch swing reading a book.

After lunch, she had asked him to help her upstairs so that she could offer her opinion about room designs Celeste intended to finalize on an upcoming buying trip. Though her knee and ankle injuries were almost healed, she still needed assistance going up and down stairs. Gabe was happy to carry her. Truth be told, he enjoyed the contact.

He ended the call, but he couldn't drag his gaze away from his wife. When he'd carried her back downstairs twenty minutes ago, he'd noticed she'd been wearing a new scent, a musky, spicy fragrance that made him want to pull her even closer. He'd supposed it was one of the custom scents that Celeste had commissioned for the healing center. If so, she'd hit a home run with the fragrance Nic wore, a combination of the peach scent that she liked and a heavier, exotic blend of spice. It had lingered in his senses for an hour now.

She'd been lingering in his thoughts for days. Weeks, even. Okay, months.

The friendship strategy had worked out well so far. They managed well together. The awkwardness between them rarely appeared anymore. He enjoyed her company. Her injury had effectively doused the sexual tension that had smoldered between them, allowing them to focus on getting to know each other. The more time he spent with her, the better he liked her. She was funny, witty, cranky in the morning, and soft and sweet in the evenings when she fell asleep on the sofa while watching TV.

Watching her now with her good leg folded up beneath her, the injured leg pushing against the porch to keep the swing in motion, he knew that the sex-not-possible-because-it-hurts-her-to-move excuse was soon to disappear. He clenched his jaw and sucked a breath past his teeth. *Damn.*

He wanted her.

She was . . . sunshine. She was warm and bright and full of life. She drew him like a moth to flame. He wanted to take her to bed and share in her light.

What was he going to do about it? Had he changed in the weeks since their California trip? Could he have sex without feeling guilty when it was over? He needed to be sure the answer was yes before approaching her. The last thing he wanted to do was to screw up what they had now.

And yet, if his head was finally on straight, what they had now could become even better.

Maybe the thing to do was to discuss it with Nic. One thing he'd learned from living with her was that she preferred to get things out in the open and face them head-on rather than pussyfoot around. Maybe talking about it ahead of time would avoid awkwardness when, and if, the right time rolled around.

"The right time," he muttered to himself. "That sounds like an erectile dysfunction commercial."

That was definitely not his problem.

Gabe exhaled a deep breath, then went into the kitchen, where he poured two glasses of lemonade. He stepped out onto the front porch. "Thirsty?"

She set her book aside. "You read my mind. Thanks."

He handed her a glass, then joined her on the swing. "What are you reading?"

She gave him a considering look. "You probably don't want to know."

He arched a brow, then reached for the book. *One*

Thousand and One Baby Names. He winced and gave her back the book, wishing he'd left well enough alone.

"Okay. That answers that question. Still not ready to deal with this particular reality, are you?"

"Let's just say that's not what I came out here to talk to you about."

"Oh? And that would be . . . ?"

Well, hell. He couldn't exactly talk about sex now, could he? Instead he brought up the other subject that had been on his mind today. "Today is my twin brothers' birthday."

"You have twin brothers?"

He nodded. "Apparently twins run in the family. I think I'd like to tell you about them. About what happened to my family."

"I'd like that very much."

So he told her. He explained about growing up in Brazos Bend, Texas, and the way the family fell apart in the wake of his mother's death. He told her about being sent off to military school and being recruited by the State Department. "I was good with languages."

Her eyes rounded. "You were a spy?"

"Officially I was an embassy worker in the wrong place at the wrong time." Then he told her about Sarajevo, the shooting, his time as a prisoner, and the rescue.

"Is that where you got the scars on your chest?"

"Yeah. Look, I don't want to go into all the gory details. All that really matters is that it was best for the good guys if I died, so I did."

"I don't understand."

"They faked my death. I went back to the States and started a new life. Think of it as a version of the witness protection program."

Nic blinked. "Whoa. Wait one minute. You're in a witness protection program?"

"No. It's nothing official. Except, of course, all my government documents are legit."

Now she gaped at him. "Are you telling me you're not really Gabe Callahan?"

"No, not at all. I didn't have to change my name. They created a past for me, issued me a new social security number, and did a little work on my face. I started going by my middle name rather than my first." He explained how he'd enrolled in grad school to study landscape architecture, met and married Jennifer, and made a name for himself—as Gabe Callahan—in his field.

"Weren't you worried someone would recognize you?"

"No. The government made my death very convincing. Plus I look different."

"Wow," she said after a moment's thought. "This just blows me away. I sensed you had secrets in your past, but I never guessed anything like this. What you are telling me is that, in effect, you gave your life for your country."

"No, not at all. That makes me sound . . ."

"Like a hero?"

"I'm no hero, Nic. Don't think of it as some big sacrifice, because it wasn't. It wasn't like we all lived in the same town and got together for Sunday dinners. The truth is that when John Callahan died, I found my life."

"You act as if John Callahan and Gabe Callahan are two different people."

He shrugged. "It's been two different lives." *At least.*

"I seldom think about John Callahan's life. It's easier that way. Although I do like to drink a toast in my brothers' honor on their birthdays. I imagine they do the same for John."

"It's weird how you speak of yourself in the third person."

"Makes me feel like a pro athlete," he dryly replied.

She grinned. "You've talked about your brothers before. There are three of them, right? Do you have any sisters?"

"No sisters. I'm told the guys have all married now, though, so there would be sisters-in-law. My . . . um . . . manager, I guess you could call him, updates me when I ask."

"You don't see your family at all?"

"No." Gabe drew in a deep breath, then exhaled heavily. "My family is politically connected. For the plan to work, they had to believe I was dead. The black hats were well aware of the Callahan family's response."

Nic's eyes rounded in shock. "That's horrible. That's just so sad."

She took his hand in hers and gave it a comforting squeeze. She seldom touched him casually, though it was something she did with others all the time. It made him realize just how careful she was around him, and he found comfort in her spontaneity now. He turned his hand, linking their fingers, and they sat holding hands and swinging gently back and forth.

After a time she asked, "Was it worth it? Are you glad you made the choice you made?"

He couldn't tell her about the high-level Al Qaeda operative whose defection his own "death" had provided cover for, or that the information the terrorist had offered up thwarted a terrorist attack on America, so all he said was, "Yeah, I am."

"Would your family think it was worth it?"

He didn't hesitate. "Yes. They would. They are patriotic to a man. I only wish . . ."

"What?" she prodded.

"At the time it all went down, I didn't know how much it hurt to lose someone. I might have looked for another way."

"So this happened how long ago?"

"Over ten years now. It's hard to believe so much time has passed, that I've gone so long without talking about them. Other than my contact, you are the only one I've told."

Surprise widened her eyes. "Jennifer didn't know?"

He hesitated, then shook his head. "No, not the whole story. When I met her, the situation was such that I couldn't. After that . . . well, it was complicated."

"So you lost your Callahan family, then you lost your wife and son. I think I'm finally beginning to understand why you have trouble with . . ." She held up the baby name book.

Gabe closed his eyes. "You married a head case, I'm afraid."

She tightened her hand around his, then released him. "Sorry, Callahan. I'm of the opinion that you're the strongest man I know. I'm glad you told me about your brothers."

The conversation lulled, but he didn't leave. He could almost hear the wheels spinning in her mind. Eventually, she picked the baby name book up again and opened it. "What are your brothers' names?"

He winced.

She noticed and said, "What?"

"It's so, well, corny. Let me put it in context. My parents were married a long time before my mom got pregnant the first time. They thought they were infertile. She named my oldest brother Matthew. Yes, my Matty was named for him. Then, when she had the twins, she decided to continue the biblical theme. They're Mark and Luke."

Nic pursed her lips, holding back a laugh. "Matthew, Mark, Luke, and John?"

"In our hometown, they called us the Holy Terrors of Texas."

Without conscious thought, she placed her hand over her stomach. "Did you all have celestial middle names?"

"Nah. Our middle names had no special meaning. Mom said she just liked the name Gabriel."

She thought about it a little longer than said, "Celeste would say it's no coincidence that you ended up in Eternity Springs. She'd say that Gabriel was meant to find his way here, where Angel Creek runs at the center of the valley."

He arched an eyebrow. "Starting the whole healing woo-woo stuff a little early there, aren't you?"

"Nope. I don't think so. Thank you for sharing this, Gabe. It means a lot."

He shrugged, uncertain why he'd said so much. Why had he told her about the Callahans? Why did he trust her so much?

While he searched for answers, she met and held his gaze. "What happened to you—losing your family, twice—that's not right. I think you need to be here. I think you need to be with me. With . . ." She reached for his hand and placed it atop her womb, pressing lightly. "Us."

Gabe felt movement beneath his hand and closed his eyes. He felt as if he were standing at the peak of Murphy Mountain and a breath of wind would push him over the cliff.

Nic continued. "Like it or not, Callahan, the twins and I are your family now. When you are ready for us, we'll be waiting."

It was, he thought, the perfect thing to say. This was why he'd confided in her. Why he trusted her.

When it came to wounded souls, Nicole Sullivan Callahan had a healer's touch.

FIFTEEN
❦

At the Trading Post Grocery and Meat Market, Lori Reese stacked cans of green beans onto metal shelves and wondered how in the world she and her mom would survive the next year without totally destroying their relationship. She loved her mom. Truly, she did. But the woman was driving her insane. From the way Sarah was acting, you'd think Lori was going to graduate from high school in a year and move to New Zealand instead of going off to college. When the latest packet of college information arrived in the mail today, Mom had made a valiant effort to appear just as excited as she, but Lori hadn't missed her trembling chin and watery eyes. It almost ruined the moment for her, and she resented it.

"If she didn't want me to go off to college, she shouldn't have taken me on a trip to visit universities and helped me investigate scholarships," Lori grumbled, sliding a can toward the back of the shelf.

"Sarah, hon?" Lori's grandmother said from the end of the aisle. "Have you seen your father? I need to tell him that Jane Waggoner wants him to cut her a nice rump roast."

Oh, Nana. Lori straightened and smiled at her grandmother. Rather than correct her, she said, "I think he's at the barbershop. I'll tell him about the roast."

"Okay, dear. Don't forget now."

"I won't. I promise. Now, can I walk you back home?"

Lori hung the Back in a Minute sign on the front door as she led her grandmother across Aspen Street to their house. Walking inside, she called out, "Mom? Nana's a little mixed up. Do you want to sit with her or shall I?"

Sarah rushed out of the kitchen, wiping her hands on a dish towel, her expression wreathed with worry. "Hey, Mom. I'm in the middle of mixing up a cake. Will you come sit with me in the kitchen and have a cup of coffee?"

Ellen Reese wrinkled her brow in confusion and glanced between Sarah and Lori. "Where's your father?"

Lori and her mother shared a pained look, and once again Lori mentally cursed Alzheimer's disease. Nana always became the most agitated when she went looking for her husband, Lori's grandfather, who had passed away eleven years ago. It was difficult to watch. "Go on back to the store, Lori. I'll take it from here."

Lori nodded, hating to leave her mom to deal with Nana alone, and at the same time, glad for the reprieve. It was her dirty little secret. She loved her grandmother dearly, but watching this slow deterioration broke her heart. It was one more reason to look forward to college, though admitting it made her feel like pond scum.

Back inside the Trading Post, she finished shelving the green beans, then reached for the box of canned corn. Kneeling, she glanced around for the box cutter, then remembered she'd left it in back. "Shoot."

"Can I help?"

Startled, she jerked back and fell on her butt, staring up at a guy who at first glance could have doubled for Christian pop-rocker Joe Jonas—except that he held a pocket knife with the blade extended. Before she could draw a breath to scream, he calmly reached down, sliced open the carton, then closed and pocketed his knife. "Here you go. Sorry I scared you."

Lori swallowed and felt her cheeks flush. "Uh . . . that's okay. Thanks." She scrambled to her feet. "I didn't hear you come in. Is there . . . um . . . something I can help you with?"

"Yeah. I'm looking for a job. Do you know if the store's owner needs any help?"

Her mom needed lots of help, but she couldn't afford any employees. At least not before the summer season started in earnest. "My mom owns the store, and I'm afraid we don't have any openings right now. What sort of job are you looking for? I might be able to give you some suggestions if you let me know what you want."

"I'll do just about anything. I'm not picky. I just need enough hours to pay for a place to stay, pay for food. I worked whitewater rafting last summer and I'm certified, so if anyone runs a trip out of Eternity Springs to the Gunnison River, I'm their man."

So if he needed a place to stay, that meant he hadn't moved here with his family? He had a backpack hooked over his shoulder. "What's your name?"

If he said anything even close to Joe Jonas, she was going to faint dead away.

"Sorry." He flashed a bashful grin that made Lori's pulse speed up. He extended his hand. "My name is Chase. Chase Timberlake."

"Nice to meet you, Chase." Lori gave his hand a quick shake and said, "I'm Lori Reese. Unfortunately, we don't have any rafting trips out of Eternity Springs. If you're licensed, you could probably get on with someone in Gunnison. It's not exactly commuting distance from here. Where are you living?"

"I don't have a place yet. I just got into town. Rode my Yamaha down the back roads from Boulder this morning. Awesome drive. I've heard really good things about Eternity Springs from my mom. Thought it would be a good place to spend the summer."

OMG, he has a motorcycle. When she got past that interesting fact, his name and mention of his mother registered. "Timberlake? Is Ali Timberlake your mother?"

"Yes. You know her?"

"I've met her, yes. She's a neat lady."

"I think so. She's the one who suggested that I'd like living here this summer. I love the mountains and I have a thing for history. Since my ancestor helped found the town, we thought it'd be neat for me to walk in his shoes, so to speak. But I need a job to make it happen."

Lori thought hard. He was too cute to lose to another mountain town. "It's still a little early for the summer season, although the Double R might be worth a try. Do you know horses? Do you ride?"

His eyes lit up and he showed her a grin that had just enough wickedness in it to make her weak in the knees. "I've ridden most of my life. Is the Double R a ranch?"

"Yes. They have the biggest trail ride program in the area, and even better for you, summer help stays in the bunkhouse. Room and board are included in the job."

"Excellent. Can you tell me how to get there?"

"Their brochure has a map. We have some up at the checkout. Come with me and I'll get you one."

"Thanks."

She handed him the brochure and was both surprised and pleased when he lingered after looking at it. "I really appreciate your help. Maybe if I land this job, I could buy you a pizza or something? To say thanks?"

Yes! She labored to keep her voice level. "You don't need to do that."

"I want to." He added with a grin, "Unless there's some big mountain-man dude who'll come after me with a fly rod or something for trying to poach his girl."

She laughed. "A fly rod?"

He flashed a grin and shrugged. Flattered and excited, Lori wanted to say yes, but told herself not to be too easy. "I don't know anything about you—who you are, where you're from, why you're here—my mom would tell me it's not safe to make a date with a stranger."

"Smart mom. Okay, so how about we meet somewhere public and talk until I'm not a stranger anymore?"

"Persistent, too, aren't you?" Lori made a show of sighing, even though inside she was giving herself a high five. She tugged the brochure out of his hands, picked up a pen, and copied down her cell number. "If you get the job, let me know. We'll figure out something."

"Awesome." He folded the brochure and stuck it in his pocket, then headed for the door. "Thanks, Lori. I'm really glad I stopped in here."

"Good luck with the job."

Lori stood smiling a bit stupidly at the door until her mom opened it and stepped inside a few moments later. "Was that Andrew?" she asked. "Is he pestering you again?"

"No." Lori pursed her lips and shook her head. "He's a summer guy looking for work. Ali Timberlake's son."

"Really? That's cool. It's early yet for summer people, though. He might have better luck in a couple of weeks." Sarah shrugged, then said, "Lori, I called Nana's doctor and she wants to see her this afternoon. Can you hold down the fort here?"

"Absolutely. How is Nana doing?"

Sarah winced. "Her meds need tweaking a bit, I'm afraid."

Lori reached out and gave her mother a hug. Poor Mom. No wonder she acted so cranky all the time. She got it from both ends, didn't she? Her baby was growing up, and a horribly sad illness was slowly stealing her mother away. At least the family's financial situation had improved in the past six months. Celeste Blessing's healing center was proving to be a great kick-start for Eternity's economy and Lori's college fund. With any luck, she'd hear good news about the Davenport Foundation scholarship in the next few weeks, and that would relieve some of her mother's concern.

Of course, if she could track down her deadbeat dad, she could sic the child support police on his butt and solve all of her mother's problems.

Lori gave her mom one more hug, then stepped back. "You concentrate on Nana, Mom. Don't worry about things here."

Sarah nodded and glanced back toward the house. "Don't forget to take the deposit to the bank."

"I won't."

"And be sure to lock the doors both here and at the house if you go out. If summer people are arriving already, we'd better be careful."

"Yes, Mom. Don't worry, Mom. Go on and take care of Nana, Mom."

Sarah flashed her a smile of amusement and relief. "I love you."

"I love you, too, Mom. Go."

"Okay. Okay. I'm gone." She kissed Lori's cheek.

"Drive carefully."

At the doorway, Sarah stopped and turned. "If you have any problems—"

"I'll call Nic or Sage."

"If it's serious, call Zach."

"Bye, Mom."

Lori shook her head and sighed, then returned to shelving the cans of corn. "Something tells me this is gonna be one interesting summer."

In the exam room at her clinic, Nic handed the older man a box of heartworm preventative and said, "Give this to Champ on the fifteenth of every month. Remember, he's liable to cough a little bit as the worms begin to die, but if it he starts spitting up or the coughing becomes too intense, I need to see him. We don't want him to throw an embolism."

"But he should be okay, right?"

"Yes. Just remember that the goal is to keep his heart rate down, especially these first couple of weeks. No walks, and outside only on a leash."

"All right, Dr. Nic. Thanks so much. I feel so guilty about letting the preventative slip my mind. Just one more thing Sue took care of that I'm having to learn about. She's probably up there in heaven wanting to kick my hind end for being so careless with Champ."

"Don't feel bad, Bart. In a month's time, he'll be good as new."

After Bart and his Lab left the clinic, Nic took advantage of the opportunity to take a seat in her waiting room and prop up her ankle. Her injuries were much improved, though if she stood too long, she tended to swell. That could be from the pregnancy as much as from the sprains. She still used one crutch when she walked, a safety precaution for added balance rather than a necessity to avoid pain.

She checked the clock. Two-fifteen. Today she planned to man the clinic until three. Though she wouldn't admit it to Gabe, she enjoyed working part-time hours, as he'd insisted. Her energy level was up. She didn't fall asleep before eight-thirty at night anymore. She no longer awoke every morning already tired.

Nic loved her profession and had no wish to give it up. However, she wouldn't miss the long clinic hours she ordinarily kept during spring and especially summer to compensate for the short winter workday. Being a rich man's wife had some definite perks.

She had flipped open a *Parents* magazine and begun

reading an article about heartburn in pregnancy when the clinic's door chime sounded. Glancing up, she saw a woman and young man whom she didn't recognize. Both were tall with blue-black hair, dark eyes, and olive skin. Mother and son, most likely. "Hello."

"Hi," the woman said, her smile tentative. "Are you the vet?"

"Yes. I'm Dr. Sul—" She gave her head a shake and grinned. "Dr. Callahan. How can I help you?"

"I'm Pam Harrington. This is my son, Nathan. We, um, have come to see Gabe. Is he around?"

His sister-in-law, Nic realized, and in an instant a flurry of impressions and questions flashed through her mind. Pam and Nathan, but where was her husband? Nic prayed they weren't here to deliver bad news in person.

They didn't appear to be sad or upset, though. They looked curious. Nic was plenty curious herself. Pam was gorgeous; she reminded Nic of a young Sophia Loren. She wondered how much Pam had resembled her sister. The boy was tall and lanky, a teenager just beginning his growth spurt, she guessed, his coloring lighter than his mother's. Both the Harringtons watched her closely.

Nic kept her smile in place. "I'm pleased to meet you. Gabe speaks of you often. I was sorry to hear about your husband's illness. I hope he's doing well?"

"Very well, thank you. He's back at work and was well enough to attend an industry conference in Colorado Springs. Nathan and I couldn't resist the opportunity to drive over here and surprise Gabe with a visit." She hesitated, then asked again. "He's not away, I hope?"

Nic glanced at the wall clock. "He's been up at Jack Davenport's place today taking care of something. I expect him back in about twenty minutes, though. I know he'll be thrilled to see you." Noting that the boy's attention had locked on Steve Cartwright's Labrador pup, who was in for his shots, she added, "You're welcome to wait for him up at the house. Or Ranger"—she gestured to the puppy—"and I would be glad for the company. Can I offer you a soft drink? Bottled water?"

A pleased glint shined in Pam Harrington's dark eyes. "Water would be nice, thank you."

"Nathan?"

"A Coke, please," he said, not taking his gaze off the dog.

Nic took their drinks from the fridge, then opened the crate door and removed Ranger. "This sweetheart just had his shots and he wants to play."

"I'll play with him," Nathan piped up.

"Thanks. You can take him outside if you'd like," she said, gesturing toward a side door. "The yard is fenced."

Once the boy and the dog were settled, Nic and Pam Harrington exchanged polite smiles and a minute or two of small talk before Nic decided to face the elephant in the vet's office.

"Gabe told me how close he is to you, your husband, and your son, Mrs. Harrington. I imagine you have some questions about me. I'm happy to answer them if you wish."

"Well. That's direct."

"I don't see any reason to be otherwise."

"Fair enough. And please, call me Pam. Okay, then, I admit Gabe caught me by surprise with his news about you, and I was worried. I love Gabe like a brother and I want more than anything else for him to be happy again. Gabe is . . . well . . . he's not been himself since the accident. He said really nice things about you. Truly, he did. I just, well, I worried you'd be . . ."

"A bimbo?" Nic suggested, her tone dry.

Pam's grin was sheepish. "Well, I didn't know what to

think. Even under normal circumstances, Gabe can be a bit thick where the opposite sex is concerned."

Nic decided she liked Pam Harrington. If the situation were reversed, Nic would have made the trip to check out the new woman, too. "I hope you will believe me when I say that I'm not out to use Gabe or take advantage of him or bring him more pain. I want him to be happy. I want to make him happy."

"Okay, you've been frank with me. Let me be frank with you. Officially I'm not his sister-in-law anymore, but I still consider Gabe family. I don't want to lose him. I know it might be uncomfortable for you, but we want him to remain in our lives."

"I don't have a problem with that."

"You don't?" Her eyes widened with surprise.

"Of course not. Gabe has suffered enough losses in his life, don't you think?"

Warmth and welcome filled Pam's smile. "I do. I absolutely do."

The two women spent the next ten minutes in frank discussion about Gabe, his first marriage, and his suffering in the wake of the accident. While Nic didn't go into private details about her marriage, she did share information about Gabe's life in Eternity Springs.

"I was too distraught to ask him much of anything when he came to Virginia after Will had his heart attack," Pam said. "Eternity Springs is certainly a beautiful spot. From what you've told me, it sounds like he found the perfect place to pull himself back together. I'm glad he came here. It sounds as if this place and these people have been just the medicine he's needed. I think I just might like you, Nicole."

"I think I might like you, too, Pam."

"Okay, then, one more question. In the last email he sent, Gabe mentioned that he had some other significant news for me next time we talked. Care to give me a hint what it is?"

Must be the news about twins, Nic surmised. Gabe still went a bit green around the gills when anyone brought up the subject. "You can ask him yourself. I think he just came home."

"I didn't hear a car."

"He parks on the street until after clinic hours." Nic motioned toward the door of the clinic, where Tiger sat waiting to be admitted. "That's Gabe's dog. He went with him up to Eagle's Way today."

"A dog? Gabe has a dog?"

"More like the dog has Gabe. Tiger has adopted him, though Gabe still tries to pretend otherwise."

With just a hint of wistfulness in her tone, Pam said, "My sister was allergic to animals."

Ah. That piece of the puzzle shed a bit more light on her husband's reaction to the boxer. Nic rose and grabbed her crutch. She opened the side door and asked Nathan to bring in the puppy, then she opened the front door for Tiger. The boxer loped into the clinic, went straight to Nathan, sat, and barked twice, his personal version of hello.

The teenager grinned, and after handing the puppy off to Nic, scratched Tiger behind his ears. "Who's this?"

"Your uncle Gabe's dog," his mother replied.

"Really? Cool. What's his name?"

Nic shrugged. "I call him Tiger, but it's just a place holder until your uncle quits being so stubborn about ownership and gives him a forever name."

"He's goofy-looking."

"He's a doll. Your uncle saved his life." Nic repeated the story of how Gabe had rescued the dog from the bear trap. "He's totally loyal to Gabe."

"Gabe always liked dogs. Matty wanted one real bad. They couldn't have one because Jen broke out in hives whenever she touched one. They had a fish tank for a while, but I have to say, it's hard to fall in love with a fish."

"Unless it's a trout on my dinner plate," Nic agreed as she walked to the clinic's front door and gazed up toward the house. Gabe had turned on the kitchen light. "If I know Gabe, he's digging into the cookie jar. Shall we join him?"

"The sign is spectacular, Colt," Gabe said as he took a tall glass from the cupboard and set it on the counter beside the fridge. He and Colt Rafferty, the wood artist with local ties whom Celeste had hired to create the healing center's sign, had been playing phone tag all day. "I've never seen such detailed, intricate woodwork. It's definitely more artwork than signage."

"Thanks. I think it turned out nicely myself," Colt Rafferty replied. "Was Celeste pleased?"

"Pleased doesn't come close. She was thrilled. I thought she was going to climb on her motorcycle and do donuts in the front yard."

Colt laughed. "Does she still plan on conducting a grand unveiling of the logo?"

"Oh, yeah. My team and I are under threat of bodily harm if we leak it or allow anyone to get a glimpse of your sign before the Fourth of July event."

Colt sighed. "I can't tell you how much I'm looking forward to my summer in Eternity Springs. I'm counting the days."

"I'll look forward to meeting you." Gabe opened the refrigerator door and removed the milk jug. "It's been a pleasure to work with you on this project."

"Same here. I'm interested to see what you've done at Cavanaugh House, or should I say Angel's Rest. From the way Celeste talks and what I've seen in the photos you sent, your work is every bit as artistic as mine is."

Gabe smiled with satisfaction at the compliment. He was proud of the work he'd done at the estate. And he was happy to feel good about working again, period.

The two men finished up their call and Gabe poured his glass of milk and turned with anticipation to Nic's canister set. What gastronomical delight did she have for him today?

Ever since she'd caught him scrounging for something sweet a week ago, Nic had made sure to keep her cookie jar stocked with treats from either Sarah's or Wendy Davis' kitchen. He and his sweet tooth appreciated the effort. Removing the jar's lid, he peered inside. "All right. Lemon bars."

He took two, wrapped them in a napkin, picked up his glass of milk, turned toward the table—and froze. The items slipped from his hands and crashed to the floor. "Pam?"

"Great. If those were the last two lemon bars, Callahan, I'm gonna be ticked. Nic tells me they're totally awesome."

Pam. Here. Oh, no. Fear sent a cold chill through his heart. Heedless of the spilled milk and broken glass, Gabe crossed the room and grabbed her by her shoulders. "You're here. Is it Will? Is he okay?"

"He's fine. He's great. He's playing golf at the Broadmoor in Colorado Springs today." She gave Gabe a hug, then said, "I'm sorry. I didn't mean to scare you. We wanted to surprise you."

"Mom wanted to check out your new wife," Nathan said by way of hello.

Gabe narrowed his eyes at Pam, who shrugged without apology, then shot an impish grin toward Nic. "It's true. I just knew you'd married a bimbo. I thought I might need to wrest you away from her evil clutches."

Worried how Nic would react to that, Gabe darted her a look of alarm.

Wistfully she said, "I always wanted to be a bimbo. Alas, I went to vet school instead."

Both women laughed, and the vise around his chest eased. *They like each other. Pam and Nic like each other.* A lump the size of a baseball appeared in Gabe's throat. He closed his eyes. His heart swelled with gladness.

You'd like her, too, Jen. I know you would.

He could almost hear her voice in his mind. *You're right, Gabe. I would like her. She's a good woman and she's good for you. Don't screw it up.*

He released a slow, heavy breath. Maybe, just maybe, everything was going to be all right.

Later, following a supper of hamburgers cooked on her uncle's old charcoal grill that Gabe unearthed from storage, Nic sat in the glider on her back patio and listened to the conversation in the kitchen as Gabe and Nathan did the dishes. She couldn't recall the last time this house had rung with so much laughter. Not male laughter, anyway. The quilt group did have fun when they met here on Tuesday nights, but that was a different sound.

She drew in a breath and caught the scent of pine in the air, and she smiled. She loved this little section of her backyard. Surrounded by a hedge of holly and lit with soft lanterns and ambient solar lights, it was her private oasis. She spent evenings out here whenever weather allowed. Though the outdoor space heater warded off the worst of the chill, she grabbed a blanket from the basket of covers and quilts she kept beside the glider during warmer months and spread it over her knees. She so enjoyed the sensation of snuggling beneath a blanket as the sky above filled with stars.

What a great evening this had been. Gabe, Pam, and her son had teased and joked and even reminisced about shared events in the past. Once or twice emotions had swelled, but grief never overtook the moment. It was, Nic thought, a hopeful sign.

Hearing the screen door creak, she glanced up to see that Pam had returned from a trip to her car to get her sweater. She did not, however, have it on. "Couldn't you find your sweater?"

"Yes, but I also looked at your clock. I didn't realize it was this late. We have to get back on the road. Gabe is on the phone with someone talking about a pump problem at Cavanaugh House. We're going to head out."

Nic started to stand and she added, "No. Stay where you are. Gabe says you've been on your feet too much."

"He's a worrywart."

"Yes, but I guess that's understandable, don't you think?"

"Yes, I—" She broke off when Gabe opened the back door and stuck his head outside.

"Hey ladies, I need to run to the site for a bit. We have a pump problem. I don't know how long I'll be."

"We need to head out anyway," Pam told him. "I was just saying good-bye to Nic. Would you tell Nathan I said to get that box for you from our trunk?"

"Sure."

Then he was gone and Pam stood staring after him, a bittersweet look on her face. Nic reached for her hand and gave it a squeeze. "I'm so glad you came, Pam. This is the happiest I've ever seen him. You've given him his smile back."

Pam sank down on the glider beside her. "I don't think it's me. I think it's you. I admit that, in a way, it's hard to see him with someone other than my sister. However, it's not as difficult as I thought it would be. You've helped him, Nic."

"Do you really think so?" she asked, the catch in her heart betraying her vulnerability.

"Yes, I do. I was worried about him. Last year was horrible. Just horrible. Having Matty linger on like he did drained Gabe. I think that despite what the doctors told us, Gabe believed he could will his son well. The weeks after the funeral . . ." She shook her head. "I couldn't reach him. No one could. When he came to Colorado, I was honestly afraid I'd never see him again. I'm glad he found Eternity Springs and I'm glad he found you. I like you, Nic. I think my sister would like you, too."

Nic basked in the glow of the warmth of Pam's words long after Gabe's family took their leave. When he returned a half hour later, he was surprised to find her still outside. "I figured the cold would have chased you in by now."

"What, you think I'm a Texan or something? This isn't cold."

"Hey now, no ragging on Texans. You'll alienate half of the property owners around here."

She nodded. "I think we're starting to speak with a drawl. How's the pump situation?"

"Fixed." Gabe sat beside her and casually draped his arm around her shoulders. "It was a valve problem I've had experience with before, so it was an easy repair."

They sat silently for a few minutes in a relaxed, companionable state. He smelled of sawdust and sandalwood, and Nic allowed herself to snuggle against him and relish the contact. Eventually Gabe said, "It was a great evening, wasn't it?"

"It was."

Gabe looked up to the star-filled indigo sky, then said, "I love it here."

"You do?"

He looked at her and smiled. "Yeah. I do. I really do." Then he leaned forward and kissed her.

SIXTEEN

Gabe suspected that kissing her was a mistake, but his body didn't care. He felt great. Spectacular.

He felt horny.

Something had changed between him and Nic during these weeks they'd lived in the same house, but not together. He didn't have a term for it, or if he did, he wasn't prepared to admit what it was. All he knew for certain was that against what had seemed like insurmountable odds, springtime had returned to his soul. Like the cottonwoods and aspen blooming on the mountainside, he'd survived the long, harsh winter. He wanted to live again. And, he wanted to do that living with her.

Beneath the starlit sky and surrounded by the clean, fresh scent of a mountain springtime, Gabe kissed her, a kiss different from any he'd shared with her before. It was passionate yet gentle. It was a kiss from his heart.

Nic responded in kind. She was so sweet. Warm. Welcoming. She was light. Brightness, when he'd lived in darkness for so long.

He broke the kiss and drew back, watching her closed eyes, the way her tongue snaked out and licked her lips as though she savored the taste of him. It was then, in that moment, that he knew. No, no mistake. It was time. It was right. She was right.

She opened her eyes, and their gazes met and held. "Nicole? Can I take you to bed?"

Her smile bloomed slow and sweet and soft. "Take me here, Gabriel. It's a beautiful, quiet night. Spread the blanket on the grass."

He grinned. "You sure? We'll freeze our asses off."

"Something tells me heat won't be a problem."

He laughed out loud at that, then rose and spread out a blanket and quilts. Then he held his hand out to her and she took it, rising and moving naturally, gracefully into his arms. He bent down to her and they kissed. She tasted of lemon bars and smelled of a Rocky Mountain spring.

His hand stroked down her back, over the curve of her hip, then up again. When she made a soft sigh of pleasure into his mouth, he groaned in reply. Then, careful of her knee, he scooped her into his arms and knelt. He lowered her onto her back as if she were the most precious of jewels, then smiled down into the deep, blue depths of her eyes and allowed himself to fall. He took the moment for himself and for her and it was . . . good.

Tender, yet erotic. Physical, yet gentle. They took their time this time, learning each other, enjoying each other, giving pleasure and receiving pleasure in return. It was more than simply sex. It was rebirth for Gabe and a new beginning for them both.

Afterward, Gabe lay on his back staring up at the starry sky, one arm tucked beneath his head, the other around his wife. He felt as if he'd just scaled a mountain pass and discovered Shangri-La on the other side. It was a place, a state, he'd like never to have to leave. He was sated, satisfied, luxuriating in boneless aprés-orgasm bliss—and, thank God, free of both guilt and ghosts.

Almost happy.

That thought threatened his mellow mood, and he told himself to turn away from it. This was not the time to analyze and fret. Not the time to resurrect those ghosts. He needed to live for the moment, in the moment. So far, so good. He hadn't invited thoughts of Jennifer into his bed—such as it was—with Nic. That's the way it should stay for both their sakes. Nice. Simple. Surface.

"Are you okay?" Nic asked, showing an uncanny ability to read his mind.

He tried to bluff his way through it. "Let me catch my breath and I could be better."

A long moment passed in silence. He thought she'd let it go, and he started to relax.

Too soon, it turned out.

Her quiet voice chastised. "Don't hide from me, Gabe. Not now."

He opened his mouth to protest, but shut it again without speaking when she rose up on her elbow. The soft light from the garden lanterns bathed her form, revealing the solemn entreaty in her eyes. "This was a big step for both of us. Look, I'm not trying to be your psychologist or your grief counselor, but I think it's important that we communicate. It's part of any healthy relationship."

"I don't like to talk about my feelings."

"Well, at least you admit you have feelings. Look, I'm not asking for details about your sex life with Jennifer. What I'm asking is for you to talk to me. Give me a clue here."

He scowled. "I think what just happened was a pretty big clue, don't you?"

"Yes, I do. But until you confirm it, I'm just guessing. I'm still learning who you are, Gabe. I could guess wrong, and that could lead to misunderstandings that could hurt us both. I need to know what to expect. Or, in this case, what not to expect. That's not asking too much."

"You're asking where we go from here?"

"Yes."

"I'm hoping upstairs to bed."

"Together?"

"Yeah."

"And what about tomorrow night? Tonight has been a change, but I'm clueless how big a change it's been. My leg is better. I can get along okay on my own. Where do we go from here, Gabe? Will you stay, here, in my bed? Or will you go?"

"You sure ask a lot of questions, don't you?" When she didn't respond to that, but simply stared at him with a steady, solemn gaze, he sighed and closed his eyes. "All right. All right. I want to stay here. I want to move into your bedroom. I'd like a regular sex life again."

He opened his eyes then and gave her a sidelong look. "So, you happy now? I spilled my guts. Did it spoil the mood?"

"You didn't spoil the mood for me." She trailed a finger down the center of his chest to his navel. "Honest talk turns me on."

Her hand continued its southward trek and his body responded to her touch. When her mouth traced the path of her hand, he gave himself up to a long-missed pleasure until his hunger grew too hot, too fierce. He pulled her up, positioned her above him, her knees straddling his hips, and took her fast, with lots of enthusiasm and little finesse. When they finished and she collapsed atop him, laughing breathlessly, he stroked the silken waterfall of her hair and wondered if the demonstration of risk-reward had been a conscious one. Somehow he doubted she did anything coincidentally.

He shook his head in wonder. "I don't know what to make of you, Nic."

She propped herself up and met his gaze. "Why do you say that?"

"You are a wonderful woman. You're gorgeous, witty, intelligent. Sexy as hell. I am a head case." Though he wasn't at all certain he wanted the answer, he finished with a quiet question. "Why are you willing to put up with this BS from me?"

She slid off him then, sat beside him, and wrapped herself in a blanket. "My turn for some honest talk, I guess."

Never mind, he wanted to say.

"The truth is that if not for the babies, I probably wouldn't be in this. The odds are against us. You are more work than I need at this point in my life. Plus I have a bone-deep aversion to being any man's doormat."

"Doormat? Excuse me?" He didn't like that all. He didn't treat her like a doormat. Did he? Guilt snaked through him, but this time he refused to accept it.

"Work with me here, Callahan. See, I need you to understand me, too. While I definitely have a wish-upon-a-star side to me, the bottom line is that I'm a pragmatic kind of girl. I like a road map. I saw what living without one did to my mother. She put up with a man's mistreatment for years, and it cost her the entire life she could have had with a man who deserved her."

"You think I mistreat you?" he asked, annoyed.

"No. That's not what I'm saying. Look, the path we've started down is uncharted territory, and there's not an atlas for us in the self-help section of the bookstore. Believe me, I've checked. Advice for WOWs doesn't really help in this case."

"Wow?"

"Wife of a widower. See, it's the added letters for the acronym that makes it dicey. I'm a PWOW or PWT-WOW or APWT-WOW. Accidentally-pregnant-with-twins wife of a widower. That puts an entirely different spin on the situation."

Technically he wasn't a widower any longer since he was married to her, but he thought it best not to bring that up. She appeared to be on edge. "Nic, maybe we should go inside. Get you some warm milk. It'll help you calm down."

Jen had always liked warm milk when she was pregnant.

She scowled at him, and he recognized he'd sounded patronizing, but she did look a little wild-eyed at the moment.

"Stop it," she snapped. "See, here's the thing. I understand that we have happened too soon for you. In a perfect world, you would have had a lot more time to let go of the past relationship before attempting to begin a new one. Unfortunately, our world isn't perfect."

"Tell me about it. My wife died."

The barb visibly hit home, and as he saw Nic flinch, his feeling of guilt intensified. Before he could apologize, she continued, "I get that the grieving process for you will be full of fits and starts. But like it or not, I'm part of your life, which automatically makes me part of your grief. I understand that Jennifer is always going to be part of our relationship. I think I can deal with that, but only if we to learn to talk about her. I won't ignore the ghost in the room. Not anymore."

Gabe rolled to his feet and shoved his legs into his jeans. "I think *I* need that warm milk."

With a shot of whiskey in it.

She followed him inside wearing only a blanket wrapped around herself. "You are healing, Gabe. Slowly but surely. I understand that you're not yet ready to move on. But that's as far as my mind reading goes. See, I don't know if you've decided to sleep with me now because you're ready for physical intimacy and any woman would do."

"Hey now." He jerked back at the low blow. "I've never given you cause to think that."

"True. So maybe it's not that I'm handier than a whore. Maybe I'm simply your rebound girl. Maybe when you finally are ready for emotional intimacy, you'll want it to be with someone other than me."

"Where did this come from?" Dammit, he'd felt so good just a few minutes earlier. Why was she ruining it? "You make me sound like a real ass, Nic."

"No, you're a man. Sometimes that's just the same thing," she fired back. She took a deep calming breath, then continued. "I can't have it be a surprise, Gabe. For our babies' sake, and, frankly, because I have strong feelings for you myself, I'm willing to roll the dice with you. But I need you to give a little in return. The times in my life when men have been able to hurt me are when I didn't see the trouble coming."

Strong feelings? What were strong feelings in her book? He skipped the milk and grabbed the vodka from the freezer since it was the closest available alcohol.

"You need to communicate, Gabe," she continued. "It's important in every aspect of our marriage, but especially when it comes to sex."

Strong feelings. He scowled at her. Was that her way of saying she loved him?

Feeling cornered, he lashed out. "You want to communicate about sex? All right. Fine. You give good head, Nic."

"You are such a jerk, Callahan." She lifted her chin and gave her hair a regal toss. "It's a good thing I'm a vet and understand how wounded animals lash out. Of course, I also know what to use to put them down. Maybe you should remember that."

He laughed at that, poured a shot of vodka, and threw it back like water. Then, without conscious thought, he filled a mug with milk and set it in the microwave to heat. Nic watched him and a tiny, sad smile played on her lips.

As he punched in the time, she approached him and rested her hand on his arm. "Gabe, I will never understand what it's like for you, the complexity of your feelings, or the depth of your grief. But you are my husband and the father of my children. I care enough about you to listen with an open mind and an open heart."

He closed his eyes. Emotion coiled within him. A part of him wanted to open up, to share how great she made him feel, to tell her that she . . . mattered. But a bigger part of him wanted to keep his mouth shut, sweep her up into his arms, and carry her upstairs to his bed so he could exorcise his demons in more mind-numbing sex.

"I'm asking you again, are you okay?"

"Didn't I already answer that question?"

"You answered the superficial question. We're sleeping together now. Surface doesn't cut it."

As the microwave dinged, he grabbed hold of the counter with both hands and dropped his chin to his chest. "You're not giving this up, are you?"

"It's too important."

Surrendering, Gabe cleared his throat. "Here's the thing about surface, Nic. Living on the surface, I can keep my head above water. Most times, treading is the best I can do."

"Treading isn't living, Gabe."

"I know. But see, every so often, my feet find the sand. I start to think I can make it to the beach. Then, invariably and without any warning, the pain will roll in like a tsunami. It'll flatten me, knock me right on my ass. Sometimes I can climb right up again. Other times I get caught in the undertow."

"That's when you need a life preserver, Gabe."

He turned his head and looked at her. "And I find that hanging on the wall here, is that what you're saying?"

"I can throw it to you if you want. I'll man the line to pull you to safety. However, I need you to ask. I need to know that you want not to drown."

"I think I'm getting a bit lost in this metaphor." Gabe punched the button to open the microwave. He removed the mug of milk and handed it to her, saying, "Here's the deal, Nic. You ask how I feel. Right now I feel pretty good. Hell, I feel great. I've missed sex. Being with you tonight was fantastic. I'd like nothing more than to have it become a regular part of my life.

"That said, I'd love to be able to say that I've put my guilt and ghosts behind me for good. But I can't promise that. I'm not trying to be a jerk here. I know it's not fair to you, and it makes me feel like a bottom-feeder to say it, but no matter how good I feel tonight, I know there's a chance I'll wake up in the morning feeling like I cheated on Jen."

"Fair enough." She nodded, and a little smile played upon her lips. "Thank you for talking to me, Gabe. That's what I need. I've thought about this a lot. I'm ready to be patient and understanding and a veritable tower of strength—as long as you don't shut me out." She sipped her milk, then set the mug down. Holding out her hand toward him, she suggested, "Now, why don't you take me to bed?"

The band around his chest relaxed, and the corners of his mouth tilted up. "A bed? Really? With a mattress and everything?"

"With a mattress and everything."

He took hold of her hand. "Your room or mine?"

"Doesn't matter." She gave his hand a squeeze. "Pick one, and let's make it ours."

If not for the lingering soreness in her leg, Nic would have skipped down the street as she made her way to Sarah's house to put the final touches on plans for Lori's upcoming birthday party. Life was good. In the week since Pam showed up at the clinic, Gabe had spent every night in her bed and burrowed his way deeper into her heart.

Today he'd come by the house for lunch and brought her flowers.

Ali Timberlake pulled up in front of Sarah's house as Nic turned the corner of Sixth and Aspen. Ali was in town visiting her son, Chase, who was working at the Double R, and Sarah had invited her to stop by and share the scoop on what was all the rage in the way of teenage birthday parties in Denver this year. Nic clucked her tongue at the sight of Ali's little red BMW convertible. That was one gorgeous car.

"And one happy woman," she murmured, watching curiously as Ali ended a phone call then threw her arms into the air and cheered. She climbed out of her car, danced a little jig, then waved at Nic. "Good morning!"

"It appears so. You look like a happy camper."

"I am. My husband, Mac, just called. He's been offered a federal judgeship. It's been his dream for as long as I've known him."

"That's wonderful news. Congratulations."

"Thank you. I'm so proud of him. Proud for him." She beamed a smile at Nic, then added, "Don't you look cute today. Love your shirt. That twist front is chic. I wish they'd had maternity tops that stylish when I needed them."

"Thanks." Nic rested a hand on the bump that these days seemed to be growing by the hour. "I don't know how long I'll be able to wear it, though. This empire waist is British Empire–size. The rate I'm going, I'll need it to be galactic empire–size."

Ali laughed. "Before I forget, I stopped to visit with Celeste for a few minutes and Gabe flagged me down on the way out. He asked me to ask you to swing by Angel's

Rest on your way home and pick up the boxer. Apparently he's too curious about the rock work being done by the hot springs, and he's making a pest of himself with the workers."

"Oh, now. That's a big fat lie. What's probably happening is that there's a dog lover or two in the group and they're spending too much time in Gabe's estimation playing with Tiger."

Ali grinned and nodded. "You might be right. Celeste did say that Gabe has been spending most of his time down by the hot springs. I know dogs are loyal creatures, but I have to say that Tiger is the most dedicated dog I've ever seen. Especially to someone who goes out of his way to pretend he's not the dog's master."

"You see that, do you? Gabe rescued Tiger from a trap last fall and the dog has been his shadow ever since. Gabe loves Tiger, but he refuses to admit it."

"What's the deal with his name?" Ali asked as they stepped up onto Sarah's front porch. "When someone asks what his name is, Gabe says he doesn't have one."

Nic rolled her eyes. "What can I say? My husband is a stubborn fool."

She rapped on Sarah's door, then, in the way of the casual habits of old friends, opened the door and stepped inside. "Sarah? Ali and I are here."

Sarah called down from upstairs. "I'll be down in a minute. Make yourselves at home."

Nic inspected the treats in the kitchen with interest and was delighted to spy not only her favorite brownies but lemon bars as well. Lemon bars now had a special place in Nic's heart.

"Would you like coffee?" she asked Ali. "Sarah always has a pitcher of iced tea in her fridge, too. Let's see what else she has." Nic opened the refrigerator door and peeked inside. "Milk, bottled water, OJ, tomato juice . . ."

"How about a glass of iced tea?"

At that moment, Sarah breezed into the kitchen, a harried look in her expression. "Sorry. Mom's having another bad day. I don't think the new meds are really helping the situation at all."

Nic took three glasses out of Sarah's cabinet and filled two of them with ice, then poured two glasses of tea and one of milk. "Sarah, honey, you are the best daughter a mother could have, but you need to start thinking about—"

"I know. I know." Sarah blinked back tears as she grabbed a spiral notebook and pen from the counter and sat down at the table. "Just . . . not yet."

Nic met Ali's gaze. "She's also a little over the top about Lori's being a senior next year."

Ali shook her head, then reached out and clasped Sarah's hand. "You're allowed to be over the top. I know I get weepy-eyed thinking about Caitlin going off to school. It's a very emotional time for both mothers and daughters."

"Yeah, well, Lori's emotional involvement revolves around her impatience to leave Eternity Springs," Sarah grumbled. "Although I will say that's changed somewhat since your son came to town, Ali. She has a serious crush on Chase."

Ali shook her head. "He's a horrible flirt."

"So what's the scoop there, Ali?" Sarah asked. "Are you glad that your son is the Double R's newest trail rider?"

"Absolutely. Last summer he worked as a whitewater rafting guide, and I swear my gray hairs multiplied like rabbits because of it."

Sarah nodded. "That would scare me, too."

"A parent can know too much," Ali told her. "It's different now than when we went off to school. Cell phones are a tether to your kids, and I'm not sure that's such a good thing. When I was off at college, my dad called me at one o'clock every Sunday afternoon. That was our time. I had to be there to take his call. But the rest of the time, he didn't know where I was or what I was doing."

"Were you a bad girl, Ali Timberlake?" Nic teased.

She paused a moment, and a wicked little grin played upon her lips. "That depends on your definition of *bad*, I guess."

Sarah groaned. "Maybe we should change the subject? I'd just as soon not think about a definition for *bad* right now."

Nic studied her friend and frowned. The tight line in Sarah's brow and the edge in her voice suggested that it might have been a really, really bad morning for Sarah, family-wise. In honor of their friendship, Nic decided to lob out a distraction. "Then I guess I'd better not say anything about Mrs. Landsbury's definition of *bad* or the grief she's been giving me."

Sarah bit. "Your next-door neighbor? What's put the bee in her bonnet?"

"She's decided I'm misbehaving, and she's keeping an awfully close eye on my house from an upstairs window." Nic paused significantly, then stared at her fingernails as she added, "It's interfering with our honeymoon."

"Honeymoon?" Sarah's eyes brightened with interest. "Are we talking figure of speech or the real deal?"

Nic rolled her tongue around her mouth. "The real deal."

Sarah slapped the table. "I knew it. I knew the man would get a brain at some point. Details, girlfriend. Dish."

Nic noted Ali's confusion and asked, "Are you not up to date on local gossip about my marriage?"

"Um . . . no. It's not really my business."

"You've never lived in a small town, have you?" Sarah observed.

"No."

"It has its challenges," Nic replied. "Having everybody know your business is one of them. Basic facts that everyone knows are that Gabe and I had to get married in the most old-fashioned sense of the word. What fewer people know but many suspect is that it hasn't been the happiest of circumstances. Very few people in town know that Gabe is a fairly recent widower, and he's had a difficult time dealing with his grief. The pregnancy happened before he was ready. However, I am happy to say that he has made great strides toward moving on in the past few weeks."

"By striding right into your bed?"

Nic grinned. "That's part of it."

"Hurrah for you, but excuse me a moment while I get bilious with jealousy," Sarah said.

Ignoring her, Nic continued. "But he's also started talking about his first wife."

"That's a good thing?" Ali asked.

"Yes. I think so."

Sarah frowned, thumping her pen against her notebook. "I don't know, Nic. Remember when I dated Danny Hardesty? It was three years after his breakup with his fiancée, but he still spent part of every date telling me how horrible she was. I felt like we needed to tell the restaurants we needed a table for three."

"It's different with a widower, I think," Nic said. "Gabe doesn't talk about her constantly, but she always has been the proverbial elephant in the room—except this elephant was a tall, dark, Sophia Loren look-alike ghost."

"Tell me he hasn't put her photo in your house," Sarah said.

"No, but I recently discovered he carries a picture of her and his baby in his wallet."

"And that's okay with you?" Ali asked.

"Sure. I don't want him to kick her out of his heart; I want him to make room there for me. I think that his ability to talk about his life with her makes that easier. Don't get me wrong—if he starts to yammer on about her like Danny Hardesty did with you, I'll reconsider. I'm walking a line here between being understanding and sympathetic and being a doormat."

"Doormat has never been a good look for you," Sarah replied, and Nic smirked in agreement.

Ali cleared her throat, then observed, "One of my husband's friends lost his wife to breast cancer after they'd been very happily married for twenty years. He told me that letting go of her was brutal; but once he'd done that, he found a special joy in discovering an equally happy relationship with another woman. He said that once he was able to commit himself to someone new, his life was richer because he had a new appreciation for life and love that made him determined to enjoy every minute of it."

"He sounds like a great guy," Sarah said. "Why can't I meet a guy like that?"

"He is a great guy," Ali replied. "And you shouldn't give up, Sarah. Who knows, your great guy could walk into the Trading Post this afternoon." To Nic, she added, "I can see Gabe being like my husband's friend."

"Me too. Gabe is a good guy, he really is. Oh, he can be a pain, don't get me wrong, but I am more hopeful today than I've been in . . . well . . . since the stick turned blue."

Sarah's teeth tugged at her bottom lip. "I hope you're right, Nic. I just . . ."

"What?"

"Never mind. I should keep my mouth shut."

"Yeah, right. Like when has that ever happened?" When Sarah scowled at her, Nic said, "Really, Sarah. I trust your instincts. I want to hear what you have to say."

"Okay. But don't get mad." Sarah sipped her tea, then said, "My fear is that you're setting yourself up for him to break your heart. I'm afraid you will always be second-best with him, and I just can't see you going through life as a consolation prize. You deserve better."

"Ouch," Ali said.

"You're right. I do deserve better and I won't hold on forever. I have too much pride for that. At some point the man will have to fish or cut bait. He'll have to make room for me in his heart, not just in his bed."

"So do you have a time period in mind, some cut-off date? And I mean that exactly like it sounds."

"I've given him until the babies are six months old to make up his mind. I won't allow him to drag his feet any longer than that. I'm trying to maintain my patience and faith. Frankly, I am making the man happy whether he wants to admit it or not. I have to believe that once he gets past the pain, he'll want the joy he had before and he'll let me, let us"—she patted her baby bump—"in. You've seen how he is with Tiger. He talks a good game, but then he slips the dog table scraps. Do you really think he'll be able to hold out against us?"

"As long as he gives you more than table scraps," Sarah said.

"Oh, that is so true," Ali agreed, her voice ringing with conviction. "A woman should never put up with table scraps."

Sarah shrugged. "Well, you make a good point. When it comes to the men in their lives, women shouldn't settle. Nic knows it. I just don't want her to forget it. She needs to think about her marriage like she does Mexican food."

"Mexican food?" Ali asked.

"We love Mexican food," Nic explained.

"And Nic deserves the whole enchilada." Sarah picked up her pen and grabbed her notebook. "Okay, enough about you. Let's talk Lori and the perfect birthday party thrown by the perfect mother."

"Not to mention," Nic said, her heart filled with love, "the perfect friends."

SEVENTEEN

Summer arrived with the influx of seasonal residents and a glorious trickle of tourists. The pace of life picked up as gift shops and restaurants opened their doors and all businesses extended their hours of operation. Between the return of the season and the spending by a constant parade of contractors working long hours at Angel's Rest, the citizens of Eternity Springs enjoyed an unusually loud jingle in their pockets.

Then the second week of June a once-in-a-generation weather system moved in over the Colorado Rockies and parked for days, dumping rain and causing significant flooding throughout the state. Eternity Springs fared better than many areas of Colorado, though early Wednesday morning Angel Creek did top its banks and only concerted sandbagging effort by townspeople along with good design on Gabe's part saved the hot springs garden from destruction. By Wednesday evening the creek returned to its banks and everyone breathed more easily while keeping a sharp eye on both the sky and radar reports.

Nic ended a busy day at the clinic: she'd released a canine heartworm patient, spayed two cats, and performed emergency surgery on the broken leg of a mountain lion kit rescued from the creek by the Cartwright boys. As she paused in the doorway of her clinic to open her umbrella, she hesitated. Something felt strange. Wrong. She set down her umbrella and made another round of the clinic looking for something, anything, out of place, but nothing stuck out. "Guess the rain is spooking me," she murmured to herself. Ordinarily this time of year, rain came from thunderstorms that moved through the valley quickly, not this dreary, steady rain that didn't stop.

She stepped outside and stayed on the path to take the long way to the house rather than step across the sodden yard to her back door. Once inside, she showered and changed into warm, dry clothes. She put chicken in the oven to bake and went into the living room, where she sat down to watch television and to wait for Gabe to come home.

The babies were active tonight, doing their kicking and punching thing that never failed to thrill her. At her appointment the previous week, her obstetrician had mentioned that by the time Nic was ready to deliver, she'd be tired of her status as a punching bag. Maybe Liz Marshall was right, but for the moment Nic enjoyed sitting quietly and feeling her babies' bump.

Except tonight she continued to be plagued by a quiet sense of unease.

Gabe and Tiger arrived home just as she pulled the chicken from the oven. Over dinner, her husband caught her up on the day's events at Angel's Rest. "As bad as this weather is, we're lucky it didn't start two weeks earlier or Celeste's grand opening might have been delayed."

"I'm glad for that, but I do worry about other businesses in town. The tourist trade is suffering."

"I know. I spoke with Henry Moreland today. He said the Double R has canceled their trail rides for the rest of the week. Even if the forecast proves true and the rain clears out tomorrow, they need three days of sunshine for things to dry out enough so that the rides won't tear up the trail."

"Will the grounds at Angel's Rest be okay for the birthday party Saturday?"

"Shouldn't be a problem," he replied.

"Good. I think—" She broke off abruptly and grimaced as she shifted in her seat to ease an ache in her back.

"You okay?" Gabe asked.

"Yeah. I think I tweaked my back bending over earlier."

He frowned at her. "You need to be more careful."

"I think my muscles are stretching—everything is out of whack."

Nic thought about that moment later as she prepared for bed and realized that the nagging backache, though mild, hadn't gone away despite the doctor-ordered stretching exercises and a doctor-approved painkiller. For the first time she felt a moment of concern.

She snapped her fingers. "I forgot to email Sage the punch recipe for tomorrow. I'll be right back."

Already in bed, worn out from a long day doing physical labor in the rain, Gabe didn't lift his head as he grunted into his pillow.

"I'm being silly," she murmured to herself as she sat down at the computer and opened the browser. She went to her favorite pregnancy website and started reading. Five minutes later, filled with unease, she drank a large glass of water, then went to bed. Lying tilted toward her left side, she rested her hands at the top of her uterus and concentrated on detecting any and all sensations.

Minutes passed without anything unusual or alarming taking place, and Nic began to relax. At some point, Gabe rolled toward her, threw an arm around her, and pulled her against him. As he snored softly into her ear, she smiled into the darkness. He made her feel protected and secure.

A quarter hour ticked by, then a half, and finally, a full hour. *Nothing is wrong. I'm imagining everything. First time being pregnant and I'm clueless and fretting over nothing. A backache by itself isn't reason for concern. Go to sleep. You'll be better in the morning. Everything will be better after a good night's sleep.*

As the constant rain beat a staccato rhythm on her roof, she snuggled up against Gabe, said a prayer for all her loved ones, and willed herself to sleep. Downstairs, the Westminster chime of the mantel clock in the parlor chimed midnight.

Gabe awoke abruptly and blinked into the darkness. All his senses went on alert. Something was wrong.

He felt the bed beside him. Nic lay there, soft, warm, and asleep. So what had woken him up? A sound that didn't belong? It was raining so hard it all but drowned out other sounds. He sniffed the air, thinking fire, but noted nothing except the subtle, sexy fragrance of Nic's peaches-and-spice lotion.

Then . . . a touch. A brush against his arm.

A paw.

Oh, for crying out loud. Sighing, he threw off the covers and sat up. He could barely make out the dog's form in the darkness. Stupid dog. Gabe had put him out before they'd gone to bed. Softly, so as not to wake his wife, he said, "I ought to let you out and leave you out."

Wearing only his boxers, Gabe trod sleepily downstairs. Halfway down, he realized the dog hadn't followed him. "What now?" he muttered. Then, in a voice just above a whisper, he called, "Hey, dog. C'mon."

Still nothing.

"Grrr," Gabe grumbled. He trudged back upstairs and reentered his bedroom. What was wrong with the mutt? For a dog, he was relatively smart. It wasn't like him to do something—

"Ouch!" Gabe yelped as his bare foot came down on something sharp on the floor.

"Gabe?" Nic asked, sitting up in bed and switching on the lamp. "What's wrong?"

"I stepped on . . . a stapler? How did that get in the middle of the floor?"

"Oh, man. I was finally asleep."

"Sorry, but I'm only partially to blame. The dog woke me up. I thought he wanted out, but apparently not. And if that weren't enough, he dragged the stapler off the desk and dropped it in the middle of the doorway, where I'd step on it."

"Tiger wouldn't do that," Nic protested. "Look, he's curled up in his bed sound asleep. You must have been dreaming."

"That dog shouldn't be sleeping in here anyway. He snores."

"Well, yes, but so do you." With that, Nic threw off the bedcovers and padded into the master bathroom.

Gabe scowled down at the dog. He had plenty of places to sleep—Nic had dog beds scattered in almost every room in the house. "It's about time I assert myself as the alpha dog in the pack," Gabe declared. From now on, the boxer would be banished from the bedroom.

As he bent over to grab the dog bed and wake the troublemaker, a frightened gasp from the bathroom distracted him. He jerked upright. "Nic?"

"Gabe, something's wrong. I think . . . oh, God . . . Gabe, I'm having contractions."

"What do you mean, CareFlight isn't available?" Gabe yelled into the telephone's receiver as he rifled through a pile of newspapers on the counter in the kitchen. Where had he left his keys?

"I'm sorry, sir. There's been a horrible accident on the highway east of Montrose. An eighteen-wheeler hit a bus. All birds in the area are tied up there."

"Then send someone from Colorado Springs."

"The weather has flights grounded along the front range. I'll send someone as soon as possible, but you need to understand it will be a couple of hours before anyone can get to you."

"Fine." He slammed down the phone with a curse, then turned to Nic, who was securing the boxer in his crate. "It'll be two hours at least," he told her. "What do we do?"

"I'm afraid to wait." She gestured toward the kitchen table, where his keys lay in plain sight. "You'd better drive me."

Five minutes later, they were on the road. For the first fifteen minutes of the trip, neither of them spoke. Tension was a living, breathing beast riding with them.

Nic sat with a small spiral notebook and a pencil in hand. When he noticed her writing something, he glanced at the dashboard, where the clock's red numerals read 3:42. "Another contraction?"

"Yes."

Damn. His natural inclination was to punch the gas pedal, but the storm, the terrain, and his own horrific history behind the wheel kept him driving at a safe speed.

"It's probably nothing," Nic said. "This whole thing is probably just a case of a first-time mom who doesn't know what she's doing. Dr. Marshall said checking me was just a precaution."

"Uh-huh."

They rode in silence for another twenty minutes before Gabe said in a grim tone. "Eternity Springs doesn't need a healing center. It needs a hospital, or at the very least a full-service medical clinic with a real staff of real doctors. If you'd had a heart attack, you'd be dead."

"No, actually we're well-equipped to deal with heart attacks. The town paid for EMT training for six people. The system usually works. It's just our bad luck that I'm having this trouble while another serious medical situation is taking place under horrible weather conditions."

Gabe wanted to argue back, but he decided to keep his mouth shut for the time being. The last thing she needed now was more stress. Besides, if this did prove to be a false alarm and she and the babies were okay, he intended to see that the situation changed. Forget Eternity Springs. For the remainder of the pregnancy, they could move to somewhere civilized, near a hospital with a neonatal unit and a perinatologist on staff.

Beside him, Nic made another mark in her notebook. Gabe felt his tension level rise from orange to red. What would he do if she started to hemorrhage? If her water broke? If she passed out?

"Do you mind if I put on a CD?" she said.

"Huh? What?" *Did she say she was bleeding?*

"I'd like music. I want to play a CD."

"Oh. Okay. Sure."

"What would you like to listen to?"

"Your choice." He bit out the words. "I really don't care."

Rain fell in sheets as Norah Jones' smoky voice drifted from the stereo. He kept his windshield wipers set at full speed, the headlights on high, and his teeth clenched tight. Despite his need for focus, his mind drifted back to another middle-of-the-night, I'm-having-contractions trip to a hospital. That night he'd been tense, too, only that tension had been fueled with anticipation rather than dread. Jen had been five days past her due date, excited and relieved that the big moment was finally under way.

He'd held her hand that night as they made the fifteen-minute trip to the hospital. Tonight, though, he needed both hands on the wheel. He and Jen had laughed and joked during the drive that night—another contrast with current events.

What a magical night that had been. Jen had awakened him with a big kiss on his mouth. Gabe had pulled on suit pants and a Jimmy Buffett T-shirt. Jen had taken one look at him and made him go back and change.

He would never forget the joy that had filled him the moment Matt slid into the doctor's hands, took his first breath, and let out his first angry cry. He'd been full. So full. When he held his son for the first time, he had truly believed that the bad times were all behind him.

Nic interrupted his reverie when she said, "Maybe I didn't hydrate well enough. Do you still keep bottled water in the back?"

"I think I have a soft cooler right behind my seat. If you can't reach it, I'll pull off and get it for you."

Nic leaned toward him and stretched her left arm behind his seat. "Almost."

He remembered how Jen used to lean over like that and lay her head against his shoulder as she reached to pick up a toy that Matty had thrown down.

Nic stretched again, then used her right arm to loosen the catch on her seat belt.

"Don't do that!" Gabe snapped when he realized what she'd done. He all but expected a car to come careening out of the darkness toward them. In their lane. "Put your seat belt back on. I'll stop and get the water myself."

"I've got it." When Nic withdrew her arm from behind him, she held a bottle of water. She buckled her belt, settled back in her seat, and calmly twisted the bottle cap, then took a long sip.

"Don't ever do that again," Gabe demanded, his voice

raised, his fingers clamped around the steering wheel. "It's stupid enough to do it under normal circumstances, but look outside. Look at the rain and the road. These are dangerous driving conditions."

"Gabe, really. It was just a few seconds."

"It only takes a second." His chest grew tight as memories flashed through his mind. "Believe me."

She stared at him for a moment, then winced. "I'm sorry. You're right. I shouldn't have unbuckled. I should have asked you to pull over. My mind is on the babies. Since dehydration can cause contractions, all I thought about was getting more water into me as fast as possible."

"I get it. Just . . . don't do it again."

"I won't." She sipped her water and added, "I promise."

I promise. His throat constricted with emotion; nevertheless, a tiny sound of pain escaped. Those two little words echoed through his mind and pierced his heart.

Hold on, Jen. Please. Help will be here soon. Don't leave me. Please, dear Lord, help us. Jen, hold on. Don't leave me!

I won't. I promise.

They were the last words Jen said to him before she died in his arms.

Grimly he attempted to push the thought aside as he stared ahead, concentrating on his driving, balancing the needs for speed and safety to the best of his ability. But as the miles and minutes ticked by, events from his past assailed him and a sense of inevitability weighted his heart and soul.

This wouldn't end well. It never did. He never should have let down his guard.

As that thought crystallized in his mind, the car rounded a curve and the animal's eyes flashed in the beam of the headlights as an elk bounded from the trees directly in front of them. Gabe instinctively braked and twisted the wheel. The tires skidded. The car began to hydroplane. Nic screamed. *Jen screamed.*

The elk bounced off the front fender and disappeared into the woods as the airbags deployed.

Airbags deployed. Metal crunched. Matt's cry stopped abruptly.

The Jeep slid off the road and came to rest softly against a stand of piñon pines. Beside him, his wife cried out, "Gabe?"

A chemical scent filled the air. "Jen, are you all right?"

She let out a little whimper of pain. "Nic. I'm Nic. Can we drive? Please tell me we're not stuck."

Nic. I'm with Nic. Gabe glanced in the backseat. No smashed car seat. No broken little boy. This was Colorado, not Virginia. Nic, not Jennifer. Twin babies on the way, not his beloved little Matt.

He looked at Nic, barely able to see her in the shadows. *She's moving. She's talking.* Gabe blew out a breath, released his death grip around the steering wheel, and dragged a trembling hand down his face, then switched on the dome light. "Nicole, are you hurt?"

She was as pale as a corpse. Urgently he asked, "Are you bleeding?"

"No. Just scraped up a bit, I think, from the airbag. Are we stranded, Gabe?"

He took stock. The windshield wipers kept up their rhythmic motion. Norah Jones still sang. The motor continued to run. They had four-wheel drive. He'd get them out of here if he had to push the Jeep back onto the road himself. "We're not stranded," he told her, opening his door. "I'll be right back."

Cold rain doused him and he vaguely noted the scrapes on his own skin stinging as he rounded the front of the car. The dent in the passenger-side front panel sucked the breath right out of his lungs. Two seconds later and the elk would have come through Nic's window. She could have died.

Nausea struck him and he staggered back a step, leaned over with his hands on his knees, and vomited. Then he stood and lifted his face into the cold, driving rain, but he knew he couldn't tarry. The clock was still ticking.

He returned to the Jeep. "The ground is spongy but not a quagmire," he told Nic. "Getting out should be no problem." With a deft touch he guided the Jeep back onto the road.

Gabe didn't protest when Nic switched on the heater and ejected the CD. He was cold to the bone, though he doubted anything so simple as a heater could warm him. He was lost in a nightmare made up of now and of then. He could smell blood on the air even while he knew he was in Colorado and not in Virginia. What if the doctor couldn't stop her labor? What if the babies died? What if Nic died? Jen had died. He'd been alone. He'd be alone again.

He was terrified.

They completed the trip to Gunnison in silence.

At the hospital, he pulled into the circular drive in front of the emergency entrance, shifted into park, and looked at her. Light from the emergency room sign turned her pale complexion bloodred. He saw both fear and urgency in her eyes and knew his own eyes must reflect the same emotions. "Wait here until I get help, okay?"

"Sure."

Even before he rounded the Jeep, the ER's automatic doors whooshed open and a man wearing scrubs pushed an empty wheelchair toward them. "Is this Mrs. Callahan?" he asked.

"Yes."

"Dr. Marshall is waiting for her."

Gabe opened Nic's door and he and the ER employee helped her into the chair. "If you'll take the first right and go down to the end of the hall, Admitting has paperwork for you to sign, Mr. Callahan. Your wife will be to the left in room three. You'll want to move your car before you join her."

"Okay."

Nic looked back over her shoulder at him, her expression rife with worry, her blue eyes pleading for him to hurry. He tried to smile reassuringly, but he simply couldn't get his lips to lift.

Gabe made his way to Admitting. In his mind's eye, he was back in a Virginia hospital, his clothing covered in blood—his blood, hers. Matt's. *Oh, God. Matty.*

"May I have your insurance card?"

A policeman saying, *His wife is DOA.*

"Sir? Your insurance card?"

"What? Oh." He winced. "Sorry."

Blindly he signed whatever papers she put in front of him. Fear was a cold stone in his gut. Nic. The babies. *What if I lose her? Lose them?*

He dragged his feet returning to the ER. He was cold, wet, frozen. Terrified. Spying a men's room, he detoured into it. He ran hot water into the sink, leaned over, and splashed his face. Words echoed in his mind. *So sorry for your loss, Mr. Callahan. Such a tragedy. She was such a joyous spirit. Our condolences, Gabe.*

He looked in the mirror, but didn't see himself. He saw the fear in Nic's eyes. *The fear in Jen's eyes. She knew she was dying.* What about Nic? What about the babies?

He reached for a paper towel and dried his face, dried his hands. Saw blood on his hands, both real and imagined.

Someone else walked into the men's room, so he

walked out. He walked past the exit and found room three. He stood outside the curtained enclosure, numb, cold, and alone as he listened to Nic's obstetrician asking a series of questions.

On the other side of the curtain, he heard Nic murmur a question he couldn't make out. The doctor responded by saying, "I won't lie to you, Nic. If you are in labor and we can't stop it, the babies won't survive."

The babies won't survive.

The boy has a traumatic brain injury. It's only a matter of time.

The doctor continued, "We don't have the facilities here to accommodate babies born at twenty-four weeks."

But the words didn't register. All Gabe heard was . . .

The babies won't survive.

Your son is dead.

My family didn't survive.

"My babies won't survive," he whispered.

Breathing heavily, his fists clenching and then releasing at his sides, Gabe backed away from the curtain and . . . broke.

He walked—almost ran—to the hospital exit. Dashing out into the rain, he climbed into the Jeep, started the engine, and shifted into gear.

Gabe drove away. Leaving his wife, his babies, and his self-respect behind.

EIGHTEEN

❧

"Nic? Honey? What's wrong?"

Nic tore her gaze away from the monitor and looked up to see her best friend in the world standing at the opening of the ER's curtained cubicle. "Honey? What's wrong?"

"Oh, Sarah." She burst into tears.

Sarah rushed to the bed and put her hands on Nic's shoulders. "Honey?"

"You came. You're here." Nic buried her head against Sarah's chest and sobbed. Sarah held her tight, cooing, "It's okay, Nic. I'm here. It's okay."

Nic cried and cried and cried. Sarah hugged and cuddled and comforted. When Nic finally wound down, Sarah softly asked, "The babies?"

"They're okay."

"Thank God. What happened? We were so worried—Celeste and Sage are with me, they're parking the car. What happened? Gabe called me and said you were here and that you needed me. Then he hung up and hasn't answered his phone since. I must have called twenty times."

"He did it again, Sarah. He ran away from his feelings, only this time I needed him. I really, really needed him. I can't believe he . . ."

"He what?"

Nic closed her eyes. What could she say? He'd hurt

her? That didn't begin to explain the devastation. Gabe had ripped her heart out. He'd left her here alone, maybe losing her babies alone. These hours had been the worst of her life, this fear the worst she'd ever known. How could he have abandoned her? How could he have left her to face it alone?

Nic told her about the tension-filled drive to Gunnison, and Sarah said, "You hit an elk? And slid off the road? Oh, Nic. You're lucky you weren't killed!"

"I know it scared him. I know he has ghosts riding his shoulder. But that's no excuse for this!"

"No excuse for what?" Sage asked as she and Celeste entered the cubicle. "What has Gabe done?"

"He left me. He basically kicked me out at the ER door to miscarry our babies all by myself."

Sage's eyes flew to the monitors. "You didn't lose the babies."

"No, thank God," Nic said, blinking back angry tears. "But Gabe didn't know that when he abandoned me here."

"He left you?" Celeste clarified, her brow furrowing in concern.

Nic nodded. "I thought . . . we both thought . . . that I was losing the babies. I'd had a backache and a general sense that something was wrong. Then I started feeling contractions, and I called Dr. Marshall and she told me to come in. CareFlight couldn't come, so he drove me. He signed the admission papers, then he left. Didn't say good-bye or anything. He just left."

Celeste clucked her tongue. "Oh, Gabe."

"We didn't know if I was in labor or not. If the babies were in danger or not. He left me to face it alone."

"I can't believe he'd do that," Sage murmured, gazing at her with what Nic could only interpret to be pity. That made it even worse.

"That's exactly what he did. At first I thought it was taking an exceptionally long time to fill out paperwork. Eventually I asked the nurse to go find him. When she returned from the parking lot with the news that the Jeep was nowhere in sight . . ." Nic closed her eyes. "I realized he'd run out on me. I swear it hurt worse than walking in on Greg and his lover in our bed."

Sarah folded her arms and tapped her toes. "That's unforgivable, Nic. Totally unforgivable."

Celeste sighed heavily and shook her head. "I do believe that men can be the dumbest of God's creatures."

Sage took hold of Nic's hand. "But you're okay? The three of you are all right?"

Again Nic nodded, swallowing against the lump of emotion in her throat. "She's going to keep us here and monitor us until noon just as a precaution, and after that . . ."

"Bed rest?" Sarah asked.

"Maybe. We discussed it. I guess the newest studies show it's often unnecessary. That said, I'd rather be safe than sorry. That's why . . ." Nic paused and licked her lips.

"I'm not going back to Eternity Springs. I've decided to go to Denver for the duration of the pregnancy, or at least until we've passed the magic twenty-eight-week mark. Dr. Marshall is setting me up with a perinatologist there, and she says they have a great newborn intensive care facility in Aurora."

Sage nodded. "The Children's Hospital has a state-of-the-art NICU."

"You shouldn't let that sorry dog run you out of town," Sarah snapped. "Eternity Springs is your home."

Nic lifted her chin. "I'm not running anywhere. I'm protecting my babies. After this, I'm a little gun-shy about trusting their lives to CareFlight." Smiling at Celeste, she added, "I'm going to hate missing the grand opening."

"Well, there is a good chance you won't." Celeste smiled at the ER nurse who brought her a chair, then said, "Zach Turner called while we were on our way here. There's been a mud and rock slide on the mountain behind Angel's Rest. It's done a substantial amount of damage to the new buildings in back. Thankfully, no one was hurt, but our ahead-of-schedule status just took a knockout punch, I'm afraid. I'm going to reschedule the grand opening for around Labor Day."

"Labor Day." Nic gave a bittersweet smile. "Dr. Marshall said I should shoot for that as my red-letter day. If I can carry the babies that long, they won't be considered premature."

"Cool." Sarah gave her a thumbs-up. "We'll plan a ribbon cutting and a cord cutting on the same day."

Celeste patted Nic's leg and said, "What can we do to help, dear? Do you want me to talk to Gabe?"

Nic shook her head. "No. Thanks, Celeste, but the things Gabe Callahan needs to hear, I need to say."

She'd started a list of them between six and seven o'clock this morning. She was already on page four.

Her friends kept her company until activity in the ER picked up and the nurse declared that two of her three visitors must leave. "I'll go," Sarah said. "I'd like to run a couple of errands before we head back."

Sage spoke to Celeste. "You mentioned you needed to pick up something at the motorcycle shop. Why don't I stay with Nic while you guys do your errands, then we can stop by Julio's for lunch before we hit the road." To Nic she added, "You are going home before you leave for Denver, aren't you?"

"Yes. I need to pack up some necessities, and I'm going to call Ali Timberlake and see if she can help me figure out a place to stay. She knows Denver better than I do."

Sarah leaned over the hospital bed and gave Nic a hug. "I'm so glad this was a false alarm. I think Gabe Callahan needs a swift kick in the butt."

"I won't argue with either point."

When Sarah moved aside, Celeste leaned over the bed and kissed Nic's forehead. "All will be well, Nic, dear. Have faith."

"I'm sorry about Angel's Rest."

"Don't be. Nothing happened there that can't be fixed." Eyeing Nic meaningfully, she added, "The same as here."

Pesky tears stung Nic's eyes again at that. She wanted to argue, but instead she said simply, "Thanks for coming."

When they left, Sage pulled up a chair beside the bed and took a seat. Nic saw her study the monitors and nod knowingly. Nic had the sense that Sage felt right at home. She blurted the question without thinking. "Have you been in my shoes before, Sage?"

"Hmm? You mean, has a man ever let me down royally?"

"The monitors. You look at them like you know what they mean. I'm sorry, it's nosy of me, but . . . it made me wonder if you've been pregnant."

Sage shook her head. "No, never pregnant, but I am familiar with fetal monitors."

She stood up and paced the room, her arms folded, her long broomstick skirt swishing around her ankles, her expression agitated. "Look, Nic. If I tell you something—a deep, dark secret—will you promise to keep it to yourself and not use it against me?"

Nic's brow knitted. Her deepest, darkest secret? Use it against her? What in the world did Sage have to confess?

"Of course I'll keep your confidence, Sage. You have my word."

Sage licked her lips. "Okay. Well. Nic, it's like this. This move to Denver . . . that's a drastic decision considering you've had a normal pregnancy so far. Are you truly worried about medical care?"

"After today, yes, I am."

"For CareFlight to be unavailable . . . that was such an aberration."

"I know, but it's more than that. Dr. Marshall wants to see me every two weeks for a while and weekly after that. That's a lot of trips to Gunnison."

"What if . . . there was a doctor in town? A specialist?"

Nic figured it out then and wondered why it had taken her so long. "You're a doctor, Sage?"

"I was. I am. I . . . oh, dear. Nic, I trained as an obstetrical surgeon. If you don't want to go to Denver, I'm well qualified to oversee your pregnancy."

"You're a *doctor*? That's your *secret*?"

Sage shoved her fingers through her thick auburn hair. "Look, it's a long story that's not worth going into if you are sure about Denver. If you want to stay in Eternity, I'll give you my curriculum vitae, but I'll need at least a full bottle of wine to get through the story."

"Oh, this is so not fair. Not only do you tease me with the story of the century, or at least the month, but you tease me with alcohol I can't drink."

Sage looked at her and laughed. "You're okay, aren't you, Nic? This incident . . . his idiocy . . . hasn't broken you."

"I'm not broken. I'm angry. In fact, I'm furious."

Sage's gaze stole to the monitors and she smirked. "Your blood pressure supports that statement. Do you want to talk about it? Would that help?"

Nic flopped her head back against the pillow. "Thanks,

but no. I think I need time to lick my wounds. Pretty good job, by the way, of deflecting the subject away from you, Dr. Anderson."

She grimaced. "Look, Nic, you've been a wonderful friend to me. When you had your accident, I failed to step up and it's haunted me ever since. For lots of reasons that have nothing to do with legalities or my license, I can't practice medicine anymore, but I can be your obstetrician if you'd like. I want you to have the choice."

"Thank you. That means a lot to me." Nic placed both hands on her belly and rubbed it. "I think, though, that I'll still go to Denver. It's not only the medical issues that make me want to leave Eternity. I need some time to myself, I think. Time away from Gabe. I need to reassess my . . . well, everything."

"I understand. Would you like me to accompany you to Denver, just to see you settled? Maybe meet with your new doctor?"

"Yes. Absolutely, Sage. I admit I was worried about the trip part of this."

"Don't worry one bit. I'm here for you."

Sage's words warmed her heart and lingered in her mind as later that afternoon she returned home to Eternity Springs. When she spied Tiger lounging on the front porch, she tensed. She hadn't expected Gabe to be home this time of day.

But Tiger's presence proved to be a false indication. Gabe wasn't home after all. Nic went about her tasks, retrieving suitcases from the attic and filling them with necessities. She wasn't taking much. She didn't need much. She didn't intend to do much more than lounge around, grow her babies, and figure out where to go from here.

She packed her suitcases lightly, carried them to her

car, then sat in the rocker in the library with Tiger at her feet.

She dialed Gabe's cell phone. When he failed to pick up, she left a message. "I'm home. I'd like to talk to you. I'll be here until six."

She thumbed the disconnect button and waited.

Gabe stopped to buy flowers.

He knew he owed her much more than a dozen red roses, but he figured this would be as good a place as any to start. He had a lot of ground to make up. Walking out on her that way had been a lousy thing to do. He was counting on Nic's forgiving nature to help him out of the hole he'd dug for himself.

Fleeing the hospital had been the single most cowardly act of his life. He still couldn't believe he'd been such an ass. He'd peeled out of that parking lot as if the hounds of hell were at his back. He'd made the two-hour trip back to Eternity Springs in ninety minutes. On wet roads.

He'd driven home, grabbed the bottle of scotch, and taken a long, hot shower. When neither the hot water nor the potent whiskey warmed him, he'd gone to Angel's Rest and worked outside, moving mud beneath a finally clearing sky. The physical work eventually chased away the numbness, and he'd nutted up the courage to call the hospital. Nic's doctor had been as cold as Murphy Mountain in January when she'd given him the good news. Hearing that Nic and both babies were fine and on their way home had made him go weak in the knees all over again.

Then he'd thought about facing Nic, and his stomach took to rolling all over again.

Now the time had come to take his medicine. He'd showered and changed into clean clothes before leaving Angel's Rest. As he pulled his Jeep into the drive, he wondered why Nic had left her car on the street. Grabbing the flowers, which the florist had wrapped in green tissue paper and tied with red ribbon, he drew a bracing breath, planned his opening sentence, and climbed the front steps. He opened the front door, spied Nic in her rocking chair looking ripe and beautiful and cold, and his smooth apology flew from his mind, leaving only the basic fact. Crossing the room, he handed her the roses and said, "Nic, I'm so sorry."

She set the flowers aside with barely a look. "Yeah, Callahan, you are."

So he was going to have to work for her forgiveness. He deserved that. He stepped back, noticing for the first time that the boxer sat at her feet. Funny—usually the mutt ran at him the moment he walked in the door. *Hope he isn't sick.*

Dismissing the dog, Gabe rubbed the back of his neck. "I don't have excuses, just an explanation. Will you listen to it?"

"Gabe, there's no—"

"Please?" he interrupted.

She closed her eyes and made a sweeping gesture with her hand.

"You probably figured out that I had what amounted to a flashback in the Jeep because I called you Jen. The two incidents were . . . totally different and yet eerily similar. Horribly similar. I snapped, Nic. That's the long and the short of it. I went a little crazy thinking about losing the babies like I'd lost Matt, losing you like I'd lost Jennifer."

He paused, expecting her to offer a word of comfort like she always did. This time, however, she remained silent. Quiet and cold.

It appeared that he'd screwed up even worse than he'd thought. Maybe it was time to pull out the big guns.

Gabe sat in the club chair opposite Nic, propped his

elbows on his knees, and leaned forward earnestly. "Here's what I've figured out, Nic. I can move on from Jen. I have moved on from Jen. Her face no longer haunts me. I don't hear her voice in my head. You are the woman who haunts me now, Nicole. I've moved on to *you*. I'm in love with *you*."

After a moment's hesitation, her mouth twisted. "So what now? Do the heavens part and the angels sing? Are the babes in my womb supposed to leap for joy?"

Gabe sat back, shocked at her bitter tone and the flash of temper in her eyes as she picked up speed. "Well, guess what? That's not happening. You had your chance, Gabe, and you blew it. I gave you everything I had—my sympathy, my compassion, my patience. I was your soft place to fall and you abused it. Abused me. You are worse than my father."

"Wait a minute—"

"At least Bryce Randall never lied to me. He never pretended to care. Never pretended that he'd be there if I needed him. When he left us, he did it honestly. He never once gave me hope. That's your sin, Callahan. You allowed me to hope and dream for my happily ever after. Let me tell you, this is more horror movie than chick flick happy ending."

"That's not fair."

"Too bad. None of this is fair." She rose from the rocking chair, put her hands on her hips, and glared at him. "I've finally figured out that grief is your lifeblood. You thrive on it."

That pissed him off. "You think I want to grieve?" He stood, his hands balled at his sides. "You think I enjoy having my heart ripped open and bleeding?"

She shook a finger at him. "See, there you go. Your grief is as much a part of you as your DNA. It's all about you. It's been all about you from day one. Well, guess what, Callahan. It's not anymore. Now it's about these babies. They are the future. You know, I never asked you to forget your past. Never. But you damn sure need to keep the past in the past and remember that you didn't die with them, Gabe." She laid a hand over her womb and added, "These babies are proof of that. But no, you cling to your grief like a lifeline. So much for moving on."

"It's the babies. Don't you see? I can move on from Jen, but not from Matt. Never from Matt. Haven't you noticed that I seldom talk about him? I can't. His smiles haven't faded in my mind. His giggles still ring in my ears. Sometimes I swear I still feel him wrapping my finger in his tiny fist. That's why these babies frighten me so much. If you'd lost them this morning . . . they are people now. They have fingers and toes and little button noses. I couldn't see that. I couldn't be part of it."

"And I could? I could do it alone?" She stood straight and tall and proud. Furious. "You left me there in a cold and lonely hospital to wait out tests to see if our children would survive. Do you have any idea how long that wait was? I'll tell you. It was the longest half hour of my life. And I did it alone. No husband. No friend. No one. Do you know how awful that was?"

He closed his eyes. He didn't have a response for that.

"Look, Gabe, it's true you've walked a path no one should be forced to travel. But, frankly, your grief and your fear are your problem. I'm done letting them be mine. I refuse to let them be these babies' problem. Once upon a time, I thought that the best thing I could do for my children was to give them you as a father. I don't think that anymore. What you did today devastated me. I won't give you the opportunity to hurt our babies."

"What are you saying?" he asked, raking his hand through his hair. "Look, Nic, I screwed up. Big-time. I realize that. Dropping you off at the hospital is one of the worst mistakes I've ever made and I'm ashamed for having done it. But I've learned from it. Nic, I'll go to grief counseling. It won't happen again."

"Fine. Good. I hope you do go to counseling because I've never known a man who needs it more. However, it's not my concern. Not anymore. I'm leaving, Gabe."

"You're what?" He'd heard her wrong, hadn't he?

"I'm moving to Denver."

He'd heard her right. *Oh, hell.* He took a step back, reeling from the blow. He'd hurt her worse than he'd realized. She was leaving him. Giving up on him.

It was his fault. He'd done this himself. To himself. To them.

"After today, I want to be near a newborn intensive care unit until the babies are born."

He blinked. "Is there a problem with the pregnancy? Did the doctor tell you to do this?" He held his breath, waiting for her answer.

"No, it's my decision."

"Okay. Good. I think that's good." He straightened his spine and declared, "I'll come with you."

She looked away from him and blinked back tears. Angry tears, he knew. She wasn't sad. She was furious. Coldly, bitterly furious.

He was losing her. Losing his family. Again. Only this time, for the first time, it was all his fault.

He knew what she was going to say before she opened her mouth.

"No, you won't," she replied, her voice calm and matter-of-fact. "I'm not just leaving Eternity Springs, John Gabriel Callahan. I'm leaving you."

NINETEEN

   Nic didn't think twice about using the credit cards and accessing the bank account Gabe had set up for her to fund her summer in Denver. She didn't spend foolishly, and besides, he was living rent-free in her house, wasn't he? Ali had helped her find a pretty duplex to rent ten minutes away from both her perinatologist's office and the hospital she'd use if she had trouble, and then she nested.

   She enrolled in classes her doctor recommended for her. She joined a Mothers of Multiples group, wandered the aisles of Babies "R" Us, and spent a good portion of every day off her feet as directed. Most of all, she tried not to think about Gabe Callahan. Doing so invariably raised her blood pressure, and that wasn't good for the babies.

   She also entertained visitors. Her friends gave her the solitude she requested—up to a point. At least one of them called her every day to check on her and update her about summer events in Eternity Springs. The most welcome news was the return of normal summer sunshine. The town had dried out, the tourists had returned, and the season was in full swing. The June art festival had been a rousing success. The summer solstice 5K run went off without a hitch, and the theater group performed the new play based on the Lost Angel murder mystery to record crowds and Celeste's disdain. Dear friends that they were, they never said a word about Gabe.

Nor did they settle for just phone calls. Ali welcomed Nic into her world and included her at weekend barbecues and on shopping trips as she and her daughter prepared for her senior year of high school. Sarah visited Nic her second week in town, Celeste the third. Even her mother and aunt flew in from Florida to visit, and they only agreed to return home when Nic promised to call at the first sign of labor. When her doorbell rang the first week of August, Nic figured the rotation was back around to Sage. Instead, she opened the door to find Lori, Chase Timberlake, and Tiger on her doorstep. Nic smiled with delight. "What a great surprise. What are you two doing in Denver? I talked to Celeste a little while ago, but she didn't mention you were in town."

Shocked, their wide-eyed gazes locked on her belly, they failed to answer her question. "Whoa, Dr. Nic," Lori said. "You look like you're about to pop."

"Or explode," Chase said.

"Gee, thanks, you two," Nic said as she looked up from greeting Tiger, who was circling her and barking with joy. She stepped back to let them in. "I'm so glad you came all this way to tell me I look fat."

"Not fat," Chase hastened to say. Unlike Lori, he didn't know Nic well enough to be aware that she was teasing. "You look gorgeous as always. Just, well, bigger. We're here because I need to visit my folks and Lori wanted to see you."

"You look like you're trying to sneak a beach ball into a rock concert, only you didn't get the memo to bring the inflatable kind," Lori said, her lips twitching. "A really big beach ball."

"Brat." Nic pulled Lori into her arms for a hug, then gave one to Chase for good measure. Stepping away, she rested her hands on the small of her back. "I am much more sympathetic now to animals who deliver litters. Carrying two is challenge enough. Can you imagine having five?"

Lori shuddered. "I can't imagine having one. I think when I decide to have kids, I'll adopt."

Nic laughed as she cleared the quilt square she'd been working on for the Patchwork Angels Quilting Bee's second project from the couch, then gestured for her visitors to have a seat. "Make yourselves at home."

"If it's okay with you, Dr. Callahan, we thought Lori could visit while I go do my errand at home. I can pick her up in about an hour?"

"That's fine."

After Chase departed, Nic sent Lori to the kitchen to pour glasses of lemonade for the two of them, then lowered herself into her chair, propped her feet up on the ottoman, and took note of the time. She needed to stay off her feet for at least half an hour.

Lori returned to the living room a few moments later, handed Nic her drink, then took a seat on the sofa. Nic studied the young woman. Ah, she knew that look. This was obviously not a simple pleasure trip. How many times had she played the role of arbitrator between mother and daughter? *Ah, sweetheart, growing up is hard, isn't it?* "So, child of my heart, what is wrong? Are you having boy trouble with Chase?"

"No. He's a good guy. I'm a little sad that he'll be leaving Eternity soon. He's been the best summer romance."

"Nothing more?"

The girl shrugged. "We're too young."

Nic nodded. "How's your mom doing?"

"Okay. She's still weird about me being a senior this year, but the summer has been so busy that she's not acting as crazy as she did there for a little while. She's not the person I'm worried about now, though. Nic, you have to do something about Gabe."

"I don't want to discuss Gabe."

"Okay, we don't have to talk about it. You just need to read this letter from Celeste." Lori pulled an envelope from her bag and handed it to Nic. "She said to tell you she thought it best you read the letter first, then you should call her if you have any questions."

Nic set the envelope down without opening it.

"She said it's important," Lori added. "A matter of life and death."

Nic pursed her lips and frowned. She didn't want to read the letter. She didn't care what defense her women friends mounted in his behalf; it wouldn't change the way she felt.

"Please, Nic?"

Nic scowled. How downright sneaky of Celeste. She knew that Nic had no will against Lori's puppy dog eyes. She'd never been able to tell that girl no about anything. Releasing a long, heavy sigh, she picked up the envelope, removed the letter, and began reading.

Pam had called Celeste because she was worried about Gabe. She'd told Celeste that when Gabe was keeping vigil with her at her husband's hospital bed, he had confessed a frightful tale about a near suicide attempt last fall. As Nic read the details, her blood ran cold.

That had been right before she'd met Gabe. *Oh, my.* The information landed a solid blow against her anger at her husband.

"Now he's holed up at Eagle's Way again all alone," Lori said. "You know how you said that Tiger had claimed Gabe as his person? Well, now the dog's cut him loose. Tiger won't stay with him. That's why we brought him down to you."

Nic worriedly eyed the dog. "Gabe didn't mistreat Tiger. I can't believe he'd do that."

"No, that's not it at all. I think Tiger is as fed up with Gabe as you are. Now, though, Gabe doesn't have anybody. As far as I can tell, he just sits around brooding. Sage went up to Eagle's Way on an errand for Celeste. She said he wouldn't talk to her, he looked like he'd been drinking, and he hadn't shaved in a while. You have to talk to him."

Nic stood up and started to pace the room until she remembered she was supposed to be sitting down and returned to her chair. Lori didn't understand what she was asking. "If he's shutting people out, what makes you think I'll be able to reach him?"

"Because he loves you! It's obvious."

Nic rubbed her belly with both hands. She didn't want to call him. She'd sworn to herself that she wouldn't contact him until the babies were born, and even then all she intended to say was that they were healthy. But if he'd really considered killing himself in the past . . .

"Please, Nic."

She blew out a sigh, took a sip of lemonade, and said, "Oh, all right. Hand me the phone."

Gabe sat on a boulder beside the bubbling mountain creek downhill from Eagle's Way and tried to work up the enthusiasm to fish. Davenport was coming out on Saturday and he'd promised him trout for supper. Considering that he'd yet to stock the freezer with a single fish since his return to Eagle's Way, he needed to get a hook in the water.

But fishing wasn't any fun anymore. Not without Nic. Without his family.

Gabe watched a small green leaf turn and swirl its way downstream

"Carried along to its destiny by forces beyond its control," came a voice from behind him. "Do you feel that way, John Gabriel?"

Startled, he almost fell off the boulder. "Celeste? Where did you come from?"

She waved toward where her Honda Gold Wing stood in the parking area, not fifty yards from where he sat. How had he not heard her arrive?

Immediately a more pressing thought occurred. Why had she come? His blood turned to ice as the likely reason exploded like a nuclear bomb in his brain. Nic. Celeste had his phone number. She'd have called unless it was something big. Something bad.

Had Nic gone into labor? It was too early. Despite the miracle of modern medicine, the babies might not survive this early. Was that why Celeste had come? To deliver that news?

Gabe shoved off the rock and turned to face her, his hands fisted at his sides, bracing himself against the news he'd anticipated for weeks. "What happened?"

"Nic and the babies are just fine, Gabe. I spoke with her this morning. You, on the other hand . . ." Celeste clucked her tongue. "Aren't you a sorry sight. Have you misplaced your razor?"

Gabe dragged his hand down the two-week-old beard he'd started growing for no good reason and ignored her question to ask one of his own. "Is there a problem at Angel's Rest?"

"No, no problem. You've brought in good people to do the necessary work."

"In that case, what brings you to Eagle's Way?"

"It's a good day for a drive, and besides, I have a gift for you."

"A gift? What for?"

"We'll talk first. Walk with me back to the house, will you? You'll have better luck fishing later. I have a feeling."

Talk. Ugh. Gabe nodded, picked up his fishing pole, and followed Celeste back toward the house. It appeared that the time had come for the talk he'd expected from Nic's friends since the day Nic left town and he'd quit answering the phone. He wasn't surprised that they'd sent Celeste. Sarah would go after him with a shotgun. Sage would look at him with those big, sad green eyes and sigh at his stupidity.

Celeste, on the other hand, was certain to ask questions. Probing, personal, rip-his-heart-out-to-answer inquiries into his emotional health. Still, he guessed he should be grateful he'd had this much of a reprieve.

"Can I get you something to eat or drink?" he asked, attempting to put off the moment.

"No, thanks. Let's sit beside the pool, shall we? It's so peaceful and beautiful there. You did a lovely job with the design, Gabe. Both here and at Angel's Rest."

"Thanks."

Rather than take a seat in one of the lounge chairs, Celeste sat at the pool's edge, removed her boots and socks, and rolled up her pant legs. She plopped her feet into the water, smiled, and said, "Come sit with me."

After working with her for months, Gabe knew it would be a waste of time to argue, so he did as she asked. "Okay, let me have it."

"You think I've come to scold you?"

"Of course. I deserve it, don't I?"

Celeste gave his leg a motherly pat and suggested, "Why don't you tell me what you think?"

"Okay, I will. If I could turn back the clock, I'd do it in a heartbeat. I'm doing the only thing I can do. I'm giving her time. Nic left me. She doesn't want to see me or talk to me, and she has every right to feel the way she feels. I can't do anything to change it. Not now. Right now my hands are tied because I will not cause her stress and put the babies at risk in any way."

"And once she has the babies? What then?"

"Then I figure out a way to fix it. Fix us. I'm going to fight for her, Celeste."

"And you intend to do that how?"

"That, I'm not so sure about. I have to convince her that I'm here for the duration. That I'm committed. That I'm not like her father or her ex or even the man I was that stormy night in June. I will not fail her again. I have to find a way to convince her that she can trust me." He paused and gave Celeste a sidelong look. "Any suggestions on how I can pull off that miracle?"

"I have a particular interest in miracles," she replied, offering a beatific smile. "Tell you what, Gabriel. Try to convince me that Nic's heart is safe with you, and I'll see what miraculous advice I have to offer. How are you a different man from the one who abandoned her at the hospital?"

Gabe took a few moments to organize his thoughts before he shrugged and said, "Maybe it's not that I'm a different man, but that I've managed to put the pieces of myself back together again. It's been a slow, steady process that occurred beneath my own personal radar, not as some great moment of revelation. Nic's leaving me was a kick to the gut that opened my eyes. I knew I had dealt with my past because I cared about the future. I'm whole again. Well, except for the fact that the person who completes me is living in Denver at the moment."

"What does your being whole have to do with the safety of Nicole's heart?"

"Everything." Gabe splashed the water gently with his heel and watched the ripples radiate outward. "I'm strong again, Celeste. When I first came to Eternity Springs, I was so weak that a snowflake could have knocked me down. Actually, a snowflake did knock me down. This town and these people helped me climb back onto my feet. I know that if we were to rerun that drive to the hospital right now, I'd still be afraid of losing the babies, of losing Nic, but I wouldn't run. I will be there for her from here on out. Every single time. I can't prove it. I have no big, splashy sign to show her. I just know it in my bones. So tell me, Celeste, how can I convince Nic of something so intangible? How can I convince her to trust me again?"

"Your instincts are good. You are smart to be patient. All her energies and concerns right now are focused on the babies. When the time does come that she is willing to revisit your relationship, Nic needs to know that she can depend on you. I suspect you'll have to win her back one small act at a time."

"I'm willing to do that. I just need her to give me the opportunity to prove myself." He lifted his gaze to where an eagle soared against the cerulean sky. "I love her, Celeste. I didn't think it could happen again, but it has. I love her."

Celeste's smile turned positively smug. "Of course you love her. You have loved her for some time now. I'm glad you finally realize it. Your heart has healed, Gabe Callahan. In fact, I consider you the first success of our healing center, and to mark the occasion, here's the gift I mentioned earlier."

She pulled something from her pocket, a silver medal dangling from a silver chain. "What's this? A Saint Christopher medal?" he asked.

"No, dear. This is the official healing center blazon, awarded to those who have embraced healing's grace. Wear it next to your heart, Gabe Callahan. Carry the grace you found here with you whatever life path you travel."

"Angel's wings?" he asked, touched by her gift.

"What else?"

"Did Sage design this? It looks like her work." When Celeste nodded, he added, "It's beautiful. Thank you."

He wasn't one to wear necklaces, but as he slipped it over his head and the medal rested against his chest, he admitted that it felt right. "I'll wear it always."

He wrapped an arm around Celeste and gave her a quick hug, then asked, "I don't suppose you have one of those ready and waiting for Nic, do you?"

Her voice rang out like church bells. "Have faith, young man. Have faith." She paused, then added, "It wouldn't hurt to say a few prayers, too."

Gabe asked Celeste to join him for lunch, but she declined, citing other errands on her schedule. He waved as she roared off on her motorcycle, shaking his head slightly at the sight. He hoped he was as active as she was when he was her age.

She'd made him feel better, he reflected as he walked toward the house. She had lifted his spirits and given him hope. The woman certainly had a way about her that spoke to the troubled areas of a soul.

He was in the middle of making a turkey sandwich when he heard his phone ring. He licked mayonnaise from his fingers, then checked the number: Nic. "Hello?"

"Are you suicidal?"

His heart leapt to hear her voice. "What?"

"People in town think you're depressed. They say you're not eating or taking care of yourself."

Gabe's stare locked on his turkey sandwich. "I'm fine. How are you, Nic? How are the babies?"

"Why aren't you in town?" she asked with an edge in her voice. "Why are you holed up at Eagle's Way?"

"I miss you."

"Answer my question."

"I just did. I miss you, Nic. Town is lonely without

you. It's crowded with tourists, too, and for some reason that only makes me miss you more."

After a long pause, she said, "Your sister-in-law told Celeste that you almost killed yourself last fall. There's some concern you've, um, relapsed. Everyone is very worried about you."

"Everyone?" He waited a long pause, but when she failed to respond, he added, "No one needs to worry. I'm not depressed and I'm certainly not suicidal. I don't want you to be concerned about my mental health. Except for missing you, I'm fine, I promise. In fact, Celeste came by a little while ago. You can talk to her. She'll back me up. Now, since I have you on the phone, can I ask how you're doing? How the babies are doing? I think about you every day and—"

"Stop it, Gabe," she interrupted. "I'm not ready for this. The only reason I called was because I can't say no to Lori."

"Then I guess that attending childbirth classes with you is out of the question?"

"Doing what?"

"I assume you're signed up for childbirth classes and I was hoping you'd let me go with you. Otherwise I'm going to go to the classes at the hospital over in Gunnison."

"Wait. Hold on. I don't get it."

"I want to be part of their lives, Nicole. I'm not going to push you, but I want you to know that I'm committed. I will be there for them, and for you, to whatever extent you'll allow. I know you have good reason not to believe me, so I'm not going to ask that of you. I'll let my actions prove my words."

He held his breath waiting for her response. For a long moment she said nothing. When she finally did speak, she broke his heart. "You hurt me, Gabe."

"I know." He swallowed hard, and in that moment he truly despised himself. "I'm so, so sorry."

He heard the line click, then a dial tone. He sighed and rubbed the back of his neck. Then, wrapping his hand around the angel's wings medallion, he murmured, "Well, at least that's a start."

Nic rejoiced in every week that crawled by. Never mind that her belly grew so big that she felt like she needed a sling to help tote it around. She refused to complain about the heartburn and insomnia and fatigue and pressure. She followed the perinatologist's instructions to the letter and had Sage on speed dial for the endless questions she had and for the reassurances she needed on a daily basis. Whatever reason Sage had for turning her back on medicine, Nic was both grateful and thankful that she'd put friendship ahead of it.

As August marched on, she began to believe she might reach her new goal of delivering her babies closer to home. Sage, her doctor in Denver, and Dr. Marshall had all assured her that if she made it to thirty-seven weeks, the Gunnison facility could care for her near-term twins just fine. The only thing preventing her from heading for the hills the moment her doctor gave her the okay was her indecision regarding what to do about Gabe.

Calling him that day had created a real chink in her armor against him. Before, she'd been able to put him out of her mind. Afterward, he had haunted her thoughts. When he called a week after Lori and Chase's visit, she'd taken his call.

He'd asked about her health and that of the babies. Then he'd told her about attending the childbirth class in Gunnison. He'd actually done it. She couldn't believe it. A little flicker of warmth sparked to life in her heart and remained burning long after the phone call ended.

Nic was watching a video when her doorbell rang during the last week of August. She hauled herself to her feet and waddled to the door. She peered into the peephole and saw Ali Timberlake standing on her front step. She swung open the door. "What a wonderful surprise."

Ali smiled sheepishly. "Sorry to show up unannounced like this, but I'm in a bind and I'm hoping you can help me."

"I'll help you any way I can, though I am a bit limited." She smiled ruefully and gestured to the huge expanse that was her belly.

"What I need is company. Caitlin is away at summer camp and Mac is working ridiculous hours with his new job. I need a distraction. Will you please come give me your opinion of the new paint color I'm considering for the family room?"

"Sure," Nic replied, glad to be able to return the favor of friendship. Ali had been a lifesaver to her this summer. "Come on in while I see if I can find some shoes I can still fit my fat feet into."

"You look gorgeous."

Nic laughed. "You're a good friend. A liar, but a good friend."

Ali lived in a lovely two-story house in an established, old-money neighborhood. Nic didn't mind tagging along on this trip, although she couldn't see herself being of any real help to Ali when it came to decorating. The woman was the epitome of style, class, and good taste.

Ali parked her car in the garage and said, "We'll go around to the backyard and enter through the back door. Follow me."

She led Nic through a whimsical black iron gate and around to the backyard. The first thing she noticed was the pool. The second was the people, and finally she saw the presents just as the crowd of friendly faces shouted, "Surprise!"

A baby shower. Her dear, wonderful friends were throwing her a baby shower. She glanced around the circle. Sage, Sarah, and Celeste, of course. Lori, LaNelle, Wendy Davis, Lisa Myers, all the members of the Patchwork Angels Quilting Bee. Choked up, all she could manage was, "Oh, you guys."

"You didn't think we'd skip giving you a shower just because we had to drive a little, did you?" Sarah asked, grabbing Nic's hand in hers and tugging her toward the chair sitting beneath the shade of a pool umbrella.

"Honestly, I never thought about it." She'd been too busy worrying about preventing labor to think about normal stuff.

For the next hour, Nic opened gifts and oohed and aahed over infant gowns, receiving blankets, booties, and bibs—two of everything, of course. Since she had chosen not to learn her babies' genders ahead of time, the gifts were mostly in either/or shades of yellow and green. Sarah gave her the coolest twin stroller ever made, and Sage presented her with car seats. Celeste gave her two gorgeous christening gowns in addition to layettes made of fabric in a pattern of gold angel wings. Nic was excited and thrilled and overwhelmed with the outpouring of affection from her friends. When she'd opened everything but the last two large, identical boxes, she saw Sage and Sarah share a look before they scooted them over to her. "What is it?" she asked.

"They weren't sure if they should bring these," Celeste said. "I told them they were exactly what you needed to see."

Nic unwrapped two hand-carved rocker cradles that were so beautiful they brought tears to her eyes. This was Colt Rafferty's work. "I thought you told me Colt didn't make it to Eternity again this summer after all."

"He didn't." Sage lifted her chin in disdain. "That's four summers in a row and he still has the audacity to enter the art contest as a local."

"Let it go, Sage," Sarah said. Turning to Nic, she explained, "Someone tracked Colt down and got him to make these special."

"Someone?" Nic asked.

Sarah's teeth tugged at her lower lip. "Read the card."

Nic opened the white envelope that was tied to the end of one cradle and slipped out a folded note card.

It's a poor second-best to being held in your arms. Love, Gabe.

"Oh, wow," she murmured. This had been a big step for Gabe, and she knew it.

During the rest of the party, Nic's gaze returned time and again to the cradles. She couldn't believe that the same man who'd ditched her at the hospital had gone to extraordinary effort to offer such perfect gifts for their babies.

Eventually, someone made note of the time and the long drive ahead for those returning to Eternity Springs that night, so guests began to take their leave. Before long, only the hostesses of the shower—Nic's four closest friends—remained, and the post-party cleanup began in earnest. While Sage and Sarah chased down scraps of ribbon and paper that had blown toward the back of the yard and Celeste began stacking gifts inside the two cradles, Ali asked Nic, "How are you doing? Can I get you anything else?"

"I'm good. I'm wonderful. This was so nice of you all to do. I can't thank you enough."

"You are very welcome. It's been a lot of fun."

Celeste walked over and smiled at Nic and Ali. "I think we're just about done. Ali, we need you to tell us where to take the trash bags, and Nic, it's time for you to make a decision. Where do you want your gifts? At your place here in town or at home in Eternity Springs?"

Nic's gaze zoomed in on the cradles. Sarah had mentioned earlier that Gabe was still living up at Eagle's Way. She licked her lips, then looked at Sage, who silently read the question in her eyes and nodded. *Yes, it will be safe for your babies to be born closer to home.*

Sarah slipped her arm through Nic's and said, "Whatever you want, Nic. Know that I have your back."

Nic drew a deep breath, then made her decision. "Home. Take it all home to Eternity Springs. We'll be there the beginning of next week."

TWENTY

On the twelfth of September, Nic returned to Eternity Springs. The trip from Denver took three hours longer than usual since she'd had to stop what seemed like every ten minutes to pee. She rode with Sage while Sarah and Tiger drove Nic's truck for her. When they pulled up in front of Nic's house, she took one look at her home and burst into tears. "Honey?" Sage asked.

"I'm okay. Just so glad to be home."

Sarah pulled the truck into Nic's driveway and opened the door. Tiger bounded out barking and bounding around the yard. "Looks like he's happy to be home, too," Sage said.

"Yes," Nic agreed. "I know he missed the freedom to roam he had here at . . ." Her voice trailed off as she noted an addition to her yard. "Is that a doghouse? With a deck?"

Sarah joined Nic and Sage and shook her head. "I told him the deck was overkill."

Nic walked closer and read the sign hanging above the opening. "'Tiger's Den'? Who built this?"

"Gabe."

"Gabe? You're kidding." She stared at her friends in disbelief. "That sounds like he's calling the dog by name."

"Something like that." Sarah shrugged. "Larry Wilson says he came into the hardware store and bought a dog collar and an engraved tag that said Tiger and listed your address. But he also bought a tag that said Clarence with your address. There's a sign on the other side of the doghouse that says Clarence's Castle."

How many times had Nic heard Gabe say that he didn't name things he didn't intend to keep? Too many to count, that's for sure. And now two names? "Why give the boxer two names?"

"Larry said Gabe wanted to talk to you first. He didn't want to change the boxer's name if it would be a problem for the dog."

Nic took another long look at the elaborate doghouse and shook her head. "Clarence?"

She heard the familiar whistle as Gabe came around the back corner of her house. He wore faded jeans and a paint-stained blue chambray work shirt that had two artist's brushes sticking up from the pocket. Seeing the women, he stopped abruptly. His gaze moved hungrily over Nic. "You look beautiful, Nic. Welcome home."

She was tired and uncomfortable and cranky. Overwhelmed. She wasn't prepared to deal with Gabe right now. "I didn't expect you to be here."

"I was finishing up a project inside. I thought you were coming home tomorrow, not today. I'm so glad—" He paused when Tiger came running up, then stopped beside Nic and barked at Gabe. His lips twisted in a sad smile and he finished, "It's good to see you, Nic."

She felt bad for him. She couldn't help it. She knew that coming back to Eternity Springs meant she had to deal with him, to allow him a place of some sort in her life. She knew that coming home was a tacit agreement to allow him to be part of the babies' births. And yet she didn't have the energy to tackle the problem of Gabe Callahan right now. She wanted to go inside, take a bath in her own bathtub, and have a nap in her own bed.

"Gabe, I'm tired. Give me a little time, and then we'll talk. Okay?"

"Sure."

He nodded to Sarah and Sage, then walked away. Nic told herself that her urge to cry was a result of fatigue, even though she didn't really believe it.

Walking into her house cheered her. Someone had cleaned and dusted the place—she smelled lemon on the air. Celeste or Ali, perhaps? Or had that been the project Gabe mentioned? Somehow she couldn't see him wielding a feather duster.

Sage and Sarah carried her bags inside for her, then prepared to leave. "See you at Angel's Rest tomorrow?" Sage asked.

"Absolutely. I still can't believe Celeste delayed the grand opening a week to give me a chance to be there."

"If you're not busy doing something else, that is," Sarah said, giving her belly a pat.

"Thanks for all the help, you guys. I love you both."

"Glad to do it." Sarah headed for the door. "Love you, too, little mama."

Feeling anything but little, Nic stuck out her tongue at her best friend in the world.

Sage laughed and said, "Call me if you have any questions or concerns and I'll be here in a jiffy. Otherwise, see you tomorrow."

Alone, Nic climbed the stairs to her bedroom, where she found the furniture rearranged to accommodate the two cradles, now trimmed with yellow gingham bedding that matched the window curtains in her room. "Oh," she murmured. "It's perfect. They're perfect."

That made her want to play with her shower gifts. Walking to the guest room she expected to use as a nursery, she found it as she'd left it and empty of presents. Thinking he must have put her shower gifts in the room he'd used before they began sharing a bed, she looked there next. But no, nothing there, either.

"Where's my stuff?" she grumbled aloud, feeling put out. "What did he—"

She broke off abruptly. Gabe. Paintbrushes in his pocket. Finishing up a project inside. In that moment, she knew where she'd find her gifts.

Nic walked to the end of the hallway and opened the door that led to the unfinished attic. She flipped on the light switch and gasped aloud. The attic wasn't merely finished. It had been transformed.

He'd chosen a mountain wildlife theme for the nursery that suited the space to a T, and he'd included two sets of everything—two cribs, two dressers, two changing tables, and even two full-size rocking chairs. Both rockers sported cushions that had been embroidered with two words: *Mama Bear* on one, *Papa Bear* on the other.

"Oh, Gabe," she said with a sigh. She sat in the Mama Bear rocker, rubbed her belly, and that's when she saw the mural on the wall. Papa Bear, Mama Bear, two Baby Bears, and a crooked-tailed boxer sprawled at their feet. Papa Bear held a T-square. Mama Bear had a stethoscope draped around her neck. In the sky to the right, a happy-faced sun shined down upon them. In the sky to the left, two silhouettes with angel wings sat perched at the apex of a rainbow.

Gabe walked as far as St. Stephen's church before turning around. Although he was determined to be patient and give Nic the time she needed to trust him again, he was up against a deadline that in the past few weeks had become vitally important to him. He desperately wanted to witness the birth of his children.

He realized he'd forfeited that right when he'd acted like an ass and deserted her at the hospital. For that matter, he'd been skating on thin ice from the very beginning with her. But he'd dealt with his demons and put them behind him, and he was ready to be a father to the twins. Nic needed to know that. Today. Now.

From the looks of her, she might pop at any moment.

By the time he reached Nic's house, Sage's car was gone. He knocked on the door and stepped inside. "Hello?"

He heard no immediate response or conversation. Sarah must be gone now, too. Good. Nic was probably upstairs. She might have lain down to take a nap, but he doubted she'd gone to sleep this fast.

He climbed the stairs and headed for what for a short time had been their bedroom. Before reaching it, he noted the attic door was open. She'd found it already. He wiped his suddenly sweaty palms on his pants before climbing the stairs to the nursery.

She sat in a rocker, the dog at her feet. In the soft light beaming through the dormer window, she appeared luminous and luscious and ripe. Staggeringly beautiful.

She opened her eyes, luminous blue pools of emotion he could not identify. "Why did you do this?"

"Is it okay? Do you like it?"

"I asked first."

"Okay." He shoved his hands in his back pockets and paced the length of the room. "I won't try to make any more excuses for my behavior, Nic. You have every right to hate me for leaving you that day. I know I can't make up for the hurt I caused you, but I wanted to do more than just apologize. Words are important, but they're not everything. Like the saying goes, actions speak louder. I looked for a way to prove to you that I won't let you and the babies down again."

"So you sent the cradles."

"Yes."

"You went to childbirth classes by yourself."

"I did."

Her gaze broke away from his and he watched her as she studied the walls. "You're an excellent artist."

"Architects learn how to draw. I considered asking Sage to paint the murals, but . . ." He shrugged. "I wanted to do them."

"Why?"

Gabe's heart began to pound. It was one thing to admit it to himself or to Celeste, but something else entirely to say it to Nic. To commit to Nic.

Last chance, Callahan. If you have any doubts at all, you need to keep your lips zipped.

He waited a beat, searched within himself, then smiled.

"Why?" he repeated. "Because it was a labor of love."

He walked over to her, went down on one knee, took her hand, and kissed it. "I'm not afraid to love those babies anymore. I love them. I want to be there when they're born. I want to help you raise them. I want to be their dad."

Tears swam in her eyes and she swallowed hard. Gabe went down on both knees and claimed both her hands. Held them tight. "I said this before, but my timing stank, so maybe you'll get the message better now. Nic, I'm not afraid to love you anymore, either. I love you. I am in love with you. Please, give me another chance. Give us another chance. I won't let you down again. You have my word. My oath." He kissed one hand and then the other. "Nic, you have my heart. Please, be my home."

A single, glistening tear slipped from her eyes and trailed slowly down her cheek. "I think this time I'm the one who is afraid."

"Don't be afraid, sweetheart. Just believe. Believe in love."

She smiled crookedly. "If you have fireworks set to go off, I'm going to think something's really fishy."

He took a risk. "I think we have to wait at least four weeks after the babies are born for the fireworks. At least, that's what they said in my childbirth class."

She gave a little smile that broke his heart but at the same time gave him hope, so he persisted. "When I came to Eternity Springs, I'd lost my ability to believe in anything but pain. This place healed me. You healed me. Your love healed me."

Her lips pouted, and with a touch of petulance in her voice she replied, "I never told you I loved you."

Not gonna make it easy for me, are you? But he had won. He could see it in her eyes, the subtle softening of her body. He kissed her hands, gently nipped her skin, and said, "Then tell me now."

She wrinkled her nose and kept her mouth stubbornly silent.

"I love you, Nicole," he repeated. "You are my heart, my soul, my world. You and Eternity Springs have taught me an invaluable lesson. Even if tragedy strikes my life again and God takes you away from me, as horrible as that would be, I know that I'd survive it. Love can hurt, but if you'll let it, love also can heal. It truly is a miraculous medicine. You believe that, too, don't you?"

When she nodded, her eyes now swimming in tears, he said, "That's why I know that eventually you'll forgive me. Love heals. Now, my love, you say it. Tell me you love me."

She reached out, grasped the silver medal that hung around his neck, and rubbed her thumb over the angel's wings. Then she released the medal and tenderly touched his cheek. "I do love you, John Gabriel Callahan. I forgive you. Just don't do anything so stupid again, okay?"

"I won't. I promise. I love you. And since I'm on a roll here, there is something else I want to ask you. Have you chosen names for the babies yet?"

"You want to name the babies?"

"I'd like some input."

Gladness filled her expression, but her lips twitched. "I don't know, Gabe. You haven't exactly made me confident with the name you chose for Tiger. I mean, really, Clarence? Why Clarence?"

"He was the angel who saved George Bailey in *It's a Wonderful Life*. Seems like an appropriate choice. That dog saved me." He kissed her hands one more time. "That dog and *you* saved me."

This time she didn't try to hide her smile. "Okay, that makes sense. And actually, Clarence fits him better than Tiger."

"Will it confuse him if we change his name, Dr. Delicious?"

She rolled her eyes but shook her head. "No, he's smart. It'll be fine. However, as far as baby names go . . . what are you thinking?"

"That my knees are too old for this hardwood floor." He rose and pulled her to her feet, saying, "C'mere. I want to hold you."

He led her over to the padded window seat, where he sat with his back against the wall and one leg spread along the length of the seat. He pulled her down between his legs, wrapped his arms around her and their children, and stared out at the view of Hummingbird Lake and Sinner's Prayer Pass beyond. So beautiful. So joyous.

He cleared his throat against a lump of emotion, then patted her tummy. "How about Beryl and Beulah? Beryl and Beulah Callahan. What do you . . . whoa! Did you feel that kick?"

"A reaction to the name, I'm sure," she dryly replied.

"So, what do you think?" He nuzzled her neck.

"I think you're a bit rusty at picking names. We'll work on it." She scooted forward, then twisted around to look at him. "Gabe, are you busy tomorrow morning?"

His brows dipped in a quizzical frown. "Celeste's grand opening is tomorrow."

"The festivities begin at noon. I'd like to schedule something else for the morning."

His eyes went wide. "You're gonna have the babies in the morning?"

"No, I hope not." She laughed softly at the panic in his eyes. "Celeste put the opening off a week so that I could be there, and as much as I want to have these little guys, I hope they'll cooperate and wait until after the party and . . . the wedding."

"Wedding?"

"Will you marry me again, Mr. Callahan? Tomorrow morning in church?"

"You're proposing to me?"

"I am."

"Cool. In that case, I will absolutely marry you tomorrow morning in church. As long as the babies don't rearrange our plans."

"They won't dare." As Clarence crossed the room and plopped himself down at Gabe's feet, Nic looked down at her belly and said, "You let me have my wedding, kiddos, or otherwise I'll let your daddy pick your names."

Shortly before nine o'clock the following morning in the rectory at St. Stephen's church, Sage and Sarah helped Nic don the flowing white silk dupioni gown that Celeste had produced for the occasion. Strapless, it had a bodice big enough to contain her bountiful breasts, an empire waist, and an A-line skirt that actually flattered her enormous belly. It fit her to perfection, and when

Nic took a look at herself in the mirror, her mouth gaped in disbelief. "I don't look like a whale!"

"You look like an angel," Celeste said.

"A wanton angel," Sarah corrected.

Sage shook her head. "You look gorgeous, luscious, and happy."

"Happy." Nic nodded and accepted the bouquet of red roses that Lori handed to her. "That I am."

She looked at Celeste and said, "I don't know what made you decide to order this dress to have on hand, but I'm thrilled you did."

Celeste gave a dismissive wave. "I believe in being prepared. With that in mind, I have a gift for you. It's not a wedding gift, but I suspect you might wish to wear it today."

She reached into her handbag and pulled out a delicate silver chain and pendant. "This is the official healing center blazon that will be awarded to those who have embraced healing's grace. Wear it next to your heart, Nicole Callahan. Carry the grace you found here with you whatever life path you travel."

"Angel's wings!" Nic exclaimed with delight. "How perfect. This is your design, isn't it, Sage?"

"Yes." Sage took the necklace from Celeste and fastened it around Nic's neck. "I have to say, the design was inspired."

"Thank you." Nic's smile encompassed them all. "I'm blessed to have friends like you, a home like Eternity Springs—"

"And a man like Gabe Callahan," Sarah finished. "Now, quit fiddling around and go marry him again."

As Nic slipped her bare, swollen feet into white rhinestone-trimmed flip-flops, a knock sounded on the door and Ali stuck her head inside. "They're all ready for you . . . oh, Nic. You look fabulous."

"Thank you. So, Gabe and Jack are waiting?"

"Yes." Ali waggled her eyebrows salaciously. "And allow me to say that both the groom and his best man are hotties in tuxes."

Moments later, Nic lived her very own fairy tale as she walked down the aisle of the pretty little church to repeat her vows with the man she loved. A man who, with his spirit now healed, loved her in return.

Gabe held his wife's hand as they crossed the footbridge over Angel Creek that led to Angel's Rest, where his friends and his family waited to celebrate . . . what should he call it? His rebirth? Renewal?

Life.

At the center of the bridge, he halted. "Nic, would you mind . . . can I have a minute?"

"Of course." She reached up and cupped his face in her palm, and as she smiled up at him with such sweet love that it took his breath away, he knew she understood. "You take as much time as you need." Resting her hand on the babies, she added, "We'll be waiting for you."

His heart full, Gabe watched her go. Then he gripped the bridge's handrail and stared down at the clear waters of Angel Creek for a long moment before lifting his gaze to the brilliant blue sky that rose about the snowcapped mountains. "I'm okay, Jen. It's been a long, ugly winter, but I made it to spring. I know that is what you wanted for me.

"I'm going to contact my father and brothers, let them know I'm still around. It'll do the babies good to have a grandfather and uncles in their lives, don't you think? I know you always wanted more family for Matty. I couldn't give him the Callahans back then, but I'll make sure they know about him now. And about you, too.

"I'll miss you forever, and I'll carry my love for you and Matty always in my heart. Right there along with

Nic and the twins and whoever else life brings me to love. I never thought it would happen, but life is good again. I found what I needed here in this valley. I think— no, I believe—that I was guided here by angels."

Gabe stood up straight, drew a deep breath, then turned toward the house. He saw Nic watching him, waiting for him. Love warmed his soul. "Come on, Clarence," he said to the boxer at his feet. "Let's go home."

ACKNOWLEDGMENTS

New beginnings are exciting things. For this one I'd especially like to thank my awesome, talented, oh-so-keen-eyed editor, Kate Collins, and my agents, Meg Ruley and Christina Hogrebe, for their support and guidance and belief in this series. You ladies rock. Special thanks to Lynn Andreozzi for the spectacular cover designs for the Eternity Springs series. I love this look! Also, thanks to my dear friends Scott and Christina Ham, who knew just the motivation to give me to find my way to Eternity Springs, and to Mary Dickerson for being my reader, my red-liner, and, most important, my friend.

*Read on for a preview of
Emily March's next novel
in her Eternity Springs series:*

Hummingbird Lake

September

The echo of the gunshot jerked Sage Anderson out of her nightmare. Her eyes flew open. She lay in the darkness, panting, sweating, her heart pounding in fear, her hands clenched into fists. *Oh, God.*

The images. The sounds. *Oh, dear God.*

It was a dream. Just a dream. One of those old, horrible, terrifying nightmares that had haunted her ever since the events she'd just dreamed about had taken place.

Slowly the past retreated. Her pulse calmed and her fingers relaxed. At that point, the shivering began, a reaction to both the chill in the room and the aftermath of the dream.

Sage rolled up and reached for the bedclothes she'd kicked off the end of the bed during the dream. This was the first time in months that she'd been plagued by one of these nightmares. She had thought she'd put them behind her.

"I am so totally done with this," she said aloud as she yanked up the sheet, tugged up the comforter, and fished for her discarded socks at the bottom of the bed. When she finally cuddled beneath goose down and Egyptian cotton, she turned her head into the pillow and tried to cry.

She badly wanted to succeed in the effort, to sob and

wail and release these vicious emotions churning inside her. As usual, the tears wouldn't come. In the past few years, she'd managed to find catharsis in tears only a handful of times.

When her eyes remained stubbornly dry and the possibility of sleep appeared completely beyond reach, she focused her attention on more pleasant thoughts. She thought about weddings. Her best friend's wedding. Well, one of her best friends, anyway.

Yesterday Nic Callahan had returned to town and reconciled with her husband. They planned to reaffirm their wedding vows at St. Stephen's later this morning prior to the grand opening celebration for Angel's Rest, Celeste Blessing's healing center and spa. Sage was thrilled for Nic and Gabe. She was pleased for Celeste and excited for Eternity Springs. Today promised to be a lovely day.

And I'm not going to let a bad dream ruin it.

With that determined thought uppermost in her mind, she glanced at the bedside clock, where 4:07 glowed in red numerals. Today promised to be a lovely *and long* day, she revised with an inner sigh. She knew she wouldn't get back to sleep at this point.

Sage sat up and took stock of her options. She could read or watch TV or surf the Net. She could catch up on paperwork or tackle the painting she'd begun yesterday for her upcoming show in Fort Worth. Except she wasn't in the mood for the first three, and she needed to let that painting sit for a few days. Something wasn't working with it, and experience had taught her that walking away for a day or two almost always helped her figure out the fix.

Her thoughts returned to the wedding, and at that point she knew what she wanted to do. She'd grab a new canvas and see if she couldn't create a gift for Gabe and Nic to mark their special day. She'd do something simple but light, bright, and beautiful.

"Perfect." She blew out a breath, rolled out of bed, and headed for the studio she'd set up in the cottage's second bedroom. This was what she needed now—something positive to think about, a task to take her out of the shadows and away from the pain and the past.

In the studio, she placed a blank canvas on her easel and studied it, opening her mind to inspiration. She shied away from one image that hovered in her head, a leftover from her nightmare. Instead, she thought about Nic and Gabe and the obstacles they'd overcome while finding their way to today. She opened her mind to the promise of their bright and happy future, and inspiration flowed. An idea took shape in her imagination. She picked up her paintbrush and went to work. When she stepped away from her easel three hours later, she studied the finished painting and smiled. "Good job, Anderson."

She had managed to shake off the lingering ugliness of her dream and create something she knew her friends would treasure. All before breakfast. "Not a bad start for the day."

She showered and dressed and had just decided to toast a bagel when, to her surprise, someone rapped at her front door. Warily Sage peeked through the window blinds.

Celeste Blessing stood on her front porch, a canvas tote bag in one hand, a relaxed smile upon her face. She had gorgeous silver-gray hair and youthful sky-blue eyes. This morning she wore a stylish bright red jacket, and gold earrings shaped like angel's wings dangled from her ears.

Sage relaxed. When she grew up, she wanted to be just like Celeste. The woman was the kindest, friendliest, smartest, and most active senior Sage had ever met. She rode a Honda Gold Wing motorcycle for fun, watched DVDs of *The Mary Tyler Moore Show* for entertainment, and she never missed a Sunday at church or failed to give her opinion about the preacher's sermon. It had been her idea to turn the Cavanaugh House estate into Angel's Rest Healing Center and Spa, and construction alone had already proved a boon to the economically depressed town even before today's official opening.

The townspeople loved Celeste for her part in rescuing Eternity Springs. Sage loved Celeste for herself. In many ways, she was the mother and grandmother Sage had never had.

She opened her door with a smile. "Celeste. What brings you out this way?"

"The Landrys offered their vacation home as an overflow facility for the center, and since we're packed to the rafters with the grand opening, we'll need to use it tonight."

The Landrys were a lovely family from Texas who owned the only other house on Reflection Point, the narrow little peninsula where Sage lived. "I wanted to stop and drop off a little welcome basket," the older woman continued. "When I saw your light, I decided to come beg a cup of herbal tea."

"I'm glad you did. I was about to toast a bagel. Care to join me?"

"Actually . . ." Celeste held up the tote bag. "I happen to have breakfast fixings with me. Care if I make myself at home in your kitchen?"

Sage blinked. "That's fine with me, but with the grand opening, aren't you swamped?"

"Everything's under control, and frankly, with all the hustle and bustle, I'm glad to have a few moments of peace and quiet out here at Hummingbird Lake. I have bacon, eggs, a loaf of day-old bread for toast, and a jar of homemade strawberry jam."

"That sounds much better than a bagel." Sage eyed the bag appreciatively. "Tell you what. My stovetop is persnickety when it comes to heat regulation. You have to talk to it just right. Why don't you let me man the frying pan while you handle the toaster?"

Celeste's blue eyes twinkled. "An excellent plan."

Sage took the tote bag and led Celeste through the cozy little cottage to the kitchen, where the women went to work. Their conversation centered around the two main events of the day, but when they sat down to eat, Celeste sipped her tea and introduced a new subject. "How are you feeling, Sage? You look a bit tired."

She attempted a dodge. "I got up early and painted a gift for Nic and Gabe."

"That's nice," Celeste said. "Although I'm sure they wouldn't have wanted you to miss sleep because of it. This wedding is a last-minute thing, after all."

"Actually, a nightmare woke me up. I couldn't get back to sleep." Sage set down her knife, surprised at herself for admitting the truth. She never talked about the nightmares.

"Oh, you poor thing." Celeste clucked her tongue. "I'm so sorry. Does that happen often?"

"No, not really." Sage took a bite of jam-slathered toast and admitted to herself that something about Celeste invited confidences. She was simply so easy to talk to. After savoring the flavor of springtime in the jam, she swallowed, sipped her juice, then added, "Since I moved to Eternity Springs, I sleep pretty well. I think the mountain air is magic."

"Eternity Springs is special," Celeste agreed. "I've said it before and I'll say it again. This valley nurses a special energy that soothes troubled souls—if those souls open their hearts and minds to the possibilities."

Sage couldn't argue against it. Heaven knows the town had been working its magic on her these past few years. She'd been a basket case, running away from life as she knew it, when she arrived at a crossroads on a Colorado mountain road and turned left, ending up in Eternity Springs.

She couldn't explain it to anyone—she couldn't explain it to herself—but she'd known in her bones that the left turn had been the rightest turn of her life. Call it instinct or intuition or a message from her very own angel, but Sage had understood that she was meant to live and work in Eternity Springs, at least for a little while.

So she'd moved here and made friends here. She'd made a life and a career here. Except for occasional nightmares and flashbacks, she was happy here.

"Eternity Springs has been good for me. I predict your healing center will be a wild success, Celeste."

"I completely agree. Those who open themselves up to all that life has to offer here will find great reward. You remember that, Sage. Now, let me help you with the dishes. Breakfast was simply divine."

"It did hit the spot. Thank you for providing both the idea and the supplies."

"You're very welcome. I'm a big believer in having protein for breakfast. You and I have a packed day ahead of us. We need our protein."

Sage didn't argue with her, but she didn't anticipate her own day being all that busy. Other than showing up at St. Stephen's thirty minutes early to help Nic dress, the only tasks on her docket were to witness the wedding and stroll Celeste's estate as a guest at the grand opening. She didn't intend to open Vistas, her art gallery, at all today.

After Celeste left, Sage wrapped her gift for Nic and Gabe in plain brown paper and fished a red marker from her junk drawer in order to draw hearts as decoration. When the memory of a homemade valentine that had giraffes sporting heart-shaped spots drifted through her mind, she sucked in a breath.

"Stupid dream," she muttered, then gritted her teeth as the pain washed over her. Following a dream, invariably the memories hung around like a hangover. Not all memories were bad, but the good ones seemed to be buried beneath the mountain of ugliness she'd brought home from Africa.

Sage set down the marker and walked to her kitchen window, where she gazed out across Hummingbird Lake toward Eternity Springs. Taking in that view went further to rid herself of that "hangover" than ingesting any aspirin or painkiller ever could.

"Forget the nightmare," she murmured. "The sadness ends now."

Well, at least for today. Today was going to be a wonderful day. This was Nic's real wedding day and the culmination of Celeste's Angel Plan for the economic survival of Eternity Springs. It was a day for celebration—not one for nightmares and heartbreaking memories—and it was time she headed for the church.

As she retrieved her car keys from her bedside table, she stared longingly at her pillow and added aloud, "A day for celebration, and maybe a nap."

A hand slapped Colt Rafferty's ass and jolted him out of his dream. It had been a good dream, too. Warm sun and a sugar-sand beach. A beer in his hand. Half-naked women jumping to catch a Frisbee, jiggling. Loved that jiggling.

"Roust your butt out of bed, boy. The trout are calling our names."

Colt growled into his pillow and bit back the caustic words he would have spoken to any other man on earth. This man, however, was his father.

He cocked open one eye and groaned. "It's still dark."

"Of course it's still dark," Ben Rafferty said. "Have you forgotten how to fish? We need to be at the water at dawn."

Colt's flight out of Washington yesterday had been delayed by weather. It had been midnight before he'd made it to Eternity Springs, almost two before he'd hit the sack. What he needed was sleep. "Angel Creek is right outside."

"I fished the creek yesterday while I was waiting for you to get here. If I'd known you'd be so late arriving, I'd have gone up toward Gunnison and tried my hand at the Taylor River. I've been itching to fish there for years. We don't have time for that today, though, so I'm thinking we should fish Hummingbird Lake this morning. It's only ten minutes from here, and with the grand opening kicking off at noon, this will be a busy place this morning. Fishing should be done in peace and quiet." Then, in a quieter tone, he added, "We only have today together, son. I don't want to miss a minute of it."

At that, Colt rolled out of bed.

Twenty minutes later they stood along the bank of Hummingbird Lake and made their first cast of the morning. With it, Colt felt the warm, gentle blanket of peace surround him. His dad must have experienced a similar sensation, because he sighed and said, "This comes close to being a religious experience."

"Yep. And I've been away from church for too long."

Ben Rafferty glanced at him. "How long has it been since you've visited Eternity Springs?"

"Four years. Haven't been back since I took the job in D.C."

His father shook his head. "That's a crying shame, son."

Colt had to agree. Colorado always had been special to him. His family had vacationed in Eternity Springs every year when he was a kid, and he'd loved everything about the town. He'd started working summers up here his last two years in high school and continued that all the way through college and even grad school. His mom always said that the reason he stayed in academics as long as he had was because he wasn't willing to give up his summers in the mountains.

"I wish this trip could be longer," he admitted. "If my appointment next week was for anything other than testifying before Congress, I'd skip it."

"That's a difficult class to cut." Ben Rafferty, high school science teacher, nodded sagely.

"It's a dog and pony show, is what it is. A pain in the ass." After a teaching stint at Georgia Tech, Colt had taken his PhD in chemical engineering to the CSB, the U.S. Chemical Safety and Hazard Investigation Board, where he investigated industrial explosions. He loved the work—solving the puzzle of what had happened in an incident and why and determining how to avoid a similar accident in the future—but he hated the hoops he and his team had to go through to get anything changed. They could write wonderful reports about their findings, but unless that led to change, what good did they do? "Let's not talk about work anymore. It'll spoil my appetite for my fish. I'm here today, and I intend to take full advantage of it. A little dose of Eternity Springs is better than nothing."

"Amen, son."

Thinking he'd had a hit, Colt tugged on the line. Nope. Nada. He made another cast, then laughed. "Know what I was dreaming about when you woke me up this morning? Senior trip."

Ben Rafferty gave a long-suffering sigh. "And people think preachers' kids are wild. Teachers' kids are ten times worse."

"Aw, c'mon, Dad. I wasn't wild."

Ben snorted. "Sure you were. You were also the most

stubborn, hardheaded, determined boy on the planet. Once you got an idea in your head, there was no stopping you. Don't see how that's changed, either."

"Being tenacious is an asset in my work."

"Sure made it a challenge to be your father."

After that, conversation lagged as the two men went about the serious business of fishing. For that stretch of time, Colt was as happy as he'd been in months. *I really need to get to Colorado more often.*

"Woo-hoo," Ben called out, snagging Colt's attention as he landed the first fish. "Better get to work, boyo. I'll be having myself a fine trout breakfast and you'll be eating cereal."

"Not gonna happen." Colt proved his claim by catching the next two, which led to some good-hearted grumbling from his father.

Time passed and Colt soaked in the peacefulness of the morning. The air carried the tangy scent of a cedar campfire, and above him a hawk soared on a subtle breeze. Worries about the upcoming committee meeting nagged at the edges of his brain, but as Ben Rafferty pulled another rainbow trout from Hummingbird Lake, Colt lifted his gaze toward Murphy Mountain, tucked his worries away, and allowed Eternity Springs to work its mojo on him. He was here, fishing with his dad. Life was good.

"I'm glad you could make it up here this week, Dad."

"I am too, son. Wish Mom could have come along, too, but she insisted that we needed some . . ." He smirked and stressed the next words. "Male bonding time. Personally, I think she's laying the groundwork to take a girls' trip with your sister. I've heard them whispering about a spa weekend."

"If Mom and Molly want a spa holiday, they should come up here. I have it on good authority that Angel's

Rest has hired the best masseuse this side of the Mississippi."

His dad glanced over at him. "Speaking of Angel's Rest, when do I get to see this sign of yours? Mrs. Blessing went on and on about it and about your artistic talent yesterday when I checked in."

"She was happy with the sign."

"Happy? Now there's an understatement if I've ever heard one. She told me that you have enough talent to make your living as an artist."

Colt shook his head at that nonsense and changed the subject. "I don't know about you, but I'm thinking it's about time for breakfast."

"Sounds good." His father jerked his head toward their fishing creels. "You clean 'em, I'll cook 'em."

"That's a deal."

Back at the carriage house with the aroma of fried trout drifting on the morning air, Colt looked through the kitchen window toward a mountainside gone gloriously gold with the color of aspens in autumn and smiled. The town's newly adopted slogan couldn't be more suitable: *Eternity Springs—it's a little piece of heaven in the Colorado Rockies.*

"I love it here, Dad. I need to visit more often."

"Then do it."

"How? My job is in D.C."

Ben Rafferty slapped him on the back. "You'll find a way to get what you want, son. You always do."

GABE GAVE IN to both their desires. He tugged off his shirt and it wasn't until he heard her shocked gasp that he realized just what he'd done. The scars had been a part of him for so long now that he forgot he even had them. He unconsciously straightened, bracing himself against the barrage of questions sure to come. Questions he had no intention of answering. That part of his life was a closed book.

The pretty veterinarian surprised him. But for that one betraying inhalation, her professionalism never slipped. Maybe her gaze was a bit softer, her touch as gentle as the snowfall, but she never once recoiled or eyed him with pity. Gradually Gabe relaxed. For a few stolen moments he allowed himself to pleasure in the sensation of human touch upon his skin.

"I'll quarantine the boxer," she said. "You should drive into Gunnison and see Dr. Hander at the medical clinic. He'll put you on prophylactic antibiotics. When was your last tetanus shot?"

"Last year."

"Good."

Next she ran through a series of basic questions about his medical history, and then asked him to lie on his back. "Your legs will hang off the table, I'm afraid, but this way will keep your pants dry."

His jeans had been wet since he wrestled with the dog, but he kept that detail to himself and studied her through half-closed eyes as she prepared to bathe his wounds with saline. Her beauty was the wholesome, girl-next-door type. He figured the lack of a ring on her finger was due to work-related safety factors rather than marital status. Bet she was married with a couple of kids.